# ENCYCLOPAEDIA OF TERRORISM IN THE WORLD

# ENCYCLOPAEDIA OF TERRORISM IN THE WORLD

(In Five Folumes)
(Volume-1)

Col. Ved Prakash (FRGS)

KALPAZ

Encyclopaedia of Terrorism in the World



ISBN: 978-81-7835-868-0 (Set)
ISBN: 978-81-7835-869-7 (Vol. 1)



Published in 2011 in India by
Kalpaz Publications
C-30, Satyawati Nagar,
Delhi-110052
E-mail: kalpaz@hotmail.com
Phone : 9212729499

*Lasser Type Setting* : Quick Media, Delhi
*Printed at* : Chawla Offset Printers, Delhi

*Dedicated to*

*My grandson, Aryan Sharma*

*with*

*a fervent plea to the international community to, through its concerted endeavour, render his generation the world over safe from the scourge of terrorism, perpetrated by some evil minds and wreaking devastation on the mankind*

# CONTENTS

# PREFACE

Terrorism is the most serious threat to the world as it exists today. Its most potent strand, and also most widely prevalent, is the Islamist terrorism, symbolised by that evil genius, Osama bin Laden.

The scourge afflicts the nations from Indonesia to the United States, and from the Scan danavians to the southern lip of the South America and Australia. It is no exaggeration to say that no nation is immune from this ideological and religious terrorism. Never in the history of the mankind, a single threat has been the cause of serious world-wide concern.

It is only natural that such an existential threat needs to he studied in all its forms and from various angles. The present book, consequently, is a comprehensive study of this all-prevailing, virulent phenomenon. It is divided into four parts for an orderly study of this vast, if crucial, subject. Three parts have already been published and this is the fourth part.

- Part 1. Terrorism in India's North-East (Three Volumes)
- Part 2. Terrorism in Northern India Jammu and Kashmir and the Punjab (Two Volumes)
- Part 3. Terrorism in India (Three Volumes)
- Part 4. Encyclopaedia of Terrorism in the World (Five Volumes)

20th was the human history's most violent century. Curious, if interesting trends have marked the era. If in the early years of nuclear age, which commenced with the Hiroshima blast, the world lived under the shadow of a nuclear holocaust, by the end of the Cold War probability of a nuclear war and exchange was lower than ever before. Likewise, after the World War II the likelihood of the clash of arms between any two major powers dwindled progressively. In a way, the 1991 Gulf War may well be the last classical war for a long time to come. The 2003 US invasion of Iraq was hardly a conventional war. It was a case of technology defeating the 'mighty' Army of President Saddam Hussain. But more significantly, after the war entered fifth year on 23 March 2007, the erstwhile all-conquering US military machine and coalition forces started losing it—almost—to the practitioners of an unconventional warfare. War through terror. Even if the US and coalition forces retrieved the situation in Iraq, the US and NATO forces are finding it hard to win the battles against the Taliban terrorists in Afghanistan.

So, in the recent years, the nuclear and classical inter-state wars seem to be becoming less likely, and the phenomenon of sub-conventional war and transnational militancy and terrorism have been on the rise. The latter belongs to the genre of "Low Intensity Conflict" (LIC). The term LIC has emerged only in the recent decades, with the US Pentagon's description of the spectrum of conflict consisting of 'high' 'medium' and 'low' intensity levels, in Klare and Kornbluh (ed). *Low Intensity Warfare*, 1988.

Contemporary warfare is predominantly of 'Low Intensity' variety. Presently, terrorism is the most dominant and most widely practised form of the LIC. It is the 'weapon' of choice for the non-state actors, who deploy it most effectively and stridently against the Conventional might of the states.

Here is some statistical information of the wide use of this variety of "Low Intensity Conflict", viz. terrorism. Since 1945, the world has seen over 160 conflicts. Of these, three-fourths have been low intensity. The victims of terrorism mostly are innocent civilians, including women and children. The real tragedy lies in the fact that victims even do not know why they are targeted and killed so mercilessly.

Majority of the material in this book is from open sources: the print and the visual media, the internet, and personal interaction with the reputed experts in the area. I owe a deep debt of gratitude to the Institute for Conflict Management, New Delhi, headed by that intrepid police officer, KPS Gill, who retrieved the Punjab for India when it had nearly gone under. I too have downloaded/used extensive data from its South Asia Terrorism Portal (SATP), like so many others in media and Academia.

This book, a multi-volume, comprehensive study, aims at spreading awareness among the civil society about the dangers posed to the international community by the ever-spreading phenomenon of the deadly pandemic called terrorism. It covers all aspects of terrorism in various parts of the world. It explains the ground realities lucidly, sans any academic and professional jargon.

Encyclopaedic in scope, the book will have served its purpose if scholars find it a useful reference work and common readers see the issues relating to terrorism in perspective and appreciate the implications of the threat to human kind in clear terms.

With this, I rest my case, sincerely the book is worth a read.

**Col. Ved Prakash (FRGS)**

# 1
# INTRODUCTORY

Terrorism is a part of human history, even if it has assumed most virulent and vicious proportions during the past some decades. The technological advances made by the world have placed in the hands of the terrorists tremendous destructive power which they used mercilessly, sans any compunctions, bringing murder, mayhem and devastation on the heads of the humans-mostly innocent.

A scholarly computation avers there are 79 Low Intensity Conflicts (LIC), 32 complex emergencies and 18 ethnic wars overplaying 175 small-scale internal wars throughout the world. What scales of misery and misfortune it has unleashed in the wide world will be clear in the text of this book. But some illustrative examples are cited below to make the point :

- 8,759 civilian and security personnel have been killed in Pakistan in 2009 till 9 June (SATPO). Nine people were killed in an attack on a hotel in Peshawar on June 10 and on June 12, 10 people were killed when bombers struck at a mosque in Noushera (NWFP) and at a mosque in Lahore (Punjab).
- At least 177 people were killed in a weekend attack (18-19 April 2009) on villages of the Lou Nuer tribe by armed men from the rival Murle ethnic group in South Sudan's Jonglei state. "We are expecting more than 300 by the time all the places have been checked" said Doyak Chol, Commissioner of Akobo county.
- UN estimates that more than 100,000 people have been killed in the 26-year-long conflict in Sri Lanka, including 6,000 in the last ferocious five months alone (Jan-May 2009) of the LTTE's war for the Eelam. Incidentally, the last and final was Eelam war IV.

- The misery of the internally displaced people (IDP), a natural consequence of terrorism-inflicted violence, cannot be over-estimated. Pakistan's armed action against its Taliban terrorists in the Swat Valley alone has resulted in more than 250,000 IDPs taking shelter in the Temporary tented camps. The numbers swelling to horrendous proportions can well be imagined when that nation's Army extends the operations to South Waziristan shortly-say in June 2009.
- The number of the IDPs in Sri Lanka as of date (June 2009) is over half-a-million, 150,000 from the last stages of the war (March-May 2009) alone.
- Afghan-Pak-India region has become the epicenter of global- terror. In 2008, the three countries accounted for a total of 5,395 killings-crossing that of lraq (a country at war and amid civil strife)—5,016. As Obama has crafted a new Af-Pak strategy to fight terrorism, it is yet to show any results. Under the US pressure, Pakistan launched anti-Taliban operations is Swat valley in May 2009, the going has been tough. The bigger fight awaits Gen. Purvez Kyani's army in South Waziristan and there is no knowing as of 16 June 2009 if he is ready for that bigger challenge.
- The break-down of fatalities caused by terrorist attacks for 2008 is given below :

| Country | 2005 | 2006 | 2007 | 2008 |
|---|---|---|---|---|
| Pakistan | 338 | 387 | 1,335 | 2,293 |
| Afghanistan | 682 | 1,042 | 1,966 | 1,989 |
| India | 1,357 | 1,256 | 1,093 | 1,113 |

- Terror deaths in Pakistan in 2008 was up by 70 per cent
- Statistics for 2008 Terrorism.

- 404 was total suicide attacks, marginally down from 525 in 2007.
- 9 per cent of all suicide attacks in 2008 were by women. In Iraq, this figure was 15 per cent.
- 50,000 were injured and killed in terror attacks. Over 50 per cent of them were Muslims.

## Defining Terrorism

Defining terrorism has been problematic from the very beginning and very roughly, and in general terms the phenomenon of terrorism can be defined as a strategy whereby violence is used to produce certain effects in a group of people so as to attain some political ends. Fear in one of the effects of such a strategy but certainly there are others.[1]

Both States seeking to maintain power and non-state actors trying to wrest it can resort to strategy of terrorism.[2] In the contemporary world, where terrorist strategies are generally linked to the non-state actors, it is good to remember that the origin of this political term was the state error of the so-called Reign of Terror in 1793-94 during the French Revolution, Robeshpierre and Committee on Public Safety executed thousands of citizens who had opposed it. The term was later applied to the case of the Great Terror of Joseph Stalin from 1936 to 1938. Both, the Frenchman and the Russian had one basic aim: to intimidate those who offered opposition to their policies. (The compliments were returned when the other dubbed USA, the biggest terrorist state when it bombed Japan in 1945. Likewise, the Umman today hold President George W. Bush as the worst criminal in the field of terrorism.

A scholar noted in 1970's a divergence of views as to what constituted terrorism. He observed that although analysts and diplomats continued to debate over the precise meaning of the term, "recent contemporary usage tends to restrict is meaning to either random or extortionate violence, aimed ultimately at the target state or a guerrilla, resistance or a liberation movement, which strike at unarmed civilians, diplomats, or non-combatants."

Of late, we are well-aware of the species called political terrorist. Terrorism which is part of a strategy for attaining political power has certain other components :

1. Terrorism is manifested in acts of socially and politically unacceptable violence.
2. There is a consistent pattern of symbolic or representative selection of the victim or objects of acts of terrorism.
3. The revolutionary movement deliberately intends these actions to create a psychological effects on specific groups and thereby to change their political behaviour and attitudes.

It may be of interest to know how the Encyclopaedia defines terrorism :

> The systematic use of terror (such a bombing, killing, and kidnapping) as a means of forcing some political objective. When used by a Government, it may signal efforts to stiffle dissent; used by insurrectionists or guerrillas, it may be part of an overall effort to effect desired political change.

EV Valter speaks of terror as an emotional state caused by specific acts or threats of violence, and terrorism as compound of three elements; the act or threat of violence, the emotional reaction and the social effects.[3] In 1934, JBS Hardman spoke of terrorism as activities involving a "systematic use of violence", but somehow sought to distinguish between mass insurrection" and the "terrorist method".[4]

David Rapoport, on the other hand, spoke of terrorists as involving individuals and acts bent on injury and unconstrained by "moral limits" and consequently argues that a moral distinction can be made between acts of political violence in general and terrorism *per se.*[5]

## A LOOK BACK

In its present incarnation, terrorism once employed by power and influence-seeking guerrillas against the imperial and colonial powers in the wars of national liberation in Africa and Asia in the 1950's and early 1960's, debouched out of the jungles and deserts into the cultural cities of the East and West. Its growth has been phenomenal, even exponential, ever since. If in 1971, there were 279 separate terrorist acts including bombing, murders, hostage-takings and kidnapping, the figure had grown to 1709 in 1980.

What Marighella clearly advocated was terrorism; the use of severe sanction or deadly force against innocents for the express proximate purpose of bending others to his will. This strategy being a given, terrorist bands commit themselves to the indiscriminate bombing of public buildings, the random drowning of Caribbean or Air India Planes in transit, the kidnapping of innocents to serve as hostages or examples.

In the Course of political revolution, one may indimidate those whose behaviour one wishes to modify. Terror, on the other hand, is not employed to alter the conduct of its victims. It is employed to influence others. Innocents are used as means to proximate ends.

## Terrorism: A Histories Perspective

A look back to the past should be of some interest for the present day scholars of the subject.

## Terrorism and the Left

Terrorism is not the sole property of the Left, but there were terrorist groups world-wide during 1970's or lo which were Marxist-oriented or influenced, and the terrorist activity of the subsequent years had resulted from the operations and teaching of such groups. The traditional Marxist-Leninist line was that terrorism was a legitimate revolutionary weapon but it should be used only when conditions for successful revolution existed and then too, as a part of a greater mass struggle under the control of "the party". As in all other fields of endeavor, "the Party" was the Prime Mover.

The major Communist State the Soviet Union selectively supported terrorist groups abroad. To wit, it supported palestine Liberation Organisation because the latters activities had accorded with Soviet international policies and perspective. It vehemently castigated Arab terrorist groups which opposed negotiations to resolve Arab-Israel conflict (namely, the Libyan-based terrorist outfits) as also the Maoist-oriented Zimbabwe African Union charged that "the Soviets tend to support only those movements it can control and manipulate in its own interest. In 1972, 94 Soviet diplomats were expelled 'from Bolivia because of their involvement in the activities of the National Liberation Army (ELN)' the local outfit founded by the "Cuban terrorist" Che Guevara.[7] September 1985, the UPI reported from Moscow that Britain expelled 12 Soviet officials six of them diplomats for working for the Soviet intelligence.[8]

Though late starters perhaps, the Chinese Communists, too were feverishly engaged in promoting terrorist groups in Africa, the Middle-East, and to a certain extent, in Latin America, during the period. China, understandably, in an attempt to establish its communist credentials was supporting rival terrorist movements to the ones patronised and sustained by the Soviet-Union in Rhodesia, South Africa, Angola and the African nations.

## The 1960s,-1980s Scenario: Exporting Terrorism

China, Pahistan and USA were involved in promoting terrorist groups in India, Afghanistan, and Sri Lanka. It must be remembered two Indian Prime Ministers - One serving, Indira Gandhi and one former, Rajiv Gandhi - tell to terrorism in 1984 and 1991.

The Peoples Revolutionary Army of Argentina cooperated with Tupamaros of Uruguay by attacking Uruguayan targets in Argentina. It is no secret that Japan's United Red Army attacked Lod Airport in Israel on behalf of its allies in the Popular Front of Liberation of Palestine (PELP). The Black September Organisation received help from the Baader-Meinhof terrorists in executing the gruesome murder of the Israli Olympians at their Munich camp. Bolivia's Army of National Liberation (ELN) murdered the Bolivian Consul in Hamburg, Germany. An IRA letter bomb seriously injured a British Embassy staffer in Washington DC.

Both the Communist Party and Socialist Workers Party (in various countries) were supportive of terrorism which they elevated to the status of "national liberation struggles" in Asia, Africa and Latin America. Then the Workers World Party, another American Trotskyst Communist Party was vociferously espousing the cause of several terrorist organizations in the Middle East and Latin America, including the Trotskyst Peoples' Revolutionary Army (ERP) in Argentina.

In the USA, revolutionary organisations had formed terrorist splinter groups of which some are listed below :

1. The Eldridge Cleaner faction of the Black Panther Party
2. The Weatherman
3. The Students for a Democratic Society
4. Proud Eagle Tribe
5. The Black Revolutionary Assault Team
6. The Americans for Justice
7. The Hoover Vacuum Conspiracy
8. Citizens Committee to Democratise Industry
9. The Black Afro Militant Movement.
10. East Coast Conspiracy to Save Lives
11. The Camp McCoy Three.
12. The New Years Gang.
13. Symbionese Liberation Army.

The development of the plastic explosives and compact automatic weapons afforded the terrorists better avenues to exploit their targest. They were, consequentily better armed than the police forces charged to counter them. In Munich, for instance, the palestinians used the Kalashnikov automatic rifles—the weapon of revolution - whereas the Police were armed with single shot rifles.

The general ambience of the 1970s favoured terrorist actions. Mao Zedong spoke of guerrillas living among the peasant population like fish in the sea. In Europe, middle class university students, indoctrinated by the eminent intellectuals like Sartre and Marcure dubbed as "false prophets" by some, created an intellectual climate that nourished urban terrorism.

It is not that all terrorist groups were informed by intellectual precepts. The hitmen of the IRA were certainly not the same political animals as the other international terrorists, being the exception to the normal terrorist profile in Western Europe. Dr. Richard clutterbuck postulated that both the IRA and their Protestant counterparts were "the only terrorist organisations in the world which even in their leadership have practically no intellectuals."[9]

The Indian terrorists' leadership, following the US and IRA desperados, was also deficient in intellectual grounding, and believed in killing everybody or anybody merely to create an atmosphere of terror and destabilize the government and create inter-religious strife. Exploding an Air India plane off the Irish Coast was the worst horror story in the world history that dispatched more than 300 passengers to their watery graves in the ocean below.

It so happened that the circumstances in various parts of the world gave rise to an upsurge of terrorism among the people who, because of modern communications, could act in concert when they desired and because they had all read the same books—Marcuse, Sartre—and drunk deep from the technicians of terror—Che Guevara, Frantz Fanon, and Carlos Marighilla.

Western analysts were convinced that the Soviet Union was interested in keeping the fires burning and the pot boiling believing that anything that destabilised the Government's and caused political and social disharmony and even internicine strife in the societal and communal groups anywhere in the world was a step closer to the ultimate desideratum—the proletarian Revolution! The Soviet Union - some would say, the Russian -

offered weapons, ideological training, and political and logistical support for the Arab groups, arguing that they were oppressed people fighting a "war of obliteration".

Commander of the PLO Squad, Adnanh Jaber, had received six months of intensive training at Sokhodnaya, near Moscow. "Palestinians, Libyans, South Yemenis, Iraqis and Algerians have been trained at Sanpzoval, near Simfarapol on the Black Sea in advanced explosive work, bomb making and in biological and chemical warfare."

The Soviets extended the work of promotion of terrorist ideals and practices to the intellectual and literary fields as well. The markets world over, particularly in the under-developed and Non-Aligned Movement Countries were floored with cheap but attractively produced books on Communism and Soviet Union, mainly written by Marx, Engels - two gods of the original ideology, and supplemented by Lenin, Trotsky, Stalin and other Soviet leaders - The lesser demi-gods of the pantheon. In the library field, for instance, the Russians funded subversive magazines, such as *Koukret* in West Germany, for which Wricke Mainhof was a star writer. The bright third world student leaders, especially chosen for training as future leaders of the "Liberalion Armies", "were run through a special course at the Lumumba University, Moscow. The infamous Veneguelan assassin Carlos spent sometime at the Lumumba before being ostensibly expelled, but there is good reason to believe that he maintained in good links with the KGB.

There was little doubt about the active involvement of the KGB and RGU in the promotion of world terror, but the were definitely not the creator of the monstor in the first place as the CIA would have liked us to believe. But the two definitely did a great deal to help spread the cancer by providing all manner of help, expertise, and technical know-how. For the KGB and the GRU/RGU, an important part of the Soviet system, helping international terrorism to spread was akin to helping out the evil capitalism.

If any country fought back the vicious terrorism and armed insurrection mounted and supported by the terrorist/revolutionary groups with links with Moscow, the communists would unleash a vicious propaganda barrage, accusing the victim of resorting to an oppressive. "State terrorism". But it was an ironic situation where a state, worst perpetrators of state terrorism even against its own citizens, was accusing another of it. It is far note that the force used by a democratic state against the terrorists is legitimate while the violence of the terrorist is illegal, inhuman, and actuated by the thirst for blood.

The United Kingdom Prevention of Terrorism Act 1976, one of the first anti-terrorism enactments, pragmatically lays down" "Terrorism means the use of violence for political ends, and includes any use of for the purpose of putting the public or any section of the community in fear". By extension, any entity that trains, arms, and finances groups that enable them to unleash terrorism on a wider scale and in a more methodical way is also covered under the provisions of the 1976 Act. So the Soviet Union is guilty of the crime of terrorism.

Even the sheer numbers were frightening. In 1981, the National Foreign Assessment Centre of the CIA avoched that during 1968-79, terrorists carried out 6,714 attacks amounting to international terrorism, 1,008 threats, 58 hoaxes, and 121 cases of conspiracy.

## TERMINOLOGY OF TERRORISM

Here are defined some terms applied to terrorism and terrorist activities. As in most cases in the recent times, the terminology has originated from the West, especially from the US. They seem to be good at coining terms relevant to a variety of situations (e.g. "shock and awe" during Iraq invasion, "collateral damage" earlier, and "veterans" for "retired" even earlier) one has to be careful while applying some of these terms to the Indian situations, because a lot depends on who is applying these terms and for what purpose! Vested interests can mischievously misinterpret some of these terms as applied to the terrorists in Punjab and Jammu and Kashmir, to serve their own ulterior motives. Peculiarities of a specific situation must be borne in mind while using and applying some of these terms coined in the context of the Western experience.

Some of these terms, relevant to counter-terrorism has been included here. What these terms mean to the terrorist and their sponsors have also been explained in amplificatory remarks.

### Revolutionary Terrorism

It is a form of political terrorism some times dubbed as agitational terrorism or terror from below. Its primary aim is to destabilise or over throw a regime by mobilising public support, beginning with the lower strata of society. The popular definition would apply more to revolution in China, Vietnam, and even Cuba and Che Guevara led and incited struggles in South America, Anti-colonial and anti-dictatorial movements too will come in this rubric. The Soviet Union exported this brand to several parts of the globe. In simple words, it may also be termed insurrectionary violence. Some analysts saw the strategy and course of terrorism in Punjab and Jammu and Kashmir following the pattern commonly identified with revolutionary terrorism. Disagreeing with this postulation, some others saw the violent movements in both states as religiously impelled. Mao Tse-dong visualised revolution in three phases :

1. Efforts are directed at organizing, establishing and preserving the solution.
2. Expansion.
3. Destruction of the regime.

But Thomas Thoronton sees an insurrection passing through five stages :

| *Phase* | *Characteristic* | *Objective* |
|---|---|---|
| 1. Preparatory | Pre-violent | Establish cause |
| 2. Initial violence | Terrorism | Morally isolate |
| 3. Expansion | Guerrilla warfare | Physically isolate |
| 4. Victorious | Conventional war | Destroy Physically |
| 5. Consolidation | Post Violent | Re-programme and maintan new regime |

At the practical level neither of the movements went beyond the third phase. After wide-spread violence for about five years in this phase, Punjab terrorism was brought to an end by the Punjab Police, greatly helped by the Army. In Jammu and Kashmir, terrorism has had a prolonged spell, essentially because of favourable conditions in the form of active help from a neighbour. Whatever may happen, Indian democracy is strong enough to ensure that it does not progress beyond phase three. In fact, in the last few years, especially after Nine-Eleven, Pakistan has felt compelled to reduce the level of support to terrorism in Kashmir, though it claims - obviously without convincing India - to have dismantled the entire terrorist infrastructure on its soil and cut off all help to it.

In Punjab and J & K, pre-violent phases were easily recognizable before terrorism properly manifested itself. In Punjab, moral isolation had largely been achieved but physical isolation was never possible, bar some districts, if we have to go by the Thoronton theory. In J & K, stages of moral and physical isolation seemed to have merged, as they neared the expansion phase by 1989-90.

The major factor to be recognized in Punjab and Kashmir terrorism is that the motive force behind either is the religious fundamentalism injected from outside sources: Pakistan in case of the latter and the overseas Sikh diaspora in the former.

## State Terrorism

Abnormal and excessive/repressive use of force by a state on a population for the express purpose of breaking its will and resolve to continue a movement qualifies to be termed as state terrorism. To a degree, all states use power to unruly crowds or anti-national movements and guiding principle here for the state is to employ minimum force, and not let loose a reign of terror, as was the practice of the colonial or dictatorial regimes. The use of force by a state beyond a certain degree proves counter-productive and inefficient, for the simple reason that the consent in the long run must form part of the calculus of power in a democratic polity. Excessive use of force against a movement is sure to create additional recruits to swell its ranks. Sometimes the term State terrorism has been applied to certain police methods in J & K (as Punjab earlier) because a section of SF used hars and indiscriminate methods. Such methods, unless used a part of state policy can only be explained in terms of lack of control and management of police resources.

However, in idealistic terms and in theoretical framework, if private armies and vigilante groups are allowed to terrorize the population or even the terrorists themselves, this too can be term as (a form of) State terrorism (Now we are entering the tricky, rather slippery ground. How shall be termed the *Salvajudum*, the victims of naxal terrorism, the tribes of Jharkhand themselves taking up arms against their tormentors? (More on it later). Such methods may prove effective for short periods, where it may not be essential to preserve cohesion and affinity with the local population, as in case of, say, an occupation Army. But in the long run, these methods are bound to create popular anger, even counter-violence. Such methods indeed, were used by Israel and Sri Lanka to fight terrorism and civil disobedience.

### State-sponsored Terrorism

This is the term applied to terrorism nurtured and fomented in a state by a neighbour or another State, aimed at destabilising the international borders of the former to sabotage its unity, integrity, sovereignty. Revolutionary, international, even micro-terrorism can be inspired and sponsored by a third power. India has no doubt that terrorism in Punjab and J & K was sponsored by a neighbour on the West, but Pakistan denies being its originator. Even when it was obvious that Pakistan has given shelter to senior Khalistani terrorist leaders, and trained and armed them as it did the Islamic terrorists in J & K, a bland and repeated denial has been its consistent response.

### Religious and Sacred Terrorism

Terrorism fomented and sustained by the followers of a particular faith focus on self-sacrifice and stringent moral codes of that religion, in this case, violence is seen as a path of salvation regardless of political out come, in terms of success and failure. This generally means a regin of terror for the non-believers and adherence of other faiths. This genre of terrorism has been in evidence in Punjab (1980s to early 1990s) and in J & K (1947 till date - 1996) in the terrorism let loose by some fanatical and radical religious groups. The terrorism practiced by the Sunni and Sikh groups against each other also comes in this category.

### The Organisational Process Theory

The theory holds that terrorism can become self-sustaining regardless of political factors that weigh with the organization. Recruits often join for reasons other than ideological conviction, and usually guided by a desire for material benefits or by an urge for an image or status. "As violence in such groups is often considered a path for individual salvation the organization may aim to achieve group cohesion and solidarity through religious or sacred terrorism". This should also explain as to why terrorism often persists in the face of its failure to achieve its political objectives.

### The Instrumental Perspective

When acts of terrorism represent a strategic choice and the

means of terrorism are directly related to these aims, it defines an Instrumental Perspective. Such terrorism should die a natural death, if it fails to achieve the stated political goal. This type of terrorism is more relevant to J & K. It is likely to be defeated here if we convince the people that their political aims cannot be achieved through terrorism.

**Counter-terrorism**

This terrorism is often and erroneously equated with state terrorism while it in fact applies to all social, economic, political and military means which are instituted to counter a terrorist threat or violence. Counter terrorism may take many shapes and forms depending upon the type of terrorism that needs to be countered by a state. In India, as in other democratic countries counter-terrorist measures have to conform to democratic and social norms of a free society. The term counter-terrorism includes counter-measures, organization, and actions necessary to defeat terrorism in a free democratic society. In Indian ethos, repression *per se* is not acceptable, but counter-measures could, however, includes strong methods necessary against the sponsors of terrorism, even if they are across the borders. This is only theoretical formulation. In practice, even in the face of substantial evidence about Pakistan arming and training terrorists in Kashmir, India till date has not proceeded against that country - whatever the reasons.

Counter terrorism should never involve repressive measures against any specific religious, linguistic, or ethnic groups in a free society. Terrorist on their part would want to create such an eventuality, as a part of their strategy to exploit the alienation of such groups for their own ulterior motives.

## Pre-emptive Measures

These are the measures initiated to incapacitate or prevent a terrorist attack before it materialises. Such pre-emption is possible only if a country has an effective and efficient intelligence system that is geared to accurately analyze and anticipate the intentions and capabilities of the terrorist organisations.

## Defensive Measures

These measures would include guarding of potential targets, erecting barriers, or border fencing. Such protective measures are taken to safeguard ones assets and vulnerable targets against terrorist attacks, but these could include certain offensive actions by the SF to engage the potential attackers before they make it to the assigned targets. In J & K the army has found it of advantage to confront the terrorists while crossing the LOC.

## Deterrence

In the field of terrorism, the term conveys the certainty of an unacceptably heavy damage to the terrorist organization and its sponsors in case of an attack. Any threats made in this context must be credible, and convince the adversary that the cost of his action would far out-weigh his likely gains. The deterrence does not seem to have worked so far J & K.

## Denial

A no concession policy can deny the gains of a terrorist attack. The denial should also shut out any benefits by raising the immediate cost of an action. It is equivalent of the "no negotiations with the terrorists" policy, stubbornly followed by Israel and US.

## Retaliation

Use of force or threat in response to a threat or terrorist attack on any target. Ideally, it should be directed against the terrorists, not against individuals or people in general - something which has been witnessed at times earlier in Punjab and presently in J & K against some suspects or suspected sympathizers, mostly flowing from the religious or ethnic affinities with the terrorists. Such actions prove not only counter-productive but also add to the alienation among the population. Even collateral damage following from counter terrorist actions will unfortunately result in similar alienation.

Retaliation may be categorized into symmetrical when it is confined to the actual area or a base from where the attack is launched, and asymmetrical which means a threat or actual attack on any sensitive target or area of the adversary.

## Some other connected Terms

**Homo-Fighters:** A term coined by Ariel Merarie in the context of the state sponsored terrorism when the terrorists target their own co-religionists on a select basis.

**Zeno-Fighters:** International Revolutionary terrorists involved in mounting terrorism against targets and areas in a "foreign" country, essential under the control of the host country, since the victims do not belong their country, the terrorists do not care if innocents are hurt. The terrorists, reportedly coming from sixteen countries and operating in J & K, obviously belong to this category.

## Latent Crisis

It is indicative of a situation when an oligarchy rules without the popular support of the masses, but with the help of the armed forces. Masses, too weak to overthrow the regime, generally express their protect through strikes, demonstrations and selective assassinations. The situation in Pakistan under the military rule perhaps tight fits the terminology. The Governor's rule in a democratic polity like India's, within certain time limits does not come under this category. Perhaps the Governors rule in J & K in 1989 - 90 imposed by the centre against mass support can be included in this category.

## Ovet Crisis

This is the situation when certain political forces rise openly and use violence against the government, the movement may not have the mass support and uses violence merely to survive. Punjab's violence was the case of such a crisis. J & K too can be included in this category as terrorist have very limited support, and that too in a certain areas of the valley, and masses of people brave the terrorist bullets to access their franchise every five years.

## Burn out and Backlash

The term is indicative of a sit when the terrorists lose public sympathy and support, consequent to having been exposed as immoral, inhuman and politically weak can invite a backlash by the counter terrorist organizations.

One should not be taken in by the surface image of incoherent' proliferation of the terrorist outfits. A deeper look would reveal a great deal of planning in raising the new outfits and rule subsequent coordination between all of them - the newly created and the existing ones. Conceptual and operational responsibility rests with the ISI and physical coond is ensured through an over arching set up like the UJC (United Jihad Council).

The trade-off between the 'national interests' and 'international interests' is increasingly open to question in the USA.

We believe that analysed is needed for arranging at info of opinions' De-mystification of militancy in JK is necessary. Truth has been sacrified at the alter of expedency in the USA and other Cs of G-8 in this regard. This needs addressing and correction.

## Network and Linkages of Terrorists : Need to understand

Terrorism is a part of human history, as delineated in latter parts of this chapter. But it has assumed vicious proportions during the past few deades, unleashing a flurry of murder and mayhem the world over. It has been helped on the may by related syndicates of narco-traders, economic criminal and political derelicts through misgovernance and corruption. Consequently, because of innovative and effective ways of money-laundering by a variety of criminals like some mentioned above, the terrorist outfits are flush with funds. Of late, the networking and linkages made possible by the advances in the technological field have added strength to the muscle of the terrorist outfits.

The insurgents and terrorists have succeeded in creating these networks not only within the countries they are operating in, but also beyond the boundaries of these countries. Consequently, the trans-national terrorism[10] (TNT) have spread its tentacles almost all over the world. This section will largely discuss the conceptual underpining of these networks and their organizational structures and operational characteristics. Some of the operational capabilities of Al Qaeda network have also been analysed as it is impacting the transnational terrorism as none of the other terrorist organizations do.

## Networking of insurgents: A conceptual understanding

A casual look at the familiar, artificial political lines drawn on a current world map and the 21st century's strategic realities suggested there at would show a complex new security paradigm. A little more careful look into that picture would afford snapshots that indicate several types of ambiguous and asymmetries conflicts.

Presently, there are 79 low intensity conflicts (LIC), 32 complex emergencies and 18 ethnic wars overlapping 175 small scale internal wars throughout the world. The consequence of this conflict-ridden scenario is unimaginable human destruction and misery, resulting in refugee flows, food and water security and resource conflicts. One study shows that since the first Persian Gulf War, anywhere between 80 to 200 million people have lost their hopes, their property and/or their lives. The consequent political alienation, reinforced by misgovernance/official corruption, criminal activity and social violence, tends to impel the survivors and their supporters/advocates towards more and more violence, insurgency/terrorism and asymmetrical tactics of despair.

People tend to hold the governments responsible for unfortunate, oppressive and unbearable situation. This results in diminished levels of popular and institutional acceptance of weak and ineffectual governments. What emerges thereafter is a broken pattern of emerging insurgencies, violence and poor governance. Ultimately, this ambience of uncertainty, confounded further by human destabilizers who exploit the situation for their own ulterior motives, create a vicious cycle of hate and dependence. In the next easy step, the armed non-state actors/groups undermine the nation-states' physical capabilities to govern. And finally, their very moral authority to govern is questioned/challenged. Political instability is the result of all this, which ends into economic and social chaop. Two apt examples of this tragic phenomenon in the current international situation are Somalia and Sudan, both in Africa unfortunately.

In the natural course of things, a state and its governing institutions should be the only authority to make laws and enforce them. The violent, intimidating and corrupt activities of illegal internal and transnational non-state actors/outfits could challenge and negate this authority of the State. A nation-state's security is under serious threat if these non-state actors come in the way of the former undertaking any of the following duties/tasks/ responsibilities: one to control its national territory, two, ensure the safety and security of its citizens, and to three, to control internal factions or non-state actors seeking illegal violent change within its borders.

The new network insurgencies/insurgents possess standing armed groups, treasury, revenue resources, and their very own intelligence services. Consequently, they own the where withals to strike alliance with non-state entities and even more importantly, intelligence agencies of other countries. They also promote a common vision by promulgating the policy, laws, and even war against the state. Brian M Genkins in his reminal essay, "Redefining the Enemy", describes the distinction between war and crime, which continues to result in a policy quandary where we underestimate the power of militarily inferior foes (insurgent), difficult terrain, unceasing hostilities and other unconventional measures of power."

Net war (the now and future past-modern war) waged by irregular adversaries including terrorists/insurgents, drug cartels and criminal gangs is a new mode of regular conflict that blends terrorism, crime and war. The trends where technological and organizational changes that benefit relatively small actors and fuel asymmetric threats, have been identified by RAND analysts Jon Arquilla and David Rond Felt. They noted that networks can prevail over hierarchies in this emerging post-modern battle or operational space. Power is migrating to small non-state actors who can organise into sprawling networks more readily than can traditionally hierarchical nation-state actors.[12] It must be realised that the enemies we face have fundamentally changed. In addition to our traditional adversaries (hostile or potentially hostile states), we now face terrorists/insurgents, weapons proliferators, organised crime affiliates, and cyber outlaws inter-twined within the context of religious, ethnic, or tribal conflicts, yielding a set of dynamic, unpredictable, diverse, networked and constantly evolving challenges.

Trans-national crime is a threat to political, economic, environmental and social systems world-wide. This threat goes beyond the substantial illegal drug trade, fraud, corruption and manipulation of both political and financial systems. The transnational crime organisations (TCO) potentially undermine not only civil society but also a political systems and state soveignty by legitimising corruption. When these criminal actors employ violence against state institutions, they become non-state actors. This leads to collapse of authority, thereby by leading to unemployment; that sends the unemployed youth into criminal activities, and their joing the insurgent outfits is the natural next step.

The organised crime and insurgency/terrorism are related in complex and diverse ways. Crime of many varieties (like drug trafficking and smuggling) are frequently used to fund terrorist or insurgent activity. Money laundering is at the core of global organised criminal enterprise. It is in this fiscal transaction or enterprise where terrorists/insurgents are most likely to cooperate. There links occasionally mature into alliances of convenience.

Terrorists or insurgents may exploit organised crime and the criminal can act as middle-man in smuggling of small arms, explosives and drugs. These criminals usually use the smuggling routes. This type of activity has been frequently used by Pakistan's ISI and Bangladesh's DGFI in Northeast India. The networks established by these groups display a remarkable capacity to transcend borders and flow around legal or geographic boundaries. These networks are based on risk reduction (joining with locals who exploit local conditions) and can expand the capabilities of criminal entities. There are four ideal types of violent actors: terrorists, rebels, criminals and warlords. Each uses violence to achieve their objective, their motives and strategies. In general terms, they, at times share common *modus operandi.* For example: criminals and warlords have economic imperatives while terrorists and insurgents have political aims. Insurgents and criminals typically target security forces and competing groups or other organisations. But terrorists and warlords generally target civilians. Warlords and insurgents seek to supplant the state's monopoly on force within a limited geographic territory, while terrorists and trans-national organised criminals operate on global scale.[13] All[14] can operate as privet armies. In addition, all can interact and blend or share attributes at given points in time. This is especially true in case of insurgents operating in northeast India.

## Network's Organisational Structure

The organisational structures used by security forces are inherently hierarchical in nature. They resemble a pyramid with key decision makers clustered towards the apex and command strata branching down like a tree root system. Information passes down from command level at a relatively slow pace. As part of the feedback loop, information is then passed slowly up the various command levels. This system suits the security force structure. Over the last decades, contemporary network (insurgent) organisational structures have gradually merged as a challenge to the hierarchical structures. They represent another aspects of modern to post-modern shift. A number of research works has been done regarding the organisational structure.[15]

These new structures are characterised as :

- Cells/nodes
- Information channels
- Ease of connectivity
- Flat information integration.[16]

Free flowing cells and nodes replaced rigid hierarchical tiers in this type of organisational structure and are best suited for insurgents. They are linked together via mutually beneficial information channels which form a web like pattern between the various cells and nodes of entity. These channels benefit from ease of connectivity which allows them to be established and terminated as required with little or no effort.

Networks require two issues to be addressed. First, the level of focus needs to be expanded from the tactical to the operational level of analysis. Second, traditional weapon systems are self contained with their own acquisition, targeting and offensive capabilities. Networks, by their very nature, are not self-contained and instead have combat functions distributed across the system of nodes.

## Operational Characteristics of Networks

The speed in their operation will be based upon Commander's decision making, information processing and reaction cycles rather than traditional forms of tactical or operational mobility.[17] Networked structures possess increased information flows due to the vast number of information channels and cross linkages that exist between the various cells/nodes. This results in many more times the amount of information being shared by the organisational structure and provides and information multiplier effect. Networked organisations reduce the amount of information hoarding by allowing a freer flow of information to take place. The required information is passed to all concerned.

The networked structures have the capability to easily create and then disconnect/drop nodes (cells), thereby they have the capability of masking their attack. Tracing who the attacker is tied to become difficult if not impossible. This method of shielding their nodes/cells from attack is by making combatants appearing to be non-combatants.[18] The insurgents merge with the masses and thus become indistinguishable from the rest of the people. The security forces operating can easily be identified. Therefore, merging with the public becomes difficult for them.

Generally the decision making is de-centralised in many networked structures, so it is difficult to identify the leader who may have passed on the orders to execute. Thereby, lot of time is wasted by the security forces to gain the information so as to react to a particular situation. Networked forces are not required to engage the security forces for longer duration during the encounter for offensive purposes. This allows them to have a higher degree of fire power for a shorter duration (required time) and thereby avoiding the counter measures by the security forces.

## TERROR MONGERS

Pakistan is known and believed—widely—to be a "most dangerous state in the world"—a phrase used by a US scholar. It not only recruits, trains, arms, nurtures, and launches terrorist attacks against its neighbors (India, Afghanistan and China)—but some nations in the distant Europe fear that its nationals are trained and equipped in Pakistan for terrorist attacks in these nations. The nations that can be included in the latter category are the UK, Spain, France, Germany etc.

There is a reason for Pakistan being dubbed as "the most dangerous place in the world". It is an unstable nation - some believe it to be a failing, if not a failed, state-possessing nuclear weapons, which states like US, UK, India etc. feel can fall in the hands of Taliban terrorists. It is not an exaggerated fear or an empty rhetoric, knowing fully well that some terror specialists have estimated that 40 per cent of the NWFP (now christened Pashtoonkhwa) is already under the Taliban control/influence. What is even worse is that the Taliban are now in a position to launch terror attacks in the major cities of the Punjab itself, the sword arm of Pakistan, viz Lahore, its capital, Rawalpindi, Islamabad, Bahawalpur et al. It is worth a note in this connection that Pakistan's President Asarf Ali Zardari himself has conceded such a possibility.

### China Fuels Terrorism

If Pakistan is a launch pad of terrorism, some other nations can be named as the ones that indirectly fuel terrorism. Saudi Arabia and China are two such nations. Saudi Arabia is the source of extremely hard line of Islam practiced by it, known as the Wahhahi Islam or Wahhabism. The country is generously financing large number of *madrassas* in Muslim countries and other countries with large Muslim populations like India. These madrassas in turn teach Wahhabi tenets of Islam, or Wahhabism, which in turn encourages terrorism among the *madrassa* students against the non-Muslim people and nations. It is no surprise that Osama is the product, and in turn, a preacher, of Wahhbli Islam. If Saudi Arabia is a potent source of terrorism among the Muslim populations, including the suicide terrorism, China fuels terrorism in its neighbouring countries by liberal supply and export of arms and ammunition to the extremists, insurgents, militants, and terrorists operating in the latter countries. India is the worst sufferer of this Chinese malfeasance. Hence the need to highlight the details of the Chinese malicious mischief in the opening Chapter of this book.

## Chinese Arms for the Indian Terrorists

An April 2008 report in *Jane's Intelligence Review* says "China has replaced Cambodia and Thailand as the main supplier of weapons to the insurgent groups in India's Northeast, Myanmar and Sri Lanka and also to the Taliban". What follows is the country-wise details on the issue.

### India

The report said insurgent groups in the Northeast get most of their arms supplies from China. The United Wa State Army (UWSA), a rebel group in Myanmar, acts as the "middleman" between Chinese arms manufacturers and insurgent groups in the Northeast, with most weapons routed through China's Yunnan province. From here, it takes the land route to Myanmar and from there, it is moved to the Indian border at Tamu, opposite Manipur.

In 2001, Myanmar intercepted a consignment of several hundred Chinese assault rifles that the UWSA was transporting to Manipur, possibly to the Manipuri UNLF and other possible factions.

### Myanmar

Much of the arms that get into India's Northeast is routed through Myanmar. Apart from the UWSA, China has allegedly stepped up its illicit arms trade with another rebel group, the Kachin Independence Army. While China maintains friendly relations with the Myanmarese junta, it has also been sustaining the UWSA with a range of Chinese weapons.

### Sri Lanka

The Sri Lankan conflict sustains almost entirely on Chinese arms. Ironically, while China's leading state-owned arms corporations, NORINCO and Poly Technologies supply to the Sri Lankan government, China's black market supplies arms to the LTTE. *Jane's* says that recent photographs of rebel troops show a range of evidently new Chinese weaponry, "including the modern 5.56 mm QBZ-95, which cannot have been captured from government forces".

## Afghanistan

The Taliban, since its revival in 2003, have had access to Chinese small arms and ammunition across either the Iranian or Pakistani territory. Apart from the anti-aircraft heavy machine guns, landmines and RPGs, the Taliban have managed to get the HN-5 MANPADS missiles, which were not in the Taliban's inventory before the US 'war on terror' in 2001. *Jane's* says that in February 2008, two HN-5 missiles, ready for firing, were reportedly got from Kandahar.

## The Route

Much of the export is shipped from the Chinese ports of Zhanjiang, Guangzhou and Hong Kong. *Jane's* says that the buyers of these arms usually take delivery of the ammunition at the Chinese docks and do the shipping themselves. But at times, the consignment is shipped to third countries where controls are lax and it is then distributed from there. Shihanoukville, on the southern coast of Cambodia was one such point, where Chinese arms, in particular headed for the LTTE, were shipped on to ports in the Gulf of Thailand for land transport to ports such as Ranong on the Andaman Sea coast.

## The Deal

A Chinese automatic rifle that is available for $ 500 in eastern Myanmar can command a price of $ 2,500 by the time it reaches the North-east.

### T 56 assault rifle (a Chinese rip-off of the AK-47) :

Rs. 2.5-3 lakh. A used one costs just Rs. 1-1.5 lakh.

### Magazines

Rs. 100 a piece

### Chinese pistols (M 20 pistol or .30 Marcos)

Rs. 1-1.5 lakh a piece

## The Expose

While the trend had been growing over the past few years, it was in 2004, when a massive arms consignment was seized in Chittagong, Bangladesh that the illegal market was exposed for the first time. The Chittagong arms seizures was one of the biggest in Bangladesh and it came to light that these weapons were meant for Northeast insurgent groups. Over 1,700 assault rifles, 400 Uzi submachine guns, 150 rocket propelled grenade launchers and a large quantity of ammunition were seized.

India has suffered the tangs of insurgency and terrorism since its very independence in 1947. For the West, especially the US, terrorism was born on Nine-Eleven. The US response to that traumatic event has been harsh. It not only created a new Department of Homeland Security, which laid down stringent rules on entry and exit of immigrants, particularly on Asians and Muslims but initiated a global war on terrorism, mainly in Afghanistan and FATA region. Likewise, most nations in Europe have enacted anti-terror laws.

The Obama administration has made a serious effort to smoothen the rough edges of the US counter-terror strategy of its predecessor, the Bush administration. The first step in this direction was Obama's announcement of his decision to shut down the Guantanamo Bay prison. Then he advanced the date of pull-out from Iraq and decided to send additional troops to Afghanistan to assure victory there against the terrorists - the Taliban. To mend the US fences with the Islamic world, Obama addressed the concerns of the Muslims and Arab nations during his visits to Turkey and Egypt in June 2009, respectively. He assured them that the GWOT was not targeting any particular religion or nations.

## References

1. Jenkins (1975), p. 1.
2. Let it be stated emphatically here that the two entities cannot and should now be placed on the equal footing, even if some fervent human rights espousers would assert that the state is a bigger danger to these rights than the outlaws it is confronting.
3. Translation from Saint-Just, Oevres Choises, pp. 251-65.
4. The *Ninth of Thermidor*; The fall of Robes pierre (NY and London 1968, edited by Richard T. Bienvenu.
5. Punanzio, Diritto, Forze e violenza, pp. 75-90.
6. The news grabbed the headlines at that time.
7. Today he is the revolutionary icon of the Leftist intellectuals as Mao seems to have been almost forgotten for whatever reasons.

8. Naunihal, 1985, p. 3.
9. Cited, Naunihal Singh, 1989, p. 5.
10. A more aggressive, destructive and suggestive acronym is difficult to imagine that "TNT".
11. Brain M Genkins *"Re-Defining the Enemy: The World Has Changed But Our Mind Set Has Not", BAND review,* Spring 2004.
12. Jon Arquilla and David Rond Felt, *A New Epoch—and Spectrum of Conflict", In Athena's Camp: Preparing for Conflict in the Information Age* (**Santa Monica,** CA: RAND, 1997), p. 5.
13. Jon P Sullivan; *"Terrorism Crime and Pravet Armies",* Networks Terrorism and Global Insurgency, p. 74.
14. There are four potential types of non-state actors: terrorists, criminals, insurgents and war lords.
15. Haward Rheingold, *"Smart Mobs: The Next Social Revolution"; Perseus Publications, 2002.*
16. Robert J Bunker and Matt Begert, *"Operational combat Analyses of Al Qaeda Network",* In Robert J Bunker ED Networks Terrorism and Global Insurgency, Routledge London and New York, p. 147.
17. Johan Voyd, *"A Discourse on Winning and Loosing".* MCA Press 1987.
18. Rober J Bunker and Matt Begert, *"Operational Combat Analysis of Al Qaeda Network";* Networks, Terrorism and Global Insurgency.

# 2

# TERRORISM : SOME ASSORTED ISSUES

Terrorism has assumed menacing proportions today. The term has come to subsume a variety of violence under its rubric. Some are mentioned below :

- Militancy
- Insurgent violence
- Ethnic violence
- Sectarian violence
- Religious conflicts
- State terrorism
- Freedom movements

Some of the genre is discussed in the succeeding pages.

## Terrorism : Religious and Secular

This Author would like to believe that the Zealots were the original terrorists. So a brief acquaintance is called for.

## Zealots

A Jewish sect noted for its uncompromising opposition to pagan Rome and the polytheism it professed. The Zealots were an aggressive political party whose concern for national and religious life of the Jewish people led them to despire even Jews who sought peace and conciliation with the Roman authorities.

Under Roman rule a number of new groups largely political emerged in Palestine. This common aim was to seen an independent Jewish state. All were zealous for, and strict in their observance of, the Torah.

The Herodians were a political group that after the death of Herod - whom they apparently regarded as the Messiah – sought the reestablishment of the rule of Herod's descendants over an independent Palestine as a pre-requisite for Jewish preservation. Unlike the Zealots, however, they did not refuse to pay taxes to the Romans.

The Zealots' party, founded 154 AD, refused to pay taxes to the Romans and advocated overthrowing them on the ground that they should acknowledge God alone as their master. A priestly, eschatologically oriented resistance movement, the Zealots were particularly dedicated to keeping the Temple and its cult pure and used guerrilla tactics towards that end. The *Sicarii* (Assassins), so called because of the dagger (*Sica*) they carried, arose, 154 AD, according to Josephus as a group of bandits who kidnapped or murdered those who had found a modus videndi with the Romans.

A census of Galilee ordered by Rome in AD 6 spurred the Zealots to rally the populace to non-compliance on the grounds that the agreement was an implicit acknowledgement by Jews of the right of pagans to rule their nation.

Extremism among the Zealots turned to terrorism and assassination and became known as Siearii (Greek *Sikarioi* = "dagger men"). They frequented public places with hidden daggers to strike down persons friendly to Rome. In the first Revolt against Rome (AD 66-70) the Zealots played a leading role. "It was they who in 73 made a stand at the fortress of Marada[1] near the Dead Sea, and committed suicide rather than surrender the fortress"[2] (and be captured by the Romans). They were still a force to be reckoned with in the first part of the following (second) century.[3]

## Religion and Terrorism : Are They Related?

There is a common belief that religious studies can help one understand better the character of secular terrorist activities, in two distinct ways.

The first approach suggests the study of appropriate analogies and parallels, because actual religious and secular terrorist movements, their political and moral contexts and the strategy and tactics employed can be compared. Kavolis and Amon compare images and metaphors used to describe rebels and their antagonists. The second approach espoused by Dugard and

Pottenger, studies particular theological concepts used consciously by the moderns to justify secular movements.

In the first century, the Jewish terrorists (briefly mentioned above) made successful efforts to provoke a popular uprising. The Sicarii/Zealot successes deserve serious attention, "if only because it occurs so rarely." No religious terrorist movement has ever been successful; and equally truely, one would be hard pressed to cite a secular movement that came close to generating a revolt by the masses, although ever since the 19th century most have conceptualised terror as the instrument to do just that (for the time being, let this postulation pass, because the recent 1980-2006. Islamic terrorism has not been ideologically sanctioned by the Muslim clergy, nor the success achieved by the groups of the native populations colonised by the western nations through egregious violence, could be called terrorism since they have been widely dubbed as freedom struggles by the oppressed.

The Zealots displayed extraordinary abilities to invent a variety of ingenious tactics from passive resistance to terrorism. Their aim was to make Jews lose confidence even in Jewish authorities and to provoke such hatred among the Jews, Greeks, and Romans that every effort at political conciliation would be frustrated. A moral and political ambience created by the Government, eager to prevent trouble made these tactics feasible.

A case-study of the 2000-year old events prove that some of the terrorist leaders of the Post-World War II movements (Palestine, Cyprus, and Northern Ireland) did learn some lessons from it, one way or the other. If Menachem Begin, aware of the harm and ill-effects brought in by the most serious crimes and mistakes committed by the Zealots, pursuaded, and even compelled the 'Irgun' to restraint itself, and thereby achieved success 2000 years after the failure of the Zealots, the Al Fatah did till to late, and the Hamas even today employ mindless terrorism to ensure continued antagonism between Israel and the neighbouring Arab nations to serve their perceived interest.

Atheists, some analysts, and even agnostics, assert that even organised religions have created more havoc through violence than all other organised groups put together. The instances of intra-Christian killing, the Crusades and the on-going post-Nine-Eleven wars of civilizations darkly hinted by a western scholar easily come to mind. The question whether religion and terrorism are related twins is best left unanswered.

## A look back in History

It is apparent that most millenarian groups do not employ terror. They are likely to be passive, even pacifist, seeking separation from the greater society in order to make spiritual preparations for the great day. But some groups, withdrawing from the pacifist bodies, as some Jewish rebels did, may resort to terrorism. This may happen when the possibility of an earthly paradise seems imminent. When Messianic impulses did result in terrorism, prior to the French Revolution (1789-99), it developed into a variety of patterns.

In Islam, messianic-inspired terror produced *Nizaris* (assassins) whose violence was essentially directed against the officials who were duty-bound to prevent their *dais* (mission) from operating openly. Their armies waged "a holy war" against the existing societal order by periodically sweeping over the country side, indiscriminately devastating, burning, and massacring. Terrorism was aimed at obliterating all physical and spiritual traces of the old order. The plans of the Fifth Monarchy men during the Puritan Revolution to capture the government to force the purification of the society were aborted.

On this and other such violent movements, Michael Walzer was to comment: "Their great achievement is what is known in the sociology of revolution as the terror, the effort to create a holy commonwealth and to force man to be godly."

The more common practice is to use terror against the millenarian cult members themselves in order to keep them isolated from the "corrupting" contact with the outside world. A recent instance is the mass suicide by the followers of Tim Tones people Temple that stunned the world in 1979.

The contact with the revealed religions resulted in a flourishing of the millenarian activity during the late 19th and early 20th centuries in the Third World, especially Asia and Africa, which accentuated into full fledged revolutionary movements.

Now comes something (paraphrased) from Moshe Anon interesting but something paradoxical: "Certain thinking leads a rebel to invoke terror against authority in the name of the very religion that establishes that authority. But these outbursts are exceptional as the same religions succeed in correcting the aberrations. The Latin origin of the term "religion" is significant here, as initially it was "religion without rules". Terror, inversely, was infringement of any rules. But the revealed religions too have antinomian in gradients which lead them to sometimes place faith above the rules or norms.

Rules command our allegiance only when we can believe in the new or better—a myth, perhaps—future that gives those rules some meaning. As the belief cannot be sustained for ever, there is an erosion of credibility in western religious beliefs since the renaissance, the genesis of secular myth of progress, and the relationship of both to each other and to present day terrorism.

The myth of progress is one of a "continuous advance towards a future utopia." It wants us to liberate ourselves from all norms derived from the proceeding myths and view all existing institutions as tentative, having utilitarian value only. Naturally, the responsible person is the one who wants to destroy the present societal structure to build an ideal future. Here enters Sergey Gennadiyevich Nechayev (1847-82), Russian revolutionary known for his organisational scheme for a professional revolutionary party and for his ruthless murder of a member of his party[4]. It is no surprise that classic works by terrorists since the mid-19th century like Nechayev's *Revolutionary Catechism* and Marighella's *Minimanuals* exclusively dilate upon the elaborate methods of destruction.

The myth - and consequent hope - of progress polarizes society, making terrorist groups attractive as the harbingers of change. Thus these groups have become Dionysian cults - the ends in themselves.

It was interesting to find a revivalist interpretation of, and possibly a perversion of the Christian concept of the "Just War" during the UN debates on the issue, as also on espousal of the Latin American "Liberation Theology," a new philosophical hypothesis that encouraged the clerical elements to regard revolutionary terrorist activities sympathetically. In "Just War," one party is believed to be morally culpable, while the other is required to rectify the wrong, without any constraints on its use of methods. The latter has even the right to destroy any person who *can*, but does not necessarily, bear arms against it.

But now comes the latest twist in the above scenario. The contemporary version of the "Just War" doctrine lays down that only self defence justifies coercion - a doctrine that stands incorporated in the UN charter. When this doctrine is applied to terrorist groups waging a war against colonial or racist governments, they are by definition, victims of aggression, and consequently are not only justified in taking up arms but are also free from the normal moral restraint incumbent upon the soldiers. But the "colonial" or racist parties however were/are subject to conventional moral restraints. In the context of this doctrine, the terrorist can only be the one whose motive is immoral or whose cause is unjust with the shifting of the criteria for culpability from action to the motive, a fundamental principal of traditional international law and one applicable for all existing domestic legal systems as well, has been overturned.

Here is an interesting speculation. The notion of a "holy war", developed in the middle ages to justify the crusades, and also used at *the same time* by Millenarian sects, is perhaps more appropriate to contemporary, evolutionary terrorist needs and practice, especially those of the more radical groups, than the idea of a "just war," even if the associated religious conotations are much too conspicuous for contemporary tasks.

It is widely accepted that modern revolutionary terrorism[5] originated in the writings and deeds of mid – 19th century Russian anarchists. The assassins of Medieval Islam who called themselves the *fidayeen* ("the faithful ones"), are the most publicised in the early movements.[6] But Thomas de Quincey, the English Romantic and first student of terrorist movements, acquaints us with others. In a bizarre essay, he tells of an imaginary club that met regularly to discuss the more "interesting" forms of assassination and terror. The terror groups mentioned are : Assassins, Zealots and Sicarii.[7]

All terrorist movements aim at producing panic and paralyzing fear. But in the modern world at least, terrorist assaults have served other possibly more important purposes too. What makes the efforts Flavius Josephus (37-95 AD; Jewish historian who was the first to write in Greek), describes so intriguingly is that they foreshadow contemporary experiences : "The aims of our society are none other than the entire emancipation and happiness of the people, convinced that their emancipation and the achievement of this happiness is brought about only by means of all destroying popular revolt."

An act of terror is invariably associated with violence that the two terms are frequently but incorrectly employed as synonyms. To make a distinction, terror is generally understood as an "extreme form of violence."[8] More accurately, terror is violence which goes beyond the norms generally accepted as regulating violence - attacking innocent or defenceless persons, mutilating prisoners and desecrating the dead are typical acts of terror in contemporary times, because they are prohibited in war and condemned as atrocities.

## Atrocities

Atrocities too serve various purposes, most obviously producing pure terror or paralyzing fear. As no terrorist group will have sufficient resources to maintain a condition of absolute uncertainty in an entire society for a long period, pure terror has a limited role in insurrectionary warfare. It is most efficacious when directed against specific critical/sensitive targets/groups.[9]

In the 20th century, to give one example, successful terrorist movements following in the footsteps of Michael Collins (IRA leader after World War I) paralysed the police early, usually by systematic assassination policies.

A second purpose of atrocities "is publicity to gain sympathy" and hence the Russian anarchist's description of terror as "propaganda by deed". Atrocity by its nature attracts considerable attention - the more spectacular the outrage, the more interest it arouses."[10]

Atrocities work both ways, as many potential sympathizers are repelled as well as attracted by them. A terrorist movement can not gain substantial strength until the government or its supporters are also seen employing similar tactics. An intelligent terrorist knows that those who identify most closely with his victims may be to enraged that they are provoked with committing counter - atrocities. So, a third purpose of atrocities is the stimulation of indiscriminate hostility - forcing the government to deal with the terrorist more harshly, if not in an equally inhuman, avenging manner.

Mindless terror will certainly prove counter-productive after a certain threshold of public patience and tolerance is crossed. ULFA movement in Assam offers a good example. During the 1990s, a number of its terrorists were nabbed by the victims kin and thoroughly thrashed before handing them over to the police, and in some cases of extreme outrage committed by these ultras, they were even lynched to death. The latest example of victims rising against the Naxal terrorists is from Chattisgarh.

Tribals willinghy agreed to (2005-6) to arm themselves with the weapons provided by the state and face the perpetrators of terror squarely significantly, the ruling party as well as the opposition are supporting them in their brave, if desperate, fight. This peace-campaign against the Naxals led by the tribals is known as Salwa. Something similar had happened earlier - late 1980's and early 1990s - when the public informed the police about the presence of the Khalistani terrorists in their area. Though the Army was called in during the last years of the insurgency, it was essentially the revival of police morale and its local-level intelligence under the gallant KPS Gill, the DGP, that won the battle. Even in the case of Kashmir insurgency, inspite the terrorists indulging in ruthless elimination of the so-called informers, often entire family, the locals are still coming forward to help the police in their anti-terrorist campaign.

No terrorist organistation can afford to win against an established government through sheer force of arms. Their initial resources are rather meagre and until they get support from a neighbouring nation, and get considerable backing of the society, convincing them of their cause, they can't even hope to conduct their movement for long. Once a certain threshold is crossed and a nation's sovereignty and integrity are at stake, a determined government will come down rather heavily and extinguish any flicker of hope which sustains all such movements. Inspite of over three – decades of its blood-spattered (splattered?) history, the LTTE has not been able to bend Colombo to achieve its desideratum. New Delhi had to enter the Golden Temple, Amritsar when the Khalistani terrorists, headed by Mr. Bhinderwale, had entrenched themselves within the holiest of the holy, even if the Nation paid a heavy cost in losing a serving Prime Minister (Indira Gandhi) in 1984. Through a mixture of political measure and use of force, New Delhi has brought most of the secessionist movement to the negotiating table. Some – like ULFA in Assam, NLFT in Tripura and PLA in Manipur are still holding out, but India can wait.

The Governments must deal firmly with terrorists. An ambivalent government, which in some ways recognises the legitimacy of their cause, and is politically embarrassed by counter-terrorist actions it is provoked into, will be ineffectual in dealing with the scourge. Ambivalence breeds uncertainty and inconsistency, and nothing disillusion the public, or excites the terrorists' hope, more!

But what is an empirical experience since the 1880's? Four generations of terrorists since that defining period have left a record of successes and failures, sufficiently clear for us to make certain conclusions. No terrorist campaign has succeeded in democratic, stable states. Nicaragua was an exception that proved the rule. Not only was the state underdeveloped, but for 45 years (1934-79) it was ruled by a repressive military regime dominated by Somozo family. So when in 1979, rebel forces - the US dubbed them as terrorists – seized power, it was a country devastated by civil war. They formed the left-wing Sandinista government, an anathema to the US. For II years (until 1990) the US sponsored the Contras-guerrilla opponent of the new Sandnista regime, trained in neighbouring Honduras by US advisers. Elections followed the withdrawl of the Contras in the 1990, in which the opposition coalition - the National Opposition Union (UNO) came to power.

Often terrorist intentions are misperceived as minor protests, and consequently inconsistent government responses gave strength to the terrorist movements. But eventually, the defenders of "the systems" learnt that the issue at state was survival. In totalitarian states terrorist activity has rarely even been attempted, the political terrorists were convinced from the beg'g that their adversaries - the ruling power - were determined to prevail, whatever the cost. Chinese use of force to decimate the protestors at Tiananmen Square comes easily to mind. Chechen rebels gained strength in Russia essentially after the dissolution of the S4.

Cynics might term the development as a gift bestowed by nascent democracy finding its feet in Russia. But it seems equally true that Russia hopes to prevail.

It is undoubtedly unfair to treat independence struggles in various colonial regimes as terrorism or terrorist activities. India offers a unique case where a Gandhi-led movement persuaded the British to withdraw peacefully, even though there was a violent struggle on the fringes, led by the Punjabi and Bengali youth. While the French followed the British pattern in relinquishing its colonies in India, Portugal exit was less graceful, as India had to mount a police-action to make her see reason. On the other end of the spectrum, US had to wage a most violent struggle to throw off the British Yoke. It was one of the most costliest war in human costs : 6 million casualties - killed and wounded. The bull dog bared its fangs again when it went to war to retake the Falkland Islands (or Isles Malvines) from Argentina which had invaded the British colony in 1982 that it had claimed since 1820. Likewise, France and Portugal two relinquished their colonies after violent struggles. An interesting fact is that with the sole exception of Ireland after World War I, all the successes in the way of the formal colonies have taken place since World War II, indicating how much that war transformed the general political ambience.

We have discussed parallels between an ancient experience and modern ones. The striking resemblance is the use of atrocities to provoke a massive uprising. Consecutive atrocities keep narrowing the room for a political or mutually agreeable solution, serving to destroy the credibility of moderates on both sides, while expanding the conflict which steadily enlists more and more participants. In the ancient example, there seems to be no master hand.

## Israeli Terrorism : Ancient and Contemporary

There was a bewildering assortment of terrorist forces : several zealots, at least two *Sicarii* organizations, and many other groups whose names and activities have scarcely survived. Then, as now, the effect of such multiplicity compelled each group to outdo others on the atrocities stakes, to prove the depth of its commitment. Consequently, in time the groups turned up and decimated each other with the same ferocity they had assailed the Romans with. Rising expectations and fierce inter-group competitive proclivities made it virtually impossible for the Jews to accept any terms the Romans could offer – a situation which is also true of the context where contemporary terrorism flourishes as well. Jewish expectations rose as there was a good possibility of mobilizing significant outside support. But the terrorists groups were sanguine about receiving divine help, and ironically, this expectation became more dominant as the actual possibilities of political support outside Judea vanished.

The terror campaign adversely impacted the Jewish consciousness, making it nearly impossible for Jews to justify violence for political purposes and until the middle of the 20th century. It was no surprise that although expectations of messianic deliverance (that would ensure an ingathering of the exiles and restoration of the political independence) survived the *Rabbies* persuaded their people to wait patiently for redemption because they would only bring further misfortune by endeavoring to expedite the process by political action and/or violence.

It is well known that the Rabbinic tradition transmitted the painful memory of how Jews lost their homeland that decisively impacted their consciousness, "But we seem to have forgotten entirely how the recollection of that senseless and avoidable catastrophe shaped the course of the insurrection which helped establish the modern state of Israel.

Ben Gurion, the leader of the Jewish establishment (The Jewish Agency and its military arm - the *Haganah*) and an avid student of the Zealot revolt, was apprehensive about history repeating itself. Another terrorist campaign would make it impossible for the moderates again to retain control. Britain, like Rome would become inflexible despite contrary inclinations. As the Greeks did before terrorism, the other local residents, the Arabs, would sponsor the dominant power, and once again the terrorists would force Jews to fight each other too.

The *Irgun* was the modern counterpart to the Zealots and the Sicarii, led by Menachem Begin. He seemed totally oblivious to Ben Gurion's fears. His book, *The Revolt*, nevertheless, speaks of a determination to avoid second *Masada*. The *Irgun's* manifestoes tirelessly reiterate the slogan "No Masada." The second *Masada* was avoided, the Civil War did not occur, and Britain yielded, partly because the Arabs did not rally to her side when support could have made the difference. One main reason was that Begin compelled the *Irgun* to remember Jewish history and accept certain restraints – first one being never to attack other Jews. In 1944, when the *Haganah* began attacking, beating and even turning *Irgun* members over to British authorities, Begin refused to retaliate, rather an unusual decision in the history of revolutionary insurrections.

Surprisingly, and inexplicably, the Arabs started fighting only after the British abandoned the mandate. One major reason was the *Irgun's* decision not to provoke them and to carefully restrict assaults on British units in Arab areas. The contrast with the Zealot policy towards Greeks is striking.[11]

Finally, the Zealots refused every political solution the moderates might negotiate short of outright victory. The *Irgun* did manage a delicate balance of maintaining its claim to entire lands while simultaneously supporting Ben Gurion's decision to accept partition. It was not an inconsiderable achievement.

## Dialectics of Rebellion : Theoretical Framework

Within the relatively enduring Indian and Chinese structures of moral thinking, the primary categories to which the substance is attributed are not "good" and "evil" and the relationship between fundamental opposites takes the form neither of "battle" nor of "dialectical transformations." In Hinduism dualistic categories both stand in a relationship of mutual recognition of each other (being in the world and world renunciation). While the categories themselves constitute permanent structure, the particular contents of Indian categories are comparatively fluid : the ascetic becomes the erotic profligate and bounces back again ; an individual moves from being in the world to world renunciation ; what is "polluting" overflows and infects the "pure."

In Confucian China polarities equal in value but unequal in power (as in the Ying-Yang paradigm) cooperate, in a manner, to sustain and develop a harmonious cosmic hierarchy. This is tell fluidity of the contents of the categories and more of a "practical" cooperation but the opposites than in the Indian structure and moral thinking.

In the medieval and early modern European tradition, polar opposition either battle energetically until the final solution, the outcome of which is pre-determined (the God-Satan Model), or are mutually interdependent in a static hierarchical relationship which it is impermissible to challenge (as in the notion of the "image" of the soul with the body, in which the "masculin" soul is entitled to the obedience of the "feminine" body).[12]

The result of the concurrent presence of both these models in the western tradition is the constant tension between "hierarchy" and "dualism" ; hierarchies are always potentially threatened by a dualistic militancy subversion of them, as they are not in either India or China.

The Greeks have provided two mythological models for rebellion : a "rational" rebellion for the priviledged individual (Prometheus) and an "emotional" rebellion for the underprivileged collectivity (Dionysus). Modern European civilization inverts the equation : an "emotional" rebellion for the priviledged individual (Tristan) a "rational" rebellion later on, for the oppressed collectively (Marx). Dionysus has been individualized, Prometheus collectivized.

Both Greece and the Modern West knew morally justifiable rational rebellions, but located them differently, and psychologically understandable, emotional rebellions, but conceived the emotions underlying such rebellions as divinely inspired in one case (Greece, where it was the emotion of the downtrodden), as artificially induced in the other (the West, where it became the emotion of the cultivated). Only the downtrodden need divine inspiration for their rebellions ; the cultivated hold the means to inspire, in their own hands (even when they do not know what they hold.)

But the medieval paradigm of the Satanic rebellion continues to insinuate itself into the modern shapes of both Prometheus and Dionysus. Greek mythological rebels should be exactly what they were : Gods, Titans, Satan (and with him, a multitude of 19th and 20th century models) are functionaries who seek to be Gods capable of creating thieves. In our times, it has become a legitimate inspiration to make of oneself, individually or collectively, an artificial God. We are condemned to discover whether the Satanic rebellion is destructive only when it is "defined as deviant" by the surrounding society, or whether it too constitutes a socio-psychological model universally valid for that which it comprehends.

There are myths and fantasies in the minds of terrorists and it must be examined how these myths are related to the ramshackle world of Western civilization, where religion is in a state of crisis and many established myths are losing there ground. Religions usually operate through myths that describe the transcendental as penetrating into our world at a certain point in history.

Social stability may be measured by the degree to which society is in tune with its dominant myth, as a society is more stable when most of the phases of life are directed according to a religious myth. The less the myth provides a rationale for all phases of daily life, social moves or mode of government, the more secular and dynamic the society becomes. When a myth withdraws from a social scene, religion seems to be anchored only in institutions and suffers a decline in authority and meaning. The more technological a society becomes, the more it "slides" away from the sphere of the prevailing myths, until this myth is seen as a mere superstition.

Such a withdrawal of religious myth occurred in the 16th century and allowed for the advancement of science and industrial revolution as well as a series of social and political revolutions. With the decline of the prevailing myths of the middle ages and advancement of technology, religion lost much of its authority and was replaced by a secular myth, that of the progress of the myth of a continuous advice towards a future utopia, as opposed to the old myth of a lost paradise. The transcendental, with all its ensuring functions, was removed from the historical scene.

With the new myth of progress came a shift towards technological needs towards a material world and material needs. The myth of the progress, which becomes a modern form of a secular religion, tends to shape a cold, mechanical world; a world that reduces emotions into their elementary components – love into sex, and compassion into utility. In this situation, human being become alienated from their human or spiritual nature and from the world of the spirit. Man acts upon nature but is no longer in a dialogue with it.

When different generations sees no need for conversing with one another, language dies. Consequently, with no medium for communication, each individual feels isolated, alienated, and out of place. Without cultural nourishment, feeling insecure and unable to sustain themselves, individuals seek the support of their government to shape and secure their lives. This only aggravates his sense of insecurity, since more a person depends on a govt., the more his own personality gets effected. Every new law, every new form of taxation, reduces his option of planning and ordering, his own life. Then the people start searching for means of break out of this unseen mould that pushed them into such confinement. The language and other traditional means of communication being unavailable, violence seems the only option. Hence the truth of the axiom : The more a society depends upon its government, the more violent it will become.

Some analysts believe that contemporary terrorists are offshoots of the 19th century revolutionists, of those who followed literally the myth of material progress and rebelled against religious myths at a period when society at large still had faith in them. "Modern terrorists" seem to be people without a knowledge of history and also without a memory of the origins of their own culture.

Can we compare the 19th century revolutionists with their 20th century kin? Perhaps not, because the former still had enough culture heritage to sustain them, enough historical horizons to find a model for identification and to evoke new myths from the past. But the 20th century modern terrorists on the other hand, are the product of a society weary unto death of the myth of progress, a society with no cultural background left to keep it viable. It is worth our while to remember the fact that if the former were called "revolutionists," the latter are simply, perhaps mere "terrorists."

**Terrorism and Communism**

Communism is synonymous with the Soviet Union. The latter might have disappeared from the political map of the world, but the former is still the darling of the Leftist intellectuals of a variety of hires. Then, the left is bouncing back into power not only in certain south American countries but also in Europe itself, circa first half of the 2000's decade. Even more importantly, it (CPM combine) is the ruling party elected democratically in three states of India (West Bengal, Kerala and Tripura in 2006), whereas it has set a world record of sorts winning the state of West Bengal 7th time in a row in May 2006. So it is important for us in India to discuss the relationship between communism and terrorism, though the chapter Heading has placed the two in reverse order, advisedly since the book is about terrorism.

Another reason for discussing this relationship is the role of the Soviet Union in exporting its ideological prediction in its every day. Then, if we are to believe certain analysts, Stalin was a political terrorist who not only exported ideology but also terror even more viciously with his country. If ever there was a case of state practising terrorism, it was Soviet Union under Stalin. But it is important to sound a note of warning here. A State subjected to terrorism by individuals and organisations fighting back the menace with violence cannot be accused of being a terrorist state, not could it be equated with Stalin's Soviet Union. It is preposterous to accuse a state, fighting off religious and political terrorists/guerrillas directly posing a serious threat to its sovereignty and integrity, of being guilty of "StateTerrorism" as some passionate human rights activists are wont to do these days, particularly in India.

It was generally know that the Soviet Union was involved in supporting anti-government guerrillas and terrorists in various countries in the garb of encouraging the indigenous independence struggles. Expectedly American scholars and strategists studied the subject rather deeply and expansively. Some of their scholars felt that the persistent strategic pattern of international destabilization and terrorism, assisted, if not controlled, by Moscow has escaped the attention of the majority of the people living in the free world. This chapter deals with some US experiences with terrorism and Soviet Union linkages with the PLO as a vehicle for exporting terrorism and destabilising, and the sources here are mostly western.

Some of the apparent examples cited about the involvement of the Soviet Union are seen—in the—of the Korean officials in Burma (now Myanmar) the US marines in Lebanon and the entire Grenada Government by a Cuban and Soviet-oriented dictatorship. Terrorism was used to foment instability. 1984 was the Orwellian year predicted long to be synonymous with political oppression and terror of the Big Brother.

On Christmas evening in 1984, some 100 highly trained FALN Puerto Rican saboteurs penetrated a number of US military installations in the US and Puerto Rico, destroying an army ammunition depot, a naval command station, barracks at a marine corps training facility, and a petroleum products storage annexe with high explosives placed at pre-selected locations. It took one whole year and millions of dollars to repair the damage.

At the same time in Washington D.C., a special hit squad operating from a moving vehicle on Massachusettes Avenue launched a rocket projectile over the fence at Vice President George Bush's official residence in the Naval observatory compound, blowing a huge hole in the back wall. The terrorist was not apprehended. Early next morning some anonymous caller reported to the Washington Post that it was an act of the brave FALN Commando Unit.

Subsequently, US Government was criticised for its inability to effectively deal with the terrorists. Some people urged the Government to grant immediate independence to Puerto Rico, suggesting that the FALN was a respectable fighting outfit for freedom, motivated only by the poverty and social inequality in Puerto Rico. Others thought the FALN was a façade, accused the Soviet Union and Cuba for the outrage and demanded that the US go to the source. Expectedly, at the UNO, the Soviet Union, Cuba, and some other Socialist and third world nations called for a special session of the General Assembly to discuss the continued "occupation" of Puerto Rico by the US Imperialists.

Terrorism is a mode of irregular warfare cheap to wage and costly to counter. It is to be accepted that a guerrilla warfare too belong to this category and for the same reason called 'low intensity conflict' (LIC) and low-cost war. Terrorism has became an effective - if gruesome and abominable method of disrupting the fabric of civilised order in an open society and even overthrowing the duly elected governments. If it can seize power internally in a nation, it has the potential to alter the balance of power on international scale, with more such successes. Unlike the earlier time when only overwhelming force - military forces using guns, tanks, aircrafts, missiles, aircraft carriers at all - could damage the west *phalean* order, today terrorism could achieve the same until the world finds effective anti-terrorism measures, and soon. With huge conventional advantage, the US could not defeat motivated guerrillas of Ho Chi Minn. History seems to be repeating itself today with America seemingly unable to win the wars in Afghanistan and Iraq, even when it has help from the "Coalition of the willing" in Iraq and of the NATO in the former.

An Aaitullan sitting in Paris succeeded in overthrowing Shah of Iran, a steadfast ally of America. Moreover, it was in for further humiliation when some Iranians seized US Embassy, making the staff including diplomats, hostage. The ignominy lasted for 144 days, inspite of US launching a military rescue mission. All this serious damaged the US prestige and credibility. It was apparent that the Soviet Union had no hand in the affair.

There is certainly a difference of opinion among the experts and scholars as to the extent that terrorism was sponsored and controlled by the Soviet Union. Some believed that Moscow's strategic thinking called for the use and manipulation of terrorism as a preferred substitute for traditional warfare which seemed to have become too expensive and far too hazardous to be waged on the conventional, set-piece battlefield, barring the special circumstances in close proximity to the "sacred" Soviet borders, as in Afghanistan. It was widely believed in the western circles that by overtly or covertly resorting to non-military way, and by exploiting low-intensity operations around the world, the soviet Union was able to continue its revolutionary endeavours against democratic pluralism in the free world as also to expand its sphere of influence.

The new doctrine adumberated in the international communist conclaves in 1957 and 1960 declared that "war was not inevitable." Instead, Communist victory would come as a result of understanding "class struggle" in capitalist nations. It was perceived that from such doctrinal concepts that continued to be enshrined in the Soviet ideology, most of the regional conflicts of the 1980s had arisen. (But now misplaced were some of these US perceptions is clear from the fact that Soviet Union was on steep decline beginning 1989, hurtling towards its perdition. We leave it at this to revert to the narration.)

Nikita Khrushchev was optimistic about the triumph of socialism over capitalism. He glibly cited the success of Fidel Castro in Cuba ; of Ho Chi Minh in Vietnam; of the National Liberation Front (NLF) in Algiers; and of radical Nationalist Patrice Lumumba in Zaire. Becoming Zaire's first Prime Minister, and having been trained by the KGB, he had made inroads into the Belgian Congo. Khrushev was sanguine. "The victory of communism was no longer far off."[13]

Succeeding Khruschev in 1964 Leonard Brezhnev urged the continuing liquidation of Western civilization after the US defeat in Vietnam, and said, "Our party supports and will continue to support people fighting for their freedom. Referring to gains in Angola, Etheopia, Mozambique, the Peoples Republic of Yemen and Afghanistan ; he committed Moscow to the consolidation of the alliance between the world socialism and national liberation movements."

One of the earliest examples of Soviet involvement in terrorism and terrorist attacks in the training of foreign revolutionaries at Tashkent in 1920. Guerrillas from India trained there were assigned by Lenin himself to conduct a terrorist bombing campaign against the British on the subcontinent. Discovering the plot, London protested to Moscow, and the mission was aborted.[14]

It is interesting that anti-British incidents, coupled with other cases involving direct and indirect Soviet involvement in political violence - ranging from open support of Irish Revolutionaries to terrorist operations in Singapore - figure prominently in Londons decision to break-off diplomatic relations with Moscow on 26 May 1927.[15] This snub did not, however, deter Kremlin from continuing its support of terrorist operation in the British Expire, including Egypt, India and Palestine.[16] (It is obvious that the Soviet sabotage - rather terrorist operations, as the Official Branch prefers to dub them - in India had an early origin, soon after the success of Lenin's revolution in Russia. Equally obviously, it was the part of the Great Game the two Empires were playing, and continued playing till 1947 - maybe even after that defining year.)

In the 1930s, the Soviets funded the National Socialist Party in Germany to destabilise that nation; they abetted the exertions of the Basque separatists and Catalan nationalists in Spain and brazenly provided funds, training, and weapons to the Leftist factions in the civil war. Again, communist agents were linked to the bandits attacking business targets in Nicaragua and the Argentinian and Brazilian insurgents were financed and trained by the Soviet Union.

The Soviets had not overlooked South America either. When it was convinced that its capital, Montivideo has been established as the centre for their subversive and destabilizing games by the Soviets, Uruguay broke off diplomatic relations with Moscow on 27 December 1935. It would be too much too believe that most terrorist operations worldwide or either Soviet sponsored, or even supported by them, as some US scholars would like us to believe. Lord Chayont was closed to the truth : " I do not believe that forces of international terrorism are centrally-inspired or centrally controlled, but I do suggest that when it suits their purpose, the force of international Communism will support terror groups throughout the world."[17] To prove that the good Lord was not too far off the mark, an instance can be quoted from distant history when Russia indeed provides evidence of its ability and political will to do something of this nature if and when its national interest demanded. In the 1920s, Russia itself was the object (and consequentially the victim) of terrorist attacks by White Guard émigrés who operated from the safety of the bases in neighbouring countries exercising the right of self-defence, the Soviet Union sent troops into mangolia and China to liquidate these bands.[18]

It must be recognised that if and when required the Soviet Union went along with the world community, for form, in opposing sub-national violence. It supported the UN Declaration on Principles of International Law concerning Friendly Relations and cooperation among states in accordance with the Charter of the UN, adopted by the General Assembly as Resolution 2625 (XXV) on 24 October 1970. The document asserts, among other things, that terrorist and other subversive activities organised and supported by one State against another are a form of unlawful use of force. The Soviet Union had often cited its support to this resolution to deny any responsibility for acts of terrorism indulged in by various leftist and sub-national groups against governments of their countries. (To be fair it needs to be said that many scholars, especially from South American, Muslim, and Arab countries, including India's Leftists led by the CPM, consider the USA as the biggest terrorist of all. Maybe, they may not be far too wrong. After all the US is the only country to have devastated a supine, nearly defeated Japan, by dropping two atomic bombs upon its cities. It too has often destabilised, through blatant use of force, its smaller neighbours, particularly in Central America and the Carribean Region. Even today (2006) it perhaps is the only country that openly speaks of "Calling for, forcing or bringing a regime change" in countries it is hostile to. Maybe it is the prerogative of the sole super power! It is the only country that has acted unilaterally, defying the UN, in recent years. It not only unsigned the CTBT, but also attached Iraq, without the UN sanction. Is there anything to choose between the actions of the erstwhile Soviet Union and the US, Democratic or Republican, ask its critics?)

It must be noted that the Soviet Union also participated in the 1970 Hague Convention for the suppression of unlawful seizure of Aircarft and the 1971 Montreal convention, for the suppression of Unlawful Acts against the safety of Civil Aviation. In addition, it concluded bilateral agreements with Iran and Finland providing for the return of hijackers to that State where the aircraft is registered.

Within the SovietUnion the following three agencies played a major role in building and guiding this operational network to achieve ideological and geo-strategic objectives :

1. The Soviet Security Agency (KGB)
2. The Soviet Military Intelligence (GRU)
3. International Department of the Central Committee of the Communist Party of the Soviet Union (CPSU). Being a party department, it expectedly plays the most important role for the support of terrorism, as also guiding the preceeding two in the execution of the tasks allotted to them in this field. It consistently promoted widespread revolutionary violence while trying to maintain the impeachable façade/image of the Soviet Union being a peace-loving nation and believing in peaceful co-existence.

A good deal of thought had gone into the subject. To facilitate spreading the work of the Communist Party, Stalin had established the Lenin Institute (also known as the Institute of Social Studies, the Institute of Social Science, and the International School Marxism—Leninism) in Moscow. Select members from western and third world communist political organisations following the Soviet line were trained there in propagands and psychological warfare, armed/unarmed combat and guerrilla tactics, with emphasis on curriculum in international terrorism.

Khruschev, though demonising Stalin to pull him down the Communist Pantheon, followed in his footsteps to further the ideological tenets of the party. He founded in 1958 Moscow's Patrice Lumumba Friendship University to serve as a base for indoctrination and training of potential freedom fighters from the third world who were not the members of the communist parties. More specialised training was imparted in Baku, Odena, Simferopol, Tashkent and in certain suburbs of Moscow. At these centres, the techniques and tactics of guerrilla warfare and other skills including the use of explosives, mining of train routes, commando field tactics, and combat capabilities of the shoulder fire rockets were taught to revolutionaries, including the first and foremost, the PLO.

Besides the above, the CPSU set up at times terrorist groups to further the same ends quite far afield from its main operational areas of concern. There was evidence in one instance, when it played a role in the establishment of the *Solidarite and Aide et Amitie* terrorist network in Paris. The network had links with some 17 illegal (underground) groups including Popular Revolutionary Vanguard (VPR) in Brazil, the movement of Revolutionary Left (MLR) the Uruguay and Chile, the Quebec Liberation Front (FLQ) and the African National Congress (ANC).[19]

The KGB and GRU were actively complementing the CPSUs exertions in this field. The KGB established relevant courses for training terrorists not only in the Soviet Union but also in East Germany. Instructions covered all aspects of terrorist activities such as comprehensive surveillance methods (following a target without being detected, escaping while being tailed, use of disguise, creating and using false identities); use of modern weapons including SAM-7, hand held missiles and anti-tank guns; and even how to organise and run a terrorist network. The KGB, when Yuri Andropor was

Chairman, operated a special cell for securiting and training of terrorists at its Moscow HQs.[20] KGB and GRU had tried to establish a number of terrorist movements or to gain control of the existing ones. VN Sakharov, a defector from the KGB, has revealed that the KGB profed chances of forming terrorist cells in Saudi Arabia, Turkey and the smaller Arab states in the Persian Gulf. The Soviets made similar landestine attempts in the early 1970s to penetrate and control the Palestinian movement from within, a campaign that paid off in Syria and Lebanon. The KGB attempted to establish links even with the IKA. It is also a known fact that the key members of the Iranian terrorist squads, the Red Brigades in Italy, the Baader - Meinhof gang in West Germany and the PELP were schooled in the Soviet Union.

The Soviet Union also helped and financed the Turkish left-wing groups[21], including the Turkish Peoples Liberation Army. Baader-Meinhoff Gang members regularly received support from the East German secret police. More specifically in the form of false papers and identity cards, money, arms ammunition and terrorist training.[22] The Settimanale, the Italian weekly, wrote : "Countries such as East Germany have a frontline position, along with Czechoslovakia and Libya, where they have training camps, frequented by the Argentineans, Italians, Palestinians, Frenchmen, Germans, and members of the IRA. KGB specialist camps were located in Bulgaria (Varna), Czechoslovakia (Karlovy vary and Dupor), East Germany (Finster wards) and Hungary (Lake Vora).

Militants, members of the hard-core____, who had taken some 50 American hostages after seizing the US Embassy on 4 November 1969, and held fast for 444 days, had been trained by Soviet and East German agents in East Berlin, Leipzing, and Prague, according to the *Diewelt*, a leading conservative daily. President Abolhassan Bani-sadr who had unsuccessfully sought to transfer control of the American hostages from the militants to his own Government told *Le Monde* that some of the militants were under communist influence. A West German daily reported that the Soviets and their allies recruited the agents from Iranian exile students groups in Europe and that some of them had taken part in demonstrations in Iranian Government missions in Switzerland in 1976 and in the Netherlands in 1978.

Terrorists from Italyknown to have visited Czechoslovakia– some repeatedly - are Giangiacome Felrinelli, Renato Curcio, Alberto Franceschini, Fabrezio Pelli and Augusto Viel. Reports had been circulating for some time, that the Czechs had set up a centre in Karlovy Vary for training of Agents in destabilising operations.

Vito Miceli, Member Parliament, who had served with the rank of General as the head of the Italian Intelligence (SID) talked on 14 May 1978 about the connections between Italian terrorism and the East European patron states. He disclosed that on 9th May 1972 the SID reported to the Ministry of Defense the proof of existing links between Feltrinelli, subversive groups of Italy's extreme Left and KGB agents working the diplomatic cover in the soviet Embassy in Rome. At the same time the SID had recommended the expulsion of 22 Soviet agents from Italy. Although, both the Defense Minister (Restivi) and the Foreign Minister (Moro) were in agreement with the proposed measure, it was vetoed by the Prime Minister (Andrecoti).[23]

Beginning 1967–69, North Korea was selected for establishing terrorist training camps, its remoteness helping the Soviet Union to conceal its leading role in the enterprise! The trainees were eventually traced to and in some cases, apprehended in Latin America (Mexico, Brazil, Bolivia and Colombia), the Middle-East and Asia (Sri Lanka, Malaya and Indonesia).[24] Some 2,500 terrorists and guerrillas, as per the evidence supplied to the congress, have been trained in the North Korean camps.[25] Terrorists arrested by the Iranian Government in 1972 admitted to having been trained and indoctrinated in North Korea.

Again, safe conduct of Singapore for Palestinians and Japanese who tried to blow up an oil refinery was facilitated by the government of North Korea.[26]

PLO had served as a conduit for Soviets' arms transactions with terrorist movements the world over. To cite one example, two terrorists belonging to Autonomy Movements and the Red Brigade were arrested in Italy in November 1979 while attempting to transport Soviet-made Strela missiles supplied by the PFLP. In an Italian court, the two confessed to the ties between the Italian terrorists and the PLO, and that most of the arms in their possession were of Czechoslovakian origin and supported by the PLO.[27] Two years earlier also (in November 1977) five tons of PLO hardware - motars, rocket-launchers, automatic weapons, and explosives - was intercepted in Belgium. The arms were concealed in electrical transformers enroute from Cyprus to Irish Republic for use by the IRA.

During his mid-February 1983 visit to Aden, the Deputy Chairman of the Soviet-State for Foreign Economic Relations

Viladimis Mordbinov obtained South Yeman's agreement to enlarge the training areas already allocated to the PLO. The PLO leader Arafat was to later inform a committee of PNC in Algiers that the Aden Government had agreed after some "Sovit Prodding" that almost all PLO training would take place on its territory.

Early March 1983, 16 querrilla warfare experts, seven Russian and nine Cubans, arrived in Aden tasked to conduct 3 and 5 month courses in the four main PLO training camps in South Yemon-at Dhali and Naqub (both north of Aden), at Shugra (on the Gulf of Aden), and at Sheikh Othman, near Aden. The subjects included in the curriculum were terrorism related : handling of explosives; preparation of the IED; use of weapons; demolition; mine laying, laying ambushes; and information gathering[28].

Now comes the brand-Quaddafi bluster in early 1979 from his secretary of information Mohamad Alzuwayy. Grandstanding Libya's support to terrorism, he declared : "We assert to the whole world that we provide material, moral and political support to every liberation revolution in the world".[28(a)] Qaddafi had been lording it over not only in Libya since 1969 as the "Revolutionary Leader", but also eyuing the leadership of the Arab World for the last few years. The US put paid to all this grandiosity when, suspecting Libyan involvement in several major terrorist incidents, it launched an air raid on Tripoli in 1986, blowing to smithreens Qaddafi's larger than life image. He has been confined to the Arab world since. The world may soon see (2006) US and Libya establishing diplomatic relations. (The sole superpower does have some positive side to its unilateral actions).

After the 1966 Tri continental conference in Havana, Col. Wardin Kotschergine of the KGB erected a number of training camps for the freedom fighters in the Cuban mountains.

A former FALN member admitted he received his terrorist training in Cuba before being assigned to the USA. Post-Castro take-over, Cuba became a favourite training ground for guerrillas and terrorists. Over 300 Palestinians were reported to be training in Cuba in 1977.[29] The Basque separatists told the Spanish police in 1978 for their receiving terrorist training and instructions in Algerian Army Camps outside Algiers from the Cuban solders[30].

## The Position of the Communist Party, USA (CPUSA)

If the US Intelligence could get so much information on activities of the pro-terrorist organisation from other countries, it surely must have taken/kept a tab on the happenings within its own borders. In any case, CPUSA was openly carrying out its revolutionary activities, as free, democratic politics do not ban them. But the CPUSA was more pragmatic and realistic, knowing the liberal sit in the country which allows freedom of expression to all its citizens.

What Gill Green wrote in a pamphlet published by the New Outlook Publishers, the official publishing house of the CPUSA; in 1970 was no surprise. Cautioning his constituency against the primitive use of terror tactics, he emphasised that "Lenin, the revolutionist is Marxist, did not reject terrorisn in principle," and then asks significantly, "Are the people of this country now ready to assault the fortress?". He criticises the New Left street fighting and rioting as inappropriate, ineffective, and inopportune, but not immoral. Then he quotes the Guru, the Guevora, to argue that the minimum conditions for a guerilla movement do not exist in the USA because "the Government has come to power by popular vote and the possibilities of peaceful struggles have not been exhausted." The role of the Communist Organiser, wrote Green, "whether in the Geittos or elsewhere, is to organise the people and give them leadership". He cited the "right of armed self-defence against the police or racist violence" to justify the violence in black communities".[31]

## CPUSA on the Palestinian Terrorists

Its position in support of certain Arab and Palestinian terrorists organisations, whose policies had met with Soviet approval, was explained by Hyman Lumer in the 5th January 1974 issue of the Daily World, noting as "especially important the growing unity and strength of the Palestinian Arab liberation movement. At its head stands the PLO, led by Yasser Arafat and embracing a number of groups, chief among them Al Fatah." Thus to the Party line, he criticised the Israeli ruling circles for seeking to brand the PLO as terrorist group, "for this is entirely groundless". He claimed that the PLO "has increasingly come to the fare as a responsible political organisation, recognising the need for mass struggle in all forms." As an instance of this mass "responsibility" we noted :

> "An even more unified fight for the right of self determination is shaping up with the PLO at its centre. The PLO warmly

endorsed the world conference of peace forces in Moscow and took an active part in its deliberation. Its members fully associated themselves, along with other Arab delegates, with the Report of the (UN) commission on the Middle East."[32]

## CPUSA and African Terrorists

CPUSA's support for terrorist movements abroad is evidenced in particular from its support of the African guerrilla outfits. This support was greatly stepped up in response to decisions made during the planning for the 10th World Youth Festival held in East Berlin, on the 28 July-5 August 1973.

## Political and Ethical Questions

Occasionally, the nations involved in fighting terrorism that threatens their sovereighnity and integrity, display paranoic proclivities while dealing with a specific immediate threat–iniagined or real. The case in point is the deliberate Soviet shooting down of a South Korean Airliner with 269 passengers aboard, including 61 Americans at 0326 Korean Times on 1 September 1983. The passenger aircraft on a regular schedule had strayed off course, passed through Soviet air space over the Kamchatka Peninsula, and then over Sakhalin Island. Apparently unaware of any navigational error, the Korean pilot reported to Tokyo at 0323 Korean time that he was on the planned track north-east of Hokkaido, Japan. But three minutes later, the plane disappeared from the radar screen at 16,000 feet attitude. After more than two hours of tracking of the Korean plane and a near approach to it by a Soviet interceptor aircraft from Sakhalin, the Soviets ordered a missile attack on the former as it was leaving Sakhalin and approaching the Sea of Japan. As per the intercepted voice transmissions, the Soviet pilot reported at 0326 hours : "The target is destroyed. I am taking off."

There was wide-spread expression of horror at the inhuman action of the Soviet Union. Some Western analysts saw in the incident the starkest differences of stance between the cultural ethos of the Soviets and the Americans while dealing with such sensitive issues. The resort to violence was roundly condemned. But the Soviet Union saw nothing wrong in the wanton destruction of innocent human lives "because the aircraft had crossed the 'sacred borders' of the Soviet territory." At a conceptual plane the political rights of a state overriding the sanctity of human life was a portentious development. This suggested politically-inspired violence of the kind the world would find hard to believe, much less accept.

But a simple question would establish the political nature of the response! "Would Moscow have reacted in the same manner if it were a North Korean plane violating the Sacred Soviet borders?"

## Fighting terrorism : Games Nations Play

Fighting and controlling – much less dominating — international terrorism is not easy, given the differing national interests, perceived or genuine, of various countries involved in it. In fact, certain international terrorist groups have adroitly exploited the different stances of some countries towards a given terrorism threat, to advance their ulterior arms and objectives. There are instances galore of one country viewing differently two terrorist groups operating in the same area. Then a certain country has changed its views of a certain group after the latter proves too strong or too obstreperous for the former. To put it simply, even as serious a problem as international terrorism is not amenable to solutions at a foreseeable future as the nations the world over play games with each other, griving precedence to their national interests against the common good of the world as a whole.

International terrorist groups have contributed in several respects to exacerbate relations between the states constituting the international system. For instance, the terrorists kidnapping a foreign diplomat from the host country can spoil relation between the two countries, with upping the ante with ever-rising ranson and other demands. A recent example in recent history is the Iranian revolutionary students ransacking the US Embassy and taking hostage the entire staff and diplomats - demanding the return of Emperor Shah Pahlavi. The US refused to give in, though the Shah died in exile in Egypt.

On 31 March 1970, the West German Ambassador to Guatemala, Count Karl Van Spreti, was kidnapped by the FAR, a native Guerrilla group. When the Government refused to accept FAR'S demand of 25 prisoners and a ransom of $ 700,000, Sprlti was killed. Augered by Guatemala's handling of the case, West Germany asked Guatemala's Ambassador to leave. Again on 31 July 1970, when Jupamaro guerillas kidnapped Brazils' Consul Aloisio Mares Diaos Gomide and demanded the release of 150 prisoners in the Urguayan jails, the demand was rejected. Brazil protested to Uruguay. Dias Gomide was finally released only in February 1971 when his wife raised a $ 250,000 ransom.[33]

These are two instances where terrorist acts estranged relations between two governments. Another way a similar estrangement can occur is when a national of a state in seized on the territory of state B and the former wants direct negotiations with the terrorists which the latter considers infringement of its sovereignty. Yet again, in this very case, if state B refuses to punish the terrorists, state a feels offended. Likehise, if a state—a la Pakistan trains terrorists on its soil and then sends them across the border for subversive acts, the relations between the two would deteriorate.

When Archdune Franz Ferdinand (heir presumptive to the Austro-Hungarian thrones) and his wife were assassinated by a Bosnian Serb on 28 June 1994 in Sarajevo, consequent outbreak of hostilities between the two countries led to the World War I. The secret Serbian terrorist group, called 'Union or Death' (also called 'Black Hand'), and formed in 1911 with the aim of uniting. Croatira and Bosnia - Herzegovina with Serbia to form "Greater Serbia," had carried out the assassination.[34] A scholar wrote on the issue: "The Austro-Hungarian declaration of war on Serbia was the decisive act : Everything else followed from it".[35]

Here is the second example of how relationship between Israel and its Arab neighbours nose-dived into wars due to terrorist actions. It is widely believed that the 1956 and 1967 West Asian wars were the outgrowth of an escalation in which raids by Palestinian terrorists played a major role. Nearer home, 13 December 2000. Pakistan inspired attack on the Indian Parliament led India ordering its Armed Forces on to its borders, "for any necessary action," and the mobilisation was designated as "operation Prakram." The situation came to the abyss twice during 2001.[36] Yet again terrorist attacks by Syrian Hezbollah Bollrh on the Israeli troops in Southern Lebanon brought the two nations into a near-war situation twice during 2005.

## Earlier International Law and Terrorism

Major impact of terrorism and terrorist activities has been felt on the international system in the area of International Law. The resurgence of terrorism during the 1970s and the 1980s brought the focus on two major aspects.

1. Is the instigation of terrorist acts by one state against another illegal under the International Law?
2. What are the legal resources permissible to a state subjected to terrorist attacks?

Here are two earliest UN Statutes pertinent to the subject, with their relevant passages.

(A) The Draft Code of Offences against the Peace and Security of Mankind (drawn up by the UN International Law Commission).

Article 2(6), which a part of the list of crimes against Peace and Security :

"The undertaking or encouragement by the authorities of a State of terrorist activities in another State, or the toleration by the authorities of a state, of organised activities calculated to carryout terrorist acts in another State."

(B) The 1965 Declaration of the Inadmissibility of Intervention in the Domestic Affairs of States and Protection of their Independence and Sovereignty (which was subsequently adopted by the General Assembly).

Its Article (2) says *inter alia*

"No state shall organise, assist, foment, finance, invite, or tolerate subversive, terrorist, or armed activities directed towards the violent overthrow of the regime of another state."

The above are the elementary and simple formulations on the subject clearly understandable even to a layman, not to speak of the legal luminaries. But nothing is allowed to be so simple in the field of international law, particularly so when the legal eagres take over the interpretation of certain terms used in various provisions of the statute, and politics and national interest of various nations affected by it intervene. Some examples follow from the distant past and some from recent times.

Using these documents, a scholar (Blum) concluded in 1974, that "the Arab support to Palestinian terrorist groups is illegal under International Law." This line of thought was sharply criticised during the UN debates on terrorism in the fall of 1972 by the Third World legal brains, claiming that the activities of such groups as Palestinians and the African Liberation Movements were not terrorism but rather were struggles for national selfy-determination and hence were legal under the International Law. This was over three decades ago. The issue continues to rankle legal opinion even today (2006), some preferring to call terrorist of a certain hue as "freedom fighters".

Another controversy haunts the International legal fraternity : What option does a State, victim of attacks by terrorists, have with regard to a state backing or tolerating terrorists? In specific terms, does a state that suffers from terrorist attacks have the right to undertake reprisals against the state harbouring/supporting these terrorists?

Discussing the Israeli attack on Beirut in the late 1960s, the scholar Folk (1970) argued that the Beirut reprisal was a violation of International Law, because it involved the use of force without any recource to diplomatic solutions and also because the Israelies failed to establish a direct link between the Lebanenes Government and the Palestinian terrorists. The opponents could dismiss this reasoning and conclusions as a mere cavil or quibble-nitpicking. Lebanon had no control over the terrorists. Who does Israel talk to, to find a diplomatic solution to this want on terrorism? Yet again, is the terrorist group involved in the act, interested in negotiations? Far from it, they do not even recognise Israel's very right to existence! Happily this scholar himself did not claim that all reprisals were forbidden by International Law, but he in a school of masterly manner, laid down a series of strict preconditions that would have to be met before any reprisal could legally be undertaken :

1. That a diligent effort to be made for a specific resolution over a reasonable period of time, including recourse to international organisations.
2. The use of force be proportional to the provocation.
3. Retaliatory action be directly against military and para military forces.
4. That the Government undertaking the reprisal provide an immediate explanation of its conduct before relevant international organisations.

When scholars lay down idealistic prescriptions for serious ills like terrorism, they not only seem to have their head in the clouds, but also seem totally ignorant of the ground realities concerning the crisis/issues and empirical experience of the victims in the recent past. The preconditions laid down above are not only impracticable but also lend themselves to be misused by the supporters of terrorists; eq. who will decide on the reasonable period of time; whether effort made is 'diligent', that the force used was proportional to provocation; retaliatory action will involve some collateral damge; and if the explanation offered by the victim is adequate and convincing. As one sees it, left to them, scholars will only offer "academic" solutions to intractable issues faced by nations. They obviously have to be tempered with the inputs from officials and politicians who have to deal with such issues and their consequences, implications for their nations. Thes are comments on the theory of pre-conditions stated above. Now some comments on the experience of some nations who have been recent victims of terrorism :

1. Falk's pre-conditions are adequate to term most of the Israeli reprisals as illegal.
2. Post Nine-Eleven US intervention in Afghanistan is illegal.
3. Prior to Nine-Eleven, there was not, even a recognition of India "bleeding from a thousand cuts" made by terrorists, most from outside its territory, not to speak of any helping hand from others.
4. What do academics like Falk have to say about a country (India) suffering recessionist and militant violence unleashed by terrorists, trained and sustained by neighbouring countries (China in case of Nagas, Mizos, and other North-Eastern rebels), (Pakistan in case of Nagas, Mizos etc. and Sikh separatist), Bangladesh in case of Mizos, Bodos and ULFA terrorists.)
5. India in still ruling its decision, over 50 years after its reference of Kashmir issue to the UNO. Having gone as a victim of aggression by Pakistan in 1949, today it is generally equated with Pakistan, some even perversely think it is the aggressor.
6. The world seems to be helpless in the face of native Africans suffering death and destruction at the hands of terrorists of different hues.
7. In recent history members of the UNO have loct territories to violent secessionist forces. Two instances immediately come to mind : Indonesia to East Timor and Ethiopia to Eritrea - through terrorism. (One uncharitably waits for a demand of a Black Nation to be carved out of USA and an independent Scotland out of the UK).

A milder variant of the act of reprisal is the right to hot pursuit. Here again, there is no agreed prescription on the preconditions that allow a victim to go in hot pursuit of the terrorists fleeings to a neighboring country. Israel has followed this policy from day one. India, on the other hand has shown excessive restraint whatever the reasons.

The emergence of terrorist groups on the world seene and their ability to network their refarious activities with the help of improved communications and destructive capabilities have placed in their hands opportunities and possibilities of creating a new form of international conflict, designated by Brian Jenkins[37] of the Rand Corporation as "surrogate warfare". Such ways are enables a state to back and support terrorist groups to launch attacks and disruptive activities against a nation without getting directly involved in the conflict. This obviously is a cheaper option, and hence attractive one for the former. It again is obvious that appropriate conditions exist in the world today to ply this kind of warfare; e.g. hugely unequal economic development among the nations, with consequent iniquitous distribution of wealth and as a result the existence of a abject poverty and deprivation along with egregious luxurious living; political and economic reasons dividing the world into groups of nations ranged against each other; some nations unable to resolve their differences because of ideological and religious beliefs; and the balance of power skewed in favour of the west, led by imperious USA, the sole Super Power. Smaller and weaker nations find it less costly and less risk-prone proposition to wage the suseogate warfare may also be called a low-intensity conflict (LIC), against bigger and mightier nations. In recent history, the Vietnamese engaged in the LIC, first against the French and then against the Americans. Presently, Pakistan is doing the same against India in Kashmir.

What is worse, even the individuals and groups of individuals, ideologically fired and blinded by religious zeal worked in by the fundamentalist clerics which turns them into the willing and even eager human-bombs, can destroy a nation, its political leadership and institutions, and economic assets. The victims-nations and individuals will take time even to identify the entitries behind these attacks. Hence the need for additional laws to deal with such specific crimes and preferably, to aim at their prevention.

It is obvious that this new form of weapon for conflict, terrorism, "affects the nations unequally" autocratic societies—

China to an extent, some former communist countries, including Russia, majority of Muslim nations Arab Sheikhdoms led by Saudi Arabia, Myanmar etc. are much less prone to terrorist-affected/ inflicted havoc that the democratic regimes, for the simple reason that the former are comparatively repressive states, granting fewer freedoms to their citizenry. After all not many other nations could have enacted Tiananmen Square. An Osama bin Laden could not have plied his heimous trade in his own country (Saudi Arabia). Saddam Hussain was so harsh in suppressing even violent dissent that majority Shias submitted meekly. The terrorists succeeded in democracies by making use of the very freedoms granted to their citizens. At a larger level, the non-democratic powers have a new weapons - surrogate warfare - which can skillfully be used by them to gain a definite advantage.

Another danger from terrorism is looming large on the horizon: the prospect of its disrupting or even destroying the existing international order. It should worry the UN that subversive potential of the terrorists is growing incrementally as the technology of the modern weaponry is getting progressively diffused. In the field of conventional weaponry, terrorists access to such technological innovations as hand-held anti-aircraft missiles and miniature sub-machine guns is an enormous addition to their destructive armoury. Fears of some strategic analysts go much beyond such possibilities : the danger of the designs and drawings of some crude nuclear devices falling in the hands of such terrorist groups. Such fears cannot be regarded as ill-founded or highly-exaggerated, knowing what that notorious Pakistani nuclear scientist, AQ Khan, has confessed in the field of proliferation of nuclear know-how. He ran for over a decade a cash-for-nuclear secrets free market. The designs of nuclear weapons were sold to certain irresponsible state-actors. How long will it be for the non-state actors to lay their hands on these deadly secrets? If the possibility is traumatising some nations and certain analysts, its quite understandable. Imagine the LTTE or al Qaeda possessing the deadly know-how! What would they not do to blackmail the nations, institutions and even individuals? It is a scary prognosis : Will the world exist as we know it today?

The consequences of terrorists wielding excessive power are there for anyone to see. A dozen determined ones could play havoc with the Sole Superpower, shattering its invincibility as never before. Billions of dollars have been spent to stem such recurrence.

Most countries in Europe have been hit in Asia, India being the worst sufferrer ever since its independence. Over 60,000 have been killed in Kashmir alone since 1979.

None is safe from Japan to Tunisia. The world over no governments are in a position to provided any semblance of security to their citizens. Consequently the people may well be compelled to take actions themselves. Terrorism will be met with counter-terrorism. Are we hurtling into private wars on the medieval model with terrorist and counter-terrorists battling it out over the gole? Iraq may be a special case, but a civil war is almost raging in that country, with terrorist groups, killing each other, serving their sectarian loyalties. Afghanistan is only a little better. At home some analysts are seeling the beginning of the civil war in Chattisgarh with tribals fighting - or, made to fight, as some journalists would like to put it. The mostly tribal terrorists are, they quote the example of Solva Judum, armed by the government to fight the terrorists. The situation becomes worse-confounded in India, which facing a multiple-terror campaigns by several outfits, is abo in the grip of Naxal Militancy, ruling the root in vast areas of rural India, stretching from the Nepal-Bihar border right upto Andhra in the south.

Kozo Okamoto, the only survivor of the three-man terrorist squad that carried out the killings at Lod Airport in May 1972, stated at his trial :

The revolutionary struggle is a political struggle between the classes. It is a just struggle. It is a just struggle we strive to build a world in which wars will be banished. But it will be a long struggle and we are preparing for World War III though killing people, destroying houses, annhilating property.

With such deeply-entrenced indeological belief impressed in the brain through brain-washing, there are chances of a break-down of international order. In the face of such imminent dangers, the community of nations may well abandon their differences over the questions of terrorism and resolve to work unitedly to quell this threat to the international order.

One of the reasons for rapid success of terrorism has been failure to offer a strong response by the world communities. Many nations not directly affected by it, are indifferent to the threat and others are infact supporting it for reasons ideological or chauvinistic, yet there is reason to hope that this tolerant attitude towards transnational terrorism will change if it possesses a genuine threat to the existing world order.

## Democracy and Terrorism

A democratic polity is deemed to be a more effectives instrument of fighting and defeating terrorism. But paradoxically, these very democratic countries provide a liberal atmosphere and the rule of law which enable the terrorist to ply his heinous trade and still survive, claiming his human and even fundamental rights! It is not a surprise that when proceeded against, the terrorists and their overground supporters scream "foul" when their legal rights are circumscribed or rescinded by the government for the greater good of the society. In autocratic countries, dissent is ruthlessly crushed and active opposition is simply unacceptable : But dissent is not only tolerated in a democracy, but is accepted as an inalienable part of a vibrant democracy. All communist countries in the erstwhile USSR had oppressive regimes, riding roughshod over their citizens who enjoyed hardly any fundamental rights. With the dissolution of the USSR, the 15 independent states do enjoy certain freedom and fundamental rights, though not as wide-spread and as well entrenched as in western countries - UK and US in particular. Presently China and North Korea are two nearly closed societies—the latter being worse between the two. China may have loosened up a bit in economic field, making rapid strides in growth paradigm, taking full advantage of globalisation and liberatlisation of trade and commerce. But it would not allow the world to forget Tienanmen Square incident in a hurry.

The world must take note that China even today (May 2006) have no plans of loosening its vice-like grip on instruments of political power. It has no intention of granting even a modicum of relaxation in the field of human and fundamental rights. As far a China is concerned, democracy can wait. Attaining a super-power status through economic and strategic strength is the only imperative they have in mind for the present - on inspirational goal set by the leadership. The speech made by Primer Wen Tiabao at the fourth session of the 10th National Peoples Congress (NPC) should make people sit up and analyze its implications. The "Report" on the work of the Government delivered by even to the session outlined the nation's ambitions, requirements, demands, and methods to achieve all these and more. He made it clear that China was no longer chasing communism or socialism. "What it aims at, is a strong unitary system that would brook no criticism or opposition in its conduct both internally and externally.[38]

As for Russia, it is no longer as autocratic as it was till 1991, but it is far from being an idealistic democracy. Politics is part of the international relations. President Putin has sought to bring in democracy. But US seems to be nitpicking. Early May 2006, US Vice-President Dick Cheney made headlines by accusing Russia, "of restricting human rights and using gas and oil as tools of manipulation or blackmail" against Russia's neighbours.[39] The *Financial Times* noted that some Russian Media presented Cheney's remarks as echoing Winston Churchill's 1946 speech in Fulton Missourie, warning that an "Iron Curtain" was descending an Europe. On 8th May 2006, President Bush talked of warm relations with Putin, but expressed concern about Russia using its economic clout is international politics! This sounds strange coming as it does from Bush. He talked of Russia's economic nationalism, and Putin using his oil companies to achieve political objectives. (All this) this all is meant to show how nations play games in international relations. The same, nations playing games while fighting international terrorism, will be discussed later in the book.

The fact remains that autocratic states seem to be dealing with terrorism more effectively in the short run; may be, because the state is not shackled by long/winded legal wrangings and intricate procedures of a democratic set up which are fully made use of by the skilled and resourceful lawyers employed by terrorists.

India, a democracy, has fallen victim to terrorism, some from within, and most from across the border. But the nation has dealt with the menace with a reasonable degree of success; be it in Tamil Nadu in the early years or the North-East and Jammu and Kashmir in the later years. Islamic terrorism in Jammu and Kashmir is testing India's forbearance.

India hopes to find a way out in the North-East even if it would take sometime. How India suffered terrorism and then combated it will be discussed in a separate chapter.

Since 1938, when Prime Minister (1937-40) Neville Chamberlaine made a deal (Winston Churchill would call it a 'surrender') with Hitler - who, some felt, headed a 'terrorist state', Munich became a symbol of political appeasement. In the later years, the same Munich was to become the watchword for what could be termed "rearment against terror." 1972 coud be the defining time when eleven Israeli athletes were Massacred at their Olympic Games Camp. Besides the determined Israeli action to eliminate the 11 Palestinians belived to have planned the crime, UK subsequently raised the famed 22 Special Air Service Regiment to combat the problems posed by international terrorism. The world seemed to be uniting to fight world-wide terror, even if these were the initial steps.West Germany formed the Grenzschutzgruppen 9(GSG9). The Dutch assigned the anti-terrorism role to their Marines. The Italians called in the paramilitary *Cara binieri, Guardia Civile*. Later, the Special Operations Group (SOG), a new force modeled on the SAS, was to spearhead the anti-terror operations. The French devised and raised some specialist anti-terrorism units from their police organisations and the Parachute Division. The Americans set up the Inter-Departmental Group on Terrorism tasked to "Coordinate information, consider tactics, and set up task forces in cases of emergency."

Of all the nations facing the danger of international terrorism, Israel was the only one to take the bull by the horns from day one. Maybe, it was the demand of circumstances of its creation, and existential problems it faced at its very birth : a state surrounded by its enemies bent upon destroying it at the very first opportunity. They simply saw no other way, except "direct action". The day of the Munich Massacre, Prime Minister Golda Meir, the real Iron Lady, if there was ever one, openly declared Israel's determination to punish the perpetrators. The next day, she unleashed the hit teams to roam the world and ferret out the eleven criminals for them it was "an eye for an eye" and "a tooth for tooth." In this game there are no second chances. A recent (2006) Spielberg film *Munich* shows graphically how they went about doing the job assigned to them. Taking the viewer on a ringside trip with the Israeli high-ups including Golda Meir, it details the psyche of violence and terrorism. Some details from the film should be educative :

1. "You are officially unofficial", Mosad agent Avner is told.
2. His four aides are Steve, a hit man; Robert an explosives expert; Hans, an expert at forging documents; and Care, a clean-up man.
3. Then there is that mysterious-case officer Ephrain who comes in and out of nowhere, merely to give the instructions and await answers, if any.[40]

Besides Israel, the US is the only nation to have made a declaratory policy of "no negotiation" with the terrorists, which boils down to "no surrender to the blackmailers." India does not belong to this category of states. She seems to have forgotten its own ancient dictum : "*Shathe shattyam same charet*" (Treat the wicked with wickedness). Indians need to remember an aphorism of Napoleon Bonaparte: " A generous king loses the reign." But India, a democracy and a plural society, has certain constraints in combating terrorism, both internal and external - to be dealt with at another place.

## Freedom Fighters Versus Terrorists

A favourite, cliche on the subject is : One Man's 'terrorist' is another's 'freedomfighter'. The debate goes on endlessly amongst the scholarly academics, analysts, and worse of it all, even among the busybodies. But as for this Author, the two cannot be confused with each other, one cannot be substituted for the other, they are certainly not synonymous, not even equivalents. If one deserves reverence, the other abomination. The Author a soldier[41], having fought the so-called freedom fighter's in the Naga Hills (1957-59), Mizoram (1974-77)—these were the periods in these two areas when the insurgency-inspired violence was at its virulent worst—and Jammu & Kashmir (1963-65 and 1984-87), considers it blasphemous even to utter the two terms in the same breath.

The difference between the two is briefly, discussed—just to make a point. A freedom fighter joins the struggle for the freedom of his country, a sacred cause. Whether the Indians fought under the leadership of the Mahatma, an apostle of peace and non-violence, to evict the British from their country, or under the young leaders like Chandra Shekhar Azad and Bhagat Singh, votaries of violent struggle, they were all freedom fighters, even if the former did not approve the methods employed by the latter. But the terrorist shed blood for causes of justice—real or imaginary. In a democracy, injustice can be undone through the power of the ballot. When human beings, brain-washed by political or religious ideology, turned into frenzied robots, they murder for the sake of murder. Sacred human values and fundamental rights guaranteed by their societies and countries mean nothing to them—being dirty shiboleths to be trampled under their feet. Human life is no more sacred. It can be snuffed out at the budding of a religious demagogue, blinded by dogma. This should suffice for the purpose of this chapter, and any further nuanced discussion on the issue is considered unnecessary. But only one more point needs to be made. When biased scholars or vested interests dub men like Azad and Bhagat Singh as terrorists, it is an unconscionable assertion or averment, indicative of a (too strong!! DAD).

Even if there is no universally recognised definition of the term, terrorism can ostensibly defined as "the deliberate and systematic murder, meaning, and menacing of the innocent to inspire fear for the political ends." This definition should explode the myth, so assiduously murtured and repeated ad nauseam, that "one man's terrorist is another's freedom fighter", and leave little scope for moral fence-sitting, even by the most squeamish. As discussed above, there exists an objective distinction between the two. By definition the men who took part in the armed uprising against the Soviet occupation in the then East Germany and Czechoslovakia and Hungary were freedom fighers. They fought for *freedom*. Their targets were instruments of tyranny, such as the secret police and the military—not the innocent civilian Russians or the bystanders. The various underground resistance movements in European nations during World War II were attacking, destroying or sabotaging the Nazi Military Machine. If certain civilians were killed, they were the overt collaborators who helped the German occupiers to maintain their oppressive hold over their sacred lands. The PLO fighters and Hamas cadres who are killing Israeli civilians are *ipso facto* terrorists. If they confront and kill some Israeli soldiers during their aggressive actions, they indeed are freedom fighters. Nearer home, the United Liberation Front of Assam, National Democratic Front of Bodoland, or Islamic Lashkar-e-Toiba cadres attacking innocent civilians are clearly terrorist.

What identifies terrorist, by contrast, is that they do not oppose political repression, rather they practice it themselves. Their methods are most dastardly and hemous of the ones employed by all the malefactors and felons who despise freedom : Wanton savagery, bordering on barbarity, designed to create fear and anarchy. Terrorists such as the ULFA, LeT, HUM, LTTE, al Qaida today and IRA, SWAPO, PLO and KCF yesterday, invariably directed their attacks against those who could pose no counter-threat to them—airline passengers, innocent civilians gathered at fairs, school children and women, vacationers, shoppers, or unprotected civilian installations like power houses and power pylons, oil and gas storage tanks, airlines, railway tracks, tea garden labour and factory workers.

No cause or grievance can provide legitimacy to terrorism or its practitioners of many hues, even some liberals feel that "no one can genuinely oppose real (or even imagined) injustices by committing even worse atrocities." One has to be very careful in interpreting and analyzing their motives when the terrorists talk of their political aims. David Patrick Noynihan is prescient when he says: "Terrorism when successful, ends in totalitarianism. The totalitarian state is terrorism come in power." A trucer averment was never made in this field.

This precisely was the goal of certain organizations during the 1970's and 1980's; namely Tupamaros of Argentina or the Red Brigade of Italy. Modus operandi was to launch a vicious campaign of bombings, kidnapping and killing in the hope of goading the government into suspending the civil and fundamental of its own citizenry by way of counter—terrorism drive against the malefactors. In the given situation, certain excesses were bound to be committed against its own population, which was exploited by the terrorist organisation to fuel civil unrest in the country—thus damaging the credibility of a lawfully established Government. The final push in this direction was given by the quasi legal branch of the same organisation which helped to rally public support behind it, citing the "atrocities" committed by Government on its own population. Consequently the discredited government stood replaced by a totalitarian model of their own. During the period, this formula was partly successful in Argentina and Uruguay and fully so in Nicaragua. In the present day situation the PLO taking power in Palestine (2005) would not fit into this formula. But the Hamas replacing it in power would be a neat-fit!

## Democracies versus Terrorism and Radical States

Terrorists, like the poor, have always been with us, to use a chiche, and from the very earliest part of recorded history. But for the present particularly since the 9/11, most nations have been able to contain their worst excesses. All States are doing their best to adopt counter-terrorism measures to resist any pressures to give into armed blackmail. This brief survey examines the stance of democratic nations towards terrorism, and actions of certain radical nations in this field.

Each country, acting on its genius, devised its own counter-terrorist policy. Most created special forces specifically equipped to fight the militant squads who shoot their way into embassies, banks, more menaingly, into nuclear installations and scientific institutions, high-security areas like government headquarters and parliaments and important public buildings. The aim of terrorists in such cases is seize and kidnap hostages, murder VIPs, create communal carnage, and to cause senseless destruction. National policies to counter these acts of desperados seem to be succeeding. Now tactics were developed to combat terrorist operations; military and police skills and capabilities were improved supplying them better weapons and modern technological devices; and public awareness was enhanced to threat panic and disruption. The need for better intelligence was recognised to pre-empt act of terrorists. The computer technology was also pressed into service for the same purpose.

In the recent years, to thwart the violent activities of militants/terrorists, laws have of necessity been modified, the security forces given greater powers to arrest, detain and interrogate suspects in most of the democratic world. In addition, another significant feature in the field of counter-terrorism has been a greater degree of international cooperation and mutual aid that has been achieved.

Consequently, terrorists no longer have things all their own way. Some significant events in the field of counter-terrorism has been :

- The (West) Germans had the Red Army Faction on the run.
- The Italians have sapped the strength of the Red Brigades and allied movements.
- Most significantly, the amazing Japanese Red Army, which operated in Europe and West Asia, has publicly admitted it had been wrong and has ceased all its terrorism-related violence.
- There has been significant withdrawals from this violent line-up, such as Hans Joachim Klein and Red Army Faction International.

Lest there is any call for premature celebrations, the battle is far from having been over. Large parts of the world is under siege. The Islamist terrorism is on aggressive path, fuelled by the anti-

American anger after Afghanistan and Iraq attacks. Democratic nations the world over are confronting the terrorist threat the best way they can—remaining within the ambit of laws or far as possible.

In Spain, for the political-historical reasons, the fight against ETA is on. Any hope of success in the near future is a distant possibility. The British and Ireland governments are tantalisingly close to the solution—but the final lap seems to be full of uncertainties.

The intractable war between the Jews and Arabs was appearing headed towards a resolution when the Palestinians, in their wisdom, in early 2006 polls, handed power to the hard-liner Hamas who steadfastly has refused to recognise Israel. Fatah chief, Chairman of the Palestinian Authority, seems to be helpless to proceed with any negotiations with Israel, as the Hamas Prime Minister is determined to block them. What is worse, the Hamas and Fatah are engaged in needless blood letting in street wars against each other in Gaza and the West Bank. Arabs killing Arabs can't be a pretty right and even OIC and Arab League have failed to stem this internicine intra-Arab killings.

Terrorists made their appearance in Greece in the summer of 1981. Leftist groups placed firebombs in At;oemoam department stores and blasted British Council offices in Salonika.

In Portugal, bombs were detonated and politicians were assassinated. Indeed, as the defences built up it seemed that assassination was again becoming a favourite tactic because it is so difficult to prevent. President Reagon and the Pope were wounded and Queen Elizabeth was the target of a boy with a replica revolver firing blanks—a replica terrorists.

In Iran, President Ali Rajai and Primie Minister Bachoner were killed in August 1981 by their own opposition terrorists. Subsequently, during his supremacy (1979-89), Khomeini (C. 1900-89) imposed puritamic rule in Iran, liquidating many of his opponents. President Bush included the country in the list of his three 'axis of evil' nations—Iran, Iraq and North Korea. In spite of elections held since the returns of Khomeinits Iran and to power in 1979, the country can hardly be called a republic.

Even the Russians, who in their Soviet Union days, had given so much help and encouragement to outside terrorists, fell victims to Afghan terrorists/guerrillas. Ironically, they were forced to train their own Red Army Special Forces in the art of combating these guerrillas before, they were forced out by in Afghanistan combined might of the US, Pakistan and the *Madrassa*-trained Taliban. Presently, once mighty Russian Army is trying hard to fight the Chechen rebels/terrorists to preserve the integrety of the country.

India has faced recessionist terrorism from the day of its birth in 1947. If in the North-East, it was started by the Nagas, followed by the Mizos, extremist Muslims took to the guns in J & K. In cause of time, the Sikhs picked up the thread in Punjab in 1980s. Besides the two major groups mentioned, there were rash of ethnic recessionist/autonomist movements in the North-East, such as ULFA, Bodos, Meiteis, Tripuris, Karbis et al.

Prime Minister Indira Gandhi fell to the bullets fired by her Sikh body guards on 31 October 1984. A newly-elected MP along with his wife and a municipal councillor were assassinated in broad daylight in New Delhi a year later (1985). India continues to fight the evil of terrorism as of today in various states—some successfully, others otherwise. If the militant Sikhs and so many ultra outfits in the North-East have been won over, Indian polity is still combating the insurgency in Jammu and Kashmir and Assam (essentially ULFA). An outstanding success has been in Mizoram where a former insurgent leader is heading the State Government presently.

The counter-terrorism battle are on in many other democracies, semi-democracies or so-called democracies which in reality are autocracies but officially designated as Republics/ Democratic Republics such as France, Germany, Egypt, Congo Kinshasa, Somalia, Bolivia, Myanmar, China, etc.

Developed countries and modern industrial societies provides many areas for attack by the determined ultras which are difficult to defend—each one of them, in any case—in an open disposition : powerlines, railway tracks, oil pipelines, reservoir and dams, electricity-generating units, and especially nuclear plants. Considering the disorder, confusion and chaos created in New York by an accidental disruption of electricity supply there in 1984, it is easy to imagine what could happen in the case of a planned electric power cut combined with other by-now-familiar terrorist horrors.

Dictated by economic considerations, many corporations have not only shifted their operations from the central cities and their suburbs to less developed rural areas but also to developing countries in Asia. Consequently, they have rendered themselves as easy targets to the terror merchants.

Another cause of concern is easy availability of weapon, particular small and medium arms, in the black market. Any one with money can buy them. Narco trade is intimately linked with illegal arms trade. A further source of anxiety is the number of armouries stacked with modern weaponry around the countryside in the US, Europe, Asia etc., with no foolproof anti-pilferage measures in place. One estimate has it that "in the 1970s, terrorists had stolen enough weapons to equip ten battalions". Yet again, "120 automatic rifles (had) disappeared in a single raid on a Norwegian Home Guard armoury, and some of were later identified in various parts of the world including EL Salvador and Bangladesh. Not all such weapons are stolen by terrorists but they can be acquired by or sold to the terrorists. Illegal trade in weaponry has been mentioned above.

In the 1980s, there were cases of countries like Libya and the then Peoples Republics of South Yemen receiving military aid from the Soviet Union, and then passing certain quantity of arms including RPG-7 rocket launchers to terrorist groups. Such sources of supply are difficult to block. More careful controls are needed over the licensing regimes for export of arms.

Even India has been amirs on this score. In mid-2005, certain arms including rifles and grenades, were recovered from a private house, and surprisingly they were all of an Indian ordnance factory manufacture.

Another form of terrorism is what can be called "Official State Terror", one well-known and well-publicised instance of it was seizure of the US Embassy in Tehran by Zealots who held 53 American hostages with connivance, if not active collaboration, of the Iranian Government. The white House and Department of State had harrowing time through the drama.

Col. Muammar Qaddafi, an outstanding practitioners of the art, sent Libyan hit squads out to the US and European countries to murder his expatriate political opponents. One of his men even gave poisoned peanuts to the children of a Libyan living in England. When asked about these murders, he said loftily: "This has nothing to do with the British people or Government—being a purely Libyan matter. The new Libya is getting rid of the old

Libya". When he performed the same act in the US, President Reagon, a tough customer, order the expulsion of the entire staff of the Libyan Embassy in Washington. Determined to act against the states extending official aid to the terrorists, he barred the countries supporting terror such as Libya, Iraq and Syria from buying American war-like stores under the provisions of the Export Administration Act of the US.

President Bush was even tougher on Libya for same 'sin', having been shaken by the 9/11 tragedy. He ordered bombing of the country, compelling Qaddafi to assume the role of an anti-terrorist ruler.

Human Rights organisations feel it is time to assess the agencies/instruments created by some States' own military and police forces to fight the terrorist lest they themselves pose a danger to the democratic states, their liberal traditions and rule of law. In earlier times, the anxiety centred, in particular, upon the crack units created for counter-assault on terror such as the Israeli unit, GSG-9 and the famed SAS of Britain. The same cantion must apply to the Delta Unit of the US and similar ones in Europe.

What is important is that they must be allowed to act within the tight framework of the law and under strict government control. In Britain, the SAS were called in at first under the authority of the police and ultimately the Government. They were in charge of the operation for a limited time, under the provisions of the law which allowed military to be called in support of the civil power. Mission completed, they handed over to the Metropolitan Police, and returned to the barracks. In America, such an operation by troops was possibly not permissible because of provisions of the Posse Comitatus Act, and the task in all probability would have gone to the FBI tactics squad, which, of course, does not have the aggressive military training to confront such situations so expeditiously and so effectively.

It needs to be emphasised that job of the special forces like the SAS is rather difficult, even risky, in the UK when they are called out for handling sensitive situations. In the aftermath of the siege of the Iranian Embassy in London by the SAS, the surviving terrorist was brought to trial before a court which not only found him guilty, but also examined the facts of the case. Had the court discovered that the SAS trooper had indeed exceeded their powers, they could perfectly well have been charged with manslaughter or murder. There are a number of precedents in British law for so charging the 'erring' soldiers, and they cannot defend themselves by claiming that they were simply obeying orders.

The same rule of law applied to the troops who fought the terrorists in North Ireland in trying conditions. "British troops do not have a licence to kill except in war." The troops on anti-terrorist operations in Ulster mould carry cards setting down clearly under what controlled circumstances they might fire.

But the face-off between the terrorist violence and military force used by a democratic government is not the only issue thrown up by the employment of the special intervention groups like the SAS. Like all soldiers, their life also consists long periods of inaction, punctuated by short burists of extremely violent action and accompanying/consequent tensions. It is not easy, in the circumstances, to maintain morale, and continuous training of various kinds, even though both are considered unavoidablly necessary. "It does not necessarily fill the gap." What is worse, there are temptations to indulge in politicking, in particular, by the special forces in Spain and Italy, where there is a long history of army involvement in political plotting, rather than in Britain and the US where military has stayed miles away from such activities.

Some analysts have raised interesting—if some what far-fetched—implications for raising and deploying special forces units to handle terrorist raids. If crack units are necessary for operations against them, surely the terrorist outfits are themselves, so to say, sort of military units, or someone kin to them. Doing this, they say, is playing into their hands. If that sounds logical, then it goes some way towards justifying their demand to be treated as prisoners of war when captured—allowing them to claim the right not to be interrogated any further after giving their name, rank and number. Captured terrorists already claimed special status for themselves in prison. IRA men had fasted to death to assert such rights but the British Government stood firm against this demand, refusing to yield on the issue.

Incidentally, the Bush administration refused to confer this status on the GITMO prisoners, held in confinement in Cuba—the worldwise clamour on this demand notwithstanding. They are terrorists, they are criminal and notthing more, was the US stand.

A strong argument in law against the terrorist in the Western Countries is that they are to be regarded as criminals and not as political prisoners. Many countries will only consider allowing extradition for those wanted as criminals. But if they can prove they are political prisoners then long traditions of asylum for political refugees comes into play, blocking the immediate extradition. "There is a distinct danger that by using the armed services in response to terror attacks, rather than uniformed police, who normally deal with criminal affairs, Western Government do provide a degree of legitimacy to the terrorists."

Such dangers notwithstanding, arguments were presented in favour of an international anti-terrorist force notably by Lord Chalfont, a former British Defence Minister, at an international conference on terrorism organised by Israel in mid-1990s. He had said inter alia : "It is at least worthwhile examining the possibilities of extending cooperation in an institutionalised form using the national anti-terrorist squads of countries like West Germany, Britain and Israel as the nuclei of a permanent force."

The inclusion of Israel, which was practising counter-terrorism of the most aggressive kind under the leadership of the then Prime Minister Menachem Begin—who had himself begun his political life as a terrorist—would have created far more difficulties than could have been solved by such on internal force. That indeed was the view of a fellow delegate at that conference—George Bush, before he became the Vice President of the US. Bush, a former Director of the CIA, said at the conference; "I do not believe the creation of a truly international force was likely, although anti-terrorist paramilitary units, closely coordinated by democratic states are a vialable answer to the threat". Bush stressed, rather, the need for cooperation in the field of intelligence and counter-intelligence among the Western Countries with the provision that "Intelligence is accountable to the people". He declared, "We should strive vigorously to shape, and utilise this important capability in the fight against international terrorism, you may be assured that I will do all I can to bring this about."

Two points deserve attention from these early observations of George Bush :

- Bush, a former CIA Director and conscious of the fact that the use of special forces by that Agency in Latin America and in Vietnam and its other shortcomings, had prompted the radical and liberal human rights campaign which hamstrung American intelligence in the early years of the terrorist threat. The restructions placed on the intelligence work affected not only the US but its allies as well.

- At personal level he was convinced of the need for an effective counter-terrorism policy and he devised one after the 9/11 attacks. It may be criticised for being too harsh, particularly some provisions of it—which critics feel trample over individual human rights and traditional American liberal values—but the fact that it has proved effective is not questioned any more as it has so far prevented a repeat of any act of terrorism, not to speak of any major ones like the 9/11 or 7/7 London bombings.

Here follow two examples of how restrictions placed upon intelligence work adversely affected the US allies as they could not obtain the urgently needed assistance :

- When the Italian Government, at the height of the Aldo Moro crisis, requested the US for special surveillance equipment, it was not provided since the Ryan Amendment forbade covert CIA operations without Presidential approval, and limited its activities against the international terrorists/terrorism only. At that point in time, the Red Brigades were deemed to be "domestic terrorists" and, therefore, outside the scope of CIA assistance.
- Yet again, when the West Germans asked for technical assistance to break into the Lufthansa Boeing aircraft hijacked to Mogadishu, their request was turned down because an Amendment to the Foreign Assistance Act in 1975 had made it illegal to use foreign aid dollars to assist with foreign policy operations". When President Reagan took over, he was keen to remove such restrictions on CIA's intelligence work and consequently William Casey, the new Director, CIA, declared, "The difficulties of the past decade are behind US", and announced that the Agency was again going secret. As more capable agents were recruited into the service, he abolished the Agency's Public Affairs Office.

> Casey intended to restore the CIA's morale and provide "desperately needed" intelligence capability. Another of his aims was to restore the confidence of friendly intelligence abroad.

A point needs to be made about bold action President Abraham took at a particular time. Within the terms of the American Constitution, it is not feasible to introduce changes in the law to enhance police powers on the scale that was deemed necessary in Britain and some other Western European countries for defence against the terrorism unleashed in the recent years. Yet Lincoln did not hesitate to suspend habeas corpus when he believed the occasion demanded it. His argument: No government, however democratic and liberal, can be expected to stand by and see itself destroyed by people who neither recognise the law nor any restrictions on their violence. That in essence was the argument offered by Britain and other European countries for removing a number of legal safeguards built into their constitutional practices to deal with an emergency like the one they face while fighting the terrorists in the recent times—and to wit, they are the people similar to the ones against whom the great Lincoln acted so drastically.

It is well to remember that Hitler had come to power taking undue advantage of liberties granted to its citizens by democracies, in this case by German Constitution. Hitler's rise to power could have been prevented if Germany had acted in Lincoln's way. Likewise, if terrorists are not stopped in their tracks, they will come into power in the country and spread the evil with greater vigour.

Besides Germany, it is the UK which has adopted most far reaching measures in this field (of Counter-terrorism) in order to combat the IRA in Northern Ireland and in the rest of the country. Those measure are—one may say, 'were', as the Irish situation is nearly resolved—the Northern Ireland (Emergency Provisions) Act, 1973, and the Prevention of Terrorist (Temporary Provisions) Act, 1974. But it is easy to see that there is a clear conflict between the imperative of preservation of civil liberties and the necessity to protect lives and property from terrorist attacks, because it is not possible to assume the powers needed to deal with terrorism without, to an extend, reducing/curbing the freedom of the common (innocent) man/citizen. Even then, this has to be done for the common good of the society.

This need to curb the civil liberties of common man gives some comfort to the terrorists, as a democratic polity is seen to be doing something undemocratic. This creates some doubt about the democratic government, and over throwing of such democratic government is the ultimate aim of the terrorists in order to impose their own views and ideas under threat of bomb and bullet. Greater the violence and inhuman atrocities perpetrated by the terrorists against the innocent, greater the curbs the governments are forced to impose on the rights of the common citizens. Hence the problems faced by the governments in striking a balance between the two contradictory requirements.

The hijacking of the italian Cruise-ship Achille Lauro by Palestinian Commandos, and their subsequent capture led to a rift between Italy and the US. Fall of the coalition government of Prime Minister Bettno Craxi was understood to be the chief motivator behind the Congress initiative to minimise similar misunderstandings in the future.

A new dimension to the international terrorism is the support some radical countries—like North Korea and Libya—extend to terrorist outfits. Even some not-so-radical countries are known to extend support to the terrorist activities. Pakistan is openly extending moral, diplomatic and political support to anti-India Islamists working for secessionism of Jammu and Kashmir.

In 1999, North Korea sent a terrorist squad to Rangoon (now, Yangon) on a mission to assassinate President Chun Doo Hwan of South Korea while he was on a state visit to Burma. The terrorists implanted bombs which killed 17 senior officials, including four cabinet ministers, and narrowly missed President Chun. The North Korean aim was to destabelise South Korea. The incident nearly led to war between the two Koreas. It was South's restraint that saved the day.

Political terrorists generally aim at replacing the existing government and associated structures with the ones of their choice. They resort to subversive activities aimed at setting in motion a chain reaction which continue till the "revolutionary" ends are achieved. Politically-motivated terrorist outfit may even aim at secessionism, a la Naga and Mizo insurections in India in 1940s and 1960s respectively. Politically motivated activists with state backing tend to be more ruthless in executing their mission, a la "Cultural Revolution" launched by Mao tse-Dong in China.

The motives of the terrorists can be personal or ideological. In Ireland and Palestine, an extreme form of nationalism blended with despair and informed by historical injustice is the motivating force behind the long-lasting terrorist movement. In the case of North Korea, the aim is to create political confusion and instability in South Korea and the region. With the backing of radical countries and unlimited access to lethal weapons, terrorists are becoming more dangerous and methodical. There is a fine pattern and acute finesse in the execution of their murderous acts as more and more sophisticated arms are falling into their hands. Terrorists today are not only equipped with the latest technological and innovative means to achieve their subversive and destructive ends but they also believe that the highest form of revolutionary terror should employ the most advanced science and technology.

It is no secret today that Islamist terrorists are the biggest and most potent threat/danger to the world peace and the existing international order. The accuracy, precision and determination with which they executed the 9/11 attack employing a number of airliners proved not only detailed, meticulous and near-perfect planning behind the macabre but was also reminiscent of precision-bombing of World War II. The terror outfits indeed are fighting a war on whatever is decent, orderly and civilized in our world. And unfortunately, there are people—so-called 'liberal' bleeding-hearts, human rights extremists and Indian Left—who are squeamish enough to object to the acronym GWOT # (Global War on Terrorism) because the term 'war' make it sound 'aggressive'!

A more serious note need to be taken of the radical states which fan and fuel terrorism. Without their active support, terrorism should be a lesser menace. The civilised world must make it clear to exporters of terrorism—through active deed, not mere pious resolutions—that murder is not a legitimate instrument of national/foreign policy. It is high time that such states are made to realise that by indulging in terrorist acts they can not achieve their policy objectives—except having the blood of the innocents on their hands.

In the past, President Reagan had publicly accured countries like North Korea, Cuba and Libya of exporting terrorism and suggested measures to check it. President Bush had included three nations in his 'axis of evil'—North Korea, Iran and Iraq. But these nations were not willing to mend their ways (in the past). Heritage

Foundation "says that North Korea alone has trained more than 2000 terrorists, belonging to various outfits since 1970."

But situation has changed post-9/11. The earlier 'rogue' states like Libya, Afghanistan, Iraq seem to have been 'defangged'. Even Pakistan is fighting terrorist of a particular hue under the US pressure, but has done nothing to stop exporting terror to India.

Most of the terrorist outfits had adopted organisational models and terrorist tactics from 'popular' foreign sources like the Maoist ideology or Che Guevara tactics.

In one world, the war against terrorism is being fought by various nations, and India remains its worst-sufferer. Unfortunately, there is a feeling that the West is more serious in its anti-terrorist drive in areas where its own interests are threatened. It simply boils down to this fact. Inspite of all the sound and fury about international cooperation in fighting terrorism, each nation musk fight its own war against terrorism in its own backyard.

## State Terrorism

State terrorism can be recognised in two categories : (1) The one practised by autocratic/dictatorial states against its own population. (2) State Terrorism deemed as such by some of the more passionate/mindless/misguided "Human Right aps"—popularly HR-Wallans—when a democratic government proceeds against terrorists and religiously impelled fanatics bent upon challenging its sovereignty and integrity. Here we start with the former variety.

State terror is an important phenomenon of recent decades. Not only is it responsible for a much larger number of casualties than inflicted by non-state terrorists, it also has much deeper and wider ramifications and political consequences. State terrors bears some affinity with the practices of Christian millenarian sects which often endeavoured to establish or capture governmental instruments to create a new world of their own perception. James Rhode's comprehensive study, ***Hiller movement** : A Modern Millenarian Revolution*, is quite opposite, germane to the issues involved. Interestingly, the Revolutionary Tribunals or People's Courts which appeared in France under Maximilien Robespierre (1958-94), French revolutionist and the Jacobin leader, also emerged in Germany under Hitler, the Soviet Union under Stalin,

China under Mao, Cuba under Castro, and more recently Iran under Khomeini.

The idea of people's courts, in the instance of hostage taking is a concept strongly identified as "enlightened terror", called so because the state conceeds its responsibility. It is not the only form state terror takes, he soldom discuss terror as an instrument of foreign policy, a 19th century phenomenon is widely used today by a number of Muslim States, and possibly also by Marxist Ones, as indicated in Claine Sterlings book *The Terrorist Network* (1986). Pakistan training and sending foreign terrorists into Kashmir is also an example of use of terror as a foreign policy option.

"Fascism's policy of violence and concept of terror" represents on explicit effort in this direction, providing a definition of terror that comprehends both state and rebel forms. Sergio Panunzio, one of Mussolini's 'principal ideologues", considered force and violence as 'similar' phenomena. Curiously, both are legitimate, though not necessarily just, forms of coercion—both radically different from terror, which he regards as so irretrievably immoral that it cannot be legitimised.

A government uses force to punish those who violate its laws and making war against those who bear arms against it. Panunzio has no doubt that a government that uses weapons of mass destruction indiscriminately is guilty of terrorist behaviour exactly the same way as a rebel blowing up a bus-load of children, because both are treating their victims as 'proximate ends."[42]

The Special Tribunals for the Defence of State set up later by Mussolini to intimidate his political opponents can be characterised in the same way, indicating that fascist Italy was a 'repressive" State, not the one that deliberately used terror. The contrast with Nazi Germany and Stalin's Soviet Union was striking, because in the latter two cases, the People's Courts followed the precedents established in the French Revolution—concerning themselves with the traits individuals were not responsible for, nor could conceivably climinate. It follows then that persons and organizations should be designated terrorist when they recognise no principles by which any of these actors could be judged arbitrarily.

Hitler arbitrarily dubbed the Jews as sub-human terrorists[43] convinced that the Jews abroad misled Germany's principal rivals to believe that Germany's limited political and military aims were a bid for world dominion.

During the course of terror unleashed by the Revolutionary Government of France on 5 September 1793, lasting till the following September only. Some 500,000 of France's 25 million citizens were jailed as political suspects. Of these 15,000 were condemned to death and 12,000 to the prisons of the New Republic.[44] Both, before and after the saga of terror, each successive leadership claimed that with them, at least, the revolution was over. But then, there were several "endings".

The Revolution 'ended" with the abolition of Feudalism. It "ended" again with the constitution of 1791. Then, the revolution was "over" when the King had fallen and the Republic was declared. The revolution was once again "finished" with the purge of Robespierre and "Complete" when a constitutional reign was established in 1795. The revolution was "fulfilled" with the crowning of "Bonaparte" as Emperor. By contrast, the terrorists were the architects of a temporary rule, not a permanent or completed revolution.

The end of Robespierre and his colleagues is often explained by an escalation of the terror so inappropriately coincident to military succusses which undermined the justifications of these temporary measures.

Terror should be characterised as total primarily because it aimed at nothing less than the complete transformation of the social and political order. For that reason, it is not sufficient to recount the history of the revolutionary consolidation of power in the capital, its organ of the instrument of repression in the provinces, its success in developing the war lines economy which led to nil victory, and its effective repression of political opposition. To comprehend terror fully, one should take into account the necessity emposed upon the revolutionary government by its own theory of legitimacy, its own justification for existence, pursuing every vestigic, physical and moral, of the France of old. The revolutioanry Government set as its task the complete recreation of France, in a Republican mould, the creation of the Republican citizen.

Over some 80 years ago, Panunzio put together a rationale for political violence (1921).[45] Given the contemporary preoccupation with political violence, that rational did have immediate relevance.

The political universe is populated by groups committed to political violence as a revolutionary strategy, "and the number of commissions and conference's devoted to current problems of contemporary violence and terrorism is region." The first Fascist felt compelled for reasons moral and pragmatic to articulate a rationale for political violence as ancilliary to their revolutionary enterprise. By the time Panunzio put his defence of violence in 1921, Fascism had already vanned out from Ferrasa to envelope the whole of Northern Italy in violence that marked the penultimate stage of Mussolini's succession to power.

The Communists have written about the issue Marx insisted on one occassion that there was only "one way" to shorten the "agonies" of the old society and the birthpangs of the—New revolutionary terrorism.[46]

Elsewhere he insisted "force is the Midwife of every old society pregnant with a new one[47]. In 1872, Marx spoke of force as necessary for revolutionary change. Lenin, in turn, seemed to *characterise* terrorism as "single, combat", individual acts of violence "unconnected with the mass of the people".[48]

Established society makes war, uses coersion against criminals, subversives, and external enemies. Revolutionaries similarly make war against counter-revolutionaries, the agents of the governmental despotism, and all declared "internal enemies". Panunzio recknoned both force and violence as sanctioned by moral principles. Force is employed to assure a common unanymity of opinion concerning certain group-sustaining values—the security of life, possessions, national integrity, continuity of government/governance, and provision necessary welfare, violence appeals, and invite you, to an alternative future, a potential reality, more capable of providing the creative and moral satisfactions than the present social system. In substance, the difference between "force" and "violence"—a difference first suggested by Georges Sorel— is the difference between the present and alternative social future. The justification for either must necessarily be the consequence of rational calculation.

As external wars are rarely undertaken without rigorous factual and moral calculations, international wars through coersive power too should be resorted to in the service of ends that promise the realisation of some ultimate good unattainable by any other means.[49]

In this sense, Panunzio, like the Marxists in general, makes an ultimate appeal to an anticipatory future ("history") as offering the moral justification for the use of coarsion. Thus Trotsky[50] sought to justify Bolshevik violence by an appeal to "the fact that the proletariat (was) the historically rising class"and "the bourgeoisie a falling class." The bourgeoisie was the proper object of violence since it was "destroying the economic structure of the world and human culture generally."[51]

Thus the employment of means for indiscriminate destruction, such as poison gas, saturation bombing and shelling of polupation centres of no appreciable—military significance, bio-chemical and mass-destruction devices, would qualify, by Panunzio's criteria, as "terroristic", and constitute "war crimes". The long distance and indiscriminate shelling of Paris by German artillery, the Zapplin bombing of London, and the use of asphyxiant arms on the Western Front were all condemned by Panunzio as criminal acts of terrorism.[52]

One of the most salient traits of terrorism is its indiscriminate and arbitrary character. Terrorist acts are like natural catastrophies—they strike anyone, the guilty and the innocent alike. There are few precautions one can take to avoid becoming the target of terror. If its onset is incalculable, its termination unpredictable for its victims. It is of interest to see the evident distinction between the Sovet and the National Socialist terror systems.

In the Soviet Union, severe punishment, including "corrective labour", which for all intentions and purposes mean death in a labour camp, could be meted out by the administrative organs of the state, in effect the NKVD. Soviet terrorism was clearly demonstrative and prophylactic in intention. Soviet terrorism is military leaders involved down to regimental command. Most of the men who fell victim to it were known to be loyal and patriotic Soviet citizens. There was nothing like this in Fascist Italy. Fascism was not a terrorist, but a repressive political system." In substance, Fascist treatment of the Jews was always attended by some restraint—given the example of Soviet and National Socialistic practices.

Some analysts believe that various aspects of modern terrorism were introduced to international affairs by a State, rather than by state-sponsored or independent organisations. Nazi Germany used a variety of terrorist methods against the Jews. The "final solution" or mass extermination, only represents the last phase of this compaign. The earlier phases? The first phase was a form of indirect terror. German and European Jews were taken hostage to ensure "good conduct" of the Jews abroad and of the foreign governments. Besides, deportation was consciously used to assure the rest anti-semitism abroad and, hence, weaken the "Jewish World Influence".

The second phase was a policy of direct anti-Jewish persecution that was execised in Germany and in her conquered territories. The Nazis made Jewish leaders hostages (Judenrate) to ensure collaboration by Jews in German territories, inflicted physical torture, created hunger and fear in ghettos, and implemented *Aktinoneu* (kidnapping for slave labour and the death camps). These terror activities were aimed at breaking normal and free people to turn them into instruments of their own decination.

The final "solution" itself was the consequence of failure, in Hilters eyes, of the two preceding phases of Nazi terror : The execution of the hostages was necessary not only as a "positive" act of solving the "Jewish Problem", but also as an act of revenge for Hitler who was convinced that the Jews had pursuaded the allies to wage a war of annihiliation upon Germany. Hitler had joined politics with the "basic mission" to resolve the struggle to expose the menace which had threatened to overshadow Germany's destiny and that of the entire Nordic race and "humanity as a whole". He feared his people's decadence and lack of will and steadfastness to assume the necessary struggle against the modern forces of false moralism, hedonism, egoism and racial degeneration. The positive aspects of his highminded resolve to create a new Nazi Reich had its negative aspects of horrendous domestic terrorism, concentration camps and Gestapo violence had implicated the German people in the "final solution" horror, which consequently rendered any deal between it and the 'enemy' powers on the lines of the November 1918 Pact very unlilkely.

A scholar has seen a silver line even in this grim scenario : "The dynamism of Hitler's actual antisemitic policy suggests, paradoxically enough, self imposed constraints on an initial, Morbid resolve to kill them all, and this may as well explain in peculiar use of terrorism before the final solution."

Andei Vishinsky was rather direct: When it is a question of annihilating the enemy: "We can just as well do without a trial."

## References

1. Masada, Hebrew.
2. Encyclopaedia, X/868 and 10/314.
3. Scholars see a possible relationship between the Zealots and the Jewsh religious community mentioned in the Dead Sea Scrolls.
4. Fyodor Dostoyevsky used Nechayev as a model for the character Pyotr Verkhovensky in *The Possessed.*
5. Revolutionary terrorism here refers only to the use of terror to promote a popular insurrection. The Russians were not the first to employ terror in this way, but through then the doctrine of its potentialities was formulated and transmitted to successive generations. See 'Assassination and Terrorism' by David C. Rapoport (Toronto, 1971).
6. The most useful studies of assassins are by Marshall Hodgson *The Order of Assassins* (Gravenhage: Mouton, 1955) and by Bernard Lewis, *The Assassins* (London, Wiedenfields, 1957). In the last chapter, Lewis offers a suggestive note on the movement's place in the history of terrorism.
7. Supplementary Paper on "Munder". It was considered as one of the Fine Arts works (Boston : Houghton Mifflin, 1877); XI, pp. 579-80. Much more than any other terrorist group, Sicarii dominates de Quincey's attention. He returns to it again in "The Essenes", "Secret Socialies", and "Supplementary note on the Essenes" VII, pp. 52-222.
8. A more extensive treatment of the definitional problems appears in "Politics of Atrocity", in "Terrorism : Inter-disciplinary Perspectives, ed. Y. Alexander and S. Finger (New York : John Day, 1977), pp. 46-61.
9. Inside the Terrorist Mind, by David C. Rapoport, Chicago Tribune "Perspective", 2 November, 1975. The film *Battle of Algiers* offers a brilliance depiction of the process.
10. P. Knopotikin, M. Moirs of a Revolutionist (Boston: Houghton Mifflin, 1989) p. 415. This peace-campaign against the Naxals, led by the tribals, is known as Salwa.
11. Lawrence Durrel, *Bitter Lemons* (London: Faber, 1957) and Gen. Grives, *Memoirs*, ed. C. Foley (London : Longman 1964): 37.
12. This brief discussion on "Dialectics of Rebellion" is culled from E. Blazs, *Chinese Civilization and Bureaucracy,* (New Haven : Yale University Press), 1964, p. 165 and Reosmond, *Body, Soul and the*

............. *Relationship.* The history of an Analogy, Journal of History of Idea, Vol. 34, 1973, p. 290.

13. NYT, 18 January, 1961.
14. GT Britain, Foreign Office, Document 37/8170 N. 476 (1922).
15. Times (London) 26 May, 1927.
16. GT Britain, Foreign Office, Documents 371/15600 N and N 3686/1970/38 (1931) and 371/15592, N 3440/4/38, N 3793/4/38 (1931) and 141/532 (1935).
17. Lord Chalfont, *Freedom in Danger, The External and Internal Threat,* Atlantic Community, Quarterly, Fall 1976.
18. See for details, I Brownie, *International Law and the Use of Force by States* (NY: OUP(1963), pp. 241-242.
19. John Barron, KGB: *The Secret Work of Soviet Secret Agents* (NY: Bantam Books, 1974) pp. 76-77; Christopher Dobson and Ronard Payne, *The Terrorist; Their Weapons, Leaders and Tactics* (NY: Facts on file, 1979).
20. Le Point, 21 June, 1976.
21. The Economist, 1 January, 1977, p. 80.
22. Washington Post, 7 September, 1975, p. B-5.
23. Vittorpranco S. Pisano, Contemporary Italian Terrorism Analysis and Counter Measures (Washington, DC : Law Library, Library of the Congress, 1979.
24. Walter Laquer, *Terrorism,* Boston : Little Brown and Co., 1977, pp. 200-01.
25. US Congress, Senate Committee on Judiciary, Hearings, 14 May, 1975.
26. Institute for Study of Conflict, Conflict Studies, No. 69, 1976.
27. Foreign Report, The Economist, 14 February, 1980.
28. Foreign Report, The Economist, 24 March, 1983.

28(a). Foreign Broadcast Information Service, 1 February, 1979.

29. Christian Science Monitor, 15 March, 1977, pp. 14-15.
30. The Herald, 7 July, 1978.
31. Gill Green, Terrorism: It is Revolutionary? (NY: New Outlook Publishers, 1970), pp. 25-37.
32. Daily World, 5 January 1974, pp. 3-4.
33. Jenkins and Johnson, 1975, p. 23.
34. Fay, 1916, p. 86-87.
35. Taylor, 1950, p. 523.
36. Indian Today.
37. Brian Jenkines (1985), pp. 19-22.
38. Rajiv Sharma, Tribune, 11-5-06.

39. AA 9, 11 May, 2006.
40. For detailed review of the Film, *see* Ervell E. Menez, Tribune, 14-5-06.
41. The Author belongs to the Sikh Regiment of Infantry, the Arm which bears the brunt of terrorist violence in a given situation. An infantryman is most qualified to understand the pain and the suffering inflicted by the mindless Terrorist Violence on the soldiers and their near and dear ones because he is first on the firing line. For the same reason he also understands the pain and grief relatives of innocent civilians slaughtered by the abominable desperados and inhuman criminals.
42. Gave Brinton, A Decade of Revolution, (NY: Harper, 1934), p. 158; The Annals of the American Academy of Political and Social Science, 450, July 1980, pp. 35-46; Yehuda Baner *Genocide,* p. 44.
43. Lectures on French Revolution (NY : MacMillan (1959), Lecture XIV, Lord Acton : Just and Unjust Wars (NY : Basic books, 1979), Michael Walzer.
44. The Incidence of Terror during the French Revolution : A Statistical Interpretation (Cambridge, Massachusetts : Harward University Press, 1935), Donald Green.
45. The Men of the First French Republic : Political Alignments in the National Convention of 1972 (Baltimore and London : John Hopkins, (1972); The Girondins (London : Athlone Press, 1961).
46. The Oenvres Choices of Saint-Just (Paris : Gullimord, 1968), pp. 162-82.
47. The Critical Spirit : Essays in Honour of Herbert Mascuse, edited by Kurt H. Wolf and Barrington Moove (Boston : Beacon Press, 1967), pp. 121-49; Ocuvres IX 350-67.
48. Les Sons—Cucottes Parisiens en L' an II : Movement Popularise eq. Government Revolutionaire, 2 June 1793-9. Thermidor An II (Paris : Clavrevil, 1959) : Albert Sobout.
49. Panunzio, Diritto, *Forza e Vielenz*, pp. 190-94.
50. Years after Trotsky's death in 1940, the famed Soviet deplomat Andreil Vishinsky was even more open and straight forward : "When it is a question of annhilating the enemy, we can just as well do without a trial."
51. Trotsky, *Terrorism and Communism* 0. 63.
52. Why is Panunzio and his ink silent on the US atom-bombing two Japanese cities and western nations, particularly Britain, carpet-bombing the German industrial town, especially Dusseldorg is rather intriguing. Is it a case of unforgiveable, blatant partisanship, or amnesia?

# 3

# WORLD TERRORISM : STATUS REPORT

There were major terror attacks in Spain (train bombing) and the UK (Metro and bus attacks). But the West was made aware of this menace more forcefully by the attack on its commercial symbol, viz. the Twin Towers, better-known as Nine-Eleven. In his address on the national network, President George W. Bush declared : "America is under attack." Consequently the US declare a global war on terror (GWOT). Due to harsh treatment of terrorists at GITMO (most of whom were Muslim) and strict regimen on migrants entering the US, the Muslim nations deemed it as America's war on Islam. A large number of nations are battling terrorists on their soils, it is the US, aided by its NATO allies, which is fighting the terrorists in Pakistan and Afghanistan - far away from its shores, and it calls it GWOT.

Even if the US has so far failed to achieve any worthwhile success in Af-Pak region, its homeland has never been under attack after the horrendous Nine-Eleven.

This chapter deals with the situation in the world on the terror front in broad terms. The terror havoc in the individual countries will be discussed in the later chapters.

Major terror attacks are enumerated on the appendix below. It will be followed by some other pieces that show various aspects of terror in the international arena.

It should be of interest here to indicate the havoc wrought by the terrorists in the worst-affected region in this context : Afghanistan-Pakistan-India.

## Afghan-Pak-India Region

Terror deaths in these countries during the last four years are detailed here :

| | Year | | | |
|---|---|---|---|---|
| Country | 2005 | 2006 | 2007 | 2008 |
| Pakistan | 338 | 387 | 1,335 | 2,293 |
| Afghanistan | 682 | 1,042 | 1,966 | 1,989 |
| India | 1,357 | 1,256 | 1,093 | 1,113 |

**Note** : The figures indicate total number of deaths.

## Failed Nations : Top 10

The Foreign Policy magazine and the Fund for Peace ranked 177 countries to work out Failed States Index in 2008.

The top ten failed states are mentioned below, according to the said survey :

Somalia

Sudan

Zimbabwe

Chad

Iraq

DR Congo

Afghanistan

Cote d'lvoire

Pakistan

Central African Republic

It may be noted that most of these nations are wracked by the curse of terrorism.

**4 January, 2007**

13 people were killed and 22 injured in a car bomb attack near a gas station in Western Baghdad's upscale, mainly Sunni district of Mansour.

**13 January, 2007**

• Somalian Parliament declares a 3-month state of emergency amid fears of a return to clan violence after weeks of war against ousted Islamists. Members of Parliament in the government's interim of Baidoa voted 154 to 2 to ratify Prime Minister Ali Mohd Gedi's plan to restore peace and order.

• More than 200 people have died in clashes between ethnic African farmers and nomadic Arabs in the south Darfur in the past week, officials said on 13 January. Sudanese government sent emissaries to reconcile the warring tribes. The fighting was the latest outburst in the nearly 4-year-old conflict that has caused more than 200,000 deaths and forced over 2,500,000 people out of their homes in Darfur.

**15 January, 2007**

A bomb explosion at an Afghan refugee camp at Jalozai in Noushera, 50 km east of Peshawar, the capital of NWFP, killed four people and wounded another.

**16 January, 2007**

• Around 30 suspected Al-Qaeda militants, including foreigners were killed when Pak military launched on aerial attack on their hidouts in Zamzula area of South Waziristan tribal region, near the Afghan border.

• Sri Lankan army claïmed to have killed 30 Tigers in the restive Est. The clash at the village of Panichchankerni in the eastern district of Battiealoa comes as the military seeks to drıve the Tigers out of a coastal pocket of territory, they control under the terms of the lattered 2002 truce.

**20 January, 2007**

Four of the five US soldiers killed by insurgents in a raid on the 20th in the southern shrine city of Karbala were kidnapped and executed by men wearing "American-looking uniforms", the military revealed on the 27th. The audacious 20 January attack had been well rehearsed by the insurgents, who got past Iraqi Checkpoints "in a convoy consisting of at least five SUVs."

**22 January, 2007**

• 78 killed and 158 wounded in Baghdad.

• Four Pakistani soldiers were attack on a military convoy in Mir Ali area of North waziristan tribal region. The convoy was going to Miran Shah, the main town in the region, from the nearby town of Bannu.

**24 January, 2007**

30 militants were killed and 27 captured in Baghdad (Iraq).

**25 January, 2007**

• Three people were killed and five injured in three separate explusions in Assam by ULFA, the latest in a wave of bombings and shoot outs that killed 86 people in the past three weeks, officials said. The blasts took place near a bus stop in Rangiya town, 70 km West of Guwahati ; in the heart of Guwahati, and third in Tinsukia districts.

**26 January, 2007 : Muslim rebels attack village in Philippines**

Moro Islamic Liberation Front (MILF) rebels attacked farming village of Rangaban on Mindanao Island. In the ensuring battle with troops, five people, including four terrorists, were killed.

**26 January, 2007 : Islamabad (Pakistan)**

A suicide bomber tried to storm the Marriot hotel hours before the Indian High Commissioner held a Republic Day reception here.

Pakistan later formed a special team to investigate the suicide attack on the Marriot and are probing possible Taliban link to the attack.

**26 January, 2007 : CRPF man dies in Maoist Mine Blast**

A CRPF jawan was killed and two others were injured in a landmine triggered by the Maosts on the highway between Motu and Kalimela, about 60 km from Malkangiri (Orissa). The blast was aimed at blocking the state highway at several places to disrupt the Republic Day celebrations.

**26 January, 2007**

• A spate of gunfire and mortar attacks in the Somali capital, Mogadishu killed five people and injured four.

• Hamas militants killed a wounded Fatah fighter in a gangland style slaying. In clashes, both sides took captives. A Hamas force firing rockets launched a pre-dawn attack on the home of Nabil Jarjir, a member of the Fatah-affiliated Al-Aosa Martyrs' Brigades in the Gaza Strip and wounded him. As the neighbours were taking the injured Jarjir to the hospital, the Hamas raiders stopped the car and killed him with a shot to the head.

• 22 killed in fresh Iraq bombings.

• Three soldiers among four killed in an LTTE-sprung ambush in north western town of Mannar.

• Islamist militants killed a police officer when they opened fire on a vehicle carrying police near Tank, a town 50 km west of Dera Ismael Khan, NWFP.

**27 January, 2007**

• 500,000 US protestors join Washington DC rally to demand Congress cut of funds for Iraq war and stop troop increases ordered by President Bush.

• The Sri Lankan Navy, employing its Fast Attack Craft, destroyed three suspicious boats in the "restricted zone" off Colbombo harbour.

**28 January, 2007**

• Hamas-Fatah battles kill 25 in the Gaza strip.

• Gunmen carjacked a US Embassy vehicle on the outskirts of the Kenyan capital (Nairobi) and killed the wife of an Embassy employ and his mother-in-law. The police later killed two of the carjackers.

Carjackings are common around Nairobi.

• Assam (India). At least three Hindi-speaking traders were seriously wounded when the ULFA militants ambushed a truck in Upper Assam's Tinsukia district.

**28 January, 2007 : Five shot dead in Southern Thailand**

Five people were shot dead and another injured in attacks by the Islamic militants in three Muslim-majority provinces of Thailand—Yala, Pattani, and Songkhla-bordering Malaysia.

**28 January, 2007 : Iraq : "No regrest for killing 182, 000 Kurds"**

"Chemical Ali" said on the 28th that he made no 'mistake' when he ordered bombing of thousands of Kurdish villages in the so-called Anfal campaign, in which 182,000 Kurds (men, women and children) were killed.

**29 January, 2007 : 46 militants arrested in Turkey**

Turkish police arrested 46 militants on the 29th for their ties to Al Qaeda in five provinces - Istanbul, Konya, Izmir, Kocaeli and Mardin.

**26,27,29, January, 2007 : Pakistan : 22 killed and 67 injured in suicide attacks**

In a third suicide attack in four days, 3/7 were killed/injured in Dera Ismael Khan district of NWFP on the 29th. On the 26th and 27th, two suicide bombers killed 19 people and injured around 67 in Islamabad and Peshawar.

**28-29 January, 2007 : India (Assam) : Four killed**

ULFA killed two Hindi-speaking migrant workers in Tinsukia district on the 29th, and a local Congress leader in Sivasagar on the 28th (fourth such attack targeting ruling party in State). Security forces killed an ULFA guerrilla on the 28th in Tinsukia (The worst was slaughter by ULFA of 73, 61 of them being Hindi-speaking migrants from Bihar (57) and Orissa (4).

**Iraq : 28-29 January, 2007 : 300 Killed**

US and Iraqi forces killed some 300 gunmen from an apocalyptic Muslim cult in a day long battle involving tanks and aircraft near the Shia holy city of Najaf. Earlier, it was reported the men killed were Sunni fighters.

Officials had uncovered a plot to kill leading Shia clerics in Najaf on the 30th, to coincide with the climax of Ashura, the annual Shia rite marking a 7th century battle that entrenched the sehism between Shia and Sunni Islam.

The leader of the cult who claimed to be Mahdi - a messiah-like figure in Islam whose coming heralds the start of perfect world justice - was killed in the battle. Up to 1.5 million pilgrims gathered amid tight security in Karbala, 70 km north of Najaf, to mark the climax of Ashura, the high point of Shia religious calendar.

Some sources put the fatalities around 150 to 200. There were Shia-Sunni clashes in other areas also (The US military had officially handed over responsibility for Najoa province to Iraqi security forces in December, 2006.

## 29 January, 2007 : Suicide bombing returns to Israel

A Palestinian suicide bomber killed 3 people in a bakery in the Red Sea resort Eilat, one of Israel's most popular holiday spots, in the first such attack in the Jewish State in nine months.

Islamic Jihad, Al Aqsa Martyrs Brigades and the previously unknown "Army of Believers" claimed joint responsibility for the bombing.

**17 February, 2007**

- At least 15 people, including a judge, were killed 24 injured when a SUICIDE BOMBER blew himself up in a court room in high security area of Baluchistan capital of Ouetta (Pakistan), "which is reeling under a spate of such attacks in recent weeks." This is the seventh attack in three weeks.

- A double car bombing killed 10 people and injured 60 in a crowded market in the northern Iraqi city of Kirkuk. The explosion occurred in Kurkuk's Rahim Awa district, a predominantly Kuzdish area of the ethnially mixed city. Several cars and shops were burnt out.

## International Terrorism : Situation is Bleak Again

Battle against terrorism had assumed vigorous drive after the 9/11 attacks. Countries like India, Russia etc had been engaged in counter-terrorism wars long years before that 'cataclysmic event' - as the west-particularly the US, would like to define it - but the latter never realised, or may be, did not want to, the grimness and gravity of the situation. After all it was a distant house on fire. But one single incident and under 3,000 deaths was all that was needed to metamorphose the perception of these countries regarding the dangers posed by the terrorism. A menacing apparition was suddenly looming large over the globe. Some terrorists acts in European nations only further fuelled the fears, adding to the forebodings. That India had suffered over 70,000 fatalities till then was merely a statistic details.

Anti-terrorism measure-legislative/legal and administrative - were instituted by most countries, most stringent by the U.S. Things seemed to be working well for a couple of years. But in 2005, the terror outlook was turning grimmer for America. The US was not winning the wars in Afghanistan and Iraq, or so some analysts believed. But today, the situation is worse the world over. "The Jihadi training centres are functioning full time once again in different parts of Pakistan. The Jihadi terrorist training infrastructure in Afghanistan which the US and NATO troops had destroyed through their airstrikes during the course of counter-terror operations, has been fully restored - al be it in Pakistani territory"[2]. This has been stated not only by outsider observers, but also by prestigious sections of the Pakistani media such as the "Herald", the monthly published from Karachi by the "Dawn" group of publications. The US has lost the war in Iraq, even if the Iraqi Government, supported and propped by it, is still trying manfully to stop the carnage resulting from the Shia-Sunni sectarian blood-letting Afghanistan, which had witnessed fairly peaceful Presidential elections in October 2004, has progressively slid back into its traditional anarchic ways of the yore. The remnants of the Taliban and the Al Qaeda, which had been driven out of Afghanistan by the US led coalition, are back with an increased force in the Pashtun majority areas of the country in its south. Others have joined them such as Gulbuddin Heckmatyar's Hizb-e-Islami (HEI), the Hizbul Tehrir (HT) and the Islamic Movement of Uzbekistan (IMK). And they are getting unstinted support of the fundamentalist political coalition of Pakistan called the Muttahida Majlis-e-Amal, which is in power in the NWFP and is a member of the ruling coalition in Baluchistan. The MMA's support for the Taliban has been corroborated by no less a person than Lt. Gen. Syed Safdar Hussain, the Pakistan Army's Corps Commander at Peshawar. Even more significantly, the MMA ruling regime has already enacted certain Taliban-style laws in NWFP which the Federal Government is wincing at being under pressure from the State Government for an early President ascent to bring them into force.

Above it all comes the so-called 'Peace' Pacts that Islamabad has concluded with the pro-Taliban tribals in North and South Waziristan agencies of the Federally Administered Tribal Area (FATA) of Pakistan bordering southern Afghanistan - ironically to thwart the advance of Taliban in this area of Pakistan and across the borders into Afghanistan. This is the reason advanced by the Pak Government for these 'Peace' Pacts which ostensibly seems to have convinced the US and the west. It is a different matter though that most analysts assert these two (agency) areas have proved to be safe havens for the Taliban fighters to be launched across the border after having been recruited, trained and equipped, by the sympathetic MMA regime, in Peshawar and other areas of the province of the province of NWFP.

## Suicide Terrorism

Suicide bombing, which had disappeared from Afghanistan's terrorist landscape, has made its reappearance after three years. Following the allegations of desecration of the Holy Quran by the American troops at the Guantanamo detention centre in Cuba, the Islamic world witnessed wide-spread anti-US demonstrations, but mostly peaceful except in Afghanistan, which saw serious incidents of anti-US violence.

Not a day passes, without clashes, raids, beheadings etc by the terrorist (Taliban-Al Qaeda) combine in Afghanistan. The

Americans, obviously, are their targets. A major 'success' come their way in 2005 when a U.S. helicopter was shot down killing all its 17 occupants, including three members of a US Special Force Unit.

In July 2005, when the US troops chased a raiding party, it crossed over into the Waziristan area of Pakistan. In an act of hot pursuit, the US troops followed them, killing all the members of the raiding party on the Pakistani soil. At was the first time the US troops exercised this right. The terrorist depredations rose to new heights of violence in 2006.

After lying low-maintaining a studied low profile - for a while in the post-9/11 heat of circumstances, Pakistan again became the most important hub of jihadi terrorism in the world, say be late 2004. It was back to being a veritable warren of jihadi terrorists of various hues, generations and nationalties - 23 in the last count. To wit, there were no less than 220 references to Pakistan in the report of the US National Commission on 9/11, released in 2004.

What is the Pakistani ranking in the world wide terror stakes (and scale) can be gauged by the fact that since the attempt to blow up the New York World Trade Centre in March 1993, there have been very few terrorist strikes during the investigation of which Pakistan and Pakistanis have not figured in some connection or the other.

Indian analysts feel that in violation of the repeated promises made by Gen. Musharraf to the US he has taken no action the Pakistan-based jihadi terrorist training infrastructure directed against India. In the same way he has also not acted against the Taliban leaders and cadres operating against Afghan and American troops in Afghanistan from Pakistani territory. The only limited action he has taken is directed against some operatives and cadres of the Al Qaeda, who pose a direct threat to US nationals and interests. Even that limited and selective action did not produce the results President Bush sorely needed, not only for the strategic interests of his country but also for the sake of his personal standing, viz the capture or killing of Osama and his deputy Aymen al-Zawahiri. The two international outlaws have continued to operate from the tribal region straddling the Pak-Afghan border and periodically disseminate video-audio recorded statements over the Al Jazeera network - threatening the US, Israel and other assorted enemies of Islam which incidentally include India since 2003 and inciting/exhorting their faithfuls in different countries to step up the Jihad against the *infidels* mentioned above. Incidentally, Al Jazeera broad cast eleventh tape of al-Zavahiri this year (2006) in December.

Musharraf keeps acting and speaking on appropriate occasions-as is his wont. If some important Qaeda leaders are captured or even killed on the eve of or during the visit of some eminent US visitors to the continent, his 'important' speeches are timed to suit some important incident or event. His televised address to his nation on 21 July 2005, in the wake of the London explosions, calling upon his security forces to crack down on the extremists and terrorists operating from Pakistani territory, did not seem to have been taken seriously by large sections of his own people, who looked upon that crack-down, incidentally third in a row since 9/11, as another eye-wash and one more example of a pantomime, even if hundreds of arrests were reported to have been made! In his usual blunt style, a well-known columnist Ayaz Amir of the Dawn, had asked a serious question dripping in cynicism : "How many crackdowns make a genuine crack-down?" When his own people' do not believe Musharraf, it is surprising how the Americans believe him. May be, answer lies in public diplomacy : avoiding public censure and telling harsh truths in private. Yet again, may be they have no options. They seem to have convinced themselves that Musharraf is their best bet - rightly or wrongly, is an irrelevant issue.

India's troubles seem to be getting deeper and more intractable. As if Pakistan on its west was not enough as a cause for India's concerns for its security and integrity, Bangladesh has turned out as second and possibly more dangerous second major hub of jihadi terrorism to its east - in the Asian region. The terrorist training camps of the Harkat-ul-Jihad-al-Islami (HUJI), a member of bin-Laden's International Islamic Front (IIF), located in Bangladeshi territory have been training Jihadi terrorists from Southern Thailand. Bangladesh continues to provide sanctuaries, funds, arms and ammunition, and explosives to various anti-Indian terrorist outfits - jihadi as well as non-jihadi. Bangladesh as a hub of anti-Indian terrorists outfits poses even a greater danger to India's security and integrity in comparison to Pakistan as it has millions of Bangladeshi emigrants—mostly illegal-settled in the dozen-and-a-half border districts of Assam and West Bengal and some of them can easily be turned into terrorists, suicide and non-suicide variation, to act as its effective vanguard in these two

Indian states. And it will be at their own peril if Indians forget a warning from no less a strategist and thinker than the farmer US Secretary of State Henry Kissinger that "there can be another Pakistan in India's North-East by 2050."

Bangladeshi exertions in the field of spreading terrorism in the region has already paid dividends : Southern Thailand has joined southern Philippines and Indonesia as another favourite play ground for jihadi terrorists in South-East Asia. Since the beginning of the 2004, over 8,000 people have been killed there -terrorist suspects as well as innocent civilians. The methods employed by the terrorists in Thailand are well-known and well-tested : Explosions using mobile phones, assassinations of officials at point-blank range and beheadings of not only Buddhists, but also Muslims suspected to be cooperating with the authorities. The terrorists repertoire is the very same one taught at the training centres in Bangladesh.

It will be worth mentioning that Pakistan is also making its contribution to the spread of terrorism in Thailand. The proof, if one is required at all, comes from a prestigious Pakistani newspaper itself, the *Daily Times* of Lahore, of 18 July 2005 : "Jihadis from Southern Thailand continue to come to Pakistan for training and the plan for the jihad in Southern Thailand was finalised at a clandestine meeting of the Jihadi leaders in Lahore."

There have been more acts of suicide terrorism in Iraq during the last two years than during the previous two decades in the entire world. More innocent civilians and government workers have been killed in Iraq by terrorists during the last two years than in the entire world during the last two decades. "In July 2005, alone, there were 55 attacks of suicide terrorism in Iraq's Sunni triangle." There has been an unending flow volunteers for suicide terrorism in Iran - about two thirds of them from Saudi Arabia and the rest from Syria, Kuwait, Pakistan and some other Muslim countries.

Saudi Arabia has continued to bleed despite the ruthless measures taken by the security forces to eliminate the Al Qaeda from its soil. Unfortunately, suspected complicity of elements from the intelligence and security agencies of the country with the Al Qaeda and other terrorists have rendered the task more difficult. The energy security of many countries, including India's, could be jeopardised if the terrorists ultimately prevails in the land of the two holiest shrines of Islam.

Jihadi terrorism has spread to Kenya, Morocco, Turkey, Spain, and the UK in the recent years and of late has reappeared in Egypt from where it had disappeared since 1997. The 'War' in Somalia has transformed into Ethiopian vs Somalian Islamast fighters, with transitional Somali Government playing a marginal role, since December 2006. The terrorists—the storm-troopers of the Somalian Islamic Courts Council (SICC)—have fled from Mogadishu and other areas of southern Somalia under their occupation under pressure from Ethiopian military. More noteworthy is the fact that the SICC leadership have for the first time called for the suicide bombers from the Muslims all over the globe. Suicide terrorism has claimed its first victims in the UK. The Muslim immigrant communities in the EU countries have become the Western hub of the international jihadi terrorism. The largest number of terrorist suspects detained for questioning in the EU countries after the Madrid blasts in March 2004 were Moroccan and Pakistanis or people of Moroccan and Pakistani origin. The Saudis, the Egyptians, the Moroccans and the Pakistanis constitute the driving force of jihadi terrorism today, whether in the East or West.

The above is the state of international terrorism, ill-omened and foreboding, in Indian's extended neighbourhood. If the US-led war on terror appeared to be succeeding for a couple of years, it is down hill journey since 2005. Even the 'victories' imagined/scored earlier are coming unstuck-or so it seems. An appeals Court in Indonesia declared 'not guilty' in December 2006 the chief conspirator, the seniormost cleric, who had just come out of the prison after completing his 30-month jail sentence. What signals such judicial pronouncements mean/convey to the counter-terrorism efforts the world over and the perpetrators of the terrorism, suicide or other variety, are not difficult to imagine. Likewise, after the military junta soon after taking over power in Thailand had assured the terrorism—affected three southern states of applying balm on their wounds, there were blasts/explosion in Bangkok on the eve of the New Year celebrations which were consequently cancelled in a hurry.

One expert posits the view that situation today is "back to 9/10". But the fact is it is far worse than that. Analysts feel the US action in Afghanistan and later attack on Iraq has made the world far more unsafe than it was before these two interventions. Frenzied reaction from most Muslim sections have fomented extremism and fundamentalist influence in the world of Islam. America have become the most-hated nation for most Muslims for its "anti-Islam policies." The Muslim intellectual circles perceive President Bush to be giving practical shape to the Huntingtonian theory of "war of civilization". As a result of the American action, the Muslim celeries have succeeded in enraging the Muslims in general and the youth in particular against the West in general and the US in particular. Consequently, these colerics have possibly given more Muslims to 'terrorist armies' and produced more suicide bombers to do their duty by Islam during the last five years (2002-06) than possibly the last two decades.

The fact that most analysts now see the US as having lost the war in both the countries and Bush is himself planning withdrawal of the US troops from there – with certain face-savers thrown here and there - have certainly emboldened the Islamist terrorist leadership to envision greater victories in near future. The frequent assertions made by Osama and his No. 2 in the tapes bread east by the Al Jazeera TV about anti-Islam war being waged by US and their exhortation to the faithful to defeat the infidel nations like the Israel, the US and of late, "Hindu" India ; the ascendance of the Hamas in Palestine and sudden infatuation for the Hezbollah of the Muslims in West Asia and beyond after its recent "victory" over Israel are but only three instances of the shape of things to come in the Muslim World. Once the "moderates" within the Islamic fold are won over or trounced, that will be the time for the non-Muslim world to be ready to face the fury of the Jihadi terrorists and suicide bombers. The time for the former to prepare for that cataclysm is today, as tomorrow would be to late!

## International Terrorism : The Looming Scourge

Terrorism is the most serious threat to the peace, stability and order in the world today. As some would say, to the world itself. One analyst put it this way : "The current 'epidemic of violence' is threatening the very fabric of international order and the most fundamental of rights."

## "Extremism will die a natural death," Rushdie : 21 January 2007

Novelist Salman Rushadie feels extremism would die a natural death the moment the community for which the battle is supposedly fought dis own it or show disinclination to continue with the strife. "The Irish Republican Army cause was defeated because the North Ireland Catholics stopped wanting to fight", Rushadie said on the 21st, "That is the way to stop terrorism in the end."

He Made Some Further Points

- The fighting going on in the name of stopping injustice is counter-productive. The fight has to be fought but there are other ways to fight than using the gun. This should be something the Muslim community and the world would have to think—the role of likes of Al Qaeda and others. The kind of fighting giving on at present is counter-productive.

An intellectual of Rushdie's stature deserves a serious attention when he speaks on terrorism. But his assumption of terrorism dying a natural death seems to be simplistic. In fact, the terrorists will look for alternative ways only after they are convinced that they cannot bend the governments. Only a state's might will force them to the negotiations table. Then only the dexterity of the political class will win the day.

## Global Terror Deaths up by 30% : US 2006 Report : 30 April, 2007

Death and injuries from terrorist attacks increased sharply in 2006, particularly in Iraq and Afghanistan, with government officials, police and security guards coming under greater attacks than ever before, the State Department's annual survey of global terrorism, concluded on 30 April 2007, and released as "Country Reports on Terrorism 2006."

The scorecard on terrorist trends found that more than 20,000 people died and over 200,000 were injured in some 14,000 incidents in 2006, an increase of 6,000 deaths, or 30 per cent, over 2005.[3]

Some of the facts/points/conclusion from the terror scene 2006 are mentioned here :

- As in 2005, the vast majority of incidents and deaths occurred primarily in Iraq and Afghanistan, where US troops and local forces are battling Islamist militants.
- The two regions, Iraq and Afghanistan, also accounted for 90 per cent of the 290 attacks considered high-casualty incidents because they killed 10 or more people.

- 45 per cent of all incidents considered terrorist attacks, about 6,600, occurred in Iraq, killing at least 13,340 people. The Iraq fatalities comprised about 65 per cent of the world-wide total of victims for the year.
- A UN report earlier in 2007 estimated there were nearly 35,000 civilian casualties in Iraq in 2006 but did not blame terrorism for all of them.
- As fighting has intensified in Afghanistan, 749 attacks were reported there in 2006, an increase of more than 50 per cent over the 491 attacks reported for 2005. At least, 1,040 people were killed in Afghanistan up from 684 reported dead from terrorist incidents in 2005.
- Russel Travers, Deputy Director of National Counter-Terrorism Centre, which compiled the statistics, said analysts used the State Departments' definition of terrorist attacks. That definition includes many attacks in Iraq that some contend are not terrorist incidents but acts of guerrilla warfare.
- The figures do not include attacks on US troops.
- More than 11,200 government officials and police were attacked in 2006, up from 9,500 in 2005. Also, more than 1,800 children were victims of attacks in 2006, an increase of 80 per cent, although officials said there was no orchestrated effort to target children.

The annual report is mandated by Congress as a way of informing policy makers, the public and the allies about tends in global terrorism. It has been controversial in recent years, as critics of the Bush administration accused it of manipulating the statistics for political gains.

## Quotable Quotes : US War on Terror

"Today we are fighting a new war to defend our liberty, and our people, and our way of life."

President George W. Bush, who compared the US war on terror to the American Revolutionary War while celebrating George Washington's 275th birthday on 19 February, 2007.

"Al Qaeda in fact is now functioning exactly as its founder and leader, Osama bin Laden envisioned it."

Terrorism expert Bruce Hoffmann, testifying before the House Armed Services Committee about Al Qaeda's recent resurgence.

"I think that Donald Rumsfeld will go down as one of the worst secretaries of defence in history."

Republican Presidential candidate John Mccaine, telling an audience in "Very Arizona that American was paying a price" for the mismanagement of the Iraq War.

"Terrorism is a Sin and Acceptance of it is a bigger sin"

Shiv Khera

International Educator

## Pakistan : An Epicenter of Terrorism

A good measure to judge the state of terrorism is to enumerate the violent incidents enacted by the desperados in Pakistan during the last couple of years.

**8 November, 2006**

Man wearing explosives attacks troops killing 42 soldiers in Dargai

**14 July, 2007**

Suicide bomber attacks military convoy in North Waziristan, killing 24 soldiers.

**19 July, 2007**

Suicide attack on minibus carrying Chinese workers near Karachi, killing 29 people.

**4 September, 2007**

Two bombs hit army bus in Rawalpindi, killing 24.

**18 October, 2007**

Suicide bombing aimed at former Prime Minister Benazir Bhutto kills 150 people in Karachi.

**29 February, 2008**

Suicide bomber strikes at funeral of slain policeman in Swat Valley, killing 40.

**2 March, 2008**

Suicide bomber attacks tribesmen discussing resistance to al-Qaeda at Darra Adam Khel, kills 40.

**11 March, 2008**

Suicide bombs rip through police HQ in Lahore, killing 24.

**19 August, 2008**

Bomb explodes outside hospital, killing 23 in Dera Ismail Khan.

**21 August, 2008**

Suicide bombers blow themselves up at a weapons factory in Wah, killing 67.

**20 September, 2008**

A devastating terror attack virtually gutted the Marriott hotel in Pakistan's capital Islamabad, killing at least 60 people.

As the only luxury hotel in the city, it was where well-heeled residents ment for a relaxed mid-morning cup of coffee, a leisurely meal post-midnight, a swim in its heated pool and even for a bit of music in its "dry bar." As the only five – star hotel, it was a virtual one stop destination for seminars and soirees, recitals and receptions, birthdays and other bashes. Over-looking the picturesque Margalla Hills, the hotel was probably an obvious target. The terrorists struck in the holy month of Ramadan.

As Pakistan gets in the crosshair of more terror groups, it was probably too much to hope that the Marriott would escape. This was perhaps stated to happen.

The last blast at this hotel was just before an Indian reception a couple of years ago. The Marriott escaped virtually unscathed then.

Huge flames billowed out of the windows and terror was home once again, exactly a week after Delhi's busiest markets (Lajpat Nagar etc) were targeted.

It was thus that Islamabad's iconic landmark was gutted.

## Terrorism : A Global Menace : FBI Chief

Chief of USA's Federal Bureau of Investigation (FBI) Robert Mueller said 3 March 2009 all countries in the world should bring the perpetrators of the Mumbai atrocity. He also condemned the attack on Sri Lankan cricketers in Lahore. He opined that terrorism is not a local, but a global issue.

## US State Department Survey : 2008

The US State Department has produced an excellent research and analysis in its annual Country Reports on Terrorism 2008, released end-April 2009. What follows is a summary of its analysis on some countries' stance on various aspects of international terrorism.

Regarding Iran, the US Government has massive evidence of its continuing role as "the most significant state sponsor of terrorism". Iran's reasons for doing so, as seen by the US : "To advance its key national security and foreign policy interests, which include regime survival, regional dominance, opposition to Arab-Israel peace, and countering Western influence, particularly in the Middle East". It must be clear to all that it is not going to change, especially once Iran has nuclear weapons. Not only does Tehran use the Islamic Revolutionary Guard Corps (the institution most supportive of President Mahmoud Ahmadinejad) "to clandestinely cultivate and support" Hamas, Islamic Jihad, and Hizbullah, but also radical Islamist groups in Afghanistan, the Balkans, and in Iraq against US forces.

As for Syria, events highlighted its ties to the world's most notorious terrorists", including the death of Hizbullah Operations Chief Imad Mugniyah, killed while under Syrian Government protection. "Among other atrocities, Mugniyah was wanted for the 1983 bombings of the Marine barracks and US embassy in Beirut, which killed over 350". Moreover, as the report shows, Syria has been tightening its alliance with Iran and continued financing terrorism.

While US efforts reduced their numbers, terrorists destabilising Iraq continued coming in "predominantly through Syria" and "receiving weapons and training from Iran."

Here is the bottom line : Not only do Syria and Iran believe that destabilizing West Asia, bullying or controlling their neighbours, and expelling US influence is in their interest, they are also directly involved in trying to kill Americans.

The report has no illusions about Hizbullah, the Lebanese Shia terrorist group : "It receives training, weapons and explosives, as well as political, diplomatic and organisational aid from Syria. It generally follows the religious guidance of Iranian Supreme Leader Ali Khamenei. Hizbullah is closely allied with Iran and often acts at its behest, though it also acts independently. The group has helped Syria advance its political objectives in the region."

Hizbullah has been involved "in numerous anti-US and anti-Israeli terrorist attacks", including "the suicide truck bombings of the US Embassy and US Marine barracks in Beirut in 1983, and the US. Embassy annexe in Beirut in 1984, and the 1985 hijacking of TWA flight 847, during which a US Navy driver was murdered".

Now, "Hizbullah has provided training to select Iraqi Shia militants, including the construction of shaped charge IEDs that can penetrate heavily-armoured vehicles..."

So, Hizbullah is an ally of Iran and Syria, involved in killing and kidnapping Americans. Should US policy, then, not actively oppose Hizbullah taking over Lebanon? And if Hizbullah is part of Lebanese Government after the June (2009) elections, shouldn't the U.S. reject dealings and stop all aid to that regime?[4]

The reports talks about "regular and indiscriminate rocket attacks on Israel from Gaza". Citing Israeli figures, the report notes that "Palestinian terrorist groups fired approximately 1750 rockets and 1,528 mortars into Israel in 2008, double the previous years total. "On December 18, Hamas leadership announced the end of the ceasefire", during which it had been firing without cease. Thereafter, rockets of longer range and in larger quantities were shot at Israel, disrupting life in the country's south. And this was the reason why Israel had no choice but to launch a major military operation in the Gaza strip.

Then the report talks about Europe becoming an area of serious concern as radicalisation continues there among "immigrant populations, youth and alienated minorities..." That means Muslims.

Terrorists and extremists are manipulating the grievances of alienated youth or immigrant populations and then cynically exploiting those grievances to subvert legitimate authority and create unrest."

Report then tells us how the terrorists should be fought in the West : "Treat immigrant and youth populations not as a threat to be defended against, but as a target of enemy subversion to be protected and supported". Then, says the analyst, it apologetically calls for dialogue.

The analyst wants Obama to read this report, because "I can't think of any more effective way for challenging the idea that apologies or dialogues with the sponsors and perpetrations of terrorism is going to change their behaviour.

Ironically, soon after the above was penned, Obama spoke to the Muslim world from Cairo. He may not have offered apologies to the Muslims, his tone was certainly apologetic.

## International Conflicts : A Broad Picture

A fact of contemporary warfare is that it has begun to lean extensively towards the "Low intensity variety. Of the 160 or so conflicts the world has seen since 1945, three fourths have been low intensity. 'Terrorism' is the most dominant and most widely practised form of the LIC as of date. Mostly perpetrated by the non-state actors, its targets are innocent civilian, including children and women. Some other relevant data/facts are recorded here :

- Only four of the 82 conflicts recorded between 1989 and 1992 were of the classic inter-state character. Every year since 1991, there have been at least ten internal conflicts around the world that caused the death of more than 10,000 where the primary weapon of war were light weapons—mostly used by the terrorists.
- Non-state actors appear to have little difficulty in accessing either the weapons or the ammunition, as prices dropped to as little as $8 for an AK-47 assault rifle—a prized possession of a terrorist.
- In all of the intra-state conflicts being waged today light weapons are the primary weapons of the war of both the combatants - the state and the non-state actor.
- The rise in sophistication was accompanied by a corresponding increase in the casualty rate in most conflict areas. The path from the .303 to the assault-rifles and rocket propelled grenades (RPG) has been a bloody one.
- All wars in Asia and some other parts of the world are funded wholly or in part by the narcotics movement - popularly known as narco-terrorism.

- Besides an inordinate number of casualties suffered by the civil society, the terrorism also causes huge refugee movement—e.g., Sri Lanka war on LTTE and Pakistan action against Taliban in the Swat Valley. By the end of the 20th century, the various conflict zones the world over had over 120 million chronically malnourished people, while there were over 28 million refugees and displaced persons, an eleven-fold increase since 1970 (Human Development Report, 1999).
- In more specific terms, in Sudan's Darfur region alone, an estimated 200,000 people have been killed and over two million rendered homeless in the terrorism-related upheavals during the past half-a-decade period.

It should be a matter of serious concern that the international community is unable to craft a joint, well thought out, concerted and effective policy frame-work to confront, control and defeat the terrorism. When a Western scholar adumbrated a "clash of civilisations" theory more than a decade ago, many analyst vigorously disagreed with him. The latter would surely have reasons to rethink their opposition. Are not we already witnessing how the radical Islam is engaged in an effort to not only dominate and over power the moderates in the Ummah but also to destabilise and defeat the nations it deems as enemies, namely the US, Israel and India? The al Qaeda has added India to the list only last year (2008).

A Pakistani scholar quotes Quran on the issue. Brig. S.K. Malik, in his *Quranic Concept of War*, says the following :

> "Terror struck into the hearts of the enemies is not only a means, it is the end in itself."

While Islamic terror outfits are active in 46 nations—(Muslim and non-Muslim) from Philippines to the US, some non-Islamic outfits are operating in countries like Sri Lanka, North Ireland, Europe, Japan and South America.

Not to speak of a joint counter-terrorism strategy to defeat the terror merchants, the UN is unable till date to cross the definitional hurdle in this war.

It needs emphasis that never before in the history were—human-beings exposed to violence of any variety as they are to terrorism during the last decade or so. The terrorists, fundamentalists, insurgents, extremists et al are focused single-mindedly to destroy the peace and harmony of the world through a wanton violence unleased by their foot soldiers, blinded and indoctrinated by their religious and ideological mentors. The latter are not only orchestrating a death dance the world over, but also transforming the tender youth into robots—the unthinking killing machines. The suicide bomber is the latest and the most lethal addition to the armoury of the hate-spewing perpetrators. It is beyond comprehension how the fanatic clerics and the nation at ideologue can so easily convert simple young men into human bombers, better known as suicide bombs—alluring them with a life of pleasure in the yonder world, surrounded by 36 virgin nymphs and other luxuries they could have only dreamt of during their sojourn on the earth. There can be no counter or answer to this unthinking robot-like killing machine.

Here are some instances of terrorist attacks in the recent past : Marine barracks bombings in Lebanon; destruction of the World Trade Centre of the US (Nine-Eleven, in day-to-day parlance) ; attack on the Indian Parliament, the representative of the largest democracy in the world ; repeated attacks on transport systems and commercial hubs of Mumbai, economic capital of India ; several attacks in Delhi, Jaipur, Hyderabad, Bangalore, Nashik etc to fuel religious and sectarian strife in India ; bombings at the tourists-filled Bali beaches in Indonesia ; killings of passengers on Metro trains in London and similar attack on trains in Madrid (Spain) ; horrendous attack on a Moscow theatre killing many students ; the latest two enormities involving Pakistan-sponsored attack on Mumbai (26/11) and terrorist attack on visiting Sri Lankan cricket team in Lahore, Pakistan ; and too frequent killings in Iraq, Afghanistan, and of late, Pakistan, which are too numerous for recording.

Above are cited some select instances to show that no place or country are safe from the terrorist depredations. The elder statesman of India, Mr. A.B. Vajpayee, put it succinctly when he addressed the US Congress in September 2002 :

> "No country in the world could enjoy immunity against terrorism on account of distance or geography."

The present situation vis-à-vis terrorism can be simply summed up in a single sentence : We are living in the most dangerous would presently.

## References

1. Sinan Salaheddin, AP, Cited Asian Age, 22 Feb 2007.
2. B. Raman, an expert on the subject, at the Round Table on "Ayodhya and London : Lessons for the future", hosted by the International Terrorism Watch Project of Observer Research Foundation (ORF), New Delhi, 29 July, 2005.
3. Josh Meyer, Los Angeles Times – Washington Post, reproduced in *Indian Express*, 2 May, 2007.
4. Barry Rubin, Director, GLORIA, Centre, Jerusalem, and Editor, MERIA Journal, in the Primer, 5 May 2009.

# 4

# TERRORIST ORGANISATIONS

## Old and New

It is fair to say that terrorism has been a part of human experience for centuries. It has been deemed a legitimate revolutionary weapon in some societies where men are prepared to make use of violence for achieving their social, economic, and political objectives. During the 1970s-1980s, terrorists assaults became fiercer, more ruthless, more sustained or carried more permanent, social, legal, and political changes because terrorism had become better organized. In subsequent years, it even became more lethal because of access to unlimited resources, advanced weaponry and improved means of its delivery and transportation, incremental availability of volunteers willing to join the violent stream, and lay down their lives if need be, and after the U.S. attacks on Afghanistan and Iraq, the theories of wars of civilization, as propounded by Huntington, gripping the imagination of the intelligentsia. Nine-Eleven shook the western world out of its indifference towards terrorism.

Here one briefly discussed various terrorist organizations existing world over. Two types of terrorist organizations existed in Western Europe prior to the dissolution of the Soviet Union. (1) Nationalist Separatist Groups (2) Marxist Revolutionary Groups, of pro-Moscow, Trotsky, or Maoist persuasion. Post Soviet collopase, Marxist groups may have been weakened in Western Europe, but left of the centre political parties all thriving. In East Europe, communism has lost out.

Under Part I are discussed terrorist organisation in the West and West Asia. Part II scans the terror outfits of Pakistan in somewhat greater detail.

## PART–I

## ITALY

Terrorism in Italy is certainly not the preserve of left-wing fanatics. In Rome and Northern Italy, Fascist groups like Ordine Nouvo are at work. The MSI, Movimento Sociale Italiano used to provide a cloak of political respectability for the extreme right. Italy had to confront terrorism on two fronts.

The first major terrorist attack in Italy was a bomb explosion in Pizza della fontana, Milan on 12 December 1969, killing fourteen and injuring 80. It was the work of the right-wing militants, but the police arrested a well-known anarchist, Pietro Valpreda, worst shock for the Italians was the trail revealing the ugly facts of involvement of Security Forces themselves in the manipulation of the right-wing terrorism. It was the time of indiscrimenate right-wint terrorism and serious rioting for the same cause in Reggio Cala bria. It came to be known as the "strategy of tension"-aimed at creating an atmosphere of panic and chaos that they hoped would enable the neo-fascists to seize power through a *coup d etat*.

The 30-year rule by one party, the Christian Democrats encouraged the security services (then known as the SID and SDS) to infiltrate both the left and the right-wing groups. It later turned out that this penetration only corrupted the security officers and also promoted inefficiency, for in neither case did the under-cover work prevent terrorism. Once the court evidence revealed the unholy links between the services and terrorists in 1974-75, there was public demand for reforms and reorganisation. The Intelligence services scandal generated popular demand for easier access for inspection of personal files maintained by the authorities a la the post-Watergate USA.

In the Mid-1970s when terrorism from both sides began to mount its most serious challenge, the Italian services were at their weakest, and most divided. "During the decade there were no less than 9361 terrorist attacks. 116 people were killed and 355 wounded."[1] But surprisingly the rate of arrest and imprisonment of those responsible was remarkably low.

Terrorism had become, in that period, a dreadful sub-culture of Italian life. What were the causative factors behind the phenomenon : the unemployment, educational crisis, or was it the result of frustration wrought in by an inefficient bureaucracy and rapid industrialisation of Italy? Scores of articles and books explored its causes, and in their enthusiasm for the new *deus ex machina* of sociology, they offered dozens of scholarly explanations, but ...ately, none of these fill the bill.

A new terrorist g... *Prima Lina*, started competing for pre-eminence with the well-estab... ...er in the field – the Red Brigades. What was even more alarming ... reports that University-oriented terrorists, the spoilt brats of the ... seemed as succeeding at last in drawing to their cause militan... from the young Italian factory workers. This, surprisingly, distressed the traditional Communists as greatly as it did the right wing.

## FRANCE

Two separatist outfits were then active in France :

(1) The Front de Liberation de la Bretagne (FLB), translating into Front for Liberation of Brittany. It announced on 8 January1974 that it was working internationally with Irish Republican Army (IRA) and the Basque Euzkadi ta Azkataswna (ETA) separatists. The FLB, composed of ethnic militants, had claimed responsibility for bombings of the Government and Police facilities in Brittany.

(2) In the South of France, the Embatta (= the wind which blows before a storm) founded in 1963, sought to unite the Spanish Basque provinces with those in France to create a separate Basque nation. The Embatta members had ties with the ETA exiles who had their headquarters in Southern France also.

France is a nation of a tradition of terrorism, part of its revolutionary inheritance, but it also has an equally strong tradition of centralised authority in government, and as is well known, a powerful police apparatus. When President Francois Mitterand took over from Giseard d' Estaing and secured a socialist majority in the National Assembly, it seemed the nation was once again turning towards the revolutionary and liberal tradition. Mitterand, as if to confirm the new stance, granted amnesty to 31 convicted terrorists of various hues with the intention of abolishing the State Security Court which, since it was established by Gen. De Gaulle in 1963, has had jurisdiction over such offences.

It were the growing activities of nationalist movements that impacted France more directly, in particular, the acts of terror organised by the Bretons and Corsicans. The two militant movements could be compared with the IRA in North Ireland and the ETA in the Basque areas of Spain. Indeed, in the South-West [illegible] campaign for France there was an overspill of the Basq[illegible] Government. To an extent, Independence from the Central Sp[illegible] helping their friends on the other side the French Basques and there were apprehensions that they might of the P[illegible] them by demanding regional independence from France. That was reason enough for Paris to monitor the situation carefully. The fears were possibly mitigated with the election of Mitterand, reputed by sympathetic to the idea of regional autonomy.

The Bretons seeking autonomy for the ancient province of Brettany made their presence felt through militant actions by the FLB, occasionally supplemented by the Breton Revolutionary Army (ARB). Unlike some other such movements, they had no friendly frontier across where some sympathy and refuge could be found. Consequently, the French police were able to prevent any but small and symbolic raids.

Corsican nationalist groups had been busy on the French mainland, as also on Corsica Island, especially the National Front in 1976. In 1980 they were reported to have been responsible for 463 explosions. When, as one of his last Presidential acts, Giscand d' Esating visited the Island before the elections, a bomb was exploded at Ajaccio airport shortly before his arrival.

## IRELAND

The Irish Republican Army (IRA), illegal till recent times, both in Ireland and North Ireland, could be traced back to the reorganisation of Irish Volunteers in 1913. Relatively inactive during the post-war years, the IRA started re-building itself in the 1960's. In 1969, it split into two factions : (1) The Officials or Regulars (2) the Provisionals or Provos.[2]

The official IRA is a Marxist Revolutionary organisation, with a legal political front, official Sinn Fein, headquartered in Dublin.[3] Under its Chief of Staff, Calhal Goulding, it had pursued a "war of national liberation," with the goal of creating a United Irish Socialist Republic. To achieve its aims, it had cooperated with the Communist Party of Ireland, and other Communist of pro-Soviet line. It observed a semi-ceasefire since 1972. Avoiding frequent clashes with the police and British troops, it continued to smuggle weapons into Ireland and wage a campaign of reactive assassination since 1972. "ceasefire".

The provisional IRA had less political cohesion compared to its rival. "Its roots are in an extremist Catholic Sectarianism and its tactics are those of undirected terror", it was said in 1973. Like the Official, the Provisional too had an overt, legal front in Eire (in the 1970), called Provisional Sinn Fein, which of course was banned in north Irland. It too aims at achieving united Irish Republic. Its chief leaders during the period included Sean Mac steobain, Chief of Staff, Joc Cahill, and Seamus Jwomey.

In addition to its transnational links with the PLA terrorists, the Provisional had alliances, during the 1970s, with several Trotskyist groups affiliated with the Fourth International.[4] These included the British, International Marxist Group (IMG); Irish Solidarity Campaign (ISC),[5] and Irish Saor Eire (Free Island) which was reputed to have provided the Provisionals with terror team which carried out numerous bombing in London in December 1972.[6]

## UNITED KINGDOM

London, given its image of being home to the Mother of Parliaments, and "the centre of the civilised world", aura, has not been able to escape the noise of terrorist bombs and assassins bullets. The anarchists of the 19th century and the recurring violence mounted by the Irish nationalists ensured that the capital had rarely been entirely free from so many incidents as in the decade of the 1980s. For not only did the Provisional IRA stepped up its violent attacks on London, the city also became a surrogate battle field where the Israelis and the Arabs engaged in fierce duels using bombs and bullets to settle their scores away from their own lands. Even more the hondoners became used to see the Arabs killing each other for the motives unknown to them.

In the following decade and half, the Muslims were to replace the erstwhile purveyors of gut and gore, by enacting their own version of "clash of civilisation", particularly so after the U.S. attacks on Afghanistan and Iraq. More on it would follow.

## WEST GERMANY

The primary urban terrorist outfit in West Germany, since 1970, was the Rote Armee Fraktion, more commonly known as the

Baader-Meinhof gang after the names of its two leading lights who had been trained in the art of sabotage and subversion in the Palestinian gurrilla camps in 1970.

The Baader-Meinhof was believed to have been responsible for a series of bomb attacks in May 1972 which killed three U.S. servicemen in Heidelberg, an Army Colonel in Frankfurt, and partially destroyed several police stations in Munich and some other cities. The three top leaders of this leftist-nihilist groups - attorney Horst Mahler, 35; Andreas Baader, 29; and Ulrike Meinhof, 38—were arrested during 1972.[7]

## UNITED STATES OF AMERICA

Among the better known terrorist organisations of revolutionary left has been the weatherman faction of Students for Democratic Society (SDS), which grew out of the reorganisation of the Students League for Industrial Democracy (SLID) in 1959 impelled by the student interest in the civil rights movement.

SDS's long association with the National Lawyers Guild (NLG), "legal bulwork of the U.S. Communist Party, began in 1964. As its legal actions increased, the SDS came to depend heavi on the NLG. This link ended its involvement with liberalism and reform and it began to more openly into a Marxist-Leninist analysis of the Class war as imperialism. The SDS then moved into the anti-war and anti-imperialist agitation on the Campuses. The obvious next step was cooperation with such revolutionary Communist organisation as CPUSA's, W.E.B., Du Bois Clubs, the then Maoist Progressive Labour Party (PLP), and its youth wings like the Young Socialist Party (YSA) and Youth Against War and Fascism (AWF). Expectedly, in June 1965 the SDS dropped its constitutional provision barring the Communists from its membership.

In Campus action, SDS members and supporters seized build, engaged in confrontation with police, disrupted Government activities, blocked in cars of Government and business recruiters, and demonstrated against government policies in South East Asia. To further its role in anti-imperial activities Third World, SDS's Radical Evacuation Programme (REP) sought help from the North American Congress on Latin America (NACLA), an organisation seeking "revolutionary change in Latin America" and which also takes a "revolutionary position" towards the U.S. society.

The Weatherman groups believed that on the subject of revolution and black self-determination, the "correct path" was to "build a white movement which will support the blacks in moving as fast as they have to and are able to but still keep itself up with the black movement enough so that white revolutionaries share the costs and the blacks do not have to do the whole thing alone."

They seemed hopelessly out of touch with the realities of the situation if we read today (2006) what A Liberation News Service report, as published in the Guardian on 10 January 1970, said : "Weatherman sees revolutionary change in America as happening almost solely, if at all, as a belated reaction to a successful world revolution including a successful revolt by the black colony inside the U.S." The Weatherman gloried in the thought of "barbarism" and praised the murder of actress Sharon Tate, eight months pregnant, by the Manson Gang others associated with the Weatherman had voiced continuing approval of the use of terror tactics to force radical social change. Bernavdine Bohrn had expressed her support to the kidnapping of Patricia Hearst by the Symbeonise Liberation Army (SLA).

## BLACK EXTREMISTS IN USA

Two organisations are discussed here :

### Black Panther Party

It was founded in 1966 by a small groups of black militants that included Huey P. Newton and Bobby Seale. Eldridge Cleaver joined a year later. It was the subject of extensive investigations by the Committee on Internal Security in 1970. The committee's report concluded that "the Black Panther Party through its delebrate rhetoric and through the actual arming and military training of its members, has contributed and increase in acts of violences and constitutes a threat to the internal security of the United States."[8]

Don Cox, a BPP Field Marshal, presenting the Panther Statement to the Second World Conference on Palestine, in session in Kuwait, 13-17 February 1971, declared in part :

> Long years of treachery, torture, bloodshed and exploitation at the hand of imperialist link the struggle of the Palestinian people and the Afro-American people for their first liberation... we both have discovered that it is only when we throw off

dependency and patience and pick up weapon ourselves to fight for our freedom that we begin taste success.

Within the United States the revolutionary movement against fascism and racism and capitalism is daily growing in momentum. Attacks on police, military and the government installations, banks and big business increase daily...Rebellions occurs even within the prisons. The U.S. Army is in a state of disarray. Bombings and sniping are regular occurrence. The progressive student movement is turning more and more to revolutionary violence...The time to attack U.S. Imperialism is ripe, while attacks are coming from each and every side, for the monster is on its death-bed and the people shall be victarious.

If the vituperative, elusive and vicious rhetoric could win the wars, the USA should have been obliterative from the surface of the earth! But where is the High Priest of the vituperatively colourful prose today?

During 1970 and 1971, the Cleaver faction tried to establish relationship with African guerrilla groups such as Zimbabwe African Peoples Union (ZAPU),[9] and the Palestinian Al Fatah guerrillas. The 15 December 1971 issue of Babylon (an RCPN newspaper) stated that the Algerian Government gave the cleaver group the same facilities it provided for those other "liberation" organisations which operate offices in Algiers - RAIGC, MPLA, FRELIMO, ZAPU, ANC, ELFATAH, NLF of South Vietnam, etc". Babylon further averred that Cleaver had established "a positive working basis with the liberation movements in Africa, Asia and Latin America, and with the progressive Governments of Asia",[10] and then it was further stated that "in September 1970, International sections of the BPP was officially recognised by Algerian Government as the representative of Afro-Asian struggle outside the United States...

## The Symbionese Liberation Army (SLA)

The term "symbionese" derives from symbiosis (= the living together of dissimilar organism) and it is hard to imagine a less lively gang of revolutionaries. A dozen or so militants reputedly constituting the SLA's main force ranged from well-to-do, educated whites to black escaped convicts. Their credo was loose blend of verbal gun smoke and pseudo - Marxian argot; their emblem a seven headed Cobra, a 170,000-year old symbol of God and life.

The SLA, "most recently identified urban terrorist organisation of the left in the USA", first achieved notority by claiming responsibility for the murder of Oakland's Superintendent of Schools Marcus Foster in an ambush, night 6 November 1973. The SLA, employing standard Marxian Jargon, complained of the school identity card system, "patterned after the system of apartheid"; of cooperation among police, probation officers and school officials; and of the projected creation of a school system security force "patterned after fascist American tactics of genocide, murder, and imprisonment practiced by American financed puppet government in Vietnam, the Philippines, Chile and South Africa."

The SLA grabbed the national headlines once again when in a fast-moving operation, informed by guerrilla tactics a la the Uruguayan Tupamaras and the Argentinean Peoples Revolutionary Army (ENP), three SLA terrorists on 4 February 1974 forced their way into the apartment of Patricia Hearst, 19, daughter of President of San Fransisco Examiner and Chairman of the Board of Hearst Corporation. They forced Patricia into the trunk of the car and drove away while a back-up squad fired M-1 carlines at the apartment building to discourage witnesses.[11]

To broadcast their proper concerns and following the precedents set by the Argentinean and Uruguayan terrorists so much in the news the past year (1973), Hearst's kidnappers demanded "charitable" donations of "quality food" to the disadvantaged before her release could be negotiated. Although the Hearst family responded immediately to meet the SLA demands, the latter expressed dissatisfaction with the massive giveaway. It demanded that $70 worth of "high quality food" be given to each poor person in California. The Hearsts created a People in Need Programme to go beyond the SLA quick giveaway demands and create a supplemental food programme that would demonstrate that the "so-called power elite could respond with a programme that could make the SLA's limited demand seem puny and self-sowing by comparison and by doing so, bring the weight of public opinion to bear against SLA and perhaps even influence the release of Patricia.[12]

A statement issued by the SLA identified its components, as also its 'concerns' and 'aims':

> We are a United Front and Federated Coalition of members from the Asian, Black, Brown, Indian, White, Women, Grey and Gay Liberation Movement.

The Symbionese Federation and the Symbionese Liberation Army is made up of the aged, youth and women and men of all races and people living in deep a loving harmony and partnership in the best interest of all within the body.

The object of this United Front is alleged struggle "for the independence and self-determination of each of their races and people and Liquidation of the Common Enemy."

## CHILE

The election of a Marxist President, Salvador Allende Gossons (1908-73) marked the beginning of the troubled times for Chile in its recent history. He was overthrown in a military coup led by Gen. Augusto Pinochet Vgarte (b 1915).

The Marxist and Communist Parties have organised underground sabotage activities to perform "acts of resistance." Most militant of these is the Movimients de Izquicerda Revolucionaria (MIR) - Movement of the Revolutionary Left. It i an extreme Castroite group which has been in alliance with th popular Unity Coalation that formed Allende's "Shock Troops"[13] when in power.

The Communist Parties the world over accused the U.S of complicity in the overthrow of Allende, whose Government in ny case had been boycotted by it. In the U.S., both the U.S. committee for justice to Latin American Political Prisoners (USLA) an the Chile Solidarity American (CSA) called for a campaign on behalf of the arrested Chilean Marxists and communists. In February 1974, the MIR announced a new transnational alliance with the Bolivian ELN, the Uruguayan Tuparmaros and Argentinean ERP. Many MIR terrorists fled to Argentina. Carlos Altaminaro, the lead of the out lawed Chilean Socialist Party, fled to refuge in Havana. He called for bloody attacks on the new Chilean Governme and the U.S., because the latter wants "to consolidate its pow through dictatorial regimes - the extreme form of which is the fascist regime in Chile." Continuing with the Marxist rhetoric, he said, "By drowning Bourgeois democracy in blood, the Bourgeois and imperialism have set the rules for the People's revolutionary struggle."[14]

The Sparatist League, calling for MIR support criticised the Communist Party of the USA, the Socialist Worker's Party, and the U.S. Committee for Justice to Latin American Political Prisoners for their "opportunist struggle" of refusal to "defend far-left militants", in favour of "those prisoners who are popular or likely to awaken the sympathies of the bourgeois liberals", such as Luis Corvalan, head of the Communist Party of Chile (Partids Communist de Chile - PCCR), and Luis Vitale, a member of the United secretarial with which the SWP has fraternal relations.

The Workers World Party (WWP) also called for support for the MIR commenting that "to this day, the MIR after the greatest resistance to the fascist terror in Chile."[15]

## West Asia : Arab Terrorist Outfits

West Asia has seen large scale exchange of terror between the Arab Palestinians and Jewish Isralies. Here is a look at the Arab terrorist organizations existing from the early times.

## Palestinian Liberation Organization (PLO)

An umbrella political structure of the Palestinian Arabs, it also controls all the main Arab terrorist groups. The PLO in turn was controlled by an Executive Committee chaired by Yasser Arafat till his death. Palestinian National Council acted as an informal Parliament for the guerrilla groups and their supporters. As of May 1974, the PLO executive committee included representatives of the following Arab terrorist groups :

| | |
|---|---|
| 1. Al Fathah | The combat arm of the PLO, it has the largest representation in the PLO executive Committee. It is the largest terrorist outfit, directly under Arafat, and consequently controls the PLO. |
| 2. Al Saiqa | Controlled by the Syrian Government, it represents its view on the PLO executive committee. |
| 3. Arab Liberation Front | Sponsored by the Iraqi Government, it represents it in the PLO. |
| 4. Popular Front for the Liberation of Palestine (PFLP) | An independent Marxist-Leninist organisation, strongly opposed to the policies of the Al Fathah and the Soviet Union. |

| | |
|---|---|
| 5. Popular Democratic Front for Liberation of Palestine (PDFLP) | Split from PFLP, it is an independent Marxist-Leninist organization but is known to have supported Al Fathah at times. |
| 6. Popular Front for Liberation of Palestine General Command (PFLP-GC) | A small independent ultra-militant organization.[16] |

The PLO was created by a decision of the first Summit at Cairo in January 1964. Till then, Arab terrorists had worked in direct association with the military forces of various Arab Governments. At the second Arab summit in September 1964, the Arab Government allocated a large sum of money for the creation of Palestinian Liberation Army (PLA). Concerned over the influence of Egypt over PLO, Syria nurtured and strengthened Al Fathah, small terrorist organisation, which had been raised earlier in 1956. However under Arafats' leadership, Al Fathah moved steadily away from the Syrian shadow towards Egypt. The offices of PLO Executive Committee were initially located in Beirut. "Liaison offices of the PLO are maintained in the capitals of various Arab countries, as also in Karachi and New Delhi."[17] In May 1974, an Executive committee Meeting of the PLO expressed strong support for the idea of a PLO - controlled Palestine state on the west Bank of Jordan and in Gaza Strip.

The World Marxist review of April 1974 explained the significance for the world communist movements of the PLO and the establishment of an independent Palestinian state under its control. The author, a senior communist leader of Jordan, noted that the PLO State would be a key step in overthrowing the Government of Jordan's King Hussain. Arafat developed a coalition within the PLO during the spring of 1974 which supported the Soviet Union's goal of setting up a PLO-controlled state in territory which Israel took from Jordan during the 1974 War.

On 10 April 1974—the anniversary of the Israeli raids on guerrilla headquarters in Lebanon where three top terrorist leaders were killed – the terrorists from PELP-GC attacked the Israeli town of Qryat Shemono, killing 18 civilians in a building. Later when the terrorists were surrounded by the Israeli soldiers, the former blow themselves up.[18]

On 15 May 1974 (the anniversary of the founding of Modern Israel), a terrorist commando squad from the PDFLP entered an

Israeli school in the town of Maalot, seizing more than 80 children. They demanded that 25 Arab terrorists be released from Israeli jails and flown to Damascus, along with the group holding the Maalot school and half of the hostage children. As the deadline for negotiations approached, Israeli military raided the school. The terrorists turned their machine guns on the innocent school children and then blew up the school and themselves. 20 children were killed immediately, and some others succumbed to their injuries later.

## Al-Fatah

It is a nationalist, pan-Arab movement which developed from the ultra-conservative, extremist Muslim Brotherhood in the post-war years. In Arabic, the initials of the movement for liberation of Palestine are HTF, which are also the root consonants for the Arabic word for death. Reversed FTH becomes the root letters for the Arabic word for 'conquest'; thus FTH becomes the acronym *Fatah* or Al Fatah, the conquest.[19]

Formed in 1956, it did not become an effective terrorist force till the late 1960s. Fatah's headquarters were in Beirut, which became almost a "free zone" for the Palestinian terrorist organisation since the November 1969 Agreement between the Lebanese Government and Arafat, as the head of the PLO. The Agreement permitted the guerilla outfits to maintain camps and bases on Lebanese soil. Gozier (1972-73) placed the number of Arab fighters in Southern Lebanon at 2000 by the end of 1972. "However, the main terrorist activities of Al Fatah have since 1971 been carried out through the Black September Organisation."

The Al Fatah received financial backing from Saudi Arabia, Kuwait and Algeria in addition to Egypt, while Iraq provided some military training. Fatah made use of the Voice of Palestine radio in Cairo during this period. It also published a newspaper, *Hissad El-Asifer.*

## Black September Organization (BSO)

The Black September Organisation was developed by the Jihad-al-Rasol Intelligence Organization of Al Fatah sometime in 1971. The BSO is believed to have recruited among the most extreme members of both the PFLP and PDFLP. Black September is thought to have taken its name from the successful campaign by

King Hussain's Jordan Government against Palestinian guerrillas operating an Jordanian soil, beginning September 1970. Understandably, the majority of its initial operations were against the Jordanian Government officials and the members of the Jordanian royal family.

At the time of the massacre of the Israeli athletes at Munich's Olympic village on 5th September 1972, the BSO was estimated to have about 60 active members and approximately 100 recruits under training in Algeria.[20]

In June 1973, a Sudanese court, trying eight captured BSO terrorists, sentenced them to life-imprisonment after they admitted to murdering the diplomats. In June 1974, however, Sudanese President Nimeiry, under domestic political compulsions, commuted the life sentence to 7 years and had the eight men flown to Cairo to be handed over to the PLO.

Earlier in 1974, Kuwait handed over to the PLO, four Palestinian gunmen who had slaughtered 30 passengers in Rome and had hijacked a Pan-Am jet in December 1973. The four were never tried by the PLO, and were allowed to line in Cairo.

## Popular Front for Liberation of Palestine (PFLP)

It emerged as guerrilla outfit in 1968. George Habash, who headed its 5-man politburo, insisted that his group was fighting a "class war" of liberation from imperialists and reactionaries. The declared aim of the PLFP "is a creation of the socialist State of Palestine along the Marxist-Leninist lines."[21]

It has been described as eclectically communist and "Solidly Marxist-Leninist". It received support from both Moscow and Beijing, but material support came (weapons and training) came primarily from Syria, Iraq, Algeria, and Peoples Republic of Yemen.

On 6 March 1972, a Maoist "Left" faction broke away to form the Popular Democratic Front for Liberation of Palestine (PDFLP), led by Naif Hawatmen.[22]

PFLP has been called a "truly transnational" terrorist organisation as it has mounted attacks on Israeli offices in many countries and has relations with the Tupamaro Urban guerrillas of Uruguay, the IRA, West Germany's Baader-Meinhofgng, the Turkish Peoples Liberation Front, and the Japanese United Red Army.

In 1969, PFLP became the first Arab terrorist group to hijack an airliner.[23] It also claimed to have trained members of the U.S. Black Panther Party but this lacks confirmation.[24]

A PFLP squad calling itself the organisation of sons of Occupied Territory, in cooperation with members of the Japanese United Red Army, hijacked a Japanese Jumbojet over the Netherlands on 20 July 1973. The five-member terrorist squad was led by a woman who was accidentally killed with an explosive device. During the 3½day incident the hijackers flew first to Dubai on the Persian (Arab?) Gulf and finally landed at Bengazi in Libya.

## ISRAEL

Israel is one nation that has faced the threat of terrorism since its very birth. Is it any surprise that the Jalmud, holy text of Jewish law, prophetically lays down : "if someone comes to kill you, rise and kill him first." And this commandment under the impact of centuries on oppression and the attempt to wipe off the Jewish race, including the most vicious one during the Holocaust, has become the watchword of Sayaret Matkal, the razor-sharp cutting-edge of Israels' counter-terrorist forces. So secretive are Israelis about the that they never mention it by name. In the manner of Yahwen, the ineffable name for God in the Old Testament, it (Sayaret Matkal) it is known to all but uttered by none. To everyone, it is Ha Yehida (The Unit), and its men, Ha Havren (the Guys). But ironically it seems so much unnecessary because everybody, especially its targets, mostly Arabs, know it is the Sayaret Matkal, the General Staff Reconnaissance Unit. Undoubtedly, it is Sayaret Matkal that raids Beirut to kill Palestinian terrorist leaders, and flies to Entebbe to rescue hijacked hostages besieged by Palestinian and German terrorists and Idi Amin's officials.

The Israeli anti-terrorist units trace their lineage to the formation of the joint British-Jewish Special Night Squad in the 1930s by Orde Wingate, that brilliant if eccentric guerrilla leader who later became famous as the commander of the Chindits Brigade operating behind the Japanese lines in Burma during World War II, only to die in an air crash in 1944, preparing for a new campaign. He obtained permission from his British Superiors to train the Jews "to protect themselves against the marauding Arabs."

Wingate, a Jalmudic scholar and imbued with its philosophy of killing rather than be killed, turned his squads into efficient guerrillas who behaved in striking at the Arabs, in their own villages rather than waiting to be attacked.

Moshe Dayan, later to become famous as the dare-devil Israeli General who twice led his nation in two wars with the Arabs, was one of the young guerrillas he led in the early operations. Dayan was to recall later : "when they returned at dawn after a nights fighting and prepared breakfast, Wingate would sit in a corner, stark naked, reading the Bible and munching raw onions as though they were the most delicious pears." However, the Jews inspired by Wingates doctrines and tactics, successfully faced the British first and then trounced the Arabs to create their homeland. The new State was subjected to guerrilla attacks from across the borders of Lebanon and Jordan, as also Gaza Strip - killing, blowing up water pumps, and setting fire to crops. Expected Israeli Army faced those terrorists. In 1951, such attacks caused 137 casualties, the figure rising to 147 in 1952, and to 180 in 1953. The Israeli Army, confronted these intruders. In 1953, "Unit 101" was raised to engage in guerrilla warfare. When the terrorists killed one Israeli woman and her two children, Unit 101 mounted a retaliatory attack on the Jordanian village of Khibye, blowing up 45 houses and leaving 66 villagers dead. This led to the condemnation of Israel by the U.N. Security Council. Israelis felt the policy of retaliation was becoming counter-productive. The Unit 101 was merged with the Paratroopers Battalion which fought most of the anti-terrorist and reprisal battles, that subsequently was to lead to the outbreak of the six day war in 1967.

A. Sharon will be remembered with awe for his anti-terrorist success in the Gaza Strip during this period. Killing the terrorists and breaking their cells, he had Gaza under the Israeli control by 1973.

The operations in the West Bank were more difficult as the terrorist could return to the safety of their shelters in Jordan and South Lebanon. Here, the Sayaret Matkal was engaged in counter-terrorist operations. It was a part of the ordinary Army and reported only to the chief of Intelligence, although unlike Unit 101, its members normally operate in uniform. Based on an airfield in the centre of Israel, its normal strength was around 200. Sayaret Matkal does not rely on the trained volunteers, but draws raw recruits from the extraordinary establishment called the Kelet, located just outside Iel Aviv, to which all young men report when called up for military service.

The Sayaret Matkal does much of its training in enemy territory-on the job training so to say. They use the Uzzi, the Israeli—invented machine-pistol, which had been adopted by most of the world's security forces, and also the Russian assault rifles, Kalashnikov, captured from the Arabs in great numbers. They also trained on the Galil, another Israeli-made automatic weapon, capable of doing anything from launching grenade to opening a battle of orange juice, but tends to be cumbersome for special operations. Pistol shooting ranks high in their curriculum, and Israelis use an unusual weapon the .22 Baretta Pistol. It is used by "007 Squad" who fly with El Al.

The recruits are trained in close combat fighting with particular emphasis on knife and all other skills necessary for the anti-terrorist operation. Special attention is paid to helicoptor-borne missions with the use of abseil ropes and joint operations with the Naval commandos who probe the Lebanese cost virtually every Night.

The Sayaret Matkal does not believe in negotiations and will not use the extended "talk-out" techniques favoured by most countries. They will attack as soon as they are ready, and will use negotiations only as a 'blind' under which to prepare an assault. They would rather attack with speed and precision and overwhelm the enemy. No siege in Israel has lasted beyond 24 hours.

They espouse the case for pre-emptive strike; it is better to kill their enemies, in their own bases and so to prevent them from mounting their operations, rather than conduct elegant sieges inside Israel. Gen. Shalome Gazit, former Director General Military Intelligence, insists on the correction of the principle of pre-emption : "whosoever adopts a defensive, passive strategy against insurgency is almost doomed to failure. You cannot fight and win any war by defensive means only." His doctrine is one of permanent counter-offensive, attacking the leaders, bases and support systems of terrorist groups.

Now there is a troubling question : when does counter-terrorism itself cross the border into terrorism? When the Mossad sent the Hit Team "Little Hammer" into Norway in 1973 to kill

Ali Hassan Salamen, the organiser of the Munich Massacre, they got the wrong man and shot down an innocent Moroccan waiter in front of his pregnant Norwegian wife. However, the Israelis blew him-up with a radio-controlled car bomb in Beirut in January 1979, turning his car into a "pile of matting metal." With him died his four body guards and four innocent people. Was Salamen's crime any greater than that of the men who set off the bomb? The two can simply not be compared, and the matter must be allowed to rest without any further discussion. The men indulging in killing the innocent wantonly should be given no quarters, and certain collateral damage has to be accepted. Anyone finding a justification for the actions of terrorists is guilty of encouraging them in their crime.

The Sayaret Matkal mounted one of their first major operations in October 1968 to convince the Egyptians to stop shelling of the Israeli positions on the Suez by proving to them that Egypt was wide open to attacks. The Unit flew into Egypt in helicopter, blew up two important bridges across the Nile, and destroyed the new power station at Naj Hammadi deep inside Egypt and hundreds of miles behind the artillery batteries on the Suez.

Such retaliatory operations successfully curbed terrorism inside Israel, foreign Palestinians into international terrorism, not only targeting Israelis abroad but also involving the rest of the world in their struggle.

The Palestinians carried the out first of their hijacks on 22 July 1968, taking over an El Al airliner flying from Rome to Tel Aviv. On 26 December 1968, two men attacked another El Al plane at Athens airport with automatic fire and grenades. It was proved that both acts of terrorism originated in Beirut. Two days after the Athens attack, the Israelis retaliated to force the Lebanese to proceed against the terrorists and prevent their using the Lebanese soil for terrorist activities. A 40-strong force of "The Guys" landed on the runway at Beirut International Airport at 9:30 PM. Arabic-speaking Israeli soldiers controlled the panic-stricken crowds, issuing instructions on the hand-held loud speakers. Another group of commandoes got all the Arab-owned planes emptied and led the passengers to safety. 13 Arab aircrafts, including a jet liner were blown up. When some Lebanese policemen opened fire, the Israelis managed to intimidate them by firing in the air and refrained from shooting back. "The air-port is only 2.5 miles from Beirut and motorised units of the Lebanese Army were sent to the scene of the raid almost at once. This column was intercepted by another squad of commandos which had set up road block on the way to the airport. Again there was no shooting and no casualties. The Israelis released some smoke canisters and this was enough to stop the Lebanese from advancing any further. At 10.30 pm, one hour after they had landed, the commandos returned to Israel.[25]

Then came the incident when the Black September terrorists, two men and two women, seized a Boeing 707 flight 517 from Brussels to Tel Aviv and boldly ordered the pilot to fly on to Lod where they threatened to blow to smithereens the plane, its 90 passengers, ten crew and themselves, unless the Israeli Government released 317 Arab prisoners. The Israelis played along with the hijackers and even with the Red Cross officials negotiating between the two sides. But throughout the negotiations a team of Sayaret Matkal men was practicing on a 707 in a nearby hanger. Once the assault techniques were perfected, they told the hijackers that they would accede to their demands. Then men in white overalls who were seen approaching the aircraft, said they were mechanics wanting to inflate in tyres let down when the aircraft first landed. Bursting in through the doors, they took over the aircraft.

This was the first time that a hijacked plane had been successfully stormed and its lessons were replicated five years later when GSG 9 performed a similar feat at Mogadishu.

The Palestinians too would not give up-looking for fresh avenues of "adventure". After Lod, came the massacre at Munich in 1972. Palestinians displayed their capability of carrying out a well-planned international operations, and their willingness to die for their cause. The Germans had shown their vulnerability to terrorism "as they lacked specially trained men needed to fight this esoteric form of warfare." The Israelis were bitter, and deeply frustrated. Moshe Dayan wanted to fly a Sayaret Matkal team to Munich but he was refused. The story of Israel subsequently liquidating each one of the eleven terrorists involved in the murders has already been told. But the war of kill and counter-kill erupted consequently, with the Israeli and Arab agents murdering each other in the streets of European cities.

## PART-II

## Pakistan Terrorist Groups and Terrorist Outfits: An Overview (List of Terrorist Groups)

Unlike other countries of the region where groups that can be defined as purely terrorist outfits exist, the dividing line between socio-politico-religious groups and terrorist outfits is very hazy. Most groups that have actively participated in street violence and acts of terrorism are also active in the political landscape of Pakistan.

These political cum terrorist outfits can broadly be classified into two groups ethnic and sectarian. The **Muttahida Quomi Movement** (MQM-A, the suffix denoting the leadership of Altaf Hussain) which evolved from the Mohajir Quomi Movement, is the foremost among the ethnic based politico-terrorist formations in Pakistan. A break-away faction termed Haquiqi Mohajir Quomi Movement (literally meaning original MQM, and termed as MQM-H) was formed by two break-away leaders of the MQM, Afaq Ahmed and Aamir Khan in June 1992. The MQM-A and the MQM-H were locked in a violent war for domination of urban territory in the Sindh province. Following strong action taken by the Pakistani state in 1997-98, the MQM-A was seriously affected in terms of loss of cadre and equipment and has, since then, largely adopted peaceful means of protest.

Sectarian violence originated in a Shia-Sunni struggle for political space within a Pakistani State that was increasingly resorting to Islam as a tool of legitimacy since 1974. In that year, sectarian elements within the Shia and Sunni sects put up a united front and agitated for official action to declare the members of the Ahmediayya sect as non-Muslims, a demand that was accepted through the adoption of a Constitutional Amendment. Having tasted this victory over the State, these Shia and Sunni elements then turned against each other in an attempt to foist their respective religious interpretations as State doctrine.

The race for setting up rival sectarian outfits started with some Shia elements formed the Tehrik Nifaz-i-Fiqah-i-Jafria (TNFJ which means Movement for the Implementation of Fiqah-i-Jafria, a school of Islamic jurisprudence professed by the Shias, later the nomenclature was modified to **Tehrik-e-Jafria Pakistan).** In response to this attempt by a minority to impose its views over a majority, a Deobandi (a sub-sect within the Sunni sect) cleric, Maulana Haq Nawaz Jhangvi founded the Anjuman Sipah-i-Sahaba Pakistan (ASSP), later renamed as **Sipah-e-Sahaba Pakistan (SSP)** in Jhang, a district of Pakistani Punjab. This outfit evolved into a dubious political organisation which reportedly has a terrorist arm too while its offshoot, the **Lashkar-e-Jhangvi** (LeJ) is a dedicated terrorist outfit. Besides these two outfits, there are several socio-religious 'Sunni organisations' which are reportedly involved in sectarian violence but cannot be strictly defined as terrorist outfits. These include the various factions of the Able-Hadith and the Mailis-e-Dawah-wal-Irshad. Among the Shia outfits the is the Muhammad Pakistan (SMP), a splinter body of the TJP, which was formed by extremists of the latter to counter what was perceived as increasing terrorism indulged in by the SSP and the LeJ.

The targets of violence indulged in by these socio-religious outfits has included opposing sectarian leaders and workers, worshippers of the 'other' sects and Iranian diplomats in Pakistan. The latter are perceived by Sunni extremists as being actively involved in aiding Shia extremism. Given the overwhelming numerical domination of the Sunni sect in Pakistan, Sunni outfits attempting to force their individual version of Sunni Islam on the State have been more active as compared to their Shia rivals.

The rise and ebb of sectarian violence also points to the political ambitions of its perpetrators. A study of Jhang, the birthplace of the SSP and all subsequent Sunni violent movements, shows that while violence was rampant in the district until 1993, it tended to move away from the district to other parts of the province after the successful election of an SSP leader Maulana Azam Tariq to the National Assembly and two others to the provincial assembly.

In the first half of its history Pakistan had experienced a violent ethnic movement for an **Independent Baluchistan.** Following strong repressive measures taken by the State in 1973, this movement has ceased to exist.

**Source** : South Asia Terrorism Portal (SATP), Institute for Conflict Management.

## Terrorist and Extremist Groups of Pakistan

### Terrorist Groups

| *Domestic Organisations* | *Trans-national Organisations* |
|---|---|
| 1. Lashkar-e-Omar (LeO) | 1. Hizb-ul-Mujahideen (HM) |
| 2. Sipah-e-Sahaba Pakistan (SSP) | 2. Harkat-ul-Ansar (HuA, presently known as Harkat-ul Mujahideen) |
| 3. Tehreek-e-Jaferia Pakistan (TJP) | 3. Lashkar-e-Toiba (LeT) |
| 4. Tehreek-e-Nafaz e-Shariat-e-Mohammadi | 4. Jaish-e-Mohammad Mujahideen E-Tanzeem (JeM) |
| 5. Lashkar-eJhangvi (LeJ) | 5. Harkat-ul Mujahideen (HuM, previously known as Harkat-ul-Ansar) |
| 6. Sipah-e-Muhammad Pakistan (SMP) | 6. Al Badr |
| 7. Muttahidda Quami Movement-Altaf Hussain (MQM) | 7. Jamait-ul-Mujahideen (JuM) |
| 8. Haqiqi Muhajir Quami Movement (MOM-H) | 8. Lashkar-e-Jabbar (LeJ) |
| 9. Baluch People's Liberation Front (BPLF) | 9. Harkat-ul-Jehad-i-Islami |
| 10. Baluch Students' Organisation (BSO) | 10. Muttahida Jehad Council (MJC) |
| 11. Jamaat-ul-Fuqra | 11. Al Barq |
| 12. Nadeem Commando | 12. Tehrik-ul-Mujhahideen |
| 13. Popular Front for Armed Resistance | 13. Al Jehad |
| 14. Muslim United Army | 14. Jammu and Kashmir National Liberation Army |

| *Domestic Organisations* | *Trans-national Organisaitons* |
|---|---|
| 15. Harkat-ul-Mujhaideen Al-alami | 15. People's League |
| 16. Baluch Students' Organisation - Awami (BSO-A) | 16. Muslim Janbaz Force |
| | 17. Kashmir Jehad Force |
| | 18. Al Jehad Force (combines Muslim Janbaz Force and Kashmir Jehad Force) |
| | 19. Al Umar Mujahideen |
| | 20. Mahaz-e-Azadi |
| | 21. Islami Jamaat-e-Tulba |
| | 22. Jammu and Kashmir Students Liberation Front |
| | 23. Ikhwan-ul-Mujahideen |
| | 24. Islamic Students League |
| | 25. Tehrik-e-Hurriat-e-Kashmir |
| | 26. Tehri-e-Nifaz-e-Fiqar Jafaria |
| | 27. Al Mustafa Liberation Fighters |
| | 28. Tehrik-e-Jehad-e-Islami |
| | 29. Muslim Mujahideen |
| | 30. Al Mujahid Force |
| | 31. Tehrik-e-Jehad |
| | 32. Islami Inquilabi Mahaz |

Only some select outfits are discussed hereafter.

## Extremist Groups

1. al-Rashid Trust
2. Al-Akhtar Truust
3. Rabita Trust
4. Ummah Tamir-e-Nau

# TERRORIST GROUP OF PAKISTAN LASHKAR OMAR

## Lashkar-e-Omar
## (The Army of Omar)

### Formation

Lashkar-e-Omar (LeO) is a new terrorist group reportedly founded in January 2002 and is a conglomerate of Harkat-ul-Jihad-i-lslami (HuJI), Lashkar-e-Jhangvi (LeJ) and Jaish-e-Mohammed (JeM) cadres. It was formed after the arrests of several front-ranking Islamist leaders in Pakistan following President Pervez Musharraf's address to the nation on January 12, 2002, in which he committed himself to dismantling the structures and networks of terrorism based in his country. The etymology of Lashkar-e-Omar is yet not clear. According to some reports, it is named after Mullah **Mohammed Omar** chief of the Taliban militia. Other reports have indicated that the name is allegedly a direct homage to Syed Ahmed Omar Sheikh, a front-ranking JeM terrorist who was, on July 15, 2002, sentenced to life by an Anti-Terrorism Court in Hyderabad, Sindh, for his role in the abduction-cum-murder of US journalist Daniel Pearl.

The LeO first came into prominence in November 2001 when it reportedly claimed responsibility for an attack on a church in Bahawalpur in Punjab. A police personnel and 17 Christians, including five children, were killed and nine others injured when six unidentified gunmen opened indiscriminate fire at a church in Model Town, Bahawalpur, on October 28, 2001.

### Ideology

Their version of Islam is akin to that of the Taliban militia of Afghanistan. The LeO's ideological underpinning is a mixture of Islamist fundamentalism and totalitarian thinking.

### Leadership and Structure

The LeO, according to media reports, was formed as a loose coalition of terrorists. While the group provides new cover for terrorist actions of LeJ, JeM and HuJI, it also includes several like-minded 'freelancers'. Omar Sheikh, currently in prison, and Amjad Hussain Faruqui of the HuJI, a fugitive accused in the Daniel Pearl case, are both closely linked to the LeO. They and their terrorist colleagues were associated with the various training camps in Afghanistan when the Taliban was in power there. Omar Sheikh was reportedly one of the instructors at one such camp. LeO cadres comprise of various Taliban members, certain **Al Qaeda** terrorists and terrorists from the HuJI, LeJ and JeM. Reports have indicated that Pakistani cadres of terrorist groups and Islamist parties allied with Osama bin Laden's International Islamic Front (IIF), who managed to survive the US air strikes in Afghanistan and crossed over into Pakistan, are also part of the LeO. According to a May 2002-report, the LeO consists of handpicked cadres of the HuJI, JeM and LeJ and was formed primarily to carry out 'punishment acts' of terrorism against Americans on Pakistani soil.

The Lashkar-e-Omar is reportedly headed by Qari Abdul Hai alias Qari Asadullah alias Talha, chief of the LeJ's Majlis-i-Shoora (Supreme Council). Qari Asadullah reportedly formed his faction of the LeJ after parting ways with LeJ founder Riaz Basra in October 2000. Basra and three of his associates were killed in an encounter in Mailsi, Multan on May 14, 2002. According to a June-2002 media report, since the LeJ was proscribed, Qari Asadullah decided on the name Lashkar-e-Omar and also succeeded in incorporating terrorist cadres from other proscribed groups like the JeM and LeT into the new group.

The LeO is stated to be patterned after bin Laden's IIF. Besides, cells of the group comprising 5-15 cadres also exist. Therefore, according to official sources, it has become difficult to infiltrate such a homogenous group of motivated cadres.

Most of the key members of the conglomerate are veterans of the 1980s jihad in Afghanistan against the erstwhile Soviet Union.

## Operational Strategies and Linkages

Official sources have indicated that what makes Lashkar-e-Omar a serious threat is the fact that most of its cadres are members of the same class and camp trained by Amjad Faruqui. Faruqui, a HuJI terrorist, is wanted for his involvement in the murder of Pearl. LeO also has suicide cadres in its ranks. The LeO is allegedly involved in the suicide bombing outside the Sheraton Hotel in Karachi on May 8. In that incident, 14 persons, including 12 French nationals, were killed. Security agencies suspect that there exist more LeO *fidayeen* (suicide) squads and that these would target foreign nationals, particularly Americans and Britons residing in Pakistan.

The LeO has close linkages with the Al Qaeda and several terrorist groups active in the Indian State of Jammu and Kashmir. Karachi based Al-Rashid Trust (ART) is reportedly funding the Lashkar-e-Omar. The ART is one of the 27 groups and organisations listed by US State Department on September 22, 2001 for involvement in financing and supporting a network of international Islamist terrorist groups.

## Activities and Incidents

- The Lashkar-e-Omar is suspected to be involved in the terrorist attack on a church in Model Town, Bahawalpur in Punjab on October 28, 2002, in which a police personnel and 17 Christians, including five children, were killed and nine others injured.
- It is reportedly closely linked to the abduction-cum-murder case of US journalist Daniel Pearl and JeM terrorist Omar Sheikh has been sentenced to life for involvement in this case.
- The group, according to official sources, is allegedly involved in the March 17, 2002 grenade attack on a church in the heavily guarded diplomatic enclave in Islamabad in which five persons, including a US diplomat's wife and daughter, were killed and 41 others injured.
- Besides, the LeO was reportedly involved in the suicide bombing outside the Sheraton Hotel in Karachi on May 8, 2002 and the June 14-attack on the US consulate in Karachi, in which 10 persons, including five women, were killed and 51 others injured.

## SIPAH-E-SAHABA PAKISTAN

Earlier termed Anjuman Sipah-e-Sahaba, the Sipah-e-Sahaba Pakistan (SSP) is a Sunni sectarian outfit that has been alleged to be involved in terrorist violence, primarily targeted against the minority Shia community in Pakistan. The outfit has also operated as a political party having contested elections and an SSP leader was a minister in the Coalition Government in Punjab in 1993. The SSP is one of the five outfits that have been proscribed by President Pervez Musharraf on January 12, 2002. The outfit is reported to have been renamed as Millat-e-lslamia Pakistan after the proscription.

## Formation

Maulana Haq Nawaz Jhangvi, Maulana Zia-ur-Rehman Farooqi, Maulana Eesar-ul-Haq Qasmi and Maulana Azam Tariq established the SSP, initially known as the Anjuman Sipah-e-Sahaba in September 1985 in an environment of increasing sectarian hostility in Pakistani Punjab. The origin of this outfit lie in the feudal set-up of Pakistani Punjab and politico-religious developments in the Nineteen Seventies and Eighties. Political and economic power in Pakistani Punjab was a privilege of large landowners, mostly Shias, a minority as compared to the Sunni sect. Urban Punjab in contrast, was a non-feudalised middle-class society and largely from the Sunni sect. The SSP is also alleged to have been set up at the behest of the then Zia-ul-Haq regime as part of the efforts to build an Islamist counter to pro-democracy forces ranged against the military regime of the Eighties.

The socio-economic rationale for SSP's origin is explained largely from the economic profile of Jhang, the home base of SSP. Located in a region that divides Central from Southern Pakistani Punjab, Jhang still has a significantly high proportion of large land holdings, leaving feudalism relatively undisturbed. Most large landlords, who are Shias, dominate both society and politics in the region. But, over the years, the area has developed as an important *mandi* (market town) gradually increasing the power of traders, shopkeepers and transport operators in the region. Seeking a political voice and role, this class, largely from the Sunni community, has been challenging the traditional feudal hold. The most serious political challenge to the control of feudal interests has been articulated in the form of violent sectarianism, with the formation of the SSP. This has meant, however, that the contest for access to resources and status and the competition for domination over the state apparatus are not framed in terms of class divisions, or modernisation imperatives, but confrontationist sectarian identities.

As in most areas affected by violence, a major contradiction has risen. While a sizeable proportion of traders and shopkeepers continue to fund the SSP in Jhang, most do not believe in the violence associated with the party, rather it is now a matter of buying security. Nevertheless, there is a decline in their support for the SSP over recent years as a result of the economic consequences of sectarian strife.

## Ideology and Objectives

The SSP wants Pakistan to be declared a Sunni state. Maulana Zia-ul-Qasmi, a leading SSP leader said in an interview in January 1998, "the government gives too much importance to the Shias. They are everywhere, on television, radio, in newspapers and in senior positions. This causes heartburn." While fervently believing in hostility towards the Shias, the SSP also aims at restoring the Khilafat system. It also aims to protect the Sunnis and their Shariat (law). The SSP has declared that Shiites are non-Muslims. The SSP came into existence as a reaction to the Iranian Revolution and increasing Shia militancy in Pakistan. There is another school of thought which says that the SSP phenomenon began from Jhang as a reaction to the socio-economic repression of the masses by Shia feudal structure in the area.

Giving his reaction to the warning given to the party by President Pervez Musharraf on August 14, 2001, SSP leader Maulana Mujibur Rehman Inqilabi said that it had nothing to do with terrorism and considered it a danger to the security of the country and people, believing in the negotiated resolution of all issues. He also said that the resolution of the Shia-Sunni issue did not lie in bans, bloodshed, hanging or cruel punishments but in negotiations. Maulana Inqilabi also pointed out that Pervez Musharraf must constitute a tribunal under his supervision comprising the Interior Minister, all provincial Home Secretaries, Chief Justices of the Supreme and High Courts, leading Ulema (religious scholars) and journalists to hear proposals from the Tehreek-e-Jaferia-Pakistan (TJP) and the SSP for the resolution of their differences. He said the tribunal should formulate a code of ethics in the light of the proposals by both the parties, give it a legal cover and then get it followed by all the concerned.

Earlier, on January 16, 2001, the SSP and its Shia rival organisation, the Tehreek-e-Jaferia Pakistan (TJP) reportedly assured the Punjab provincial Government of co-operation in the elimination of terrorism from the country. Similarly, on February 3, 2001, the Punjab leadership of the SSP and another Shia outfit, Sipah-e-Muhammad Pakistan (SMP) announced its willingness to overcome differences and to withdraw cases filed against each other.

The SSP also actively opposes the US-Pakistan alliance formed in the aftermath of the September 11 terrorist attacks on US targets. The alliance was targeted against the erstwhile Taliban regime in Afghanistan, a major supporter of Sunni extremists and terrorist outfits in Pakistan. The outfit joined the Jamaat-e-lslami (JeI), Jamaat-e-Ulema-e Pakistan (JUP), Jamaat-e-Ulema-e-lslam, and Fazlur Rahman faction of JuI and Jamaat-e-Ahle Hadith in forming the Afghan Jehad Council and claiming the U.S. action was not a war against Taliban but against Islam and therefore it was essential for the Muslims to declare Jehad against the U.S. its allies.

## Leadership and Structure

Maulana Azam Tariq, SSP chief and a Member of the National Assembly, was assassinated along with four other persons by three unidentified gunmen in Islamabad on October 6, 2003. He had won the October 2002 National Assembly elections from Jhang as an independent candidate. Azam Tariq, educated in the *Madrassas* (seminaries) in Faisalabad and Karachi, was a frequent visitor to Afghanistan during the Taliban militia's rule. Although the Maulana had claimed that the SSP had no links with any terrorist groups, security agencies believe that the SSP and LeJ are closely linked. In October 2000, the Maulana while speaking at an international Difah-e-Sahaba conference in Karachi said that the SSP aims to transform 28 large Pakistani cities into 'model Islamic cities' where television, cinema and music would be banned. Azam Tariq was also a supporter the terrorist violence in the Indian State of Jammu and Kashmir (J&K). When Maulana Masood Azhar formed the Jaish-e-Mohammed (JeM) in the aftermath of his release in Kandahar, Afghanistan, following the hijacking of an Indian aircraft in December 1999, Azam Tariq reportedly 'pledged' to send 500,000 Jehadis to J&K to fight Indian security forces. According to an October 2003 report in the *Daily Times,* 65 cases were registered against him, including 28 cases relating to terrorist acts.

Allama Ali Sher Ghazni is the Patron-in-Chief of the outfit. Maulana Zia-ul-Qasmi serves as the Chairman, Supreme Council. Other important SSP leaders are Qazi Mohammed Ahmed Rashidi, Mohammed Yousuf Mujahid, Tariq Madni, Muhammad Tayyab Qasim and Maulana Muhammad Ahmad Ludhianvi.

Maulana Haq Nawaz Jhangvi, one of the founder members of SSP was assassinated on February 23, 1990, reportedly by Shia terrorists. He was considered to have been the most prominent

SSP leader, belonged to the Deobandi sect and was very popular in Jhang for his speeches. Maulana Jhangvi aimed to make Pakistan a Sunni state. He contested and lost the election for a National Assembly seat in 1990. Haq Nawaz's avowed mission was to declare Shias as Kafir (infidel) and in this pursuit, he publicly instructed his followers to destroy peace in Pakistan, if it became necessary to get Shias declared as Kafir.

Kaka Balli, kin of a former member of the National Assembly from Jhang, Amanullah Khan Sial, was convicted to lifetime imprisonment for the assassination of Maulana Jhangvi. After the assassination, Maulana Zia-ur Rehman Farooqi took over the leadership of the outfit. He was later killed in a bomb explosion in the Lahore Sessions Court on January 19, 1997. Maulana Azam Tariq succeeded Maulana Zia-ur Rehman Farooqi.

The SSP is reported to have approximately 3,000 - 6,000 trained activists who indulge in various kinds of violent sectarian activities, which are primarily directed against the Shias. Most SSP cadres hail from Punjab.

## Operational Strategies

SSP extremists have primarily operated in two ways: The first involves targeted killings of prominent opponent organisation activists. In the second, terrorists fire on worshippers in mosques operated by opposing sects.

By 1992, the SSP was reported to have gained access to sophisticated arms as also the ability to use these weapons even against law enforcement agencies. In June 1992, its activists used a rocket launcher in an attack which killed five police personnel. In Punjab, 1994 was one of the worst years in terms of sectarian violence when such incidents claimed 73 lives and more than 300 people were injured. Many of these killings were the result of indiscriminate firing on people saying their prayers. The SSP along with several other Sunni and Shia organisations were suspected to have participated in this violence.

In 1996, the outfit joined peace efforts initiated by the Milli Yakjeheti Council though violence continued unabated. The second half of the year was notable for the fact that while the number of incidents decreased, average casualties in these incidents increased. In one such instance where SSP was suspected as the perpetrator, ten persons were killed in indiscriminate firing at a mourning procession in Mailsi in Vehari district in July 1996.

News reports have indicated that the SSP and other Sunni outfits hold Iran as the sponsor of Shia extremist outfits in Pakistan. Hence when any major Sunni leader is assassinated, Iranians in Pakistan are targeted for retribution. For instance, the Iranian Counsel General in Lahore, Sadeq Ganji, was killed in December 1990 in what was reported to be a retribution for the February 1990 killing of the SSP co-founder Maulana Haq Nawaz Jhangvi. Similarly, in January 1997, the Iranian Cultural Centre in Lahore was attacked and set on fire, while in Multan seven persons were killed including the Iranian diplomat Muhammad Ali Rahimi. Earlier, in the month, a bomb blast at the Sessions Court in Lahore left 30 persons dead, including the then SSP chief Zia-ur-Rehman Farooqi along with 22 policemen and a journalist. News reports said that the retribution continued in September 1997 when five personnel of the Iranian armed forces who were in Pakistan for training were killed by suspected Sunni terrorists.

As with other sectarian outfits in Pakistan, the SSP has chosen to lie low after the military coup of November 1999. This lends credence to the hypothesis that SSP like other sectarian and ethnic groups, indulge in violence only when a passive state guarantees an environment of neutrality and even tacit support to this violence. With a hard-line stance being taken by the military regime against internal violence within Pakistan, these organisations have chosen to keep a low profile.

As part of its opposition to the US-Pakistan alliance against the erstwhile Taliban regime, the SSP joined other members of the Afghan Jehad Council on September 20, 2001 in announcing a Jehad against the US forces if they used Pakistani soil to carry out military attacks on the Taliban regime. The SSP leadership while criticising the Pakistan Government's decision of extending support to the US-led air attacks on the terrorist training camps in Afghanistan also indicated that they would fight alongside the Taliban militia.

## Links

In 1996, protesting against what they termed as the moderating nature of the organisations, the more radical and extremist elements of the SSP walked out of the outfit to form the Lashkar-e-Jhangvi (LeJ), a sectarian terrorist outfit that was proscribed by President Pervez Musharraf on August 14, 2001. In contrast, the SSP has always retained an explicit political profile, contesting elections and having been a constituent of a Punjab coalition government. Despite SSP denials, the LeJ is widely considered to be the armed wing of the Sipah-e-Sahaba.

Many SSP cadres have received arms training from the Harkat-ul-Mujahideen (HuM) and the erstwhile Taliban regime in Afghanistan.

The SSP is also reported to be closely linked to the Jaish-e-Mohammed (JeM), a Pakistan-based terrorist outfit active in Jammu and Kashmir. Maulana Masood Azhar, JeM chief, speaking at a Jehad conference in October 2000 said, "now we go hand-in-hand, and Sipah-e-Sahaba stands shoulder to shoulder with Jaish-e-Muhammad in Jehad."

The SSP draws support, inspiration and assistance from various political parties in Pakistan, primarily the Jamaat-e-Islam (JeI) and the Jamaat-Ulema-e-Islam (JuI). The JuI is associated with running a large number of *Madrassas* all over Pakistan from where recruits for the HuM, SSP and Taliban are provided.

The SSP reportedly receives significant funding from Saudi Arabia through wealthy private sources in Pakistan. Funds are also acquired from various sources, including Zakat and donations from various Sunni extremist groups. Other sources include donations through local Sunni organisations and trusts, *Madrassas* and study circles, and contributions by political groups. Most of the foreign funded Sunni *Madrassas* in Pakistan are reportedly controlled by the SSP.

The SSP has also been linked to Ramzi Ahmed Yousuf, an accused in the New York World Trade Centre bombing of February 1993, who was later captured by the US authorities in February 1995.

## Areas of Operation

Towns like Sargodha, Bahawalpur, Jhang, Multan and Muzaffargarh are the SSP strongholds. The dynamic leadership of Haq Nawaz Jhangvi is reported to have popularised an anti-Shia campaign in their backyard, southern and western areas of Punjab.

The SSP has influence in all the four provinces of Pakistan

and is considered to be the most powerful extremist group in the country. It has also succeeded in creating a political vote bank in the Punjab and North West Frontier Province (NWFP). The SSP has reportedly 500 offices and branches in all 34 districts of Punjab. It is also reported to have approximately 1,00,000 registered workers in Pakistan and 17 branches in foreign countries including the UAE, Saudi Arabia, Bangladesh, Canada and England.

## Tehreek-e-Jaferia Pakistan

Tehreek-e-Jaferia Pakistan (TJP) meaning 'movement of the followers of Fiqah-e-Jaferia', the dominant Shia outfit in Pakistan was formed in 1992. The origin of TJP can be traced to the Tehreek Nifaz Fiqah-e-Jafria (TNFJ) meaning 'movement for the implementation of Fiqah-e-Jafreia' (a school of Islamic jurisprudence which is traced back to its founder Imam Jafar Sadiq) which was formed in 1979 to protect the interests of the Shiite minority and to spread the ideas of Ayatollah Khomeini, the Iranian leader who led the successful Islamic Revolution that overthrew the Shah of Iran in 1979. It is widely believed that the Sunni clergy considered the name of Tehreek Nifaz-e-Fiqah-e-Jaferia as being offensive and opposed the Shias, a minority sect demanding the imposition of their *fiqah* (a school of Islamic jurisprudence) in a Sunni majority Pakistan. Following this backlash, the Shia leadership is reported to have changed the name from TNFJ to Tehreek-e-Jaferia Pakistan (TJP) in 1994. It is also believed that the outfit changed its nomenclature because the party, under Allama Arif Husseini, wanted to extend its membership to the non-Shias also.

An ideological split divided the movement into two groups: one headed by Hamid Musawi, the follower of Ayatollah Sheriate-Madari; the other headed by Arif Husseini, the follower of Khomeini's teachings. Allama Hamid Ali Musawi's group continues to function under the old nomenclature of TNFJ. The TJP had, during the period of Allama Arif Husseini, undertaken upon itself to change the party's complexion from a religious organisation to a progressive political party acceptable to non-Shias as well. Towards this goal, a political committee was constituted to work out the future strategy in a given situation and negotiate with political leaders of standing to join hands to achieve the objective. But the leadership, predominantly religious scholars, dispensed with the committee to signal that the TJP was and will remain a religious organisation.

Allama Husseini was killed on August 6, 1988 in Peshawar. Amongst others, Captain Majid Raza Gilani, who belonged to Jhang, was accused of the incident. As he was one of the former staff members of President Zia, the TNFJ blamed Zia-ul-Haq for his murder and launched vigorous protests.

The objectives projected by the TJP are : the creation of a society based on 'pure Islam', the protection of social, political and religious rights of Shiites, the propaganda of Shiite ideas, coordination of all Pakistani Shiite organisations and the fight against imperialism. It also believes in Islamic egalitarianism and social justice. Two TJP members are also members of the Pakistani Parliament. The TJP is reported to have links with the Iranian clergy. The outfit source its finances from the Shiite community in Pakistan, Iran as well as certain commercial groups.

The Tehreek-e-Jaferia Pakistan, led by Allama Syed Sajid Ali Naqvi, is a well-organised outfit, which effectively represents the interests of the Shia community in Pakistan with a significant following in Jhang. In recent years, as a result of increased pressure from the Sunnis, the TJP has preferred to adopt a more reconciliatory and accommodating posture than in the past when it appeared more assertive and threatening vis-a-vis the government and Sunnis. The TJP has several affiliated organisations, including Sipah-e-Abbas, Sipah-e-Ahl-Bait and youth bodies like the Imamia Students Organisation and the Imamia Organisation, which are reported to play an active role. Since 1994, the Sipah-e-Muhammad Pakistan (SMP), a splinter group of the TJP with a significant following in Jhang has emerged as a prominent Shia terrorist outfit involved in anti-SSP campaigns, violence and target killings. The TJP is one of the five outfits that have been proscribed by President Pervez Musharraf on January 12, 2002.

The current violent phase between the two communities, who had lived in relative harmony for many centuries, is traced to the 1980s when a group of Deobandi militants formed the Anjuman Sipah-e-Sahaba (ASS), to wage 'war' against the Shia landholders in Jhang. The ASS, later re-named as the Sipah-e-Sahaba Pakistan (SSP), was established during the Islamisation campaign of the then

President Gen. Zia-ul-Haq, and coincided with the Iranian revolution led by Ayatollah Khomeini. The Shiite Ulemas (religious scholars) perceived his measures as an attempt to spread Sunnite norms of Hanifite type in the Shiite community. According to analysts, sectarian violence among the rival outfits intensified in the wake of the *'jihad'* in Afghanistan as Pakistan, particularly the central and southern Punjab, served as a base for 'mujahideen' recruits. Most of these 'mujahideen' returned to Pakistan after the Russian forces pulled out in the late 1980s, and brought with them a sizeable supply of arms, ammunition and a proclivity for violence. They joined the extremist sectarian outfits and since then, sectarian rivalry was largely expressed through extreme violence. Rivalry between the two outfits intensified when the SSP founder Haq Nawaz Jhangvi was killed in March 1990. The same year also witnessed the killing of an Iranian diplomat, Sadiq Ganji in Lahore. In 1997, Jhangvi's successor Zia-ur-Rehman Farooqi and 26 others were killed in a bomb blast at the Lahore Sessions Court. In the aftermath, Iranian diplomat Muhammad Ali Rahimi and six locals were killed in an attack on the Iranian Cultural Centre in Multan. On April 12, 2000 three hand grenades were lobbed at a gathering in a Shia mosque in Mulawali, the hometown of Syed Sajid Naqvi, killing 13 persons, including five members of the family of Syed Sajid Naqvi. The grenade was reportedly hurled from an adjacent Sunni mosque. Shortly thereafter, a TJP leader, Syed Farrukh Barjees was killed at Khanewal near Multan on April 26. On November 23,2000, Anwar Ali Akhunzada, the central general secretary of TJP in Peshawar was assassinated by the Lashkar-e-Jhangvi (TeJ).

To counter the Sunni militancy, the Shias formed Sipah-e-Muhammad Pakistan (SMP) in 1993. It is aenerallv believed that Maulana Mureed Abbas Yazdani created it in 1993 after he was convinced that the TJP would not allow its young cadres to physically counter the SSP. The Shia youth had been asking the TJP to take notice of what they called excesses of the SSP whose members were alleged to be targeting some of the Shia's beliefs. Allama Hamid Ali Musawi did not endorse the move. Subsequently, the Sipah-e-Muhammad Pakistan (SMP), headquartered at Thokar Niaz Beg, was created out of the TJP reportedly by Maulana Mureed Abbas Yazdani in 1993 and it adopted a more militant stance against the SSP than the TJP would allow.

## Tehreek-e-Nafaz-e-Shariat-e-Mohammadi (Movement for the Enforcement of Islamic Laws)

The Tehreek-e-Nafaz-e-Shariat-e-Mohammadi (TNSM) is one of the five outfits that have been proscribed by President Pervez Musharraf on January 12,2002.

### Formation

The Tehreek-e-Nafaz-e-Shariat-e-Mohammadi (TNSM) was founded in 1992 with the objective of a militant enforcement of Islamic law. It came into prominence in November 1994 when it laid siege to the Saidu Sharif city Airport demanding imposition of the *shariat.*

### Ideology and Objectives

It is a militant, Wahabi tribal outfit. The primary objective of the TNSM is the imposition of *shariat* in Pakistan. Ideologically, it is dedicated to transform Pakistan into a Taliban style state. In an August 1998-speech in Peshawar, Maulana Sufi Mohammed, its leader, reportedly declared that those opposing the imposition of *shari'a* in Pakistan were *wajib-ul-qatl* (worthy of death). The outfit while outrightly rejecting democracy has termed it as 'un-lslamic'. In an interview Sufi Mohammed said, "We want enforcement of the Islamic judicial system in totality: judicial, political, economic, jihad, fi sabilillah, education and health. In my opinion the life of the faithful will automatically be moulded according to the Islamic system when the judicial system is enforced." TNSM rcjccts all political and religio-political parties as, according to it, they follow the western style of democracy. Its Chief frequently uses the term *talaq* (divorce) for his opponents when he criticizes any of their acts of infidelity, such as voting in the election. TNSM openly condones the use of foree in what they see as a *Jehad.*

### Leadership, Structure and Headquarters

Maulana Sufi Mohammed is the leader of the Tehreek-e-Nafaz-e-Shariat-e-Mohammadi (TNSM). Maulana Abdul Ghafoor is the Deputy Chief of the outfit while Muhammad Abdullah is its spokesman. The executive body is the highest policy making organ of the TNSM. The outfit has a large number of ex-servicemen, including many retired Commissioned Officers, in its ranks and, thus, poses the greatest concern to the military regime in Pakistan.

Many serviing senior officers of the Pakistani Army are also related to these ex-servicemen. According to a media report, many TNSM cadres are alleged to be persons with criminal background. Dissension within the TNSM ranks has led to the expulsion of many senior leaders. Maulana Fazal Dian, a central leader was expelled by Sufi Mohammed for violeating TNSM rules. Maulana Israil, the then spokesperson of the TNSM, said, on September 5, 2000, Maulana Fazal Dian had attended the meeting of Jamaat-e-Islam (JeI) held in Timergara Dir, which was a violation of the TNSM's rules and regulations. Fazal Dian later formally joined the JeI. Rham Wajid, who was the TNSM General Secretary during the May 1994-demonstrations against the provincial administration, later applied for refugee status in Canada. The TNSM headquarters is located in Maidan, lower Dir district. Media reports have indicate that the TNSM has now attained the status of a well-trained and well-equipped militant organization by getting hundreds of its youths trained in Afghanistan.

## Area of Operation

The TNSM operates primarily in the tribal belt, such as in Swat and the adjoining districts of the North West Frontier Province (NWFP). Although well established in the NWFP, the TNSM has had only limited success in expanding its activities beyond the tribal areas of the province. The strategy of the then NWFP government of Mehtab Abbasi, in 1999, to reportedly work with the TNSM rather than confront it assisted the outfit in expanding its activities in the region. News sources indicate that the government reportedly announced concessions with regard to implementation of *shari's* in the area.

The TNSM and the JeIare locked in a turf war in the Malakand division and the Jamaat-Ulema-e-Islam, JeL and TNSM are in conflict with each other in the tribal areas.

Media reports of April 2001 indicated that the TNSM's operations shifted from its earlier strongholds in Mingora in Swat and Dir to the tourist resorts of Madyan, Bahrain and Kalam where hundreds of armed youths with black turbans were reportedly seen roaming around. Turism operators, especially hoteliers, who have invested large amounts of mone in constructing some three dozen standard hotels and other tourist attractions are facing threats of attacks on tourists. Reports were circulating in the area that no unveiled woman would be allowed to enter or move about in the summer resorts, giving credence to the fears that all government efforts to promote tourism in the area would suffer a setback.

## Activities and Incidents

It first came into prominence in November 1994 when it led an armed uprising in support of *shariat* in the Malakand division, North West Frontier Province (NWFP) The TNSM's call to arms reportedly drew large numbers of experienced Afghan Mujahideen from nearby Peshawar and Bajaur areas. Approximately 40 persons, including 12 security force personnel, were killed in a week of fighting before the government was able to re-establish law and order. The Frontier Corps. was employed to regain control of the Saidu Sharif airport, roads, police stations and judicial courts in the area.

The TNSM's siege against the provincial administration is withnessed mostly during the summer, every year, and there has been no change in this routine since 1994 when violent clashes took place between its cadres and the law enforcement authorities.

The TNSM, Malakand division, organized a protest procession in Mingora on September 20, 2001 where the speakers called for raising a 'voluntary army' in order to extend support to the Taliban militia against the then impending US strikes.

The outfit has also established parallel 'courts' in the Malakand division to protest against what it perceives is the non-cooperation of the government. A media report of December 2000 indicated that these courts had so far decided approximately one hundred cases in all the districts of the division. According to the TNSM leadership, the legal system in Pakistan was based on English laws and hence was not acceptable to the outfit. Further, these 'courts' are reportedly pronouncing 'decisions' on many cases free of charge. The TNSM has also demanded the use of Pashtu language for court proceedings instead of the national language, Urdu.

In the US military campaign in Afghanistan, the TNSM is reported to have sent thousands of armed cadres to Afghanistan to fight alongside the Taliban militia. News reports of October 27 from Bajaur, NWFP, indicated that approximately 10,000 TNSM cadres led by their Chief, Maulana Sufi Mohammed, crossed the Pakistan-Afghan border. They were armed with Klashnikovs, rocket launchers, missiles, anti-aircraft guns, hand grenades and swords.

Their convoy comprising 300 vehicles had left the TNSM headquarters in Maidan, lower Dir district, and reached Bajaur Agency. 4,000-armed tribesmen are also reported to have joined the TNSM cadres and they have reached the Ghaani Pass on the Pakistan-Afghan border. News reports added that the political administration of Bajaur Agency allowed the TNSM cadres to pass through the agency jurisdiction on their way to Afghanistan. According to the TNSM Chief, the cadres were proceeding to Kandahar, headquarters of the erstwhile Taliban regime. Qazi Ihsanullah, a TNSM spokesperson said in Bajaur, on October 27, "We will resist if the authorities try to stop us. The jihad (holy war) will start here... Initially Mullah Omar advised us to wait and come to Afghanistan only when necessary but we have told them that we will stay in Afghanistan as a reserve force." TNSM sources indicated that scrutiny of cadres was carried out to send only the able-bodied and young people to fight along side the Taliban. TNSM said in Maidan Dir (Lower) on October 24 that he had "urged all of his followers to prepare themselves for the jihad that was binding on them." He opined, "It was compulsory for the faithful to participate in the jihad against the aggressors", and added, "non-Muslims should be taught an exemplary lesson." He said it was *Jehad* in the way of Allah and not for the Taliban. He claimed that the TNSM cadres were in possession of all kinds of heavy weapons like anti-aircraft guns, mortars, missiles, and klashnikovs. He added that the TNSM was in contact with the then Jalalabad Governor, Abdul Kabir and Taliban supreme Mulla Mohammed Omar.

The TNSM while condemning the Afghan policy of the Musharraf regime termed it as a total failure.

Media reports have indicated that a sizeable number of TNSM activists have joined the Taliban ranks since 1994.

In April 2001, the TNSM demanded that the provincial administration of Malakand put in place a 'true Islamic judicial system' by dismantling the present set-up. It rejected the government's judicial system which, in its perception, lacks in authority and finality under Islamic injunctions. It also opposed the military regime's plan to hold local council elections. In his speeches at Ushu, Kalam and other places, in April 2001, the TNSM Chief said, "There.is no room for vote in Islam and the concept of democracy which some religio-political parties are demanding is wrong."

The TNSM is also reported to have set up approximately three FM radio stations in the Bajaur area of North West Frontier Province of Pakistan, bordering Afghanistan, to campaign for funds and volunteers to fight alongside the Taliban militia. These radio stations were also used to air TNSM leaders' address to pro-Taliban rallies.

On November 5, 1994, 15 persons were killed and 17 others injured TNSM cadres clashed with security forces in the NWFP region. The TNSM was demanding the enforcement of *Sharia* in the tribal Malakand region, which borders Afghanistan. The TNSM movement to introduce *Sharia* in the region was strengthened following a Supreme Court decision in February 1993 that removed British colonial laws in tribal areas.

On November 8, 1994, TNSM released 50 government officials in the town of Matta, NWFP, following a cease-fire between the outfit and the provincial government. NWFP Chief Minister Sherpao consequently agreed to enforce *Sharia* in Malakand.

On December 4, 1994, police fired tear gas to halt a march by 5-10,000 members of the TNSM who were seeking the release of 85 colleagues who had been arrested during the past month's protests.

On June 19, 1995, the TNSM Chief and twenty of his senior followers were arrested following a clash with the security forces. At least 26 persons were injured when hundreds of TNSM cadres occupied government offices in the Swat district. They were demanding the implementation of an agreement reached with the government in 1994 to enforce *Sharia* in Malakand.

On September 6, 1998, the TNSM threatened to attack American property and also abduct American citizens in Pakistan unless the USA apologised to the Muslim world for the August 1998 missile strikes in Afghanistan.

## Lashkar-e-Jhangvi

### Formation

Lashkar-e-Jhangvi (LeJ), a Sunni-Deobandi terrorist outfit was formed in 1996 by a break away group of radical sectarian extremists of the Sipah-e-Sahaba Pakistan (SSP), a Sunni extremist outfit, which accused the parent organisation of deviating from the ideals of its slain co-founder, Maulana Haq Nawaz Jhangvi. It is from Maulana Jhangvi that the LeJ derives its name. It was formed under the leadership of Akram Lahori and Riaz Basra. The LeJ is one of the two sectarian terrorist outfits proscribed on August 14, 2001, by President Pervez Musharraf.

## Ideology and Objectives

The LeJ aims to transform Pakistan into a Sunni state, primarily through violent means. The Lashkar-e-Jhangvi is part of the broader Deoband movement.

## Leadership and Command Structure

Muhammad Ajmal alias Akram Lahori is reportedly the present Saalar-i-Aala ('Commander-in-Chief') of the LeJ. Lahori was originally with the Sipah-e-Sahaba Pakistan (SSP), which he had joined in 1990. Subsequently, in 1996, he along with Malik Ishaque and Riaz Basra founded the LeJ and launched terrorist activities in Punjab. He has also reportedly established a training camp in Sarobi, Afghanistan after securing support from the erstwhile Taliban regime there.

Lahori succeeded Riaz Basra, who was killed in Mailsi, Multan on May 14, 2002. Lahori is himself in police custody following his arrest in Orangi Town, Karachi, on June 17, 2002 based on information provided by Shabbir Ahmed—an LeJ cadre who arrested by Karachi police in Gulzar-i-Hijri on the same day. Police also recovered two Kalashnikovs and two TT pistols from the possession of Lahori, who was carrying head money of Rs. five million announced by the Sindh government and another Rs. five million announced by the Punjab government. Five accomplices of Lahori were also arrested on the same day. At his arrest, a senior member of the LeJ, Qari Ataur Rahman alias Naeem Bukhari, issued a press statement expressing the apprehension that Lahori might the killed in a fake encounter. Rahman was himself later arrested from his hideout in Gulistan-i-Jauhar, Karachi. Rahman is allegedly involved in the abduction-cum-murder of US journalist Daniel Pearl. It is, however, not clear if Lahori has passed on the mantle to any one else, or continues to head the outfit while being in detention.

Lahori, according to reports of July 2, 2002 quoting senior police officials, was involved in 38 cases of sectarian killings in

Sindh. These included the killing of Ehtishamuddin Haider, brother of Federal Interior Minister Moinuddin Haider, Pakistan State Oil Managing Director Shoukat Raza Mirza. Besides, he was also involved in the massacre at Imambargah Mehmoodabad and in the murder of Iranian cadets in Rawalpindi. Lahori reportedly confessed during interrogation that he was involved in 30 cases of sectarian killings in Punjab, including those of 24 persons who were attending a Majlis in Mominpura. Also he revealed that his group had planned to kill Interior Minister Moinuddin Hiader, but due to tight security measures, murdered his brother instead. Consequent to the death of Riaz Basra, Lahori was acting as LeJ chief and he himself reportedly monitored and perpetrated sectarian killings in Karachi where he was residing for the last one and a half years.

Lahori's predecessor was Basra. He was involved in more than 300 terrorist incidents, including attacking Iranian missions, killing an Iranian diplomat Sadiq Ganji in December 1990 and targeting government officials. He was arrested and tried by a special court for Ganji's killing, but escaped during trial in 1994 from police custody while being produced in court. He was Chief of the Khalid bin Walid unit of the Afghan Mujahideen in Afghanistan.

Media reports said Riaz Basra, along with three of his accomplices, was killed in an encounter on May 14, 2002. The encounter occurred at Dakota, which had been targeted twice in the past by the proscribed LeJ. Basra was allegedly in police custody in Faisalabad since January 2002 and was being interrogated for the activities of his group. According to reports quoting police sources, four armed terrorists came to Chak Kot Chaudhry Sher Mohammad Ghalvi on May 14 and stopped near the house of Chaudhry Fida Hussain Ghalvi, district chief of the banned Shia group Tehreek-e-Jaferia Pakistan (TJP). Consequent to a shoot-out between the two groups the police intervened and in the ensuing encounter Basra and his associates were killed. Ghalvi asserted that the LeJ cadres had come to kill him and to emphasise his belief also pointed out that the Lashkar-e-Jhangvi had killed his brother, Mukhtar, in year 1997. Police sources said that Basra's identity was established by one of his accomplices, Kashif, who is under detention for alleged involvement in another sectarian killing.

Consequent to Basra's killing, reports on his arrest in January 2002 have indicated that he was arrested after the Faisalabad police captured Ajmal alias Sheikh Jamshaid, an associate of Basra. Ajmal assisted the police in arresting Liaquat Ali of Kehror Pucca, who was wanted for his alleged involvement in a triple murder case. After interrogating Liaquat, the police raided a number of locations in Faisalabad, Lahore, Jhang, Sargodha and certain other parts of Pakistan. Based on information received from Ajmal and Liaquat, Riaz Basra was arrested.

Basra is described as a religious fanatic with extraordinary religious enthusiasm. Motivated by the Sipah-e-Sahaba Pakistan and politically active since 1988, he contested elections to the provincial assembly from Lahore as an SSP nominee. It is under Basra's leadership that the LeJ rose to become the most dreaded sectarian terrorist outfit in Pakistan. The intensity of its threat was such that Nawaz Sharief, the former Prime Minister of Pakistan, who was served a threatening letter by Basra, stopped attending open courts.

The entire leadership of the Lashkar-e-Jhangvi consists of Jehadis who fought against Soviet forces in Afghanistan. A majority of its cadres are drawn from the numerous Sunni madrassas (seminaries) in Pakistan.

Media reports indicate that the LeJ is an amalgam of loosely co-ordinated sub-units in various parts of Pakistan, particularly in the districts of Punjab with autonomous chiefs for each sub-unit. Riaz Basra reportedly controls the LeJ's units in Lahore, Gujranwala, Rawalpindi and Sargodha. Another top LeJ terrorist, Malik Ishaque, currently under detention, was the chief of the units in Faisalabad, Multan and Bahawalpur divisions and in Bhakkar district. The success of most of its terrorist operations is attributed to its multi-cellular structure, whereby the outfit is divided into small groups that are not in constant contact with each other.

The LeJ is organised into small cells of approximately five to eight cadres each, who operate independently of the others. Individual LeJ cadres are reportedly unaware of the number of cells in existence similar to their own or the structure of operations. After carrying out an attack LeJ cadres often disperse and then reassemble at the various training camps to plan future operations.

A news report of October 2000 claimed that the LeJ had split into two factions—one headed by Riaz Basra (since deceased) and the other by the chief of the outfit's Majlis-i-Shoora (Supreme Council), Qari Abdul Hai alias Qari Asadullah alias Talha. The split reportedly occurred due to differences between the two over resumption of ethnic strife, which had receded after the military coup in Pakistan in October 1999. While Basra favoured resumption of terrorist attacks against Shia targets in order to force the government to comply with the demands of the outfit, Talha opposed the plan as he reportedly felt it was suicidal not only for the organization but also for national solidarity. Talha based his opinion on the assumption that, with a military regime in power, any armed activity would invite stern action against the LeJ. Qari Hai was Basra's lieutenant and ran the letter's training camp in Sarobi, Afghanistan, until the two fell out and formed their own respective factions. While the majority of Hai's supporters are Karachi-based, Basra's cadres have their roots in the Punjab.

Basra figured on a US State Department list of terrorists who "live in or have lived in, have trained in, are headquartered in or financed from Afghanistan". Riaz Basra, who escaped from police custody was wanted by Pakistani authorities in connection with sectarian terrorism, and had been described in the US State Department list as a "would be assassin" of the deposed Pakistani Premier Nawaz Sharief. Basra was allegedly involved in a terrorist incident on January 3, 1999 in which a bridge on the Lahore-Raiwind road, close to Nawaz Sharief's house, was blown up shortly before the then Prime Minister was due to pass by. Basra was also reortedly sighted at various places in Pakistan in the past five years, and Pakistani newspapers have often received messages purportedly sent by him claiming responsibility for certain sectarian terrorist attacks. Although police sources in Sargodha, on April 5, 1999, reported that he was killed in an encounter, his mother's testimony and forensic tests have since disproved this.

Riaz Basra was allegedly permitted to escape from the annual Tableghi congregation in November 2000, in Raiwind. Reports indicate that security force personnel allowed Basra to escape fearing large-scale bloodshed if he were arrested at the congregation. Official sources point that Basra is adept at changing his appearance, and that he has a number of lookalikes within his ranks and on a number of occasions he has mistakenly been reported killed.

The outfit had suffered the loss of several of its top leaders and other cadres due to a crackdown initiated by the Nawaz Sharief administration in 1998.

Pakistani reports indicate that the active cadre strength of the LeJ is approximately 300. Most of these cadres are either under arrest in Pakistan or were based in the various training camps in Afghanistan, from where they regularly came to Pakistan to carry out terrorist activities. Media reports have also added that the outfit is never short of cadres, in spite of the large-scale arrests or the deaths of cadres in encounters. Media reports in September 2001 have indicated that the LeJ has been fielding newer cadres to evade arrests.

Two of the LeJ's most important training centres are located in Muridke (Sheikhupura) and Kabirwal, in Khanewal district. It also has a training camp in Afghanistan located near the Sarobi Dam, Kabul. The present status of the camp is not known. Qari Asadullah, a top LeJ terrorist has reportedly been supervising and ensuring the training facilities of Pakistan-origin terrorists at this camp in collaboration with and support of the erstwhile Taliban regime. However, in the light of US attacks on Afghanistan, the fate of LeJ camps in that country is not immediately known. Lashkar-e-Jhangvi cadres are reportedly using police uniforms for their operations in order to secure easy access to mosques and for easy extrication after committing a terrorist act.

Media reports indicate that the occasional successes against the LeJ by the security agencies have forced the top leadership to remain underground. Rather than risk arrest by engaging in attacks themselves, they have begun training new recruits and directing operations.

## Linkages

Although SSP chief Maulana Azam Tariq has repeatedly dissociated himself publicly from the terrorist activities of the LeJ, security agencies and media reports indicate that the two outfits are closely linked to each other. For instance, when LeJ terrorist Sheikh Haq Nawaz Jhangvi was due to be hanged in February 2001 for terrorist offences, Maulana Tariq, instead of dissociating himself from the terrorist, led a campaign for the remission of his sentence and also offered diyat (blood money) to Iran. Sheikh Haq Nawaz Jhangvi, was nangeo in the Maiwall Jai. Nawaz was 19 years old when he murdered the Iranian diplomat in Lahore on December 19, 1990. It took the courts and the authorities 11 years to decide his fate. During his trial he was kept at different jails in the Punjab. Prior to his hanging, the Supreme Court of Pakistan dismissed two review petitions filed by him against the death penalty.

Both the SSP and LeJ maintain that they are not organisationally linked. But, few analysts of the sectarian conflict in Pakistan believe this to be true. Their cadres come from the same madrassas as also a similar social milieu. The SSP leadership has never criticized the Lashkar-e-Jhangvi because the two organizations share the same sectarian belief system and worldview. They also have a similar charter of demands, which includes turning Pakistan into a Sunni state. Both the outfits have consistently resorted to violence and killings to press their demands, though the SSP has also been attempting to adopt a political path.

The SSP and LeJ have very close links with the Taliban militia. They assisted the Taliban in every way they can both in Afghanistan and within Pakistan. They have fought alongside the Taliban militia in Afghanistan against the Northern Alliance. Besides, all three groups are closely linked in their fight against the Shias, be it in Afghanistan or in Pakistan. LeJ and SSP cadres reportedly played an active part in the massacres of Shias by the erstwhile Taliban regime in Afghanistan.

Many hardcore LeJ terrorists were given sanctuary in Afghanistan by the erstwhile Taliban regime. The Taliban leadership had consistently refused to hand over 21 wanted Pakistani terrorists to Islamabad, saying the fugitives, belonging to the SSP and the LeJ, were not on their soil. Pakistani authorities, however, repeatedly emphasised that these terrorists continued to live in the Afghan capital, Kabul before the US attacks in Afghanistan commenced. The whereabouts of these Afghanistan-based LeJ terrorists, after the US launched attacks on Afghanistan, is not clear. Although the Taliban refused to acknowledge the presence of these terrorists, the Pakistani establishment pointed that they were enjoying its hospitality.

Pakistani Interior Minister Moinuddin Haider visited Kabul and

Kandahar in March 2001 and, among other things, discussed with the Taliban regime the extradition of Pakistani fugitives. The Taliban declined to sign an extradition treaty but promised to search and surrender them. At the time, topping the list of wanted persons was the then LeJ chief, Riaz Basra, who, like the others on the list carried a handsome reward on his head. In fact, official sources later said Basra had visited Karachi and southern Punjab during the year 2001 for medical treatment. The authorities also added that Basra had narrowly escaped arrest in the Punjab during his visit when he had stayed in Pakistan for almost six months.

Besides, Basra Zakiullah and present chief Lahori, too, figured on the list of most wanted persons. Official sources hold that LeJ terrorists frequently cross over into Pakistan from Afghanistan using unfrequented routes, commit bank robberies and sectarian-related killings.

Being part of the broader Deobandi movement, the LEJ secured considerable assistance from other Deobandi outfits. It also has an effectual working relationship with other Deobandi political and terrorist outfits at a personal level, if not at the organisational level. In Afghanistan, they reportedly trained along with the Taliban and other Deobandi terrorists from Pakistan at the same training camps.

The LeJ is also reported to have links with the Harkat-ul-Mujahideen (HUM), Pakistan-based terrorist outfit active in India's Jammu and Kashmir. Many front ranking LeJ terrorists are have reportedly received training at HuM camps in Afghanistan. According to a media report, many LeJ cadres secured training at the HuM's Khalid Bin Waleed camp in Afghanistan. According to the same report, the standard training period consists of 4-8 weeks during which the trainees are provided extensive training in handling sophisticated small arms, assembling and handling of Improvised Explosive Devices (IEDs), other varieties of explosives, as well as in hit-and-run tactics.

The LeJ also maintains links with another Pakistan-based terrorist outfit, the Jaish-e-Mohammed (JeM). Jaish Chief Maulana Masood Azhar reportedly wanted to name his outfit Lashkar-e-Muhammad but was 'advised' to avoid the association with the Lashkar-e-Jhangvi.

Reports hold that the LeJ has been securing financial

assistance from Saudi Arabia. Evidence of private Arab funding was disclosed with the arrest of several LeJ cadres responsible for the May 1997 killing of Ashraf Marth, a senior Police officer who had arrested the killers of Agha Mohammed Ali Rahimi, the Iranian Cultural Attache in Multan. A substantial portion of LeJ's funding is reportedly derived from wealthy benefactors in Karachi, Pakistan.

## Activities and Incidents

The LeJ's chief area of operation is within Pakistan, where it has admitted responsibility for numerous massacres of Shias and targeted killings of Shia religious and community leaders.

More than 70 doctors and 34 lawyers, various Ulema (religious scholars), teachers and students of seminaries, politico-religious parties leaders and activists, officials of various government and private institutions have been assassinated between June 2000 and June 2002 in Pakistan by the SSP and the LeJ. All of them were Shias.

The LeJ has also carried out numerous attacks against Iranian interests and Iranian nationals in Pakistan. The outfit uses terror tactics with the aim of forcing the Pakistani State into accepting its narrow interpretations of Sunni sectarian doctrines as official doctrines. The victims of its terror tactics have been leaders and workers of rival Shia outfits, bureaucrats, policemen, and worshippers of the 'other' sect. The Lashkar-e-Jhangvi is widely considered to be the most secretive sectarian terrorist outfit in Pakistan. It has never exposed itself to the Pakistani public or media. The only means of exposure is through the fax messages and press releases it sends to newspaper offices claiming responsibility for an act of terrorism.

In 1999, the LeJ, in a press release, offered a reward of 135 million Pakistani rupees for anyone who would undertake the killing of Nawaz Sharief, the then Prime Minister; Shabaz Sharief, his younger brother and the then Chief Minister of Punjab, and Mushahid Hussein, the then Information Minister. An attempt was, indeed, made on the life of Nawaz Sharief when a bomb exploded and destroyed a bridge between Lahore and Raiwind, barely an hour before he was to pass by on January 2, 1999.

The LeJ reportedly also uses rafts across the Attack River for shipping arms and ammunition from the North West Frontier Province (NWFP) into Punjab. The new modus operandi was chosen to hoodwink the authorities after permanent pickets were set up by the Punjab police on all land routes coming into the Province from the NWFP, in addition to intensifying patrolling along all such routes. Earlier, the LeJ had been using two bridges, one near Taunsa and another near Bhakkar, to transport arms and ammunition.

The LeJ is currently reported to be finding it hard to execute terrorist strikes because it has become difficult to smuggle arms into Punjab and also due to the differences between Riaz Basra and Qari Asadullah.

In October 1997, a Pakistani news report quoted Malik Ishaque, a top LeJ terrorist currently under detention, as saying, "I have been instrumental in the killing of 102 human beings."

The LeJ was responsible for the Lahore Mominpura Cemetery massacre on January 11, 1998, in which 25 Shia Muslims were killed and 50 others injured. Most of the victims were women and children who had gathered for Qur'an-Khwani (Quranic recital) at the cemetery. Aziz Gujar, Haroon Mansoor, Riaz Basra and Akram Lahori were the main accused in this massacre. While the first two were arrested, Basra and Lahori evaded arrest.

Acting upon information secured from LeJ chief Lahori and Rahman, both of who are now under detention, police recovered 134 Kalashnikov rifles, rockets, landmines, explosives, chemicals, and poison-filled capsules. Karachi Police have also arrested the wife and a son of Lahori. Lahori was also taken to Punjab and, based on his information, police and agents of US Federal Bureau of Investigation (FBI) raided various places and arrested several suspected terrorists.

The Sindh government on October 15, 2001 announced head money for the arrest of 12 proclaimed offenders involved in heinous sectarian terrorist attacks. According to the announcement, seven absconders belong to Lashkar-e-Jhangvi while five are activists of another proscribed terrorist outfit, the Sipah-e-Muhammad Pakistan (SMP). The Sindh government announced Rs. 1 million cash reward for each of the three Lashkar-e-Jhangvi terrorists, Qari Abdul Hai alias Qari Asad alias Talha, resident of District Alipur, Muzaffargar; Atta-ur-Rehman alias Nadeem Bukhari, resident of Paposh Nagar, Karachi, and Asif Ramzi, resident of Karachi. Half a million rupees cash reward each was fixed for another three LeJ cadres - Asif Ramzi alias Chotto alias Hafiz, resident of Muhammad

Nagar, Karachi. Mohad Rashidi and Lal Mohd alias Lal Bhai Faqeer, resident of Orangi Town, Karachi. Rs. 0.25 million cash reward was fixed for Lashkar-e-Jhangvi cadre Muhammad Umer alias Haji Sahib, resident of Shah Faisal Colony, Karachi.

Karachi Police on June 29 published photos of 10 terrorists wanted in connection with the murder of US journalist Daniel Pearl and for the two car-bomb attacks on Western targets in Karachi. At least 16 persons, including 12 French nationals, were killed and 26 persons injured in a bomb blast in Karachi on May 8, 2002. In the second attack, near the US Consulate in Karachi on June 14, 12 persons were killed. At least five of the 10 terrorists identified are believed to be LeJ cadres. It was also the first occasion that police identified LeJ as being involved in all the three incidents. One of the photographed men, Asif Ramzi, is listed as wanted in the Pearl murder case and also for sectarian killings, with a three million rupees-reward offered for his capture. Another suspect, Naveedul Hassan, is listed as wanted in the June 14 terrorist incident and his capture carries two million rupee-award. Sharib is listed as wanted in both the Consulate-attack and the May 8-attack.

According to senior investigators, the Al Qaeda network is suspected to have worked with LeJ cadres to plan both the car-bomb attacks. Intelligence sources have indicated that certain LeJ terrorists arrested in Karachi in June 2002 have been allegedly working with the Al Qaeda to strike at targets in Pakistan.

## SIPAH-E-MOHAMMED PAKISTAN

Sipah-e-Mohammed Pakistan (SMP) literally meaning 'Army of Muhammad' refers to a Shia group which is involved in sectarian terrorist activity primarily in Pakistani Punjab. The SMP is one of the two sectarian terrorist outfits proscribed on August 14, 2001, by President Pervez Musharraf.

### Formation

The exact date of formation of the SMP is not certain. But it is generally believed that Maulana Mureed Abbas Yazdani created the outfit in 1993 after he was convinced that the predominant Shia organisation, Tehreek-e-Jaferia Pakistan (TJP) would not allow its young cadre to physically counter the Sunni militancy of the Sipah-e-Sahaba Pakistan (SSP) and the Lashkar-e-Jhangvi (LeJ). The Shia youth had been urging the TJP leadership to take notice of the alleged excesses of the SSP whose members were alleged to be targeting Shia's and their beliefs.

## Objective

The primary objective of the SMP is the protection of the Shiite community from Sunni fundamentalist and terrorist outfits. Its main rival is the Lashkar-e-Jhangvi (LeJ). SMP chief Ghulam Raza Naqvi is also reported to have visualised the creation of a Quds force comprising both Shias and Sunnis to 'liberate' Jerusalem.

## Leadership and Structure

Ghulam Raza Naqvi is the Saalar-i-Aala (chief) of SMP. A dreaded hitman, when arrested in 1996, the government had placed a reward of Rs. 2 million for his alleged involvement in about 30 cases of murder and dacoity. He is now in prison. He is known for turning Thokar Niaz Beg, a village in the suburbs of Lahore, a no-go area for the police who failed in at least four attempts to break this Shia stronghold. Thokar Niaz Beg also serves as the SMP headquarters. Munawwar Abbas Alvi is a front ranking SMP leader who is also in prison.

The SMP is estimated to have a cadre base of 30000 Shia followers. This mainly comprises former members of the Tehreek Nafaz Fiqh-e-Jafariya (TNFJ) and TJP. The SMP has a strong following in the Punjab province.

There are apparently no terrorist training facilities for the SMP cadres outside Pakistan and neither are its cadres been allowed to operate from outside Pakistan.

## Linkages

The outfit reportedly maintains close links with the Shia regime in Iran.

## Major Incidents

The SMP is involved in a number of massacres, targeted killings and dacoities. However, the phase following the October 1999 military coup in Pakistan saw a decline in sectarian violence. In February 2001, at a meeting of the Milli Yekjehti Council (MYO), the SMP and the SSP announced their willingness to shun all differences and to withdraw cases against each other. Meanwhile, several Shia organisations have been petitioning the government for the release of SMP chief Ghulam Raza Naqvi, though the government is yet to respond. The TJP President Allama Syed Sajid Naqvi commenting in the context of the August 14, 2001 order proscribing SMP and Sunni terrorist outfit LeJ, said that there should be uniform policy vis-a-vis the release of cadres. He opined that as the SSP Chief Azam Tariq has been released despite his alleged involvement in many sectarian related crimes, the Federal government should release the SMP chief also.

The SMP, in February 2001, was reported to have sought membership in the Grand Democratic Alliance, formed to launch a movement for restoration of democracy in Pakistan. Even as these apparent gestures towards peace are made, the SMP was suspected to be involved in the attack on an SSP controlled mosque in which nine worshippers were killed and 12 others injured on March 12, 2001.

The SMP's connection with the Shia regime in Iran led to the assassination of Iran's Counsel General in Lahore, Sadeq Ganji, in December 1990 by suspected Sunni terrorists. The assassination was apparently a reprisal for the murder in February that year of SSP founder, Maulana Haq Nawaz Jhangvi. Similarly, soon after a bomb explosion at a Lahore court in January 1997 in which the then SSP chief, Zia-ur-Rehman Farooqi was killed along with 29 others, an Iranian diplomat Muhammad Ali Rahimi was killed in Multan in the same month. The Iranian Cultural Centre in Lahore too was attacked and burnt down in that month. Besides, five personnel of the Iranian armed forces who were in Pakistan for training were murdered in September 1997. An SSP activist Sheikh Haq Nawaz Jhangvi, was convicted and hanged on March 1, 2001 for the Iranian diplomat, Sadeq Ganji's assassination.

In 1996, a faction of the SMP cadres opposed their Chief Maulana Yazdani for his conciliatory attitude towards the MYC, which to them amounted to a compromise on their faith and fundamental beliefs. The present Saalar-i-Aala ('commander') of the SMP Ghulam Raza Naqvi reportedly ordered the assassination of Maulana Yazdani, which was executed in September 1996. Another faction was formed under the leadership of Major (Retd.) Ashraf Ali Shah in 1996 and confronted Ghulam Naqvi's group which led to internecine clashes.

Ghulam Naqvi, had, in 1996, ensured that the outfit had its headquarters, Thokar Niaz Beg, a village in Lahore, completely under their control and impossible for security agencies to penetrate. Following the factional clashes, the SMP commander was forced to flee and was later arrested by police in December 1996. The year also saw the broadening target base of sectarian terrorists with several bureaucrats being attacked and killed including the Commissioner of Sargodha and the Deputy Commissioner of Khanewal.

SMP for all practical purposes stopped operating in 1996 after Ghulam Raza's arrest. Its cadres now reportedly operate on their own. Lack of financial resources and training are also key factors in the SMP's relative oblivion. Though pro-violence Shia activists supported the Sipah-e-Muhammad, it could not get any organisational support from the TJP, which restricted itself to providing legal aid to arrested SMP cadres.

Law-enforcing agencies launched a massive crackdown on the outfit on August 15, 2001. But they could not ascertain the hideouts of the top leadership of the SMP. Approximately 200 leaders and activists of the Lashkar-e-Jhangvi (LeJ) and Sipah-e-Muhammad Pakistan (SMP) were arrested in a crackdown launched by the police on August 15. Punjab Police, on August 16, registered cases under the amended Anti-Terrorism Act (ATA) against the arrested activists of SMP. Arrests were also reported from various parts of Faisalabad, Jhang and Toba Tek Singh districts.

The State Bank of Pakistan (SBP), through a circular issued on August 23, 2001 ordered all banks and financial institutions to freeze the accounts of SMP with immediate effect. However, since the outfit was operating underground, official sources indicated that they might not be operating their bank accounts under the outfit's name. Pakistani news reports have indicated that the SBP is yet to locate details of bank accounts of proscribed sectarian outfits, the Lashkar-e-Jhangvi (LeJ) and the Sipah-e-Muhammad Pakistan (SMP). News sources observed that SBP has confirmed reports that the banned outfits were not maintaining accounts with any of the banks or financial institutions anywhere in the country.

The Milli Yekjehti Council (MYC) was formed in March 1995 by 11 religious/sectarian outfits to foster sectarian harmony, point out causes of any misunderstanding between sects and resolve any conflicts which result from these differences. The Council agreed in May 1995 on a 17-point code of conduct. As a result, the situation vis-a-vis sectarian violence significantly improved in 1995 and 1996. However, the extremists in both the Shia and Sunni camps blamed their leaders for compromising on their respective basic beliefs and principles and, therefore, were not happy. After a lot of grumbling, they lost patience by the middle of 1996 and started another extremely violent phase of violence. Ever Since, though the MYC has been around and periodically asserts that it has successfully deflated tensions between extremist outfits, violence continues.

## Muttahida Quomi Mahaz

### (Previously known as Mohajir Quomi Movement)

The most potent threat to Pakistan's internal security in the late Nineteen Eighties and early Nineties was posed by militia from the Mohajir community. Originally formed as the Mohajir Quomi Movement (MOM), it is now split into two factions. The faction led by the founder Altaf Hussain was renamed Muttahida Quomi Mahaz and is commonly referred to as MQM (A). A breakaway faction, created in 1992, retains the original name Mohajir Quomi Movement - with the suffix Haqiqi which means real - and is commonly referred to as MQM (H). The two factions have been responsible for several incidents of urban terrorism even as the MQM (A) participates in Pakistan's electoral process. After a series of strong measures taken by the State in 1998, the MQM (A) has largely reoriented itself into an exclusively political outfit. In its latest display of clout in Mohajir dominated areas, it called for a boycott of local body elections held in July 2001 and ensured a low turnout in areas dominated by its cadre.

The MQM sought to portray itself, in its initial years as an organisation of Mohajirs. This ethnic term refers to refugees from India who settled in Karachi and other urban centres of Sindh province. They now constitute the largest segment in Sindh's urban population. Largely natives of India's Bihar and Uttar Pradesh provinces, this community maintains a distinct identity for itself. In the immediate post-partition period, the community formed one of the most influential lobbies in Pakistan having been closely associated with the movement for the country and its founder Mohammad Ali Jinnah. With the increasing power of the military over the State apparatus, the community found its pre-eminent position being increasingly usurped by the Punjabi dominated military-bureaucratic formation that effectively ruled Pakistan since Gen. Ayub's coup in 1958.

The first assertions of a distinct ethnic identity were made by the "All Pakistan Mohajir Students Organisation" (APMSO) founded by Altaf Hussain in Karachi in 1978. Altaf Hussain went on, in 1984, to form the MQM. For two years, the outfit maintained a low profile reportedly concentrating on building its cadre base in Karachi and Hyderabad. It came on the national stage with a massive rally in Karachi on August 8. Ever since it has been a major actor in Pakistan's politics even as it maintains an armed cadre that has repeatedly indulged in urban terrorism. In 1992, going against the civilian political executive, the army reportedly encouraged a split in the outfit helping create the MQM (H) under the leadership or Ataq Ahmed and Aamir Khan, who were earier top members or MOM's armed wing. To disguise itself as a broad social formation, the outfit dropped the term Mohajir from its title and renamed itself the Muttahida Quomi Mahaz (United National Front).

Violence has always accompanied the outfit's political activities. It began with the first public meeting on August 8, 1986, which was accompanied by aerial firing, street violence and damage to public property by participants. Two months later, on October 31, rioting in Karachi and Hyderabad, another MQM (A) stronghold, left 12 persons dead. Altaf Hussain and ten other leaders of the outfit were arrested on November 2 that year which only increased the street violence in Mohajir dominated cities. On December 14, the outfit's secretary general Dr. Imran Farooq claimed that the situation can come under control only if Altaf Hussain is released. Almost on cue, violence flared up that night and the next day leaving 120 persons dead in Karachi.

Violence continued, allegedly perpetrated by MQM, despite the outfit entering into an alliance with the Pakistan People's Party (PPP) in 1988 and participating in a coalition government at the Federal level. The two parties had signed a 54 point agreement commonly known as the Karachi Accord just before the elections held in December that year. News reports suggested that most violence was between supporters of the MQM and the Jiye Sindh Movement, an organisation purportedly fighting the cause of native Sindhis. Another rival with which the MQM frequently indulged in violent clashes was the Punjabi-Pukhtoon Ittehad (PPI), an outfit comprising of armed extremists from the Pukhtoon and Punjabi communities. Random attacks by armed activists of the warring groups on unarmed civilians were the major cause for casualties. In May 1989, the MQM walked out of the PPP led coalition in Sindh and five months later, from the federal government, accusing the PPP of failing to honour its promises outlined in the Karachi Accord.

The press to was a victim of the MQM's terror strategies. Several newspapers, including the *Dawn, Jang,* identified by the outfit as non-symphathetic to the 'movement' were targeted for enforced boycotts.

Following reports of an imminent army crackdown on the outfit, Altaf Hussain left for UK on January 1, 1992 and has been in exile since. Despite the flight of its leader, the outfit's terrorist arm continued to operate until 1998. Its political arm too faded into insignificance after the October 1999 coup in Pakistan.

The mid nineties in urban Sindh was marked by consistent strike calls from the MQM which included an announcement in July 1995 that weekly strikes on Fridays and Saturdays would be observed. Most MQM strikes were accompanied by violence leaving scores dead in their wake.

The outfit's leadership, particularly Altaf Hussain, has been described by most analysts, as opportunists. The political platforms adopted by the outfit have been forwarded as evidence. After striking a deal, termed as the Karachi Accord, with Benazir Bhutto's PPP, the outfit switched alliances and teamed up with Nawaz Shariefs, Pakistan Muslim League (PML) in 1992. In Pakistan's predominantly two party set-up, MQM which has time and again proved itself as the third largest political force, has swung between the two dominant parties and joined several ruling coalitions at the federal level and in Sindh. The elected local bodies in Karachi and Hyderabad have been overwhelmingly dominated by the MQM (A).

## Baluch People's Liberation Front (BPLF)

The Baluch People's Liberation Front (BPLF), was formed by Mir Hazar Ramkhani, a prominent Baluchi leader in 1976 after developing irreconcilable differences with the dominant leadership of Baluch Students Organisation (BSO) led by Sher Mohammed Marri. The differences emerged on the question of strategies to be adopted.

The BPLF gained the support of the Baluch Students Organisation-Awami, a product of an earlier split within the Baluch Students Organisation. BPLF, a Marxist oriented outfit was provided logistic support by the then Afghanistan government. Some of its cadres were trained in Beirut by the Popular Front for the Liberation of Palestine. It relied heavily on the support it received from the Afghan authorities.

The BPLF did not possess any command structure and was a loosely based outfit. In the 1970's as the Pakistani security forces improved its counter-terrorist measures, the BPLF was increasingly forced to fall back to the camps inside Afghanistan. The current status of the outfit is not known.

## Jamaat Ul-Fuqra

### Formation

Jamaat ul-Fuqra (JF) or "community of the impoverished", a terrorist outfit operating in Pakistan and North America, was formed by a Pakistani cleric, Sheikh Mubarak Ali Gilani, in New York in 1980, on his first visit to the US. Mubarak Gilani's intention in forming the outfit was to 'purify' Islam through violence.

### Ideology, Leadership and Structure

The JF, in its early phase, sought to counter what is perceived as excessive Western influence on Islam. It also concluded that violence was a significant aspect in its quest to purify Islam. In its ideological moorings, the Fuqra regards as enemies of Islam all those who do not follow the tenets of Islam as laid out in the Koran, including those Muslims who they consider as heretics as well as non-Muslims. One of Gilani's works published by the Quranic Open University in the US and seized in a 1991-investigation instructed his cadres that their foremost duty was to wage *Jehad* against the 'oppressors of Muslims'. Members of the group are described as Islamist extremists with much hatred toward their 'enemies'.

The JF is loosely structured with certain elements working

openly through social service organizations to recruit members, raise money, organise activities and carry out propaganda. Individuals selected to live on JF premises agree to abide by the law and discipline of the Jamaat ul-Fuqra. Investigations by the Colorado Attorney General's Office in the 1980s indicated that the JF was composed of approximately 30 different 'Jamaats' or communities, more or less mobile in nature. Most of these 'Jamaats' are reportedly existent even today along with what investigators discerned to be several covert paramilitary training compounds, one of which had been located in a mountainous area near Buena Vista, Colorado prior to the Colorado prosecutions in the mid-1990s.

Within 10 years of its formation, Fuqra's communes in the US attracted many Muslim converts-including some of those recruited in prisons. The JF is said to comprise of some 1,000 to 3,000 members in the US. Secrecy is the hallmark of the outfit and cadres are reportedly well versed in the use of aliases. The Fuqra's structure is well concealed behind front outfits and consists of a network of safe houses and cells. Furthermore, the JF founder as well as cadres consistently maintain that it does not exist. JF members occasionally travel abroad for 'paramilitary and survivalist training' under Gilani's supervision.

Sheikh Mubarak Ali Gilani, who also calls himself the sixth Sultan Ul Faqr, is the chief of JF. Jamaat ul-Fuqra is headquartered in Hancock, New York.

## Areas of Activity and Influence

Although Gilani, the reclusive chief of Fuqra resides in Lahore, Pakistan, most JF cells are located in North America. Fuqra members have purchased isolated rural properties in North America to live as a community, practice their faith, and insulate themselves from Western culture. The group has set up and funded rural communes that the US authorities allege are linked to murder, bombings and other felonies throughout the US and Canada. Currently, there are half a dozen Fuqra residential compounds in rural hamlets across the US sheltering hundreds of cadres, some of who have reportedly trained in the use of weapons and explosives in Pakistan.

Muslims of the Americas, a tax-exempt group established in the US in 1980 by Gilani, operates communes of primarily black,

American-born Muslims in many states in the US, including in Binghamton in New York, Badger in California, York in South California and Red House in Virginia. JF is reportedly linked through court documents to the Muslims of Americas. There is also a road in the name of Sheikh Gilani in the vicinity of Virginia. The cult houses between 100 and 200 people, many of them women and children in about 20 huge trailers. There is also a Virginia newspaper, the *Islamic Post,* founded by Sheikh Gilani.

## Linkages and Incidents

Jamaat al-Fuqra, also described as a cult, is currently the focus of a probe by US authorities for charges ranging from links with terrorist groups to laundering money into Pakistan.

In the 1980s, they carried out various terrorist acts, including numerous fire-bombings across the United States. JF's early targets in North America were ethnic Indians and targets linked to various Indian sects. In July 1983, Stephen Paul Paster, a front ranking JF member, was responsible for planting a pipe bomb at a Portland hotel owned by followers of the Bhagwan Rajneesh cult. After his arrest in Colorado, Paster served four years of a 20-year prison sentence for the bombing. He was suspected but not charged in two other bombings in Seattle in 1984 - the bombings of the Vedanta Society temple and the Integral Yoga Society building. Currently, Paster is reported to be based in Lahore, Pakistan, from where, intelligence sources say, he provides explosives training to Fuqra cadres.

After the Portland bombing, two Fuqra cadres allegedly killed Mozaffar Ahmad, a leader of the minority Ahmadiyyah sect in Canton, Michigan. Both the suspects reportedly perished in a fire they had set at the Ahmadiyyah mosque in nearby Detroit. The JF is also reported to have been involved in the killing of three Indians on August 1, 1984 in a suburb of Tacoma, Washington. Besides, the JF is suspected to be involved in a series of fire bombings of Hindu and Hare Krishna temples in Seattle, Denver, Philadelphia and Kansas City.

US officials in 1989, during a search of a storage locker in Colorado Springs, recovered a large cache of armaments and documents with multiple links to the JF. Among the arms recovered were handguns, semi-automatic firearms, explosives, pipe bombs, bomb components and several bombs. Some of the seized documents described the activities and code of the "Muhammad Commandos of Sector 5," who were reportedly involved in arms training and intelligence gathering. The documents, including maps and lists, contained details of potential JF targets and victims in Los Angeles, Arizona and Colorado—oil and gas installations and electrical facilities, US. Air Force Academy and other military sites, people in 12 US states and Canada with Jewish or Hindu-sounding names. Various JF publications were seized during this search. Titles of some of the publications seized included "Guerrilla Warfare", "Counter Guerrilla Operations", "Understanding Amateur Radio", and "Fair Weather Flying," and "Basic Blueprint Reading and Sketching."

In 1991, JF's plans to bomb an Indian cinema and a Hindu temple near Toronto were unsuccessful. Five JF cadres were arrested at the Niagara Falls border crossing after US Customs agents searched their cars and found visual evidence and plans of the interiors of the targets and a description of time bombs. A Canadian jury convicted three American JF cadres of conspiracy to commit mischief and endanger life. A fourth suspect, who had come to Canada from Pakistan shortly before the planned bombing, fled to Pakistan after his colleagues' arrest, according to evidence presented at the trial.

In the 1990s, JF was more often than not operating under the guise of two front groups, 'Muslims of the Americas' and 'Quranic Open University'. The latter portrayed itself as a religious and charitable educational institution dedicated to studying the Quran.

Gilani has reportedly admitted to receiving hundreds of thousands of dollars a year in donations from America. A large segment of JF members have been convicted of criminal acts, including murder and fraud. With the US State Department outlawing Fuqra and listing it as one of the proscribed groups in its annual reports, the activities of the outfit decreased relatively. The JF supports various terrorist groups operating in Pakistan and in the Indian State of Jammu and Kashmir. Sheikh Gilani has linkages with Islamist terrorist groups like the Hamas and Hezbollah. Although dormant in terms of real activity, JF has an active link with the terrorist groups in Pakistan and provides both moral and material assistance to these groups.

JF cadres are suspects in at least 10 unsolved assassinations and 17 firebombing cases between 1979 and 1990.

In 1993 Fuqra members in Colorado were convicted of participating in a conspiracy resulting in the killing of a Muslim religious figure in Arizona.

One of the persons convicted in the World Trade Center bombing in 1993 was Clement Rodney Hampton-el, a Fuqra member. JF was linked in a Congressional testimony to the planning of the 1993 World Trade Center bombing.

Gilani is now in Pakistani custody for the abduction of US journalist Daniel Pearl. Official sources in Pakistan have indicated that Daniel Pearl was attempting to meet Gilani in the days before he disappeared in Karachi. Pakistani police arrested Gilani in Rawalpindi on January 30, 2002 and shifted him to Karachi for questioning. Although he denied any link to the abduction, police also detained several of his colleagues. Consequent to his arrest, he reportedly told his interrogators that he had links with the Pakistani intelligence agencies.

A media report has indicated that the JF is also being probed for links with Richard Reid, a Briton, accused of trying to use explosives in his shoes to blow up a Paris-to-Miami jetliner on December 22, 2001.

A house in Virginia believed to be linked to the JF was raided by police in December 2001 and two persons were arrested for illegally purchasing guns.

Three suspected US-based JF members have been arrested on weapons charges in the year 2001, including two following the September 11 multiple terrorist attacks. Vicente Rafael Pierre, a 44-year-old native of Brooklyn and his wife Traci Upshur, both JF cadres, were arrested on gun charges and convicted on November 30, 2001. Pierre's Virginia compound, near the Red House Commune, is reported to have served as a JF base.

A money laundering scheme run by the Red House Commune is reportedly similar to a Colorado operation that was shut down in 1993. Colorado law enforcement agencies convicted five JF cadres for defrauding the Colorado government of approximately $350,000 through bogus workers' compensation claims. Prosecuting agencies have indicated that the amount had been laundered through Professional Security International (PSI), a JF security firm, and Muslims of the Americas. A portion of the funds was tracked through PSI to JF couriers who traveled to Pakistan. The

PSI reportedly enabled JF cadres to obtain federal licenses to buy weapons. The Fuqra is also suspected of having two more security firms located in New York.

The Fuqra also reportedly has various broad schemes to take government entitlement money and utilise it to fund terrorist activities. The commune in Colorado is spread across 101 acres and police recovered bombs, weapons and plans for terrorist attacks in a raid in the year 1993. Two other communes in New York and California have shooting ranges. The 1,800-acre settlement in the Sierra Mountains in California also reportedly has an airstrip.

In a February 22, 2002 interview, Gilani said his 'contribution' to the 'Kashmir cause' since 1947 and to the Afghan *Jehad* were on record. In the same interview, Gilani claimed that both the governments of Pakistan and Pakistan occupied Kashmir (PoK) had requested him to mobilise his university students to project the cause of Kashmir in the US through the media by holding rallies and informing the public. To this end, he claimed that the Kashmir-American Friendship Society was formed in 1993.

Gilani is currently under investigation for his alleged links to the al Qaeda terror network of Osama bin Laden and for money laundering from the US into Pakistan and vice versa. The US Federal Bureau of Investigation (FBI) is investigating connections between a small black Muslim community in California's Sierra Nevada valley, called Baladullah and the JF. The FBI reportedly looked into Baladullah, a community of 30 Muslim families, while investigating into JF's activities at a remote Virginia settlement, where one person was convicted in November 2001 on charges of federal firearms violations.

## Nadeem Commando, Terrorist Group of Pakistan

A relatively small terrorist outfit, Nadeem Commando (NC), comprises largely of Mohajirs (Muslims who migrated to Pakistan in 1947 from areas in India). It professes the ideology of the Mohajir Quami Movement (MQM) and fervently advocates the rights of Mohajirs.

The origins of the outfit are not well documented but it is reported to have become active in the early 1990's. NC is alleged to have close links with the Muttahida Quami Movement-Altaf (MQM-A).Their main areas of operation are Karachi and Hyderabad, the chief concentrations of Mohajir community in Pakistan.

The outfit's supply lines and funds have been traced to expatriate Mohajirs, particularly those based in London. The city is also the main base for the MQM-A with its leader Altaf Hussain living in exile there. NC's terror tactics are based on random shooting of carefully selected targets and staging violent incidents during political strikes called by MQM-A in Karachi and Hyderabad.

Pakistani authorities have alleged that the NC was responsible for the assassination of two US diplomats in Karachi in April 1995 is among the outfit's most publicised terrorist strikes. Pakistani officials have also reported that most of the outfit's cadres were either killed or arrested in Karachi during the Pakistan government's counter-terrorist operation in May 1996, called 'Operation Clean Up'.

Even though their current status is not clear, Nadeem Commando is alleged to provide its cadres and material during periodic strikes called by MQM-A in Karachi and Hyderabad. The disruption that NC cadres are alleged to be causing in Karachi during the strikes called by MQM-A have been a source of serious concern to the Pakistani government since Karachi is also the commercial capital of Pakistan.

## Muslim United Army

### Formation

Although the exact formation date of the Muslim United Army (MuA) is not known, it came into prominence on October 16, 2002, in connection with a series of parcel-bomb attacks in Karachi that left nine persons injured, including eight police personnel. These letters were sent to the offices of the provincial Home Secretary and some front ranking police officials connected with the operations against sectarian and terrorists groups in Pakistan. Reports of June 2003 quoting Pakistani security agencies have indicated the MuA is an alliance of a number of terrorist outfits, including the Harkat-ul-Mujahideen al Aalmi and Lashkar-e-Jhangvi.

### Ideology and Objectives

In an email message sent on October 16, 2002, Asif Ramzi, the then self-styled supreme commander of his own faction of the proscribed Sunni group Lashkar-e-Jhangvi (LeJ), wrote: "...all the rightwing organisations, including the Lashkar-e-Jhangvi, have formed the Muslim United Army to organise the groups against the United States. We are going to launch a war against...anti-Islam forces, police and other non-Muslims on [sic] the platform of the MUA." The message also reportedly made an appeal to Muslims living in the United States to leave that country since "the Mujahideen have completed preparations to strike the United States again in which more than 3.5 million people could be killed".

Another MuA letter refers to Jaish-e-Mohammed terrorist Sheikh Omar (convicted in the Daniel Pearl murder case), Mohammad Imran, chief of the Harkat-ul-Mujahideen al Aalmi, his deputy Hanif, Akram Lahori, supreme commander of his own faction of Lashkar-e-Jhangvi, as the "greatest leaders of the Ummah".

### Leadership

Asif Ramzi, self-styled supreme commander of his own faction of LeJ, is reported to have been one of the key leaders of the MuA till his death on December 19, 2002, along with three accomplices in a bomb blast at a warehouse in Karachi's Korangi area.

A hitherto unknown Sheikh Ahmed currently leads the MuA, according to Pakistani reports of June 2003.

The Harkat-ul-Mujahideen al Aalmi, a splinter group of the Harkat-ul-Mujahideen (HuM) is reportedly part of the Muslim United Army.

## Harkat-Ul-Mujahideen Al-alami

### Formation

The Harkat-ul-Mujahideen Al-alami (HuMA; Al-alami, meaning International) is an offshoot of the proscribed Deobandi terrorist group, the Harkat-ul-Mujahideen (HUM), and was formed sometime in the year 2002 after parting ways with the latter on a dispute over organisational affairs. According to *The Friday Times*, there was reportedly some pressure on the HuM after its proscription in Pakistan in November 2001 to merge with the Jamiat-ul-Mujahideen, another *Jehadi* group based in that country. However, this plan met with stiff resistance from within the HuM and reportedly, the dissent led to a group breaking away from the parent outfit and calling itself the Harkat-ul-Mujahideen Al-alami.

It is based in the Pakistani port city of Karachi.

## Objectives and Activity

Pakistani officials reportedly told a US delegation in Islamabad in September 2002 that the HuMA was involved in some of the attacks on Christians and Westerners in the country since 9/11. Officials reportedly pointed out to the American delegation led by Undersecretary for Defence, Douglas J. Feith, that the group had the potential to carry out high-intensity attacks, as it was equipped with sophisticated weapons, including rocket launchers and detonators.

It is suspected to be involved in the failed attempts to assassinate President Pervez Musharraf and the former Interior Minister Moinuddin Haider. Sharib alias Asadullah led a group of eight HuMA terrorists in the failed plot to assassinate President Musharraf in Karachi on April 26, 2002. Rangers Director-General (DG) in Sindh, Maj. Gen Salahuddin, was quoted as saying in a July 2002 report that two cadres of the HuMA group had parked their vehicle near the Falak Naz Centre on Sharea Faisal on April 26 when the President was scheduled to visit the Army House from the airport. However, the remote control to set-off the device failed. The DG also said that Inspector Wasim of the Rangers had abetted the accused in their attempt and was subsequently arrested.

Sindh Police has suspected the involvement of the group, among others, in the US Consulate bombing case, the April 26 conspiracy to assassinate the President, the May-8 Sheraton Hotel blasts and the Aga Khan flats blast in the limits of Pirabad.

The HuMA cadres reportedly decide upon their targets after consultations at the meetings of an 'consultative committee' headed by Muhammad Imran, who was arrested on July 7, 2002.

Among other objectives, the group has declared that it intends to damage the United States, its interests and all those who are friendly to the US.

## Leadership and Cadre

Most of its activists and its top leadership are currently under arrest. While Muhammad Imran functioned as the *Amir* (chief) of Harkat-ul-Mujahideen Al-alami, Muhammad Hanif was the deputy chief and in charge of its *Askari* (military) wing. Both Imran and Hanif were arrested on July 7, 2002, for their alleged involvement in the plot to assassinate President Musharraf. Subsequently, on April 14, 2003, an Anti-Terrorism Court in Karachi held both guilty and sentenced them to death. "This death sentence is a blessing for me, although our deaths have been planned by the government to please America," said Imran in response to the judgment.

Zubair Mufti, arrested on September 18, 2002, in connection with the assassination attempt on President Musharraf, has been described by the Sindh Police as a technical mastermind of the group. Mohammad Ashraf Khan, arrested by the Karachi police on July 24, 2002 in connection with car-bomb explosion near the US Consulate on June 14, functioned as the treasurer of the organisation.

The group reportedly consists of approximately 60 cadres working independently in their respective areas. None of them was responsible to a central body but a 'consultative committee' led by Mohammad Imran decided the implementation of terrorist strikes. The *Daily Times* reported on April 15, 2003, that security agencies had arrested 24 HuMA terrorists and at least 40 were still at large.

## Linkages

Reports of October 2002 pointed out that the Federal Government had found evidence of the involvement of some tribal leaders supplying weapons to the Al Qaeda fugitives and Harkat-ul-Mujahideen al-Alami in Karachi. Further, interrogation of eight HuMA terrorists arrested on September 18, 2002, has revealed that they had bought arms and ammunition in the tribal areas of the North West Frontier Province (NWFP).

Saud Memon in the Sindh province is reported to be one of the prominent financiers of the HuMA. The Sindh Government had declared him among their 10 most-wanted terrorists on June 29, 2002. Reportedly, it was on the land owned by Memon that the body of murdered US journalist Daniel Pearl was discovered. Till April 2003, according to the *Daily Times,* Memon was at large.

The HuMA has links with the Al Qaeda, which has been established primarily through the proscribed Sunni group, Lashkar-e-Jhangvi (LeJ), and other terrorist groups like the Harkat-ul-Mujahideen (HUM) and with some Arab nationals individually. Official sources in Sindh province were quoted as saying in a April 2003 report that despite having de-linked themselves from the public as an independent outfit, the HuMA continued to maintain contacts with its parent outfit, the Harkat-ul-Mujahideen as also the LeJ. Some of the HuMA cadres reportedly also have close links with the Taliban militia.

## Hizb-ul-Mujahideen

Of the terrorist outfits currently operating in Jammu and Kashmir (J&K), the Hizb-ul-Mujahideen (HM) is the one of the largest, with a cadre base drawn from indigenous and foreign sources. It is one of the most important terrorist outfits in terms of its effectiveness in perpetrating violence across the State at regular intervals. The HM is one of the 32 outfits proscribed under the Prevention of Terrorism Act, 2002.

### Formation and Objectives

The HM came into being in the Kashmir Valley in September 1989 with Master Ahsan Dar as its chief. Dar was later arrested by security forces in mid-December 1993. It was reportedly formed as the militant wing of the Jamaat-e-Islami (JeI), an Islamist organisation. The Jamaat-e-Islami is reported to have set up the Hizb at the behest of the Inter Services Intelligence (ISI), Pakistan's external intelligence agency, to counter the Jammu and Kashmir Liberation Front (JKLF), which had advocated complete independence of the State. Many of the early Hizb cadres were former JKLF members.

In June 1990, the HM 'Constitution' was approved and Mohammed Yusuf Shah, popularly known as Syed Salahuddin, was appointed Patron and Hilal Ahmed Mir as Amir (chief). Apparently, differences between JeI elements and the non-JeI faction started developing within the HM which led to a split with one faction being led by Salahuddin whereas the other was led by Hilal Ahmed Mir (killed in 1993).

The Hizb-ul-Mujahideen stands for the integration of J&K with Pakistan. Since its inception, the HM has also campaigned for the Islamisation of Kashmir.

### Leadership, Command Structure and Areas of Operation

Headquartered at Muzaffarabad in Pakistan occupied Kashmir (PoK), the Hizb-ul-Mujahideen with an estimated cadre strength of at least 1500, is presently headed by Syed Salahuddin. The patron of HM in PoK is Ghulam Nabi Nausheri.

Ghazi Nasiruddin is the outfit's 'chief commander of operations' in the Kashmir Valley. He succeeded Saif-ul-Islam alias Ghulam Rasool Khan alias 'Engineer' Zaman, who was killed in a major counter-insurgency operation on April 2, 2003, at Nowgam Chowk, on the outskirts of capital Srinagar. Saleem Hashmi is the spokesperson of the outfit.

Currently, the HM is organised into five divisions; central division for Srinagar, northern division for Kupwara-Bandipora-Baramulla, southern division for Anantnag and Pulwama districts, Chenab division for Doda district and Gool in the Udhampur district, and Pir Panjal Division for the Rajouri and Poonch districts.

The HM has its own news agency, Kashmir Press International, and a women's wing, Banat-ul-Islam.

The Hizb reportedly has a substantial support base in the Kashmir Valley and in the Doda, Rajouri, Poonch districts and parts of Udhampur district in the Jammu region.

## Internal Dynamics

The HM came into the spotlight when it's Salar-e-Ala or 'chief commander', Abdul Majeed Dar, made a conditional offer of cease-fire to the Indian Government at a press conference in Srinagar on July 24, 2000. The endorsement of this offer by the group's supremo Syed Salahuddin followed in an Islamabad press conference on July 25. On August 3, 2000, a high-level official team of the Government of India visited Srinagar and conducted a meeting with Dar and his associates at the Nehru Guest House. However, on August 8, 2000, Syed Salahuddin 'withdrew' the cease-fire at a press conference in Islamabad, reportedly under pressure from the other terrorist groups and their handlers in Pakistan.

On March 23, 2003, Majeed Dar was shot dead by unidentified gunmen in the Noor Bagh area of Sopore Township in north Kashmir when two gun-wielding youth barged into his ancestral house and fired indiscriminately. Two terrorist groups claimed responsibility for Dar's killing: the hitherto little-known, 'Save Kashmir Movement', believed to be a front of the Al Umar Mujahideen, while claiming responsibility, labeled Dar as "an informant of Indian agencies" and "an enemy of the Kashmiri people." Separately, a person describing himself as the spokesperson of Al Nasireen, another obscure group, in a message to a local news agency, said that activists of his group killed Dar for his 'anti-movement activities'. Meanwhile, another person claiming to be a spokesperson for the HM called up the news agency and condemned Dar's killing. Dar had been a front ranking terrorist in the HM before his 'expulsion' in May 2002. In his capacity as 'deputy supreme commander', 'Military adviser' and 'chief commander of operations', Dar played a significant role in the indoctrination, recruitment, launching and training of Hizb cadres. Reports suggest that, while managing the Hizb training camps in Pakistan, he was the only Kashmiri terrorist who had direct access to Prime Minister Nawaz Sharief as also General Pervez Musharraf.

Dar's killing is the culmination of an almost three-year old battle for supremacy being waged by his followers against the faction led by Syed Salahuddin, the HM 'supreme commander[1] and chief of the 14-member United Jehad Council (UJC), a conglomerate of Pakistan-based terrorist organisations. The Dar initiated 'peace talks' led to dissent within the Hizb, with the Pakistani ranks fearing that an effective process of negotiations may actually be established, to the detriment of Pakistani interests. Subsequently, a war for supremacy ensued within the HM, and a distinctive 'bimodal' operating structure emerged, with separate factions owing allegiance to Dar and Salahuddin. Since the ill-fated peace talks, followers of Salahuddin - who operates from Pakistan - and Majeed Dar, who remained 'underground' in the Kashmir Valley, had a series of internecine clashes. In November 2002, two Salahuddin loyalists were killed in factional conflict reported at the Mirpur and Tarbela camps in PoK. The Hizb leadership in Pakistan has also issued statements claiming Dar's alleged alignment with Indian intelligence agencies. Reports suggest that Dar had been disillusioned with the Pakistani Inter Services Intelligence (ISI) and its military leadership. Dar was 'suspended' by the Salahuddin faction and replaced by Saiful Islam as the Hizb 'chief commander of operations' in Kashmir, on May 4, 2002. Two of his close associates, Assad Yazdani and Zaffar Abdul Fatah, were also 'removed' from positions of command. Again, on May 9, 2002, the Hizb leadership expelled another two 'divisional commanders' in south Kashmir. Even as Dar and his associates were accused of assisting Indian security forces, many of his loyalists were killed by cadres of the Salahuddin group. Faced with Dar's rising popularity within the HM ranks, Salahuddin and the ISI had, in the recent months before the former's death, initiated several moves to marginalize and target Dar and his associates in the terrorist ensemble.

The Salahuddin faction is also widely believed to have carried out the January 31, 2003, killing of the editor of *News and Feature Alliance* (NAFA), Parvaz Mohammad Sultan, in Srinagar. NAFA had been prominently reporting on the internal feud in the HM for the preceding two weeks prior to Sultan's killing. The NAFA reports had mentioned that the Valley-based faction led by Dar had 'overthrown' the Salahuddin faction. Within hours of Majeed Dar's murder clashes broke out at HM camps in PoK between the slain leader's followers and the faction led by Salahuddin. Violent confrontations are believed to have taken place at camps in Kotli, Mirpur, Oggi, Jungal-Mangal, Haripur and Gadhi-Dupatta. Reports have indicated that Salahuddin was fidgety over the prospect of an imminent test of strength in the camps.

In a major counter-insurgency operation on April 2, 2003, HM 'chief commander of operations', Saif-ul-lslam was killed at Nowgam Chowk, on the outskirts of Srinagar. Within a span of 10 days, two front ranking cadres of the HM had been liquidated. An emergency meeting of the 'command council' of the HM in Muzaffarabad named Ghazi Nasiruddin as the new chief for Kashmir, to succeed Saif-ul-Islam, on April 3. However, sources indicate that a process of churning is underway within the HM and its guardians in Pakistan. The HM has for long been regarded as having a considerable number of Kashmiris in its ranks. However, the relative dominance of foreign cadres within the HM has, in the past, progressively impaired the operational capacity of the group. Strained relations between local and foreign cadres have, at times, culminated in violent clashes in some places. Prior to his elevation as the 'chief commander', next only to chief Syed Salahuddin, Saif-ul-Islam had functioned as a 'divisional commander' in south Kashmir for seven years. When Salahuddin removed Abdul Majeed Dar and some 'divisional commanders' loyal to him in January 2002, Saif-ul-Islam was installed as 'chief commander of operations'. Dar had fallen out of favour with Salahuddin and the ISI ever since he announced an ill-fated cease-fire in July 2000.

Media reports have indicated that, two months prior to his death, Pakistani intelligence officials had been urging Majeed Dar to return to Pakistan. Although the Salahuddin-led faction was hostile to Dar, the ISI was keen on a rapprochement. More important, Dar believed that American pressure on Pakistan to move forward with the dialogue process would ensure his safety. But, subsequent events have proved otherwise and the recent killings have led to a split in the HM, with followers of the slain Dar saying that they were parting ways with 'supreme commander' Salahuddin. "We have launched our own faction of Hizbul Mujahideen," Tufail Ahmed, a former 'operational chief of the Hizb, and Dar supporter said in a March 27, 2003, report. Ahmed is the younger brother of Zafar Abdul Fateh, who was expelled along with Majeed Dar by Salahuddin in May 2002. He claimed that commanders of the new faction on both sides of the border had 'unanimously' appointed Ahmed Yasin as their 'chief commander'. "Around 40 per cent of the Hizb activists are with us," claimed Ahmed.

The two Hizb factions have often blamed each other for the arrest and deaths of their leaders in J&K. Seven Hizb 'chief operational commanders' have been killed in J&K since 1989, according to the *Daily Times*. They include Ahsan Dar, Ashraf Dar, Maqbool Allai, Commander Baangro, Naseerul Islam, Masood Nantary, and Abdul Majeed Dar. Barring Majeed Dar, all these 'commanders' were killed in encounters with the Indian security forces. Saif-ul-Islam's name now also belongs to this list. At least two of these 'commanders' were reportedly killed after they formed splinter Hizb factions.

## Links

The HM is closely linked to the Jamaat-e-Islami, both in the Kashmir Valley and in Pakistan. Overseas, it is allegedly backed by Ghulam Nabi Fai's Kashmir American Council and Ayub Thakur's World Kashmir Freedom Movement in the USA. Early in its history, the Hizb had established contacts with Afghan Mujahideen groups such as Hizb-e-Islami, under which some of its cadre is alleged to have received arms training.

The HM is reported to have a close association with the Pakistani Inter Services Intelligence and the United Jehad Council, and other terrorist organisations operating out of Pakistan. Hizb chief Syed Salahuddin also heads the UJC.

The proscribed Students Islamic Movement of India (SIMI) is also believed to have links with the Hizb-ul-Mujahideen.

## Lashkar-e-Toiba
## 'Army of the Pure'
## (Also spelt : Lashkar-e-Tayyaba)

### Formation

Formed in 1990 in the Kunar province of Afghanistan, the Lashkar-e-Toiba (also known as Jama'at-ud-Da'awa) is based in Muridke near Lahore in Pakistan and is headed by Hafiz Muhammad Saeed.

Its first presence in Jammu and Kashmir (J&K) was recorded in 1993 when 12 Pakistani and Afghan mercenaries infiltrated across the Line of Control (LoC) in tandem with the Islami Inquilabi Mahaz, a terrorist outfit then active in the Poonch district of J&K.

### 1. Proscription

The LeT is outlawed in India under the Unlawful Activities (Prevention) Act.

It was included in the Terrorist Exclusion List by the US Government on December 5, 2001. The US administration designated the Lashkar-e-Toiba as a FTO (Foreign Terrorist Organisation) on December 26, 2001. It is also a banned organization in Britain since March 30, 2001.

The group was proscribed by the United Nations in May, 2005.

The military regime of Gen. Pervez Musharraf banned the Lashkar-e-Toiba in Pakistan on January 12, 2002.

### 2. Objectives/Ideology

The LeT's professed ideology goes beyond merely challenging India's sovereignty over the State of Jammu and Kashmir. The Lashkar's 'agenda', as outlined in a pamphlet titled Why are we waging jihad includes the restoration of Islamic rule over all parts of India. Further, the outfit seeks to bring about a union of all Muslim majority regions in countries that surround Pakistan. Towards that end, it is active in Jammu and Kashmir, Chechnya and other parts of Central Asia.

Hafiz Saeed, a scholar of Islam, has said that the purpose of Jihad is to carry out a sustained struggle for the dominance of Islam in the entire world and to eliminate the evil forces and the ignorant. He considers India, Israel and US to be his prime enemies and has threatened to launch Fidayeen (suicide squad) attacks on American interests too.

The Lashkar-e-Toiba does not believe in democracy and nationalism. According to its ideology, it is the duty of every 'Momin' to protect and defend the interests of Muslims all over the world where Muslims are under the rule of non-Muslim in the democratic system. It has, thus chosen the path of Jihad as the suited means to achieve its goal. Cadres are drawn from the Wahabi school of thought.

Jihad, Hafiz Saeed said during the All Pakistan Ulema Convention held on July 17, 2003, at Lahore, is the only way Pakistan can move towards dignity and prosperity.

The LeT has consistently advocated the use of force and vowed that it would plant the 'flag of Islam' in Washington, Tel Aviv and New Delhi.

**3. Leadership and Command Structure**

The outfit's headquarters (200 acres) is located at Muridke, 30 kms from Lahore, which was built with contributions and donations from the Middle East, with Saudi Arabia being the biggest benefactor.

The headquarters houses a Madrassa (seminary), a hospital, a market, a large residential area for 'scholars' and faculty members, a fish farm and agricultural tracts. The LeT also reportedly operates 16 Islamic institutions, 135 secondary schools, an ambulance service, mobile clinics, blood banks and several seminaries across Pakistan.

LeT publishes its views and opinion through its Website (http://www.jamatuddawa.org/), an Urdu monthly journal, Al-Dawa, which has a circulation of 80,000, and an Urdu weekly, Gazwa. It also publishes Voice of Islam, an English monthly, and Al-Rabat - monthly in Arabic, Mujala-e-Tulba - Urdu monthly for students, Jehad Times - Urdu Weekly.

Hafiz Muhammad Saeed is the Amir (chief) of Lashkar-e-Toiba. While Yahiya Mujahid serves as the spokesman of the outfit, Maulana Abdul Wahid is one of the senior leaders. Abdullah Muntazer is the 'Spokesman for International Media' and editor of the outfit's Website. Saeed's son Talha reportedly looks after the LeT activity at its base camp in Muzaffarabad, capital of Pakistan occupied Kashmir. Saeed's son-in-law, Khalid Waleed, is reportedly part of the LeT office in Lahore.

According to a November 2005 report of Rediff, the LeT

leadership consisted of: Hafiz Mohammed Saeed (Supreme Commander); Zia-Ur-Rehman Lakhvi alias Chachaji (Supreme Commander, Kashmir); A. B. Rahman-Ur-Dakhil (Deputy Supreme Commander); Abdullah Shehzad alias Abu Anas alias Shamas (Chief Operations Commander, Valley); Abdul Hassan alias MY (Central Division Commander); Kari Saif-Ul-Rahman (North Division Commander); Kari Saif-Ul-Islam (Deputy Commander); Masood alias Mahmood (Area Commander, Sopore); Hyder-e-Krar alias Cl (Deputy Commander, Bandipora); Usman Bhai alias Saif-Ul-Islam (Deputy Commander, Lolab); Abdul Nawaz (Deputy Commander, Sogam); Abu Rafi (Deputy Divisional Commander, Baramulla); Abdul Nawaz (Deputy Commander, Handwara); Abu Museb alias Saifulla (Deputy Commander, Budgam).

Its cadres are organised at district levels with 'district commanders' in charge. Within Pakistan, the outfit has a network of training camps and branch offices, which undertake recruitment and collection of finances.

It comprises cadres mostly from Pakistan and Afghanistan and a sprinkling of militants from Sudan, Bahrain, Central Asia, Turkey and Libya. Funded, armed and trained by the Inter-Services Intelligence (ISI, the external intelligence agency of Pakistan), it has presently a little over 750 cadres (this number keeps changing) in Jammu and Kashmir (a vast majority of the foreign mercenaries operating in the Valley).

The policy making apex body consists of Amir (chief), Naib Amir (deputy chief) Finance chief etc. At the field level, it has Chief Commander, Divisional Commander, District Commander, Battalion Commander and down below on army pattern.

**4. Area of Operation**

While the primary area of operations of the Lashkar-e-Toiba is Jammu and Kashmir, the outfit has carried out attacks in other parts of India, including in New Delhi, Mumbai, Bangalore, Hyderabad, Varanasi, Kolkata, Gujarat, etc. It reportedly has cells in many cities/towns outside Jammu and Kashmir.

The LeT has been able to network with several Islamist extremist organizations across India, especially in J&K, Andhra Pradesh, Tamil Nadu, Karnataka, Maharashtra and Gujarat. LeT is actively engaged in subversive activities in the States of Maharashtra, West Bengal, Bihar, Hyderabad, Delhi, Haryana and

Uttar Pradesh at the instance of ISI to expand the frontier of violence outside J&K by subverting fringe elements. Of all the Pakistan-based terrorist groups, the LeT is the only group with support bases across India.

The Lashkar-e-Toiba has training camps spread across Pakistan and Pakistan occupied Kashmir (PoK). Its camps, recruitment centres/offices are spread across the length and breadth of Pakistan and PoK in Muzaffarabad, Lahore, Peshawar, Islamabad, Rawalpindi, Karachi, Multan, Quetta, Gujranwala, Sialkot, Gilgit (in the Northern Area of PoK), etc. LeT reportedly has 2,200 offices across Pakistan.

The LeT allegedly carried out the terrorist attack at the Indian Institute of Science campus in Bangalore on December 28, 2005, in which one person was killed. Earlier, on October 29, 2005, it engineered the serial explosions in New Delhi killing at least 62 persons. It is also suspected to have carried out the Varanasi attack on March 7, 2006 in which 21 civilians died and 62 others were injured; Three suspected LeT terrorists were shot dead during an abortive attempt to storm the headquarters of Rashtriya Swayamsevak Sangh (RSS), a right-wing Hindu organization, at Nagpur in Maharashtra on June 1, 2006; The LeT, according to Mumbai Police, carried out the 7/11 serial bombings in Mumbai in which at least 200 people were killed.

Arrests made during March-April 2004 near Baghdad brought to light links between the LeT and Islamist groups fighting the United States military in Iraq. In March - and possibly even earlier- United States forces detained Pakistani national Dilshad Ahmad and four others in Baghdad. Ahmad, a long-time Lashkar operative from the Bahawalpur area of the province of Punjab in Pakistan, had played a key role in the Lashkar's trans-Line of Control (LoC) operations, serving between 1997 and 2001 as the organisation's commander for the forward camps from where infiltrating groups of terrorists are launched into Jammu and Kashmir with Pakistani military support. Ahmad is believed to have made at least six secret visits to Lashkar groups operating in J&K during this period.

### 5. Training and Operational Strategies

The outfit provides training to both militant cadres and the Ulema (religious scholars). Its militant cadres are given two months training in the handling of AK series rifles, LMGs, pistols, rocket launchers and hand grenades. It also provides a 21-day training programme called Daura-e-Aam and a three months specialized training programme called Daura-e-Khas.

The Ulema are provided with a 42-days course. At the time of induction, the young recruits are made to go through a fresher course called Bait-ur-Rizwan.

Lashkar-e-Toiba is credited for having initiated the strategy of Fidayeen (suicide squad) attacks in J&K. It has formed two sub-groups called 'Jaan-e-Fidai' and 'Ibn-e-Tayamiah'. While the first group consists of highly motivated terrorists, the second comprises terrorists suffering from incurable diseases.

Compared to other terrorist outfits in J&K, the LeT has commanded significant attention primarily due to two reasons. First, for its well planned and executed attacks on security force (SF) targets and secondly, for the massacres of non-Muslim civilians. After the Kargil War of May-July 1999, (when Pakistani troops and mercenaries, including those of the Lashkar, were forced to withdraw from peaks on the Indian side of the Line of Control - LoC), the outfit launched its Fidayeen strategy whereby small groups (2-5 members) of Lashkar cadres would storm a security force camp or base. In another frequently used strategy, groups of Lashkar cadres, dressed in SF fatigues, would arrive at remote hill villages, round up Hindu or Sikh civilians, and massacre them. These two strategies have been designed to achieve maximum publicity and extract public allegiance, mainly out of fear. On December 8, 2001, two LeT suicide squad cadres managed to penetrate inside a SF convoy and opened fire killing one soldier. They were able to generate adequate confusion to escape from the convoy after the attack but were later killed in an encounter with another SF unit.

**6. Links**

It is closely linked to the Inter-Services Intelligence, the Taliban and **Al Qaeda.**

India's National Security Adviser M.K. Narayanan said on August 11, 2006, that the Pakistan-based Lashkar-e-Toiba is part of the "al Qaeda compact" and is "as big as and omnipotent" as the international terror network. "The Lashkar today has emerged as a very major force. It has connectivity with west Asia, Europe....Actually there was an LeT module broken in Virginia and some people were picked up. It is as big as and omnipotent as al

Qaeda in every sense of the term," he told a private news channel. Asked how significant the al Qaeda connection was in India, Narayanan said LeT was the "most visible manifestation" of the al Qaeda in India.

LeT has an extensive network that run across Pakistan and India with branches in Saudi Arabia, United Kingdom, Bangladesh and South East Asia.

The outfit collects donations from the Pakistani community in the Persian Gulf and United Kingdom, Islamic Non-Governmental Organizations, and Pakistani and Kashmiri businessmen. It receives considerable financial, material and other forms of assistance from the Pakistan government, routed primarily through the ISI. The ISI is the main source of LeT's funding. Saudi Arabia also provides funds.

The LeT maintains ties to various religious/military groups around the world, ranging from the Philippines to the Middle East and Chechnya primarily through the al Qaeda fraternal network.

The LeT has also been part of the Bosnian campaign against the Serbs.

It has allegedly set up sleeper cells in the U.S. and Australia, trained terrorists from other countries and has entered new theatres of Jihad like Iraq.

The group has links with many international Islamist terrorist groups like the Ikhwan-ul-Musalmeen of Egypt and other Arab groups.

LeT has a unit in Germany and also receives help from the Al Muhajiraun, supporter of Sharia Group, (Abu Hamza Masari - of Mosque Finsbury Park, North London) and its annual convention is regularly attended by fraternal bodies in Saudi Arabia, Kuwait, Yemen, Bahrain, Oman, Kosovo, Bangladesh, Myanmar, USA, Palestine, Bosnia, Philippines, Jordan, Chechnya, etc.

It also has links with the International Sikh Youth Federation (Lakhbir Singh Rode).

**7. Finances**

The outfit collects donations from the Pakistani community in the Persian Gulf and United Kingdom, Islamic Non-Governmental Organizations, and Pakistani and Kashmiri businessmen. It receives considerable financial, material and other forms of assistance from the Pakistan government, routed primarily through the ISI. The ISI is the main source of LeT's funding. Funds also come from some sources in Saudi Arabia.

Finances are also generated through Hawala transaction and through infiltrating groups and other conduits.

According to Mohammad Omar Rana, the expenditure on its militia alone is around 35 crores of rupees per annum.

**8. Weapons and Training**

AK series rifles, LMG/HMG's, Hand Grenades, Rockets, Pistols, Mortars, Anti-tank mines, Anti personnel mines, Anti Aircraft Gun, Remote Control Device, explosive devices and sophisticated communication system.

Lashkar-e-Tayyaba was proscribed in 2002 but continues to operate till date under the new name of Jamat-ul-Dama. There appears to be "globalized" elements within the LeT that are suspected to the pursuing an operational agenda that extend well beyond India.[26] The arrest of Abu Zubaydah in 2002 at a LeT safe house in Faisalabad, high lights the fact that the members of the Group have actively cooperated with Al Qaeda and possibly assisted with the movement of cadres through out Pakistan.[27]

Besides the above, there have been claims that the LeT has been instrumental in recruiting and training Islamists to engage American forces in Iraq.[28] Again, there were claims in the wake of the July 2005 London bombing that the LeT had provided some form of training to foreign jihadis who were keen to carry out terrorist attacks in western capitals. Three of the four 'British citizens'—note the fact that the Western analysts would not like to use the term 'British terrorists' which in fact these so-called 'citizens' were!—involved in the 5/11 bombings had ethnic ties to Pakistan. At least one, Shehzad Tanweer, visited the LeT headquarters in Muridke, some 20 miles from Lahore.[29]

## "Lashkar as big a threat to U.S., U.K. as Al Qaeda" CIA

The CIA has told President Barack Obama that the British-born Pakistani terrorists, who have extensive contacts with LET, are the biggest threat to the US, a British daily reported in February 2009.[30] American spy chiefs have told the President that the CIA has launched a vast spying operation in Britain to prevent a repeat of the 9/11 attacks being launched from Britain.

U.S. intelligence Chiefs believe that a British-born Pakistani extremist entering the U.S. under a current visa waiver programme for all Britons is the most likely source of another terrorist spectacular on American soil. A former CIA officer, who has advised Obama, told the daily that the CIA has stepped up its British operations after the November 2008 Mumbai massacre by the LeT, which has an extensive web of supporters in Britain, and is now as big a threat to the U.K. and U.S. as the al Qaeda.

Bruce C Riedel told the daily : "The British Pakistani community is recognized as probably al Qaeda's best mechanism for launching an attack against North America".

"The Americans run their own assets in the Pakistani Community; they get their own intelligence. There is close cooperation with MI5 but they don't tell us the names of all their sources," he said.

## Jaish-e-Mohammed (Army of the Prophet)

The Jaish-e-Mohammed (JeM) has been held responsible for the December 13, 2001 terrorist attack on the Indian Parliament in New Delhi. The outfit has been banned by the Indian government under provisions of the Prevention of Terrorism Act (POTA) on October 25, 2001. The US Secretary of State, Colin Powell, in a notification on December 26, 2001, designated the outfit as a foreign terrorist organisation.

### Evolution of Group

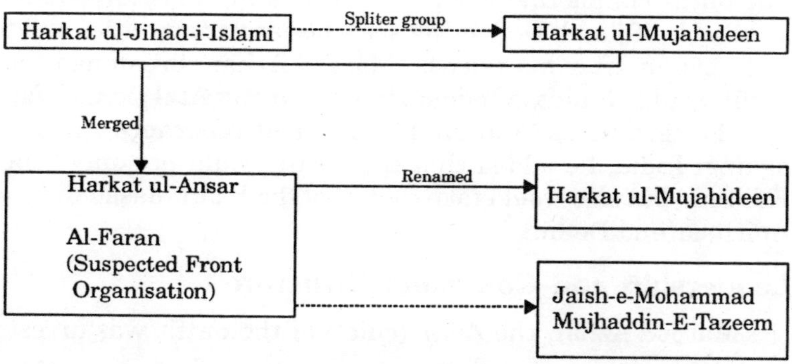

## Formation

The Jaish-e-Mohammed (JeM) is a relatively new terrorist outfit, compared to other major outfits active in Jammu and Kashmir (J&K). Like the Lashkar-e-Toiba (LeT), the JeM too is an outfit formed, controlled and manned by Pakistan. The outfit was launched on January 31, 2000, by Maulana Masood Azhar in Karachi after he was released from an Indian jail during the terrorists for hostage swap of December 31, 1999, following the hijacking of the Indian Airlines Flight IC 814.

The formation of the outfit was endorsed by three religious school chiefs, Mufti Nizamuddin Shamzai of the Majlis-e-Tawan-e-Islami (MT), Maulana Mufti Rashid Ahmed of the Dar-ul Ifta-e-wal-Irshad and Maulana Sher Ali of the Sheikh-ul-Hadith Dar-ul Haqqania.

The outfit's creation can be linked to the popularity surrounding Masood Azhar after his release from India. Maulana Masood Azhar was the general secretary of the newly established Harkat-ul-Ansar (HuA) in 1994 and was on a 'mission' in J&K when he was arrested on February 11. When he was released, the HuA had been included in the US list of Foreign Terrorist Organisations which had compelled the outfit to rename itself as the Harkat-ul-Mujahideen (HuM). However, Masood Azhar decided to float the new outfit JeM rather than rejoin his old outfit. He was also reported to have received assistance in setting up the JeM from Pakistan's Inter-Services Intelligence (ISI), the then *Taliban* regime in Afghanistan, *Osama bin Laden* and several Sunni sectarian outfits of Pakistan.

## Objectives

The Jaish-e-Mohammed is part of the Islamist terror network with its base in Pakistan and active in the terrorist violence in J&K. The outfit, like other terrorist outfits in J&K, claims to using violence to force a withdrawal of Indian security forces from J&K. The outfit claims that each of its offices in Pakistan would serve as schools of jihad. Delivering speeches at various cities and towns in Pakistan after his release, Masood Azhar threatened that the outfit would eliminate Indian Prime Minister Atal Behari Vajpayee who he termed as 'Abu Jahl' (Father of Ignorance). In its fight against India, he added that the outfit would not only "liberate" Kashmir, but also would take control of the Babri Masjid in Ayodhya, Amritsar and Delhi.

## Leadership and Command Structure

Masood Azhar, the *Amir* (chief) of the outfit was arrested by

Pakistani security forces on December 29, 2001, after pressure from India and other foreign countries following the December 13, 2001 attack on India's Parliament. However, a three-member Review Board of Lahore High Court ordered on December 14, 2002, that Azhar be released.

There are no reports of any formal governing bodies or councils within the outfit. Unconfirmed reports indicate that the prominent office bearers of the organisation include.

(*a*) Maulana Masood Azhar - Amir

(*b*) Maulana Qari Mansoor Ahmed - Nazim Propaganda Wing (he is a resident of Bhurewala, Punjab)

(*c*) Maulana Abdul Jabbar - Nazim, Military Affairs (Former Nazim military affairs, (HuM)

(*d*) Maulana Sajjad Usman - Incharge, Finance (Former HuM Nazim Finance)

(*e*) Shah Nawaz Khan alias Sajjid Jehadi & Gazi Baba - Chief Commander J&K (Former Supreme Commander HuM, J&K)

(*f*) Maulana Mufti Mohd. Asghar - Launching Commander (Former Launching Commander of HuM)

## Operational Strategies

Most Jaish-e-Mohammed attacks have been described as *fidayeen* (suicide terrorist) attacks. In this mode, terrorists of the outfit storm a high security target, including security forces' bases, camps and convoys. After storming, they either fortify themselves within the target, killing as many security force personnel and civilians as possible before they are killed by retaliatory action. In other cases, they kill and injure as many as possible before attempting to escape.

## Area of Operation

The Jaish-e-Mohammed has largely confined its operations within J&K. The only recorded instance of its operations outside J&K has been the December 13, 2001, Parliament attack in New Delhi. However, several of its cadre have, on occasions been arrested or killed by security forces in states other than J&K.

## External Linkages

The outfit is closely linked, through the Binoria Madrassah in Karachi, with the former *Taliban* regime of Afghanistan and its protege, *Osama bin Laden* and his *Al-Qaeda*. JeM chief, Masood Azhar was released by Indian authorities in Kandahar and has reportedly met Taliban and Al Qaeda leaders in Afghanistan on various occasions.

The JeM is also reported to have links with Sunni terrorist outfits operating in Pakistan such as the Sipah-e-Sahaba Pakistan (SSP)and Lashkar-e-Jhangvi (LeJ).

Bahawalpur in Pakistan's Punjab serves as headquarters of the JeM. The outfit maintains two physical mailing addresses for its Central Office in Bahawalpur[30] :

- Post Box No 7, GPO Bahawalpur
- House No. F-16
  Ehsan Colony
  Bahawalpur

## Harkat-ul-Mujahideen (Formerly known as Harkat Ul-Ansar)

The Harkat-ul-Mujahideen (HuM), a Pakistan-based terrorist outfit, has been in existence twice in the history of that country's involvement in cross-border terrorism. In the interim between the two phases, it continued to exist, but under the name of the Harkat-ul-Ansar (HUA). While the first renaming was an outcome of a reorganisation effected by the Inter-Services Intelligence (ISI), Pakistan's external intelligence agency, among its various sponsored terrorist outfits in Jammu and Kashmir (J&K), the second renaming was necessitated by a US proscription of the outfit.

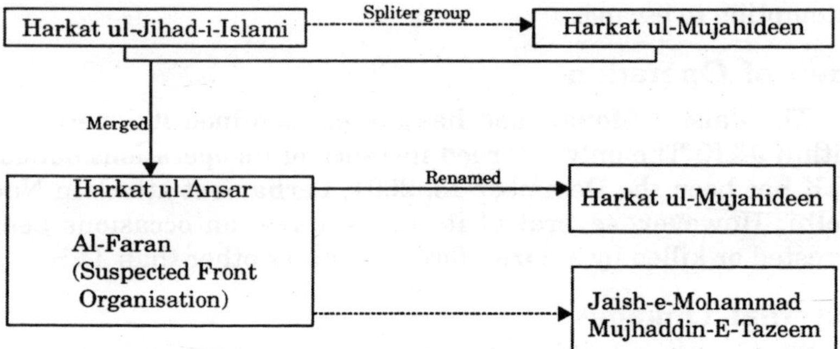

The HuA was categorised as a terrorist outfit by the US in 1997 following reports that it was linked with Osama bin Laden, and his Al Qaeda, a global terrorist network that has struck at several US targets around the world. The outfit immediately adopted the name of Harkat-ul-Mujahideen to escape the ramifications of the proscription. Despite public knowledge that the HuM was a recast version of the HuA, the US had refused to categories the outfit as a terrorist outfit. However, following the September 11, 2001 terrorist attacks on New York and Washington in the US, the outfit came under scrutiny of the US government for its extensive links with Osama bin Laden, the prime suspect in the terrorist attacks. On September 25, US President George W. Bush signed an order officially banning the outfit.

The HuM was originally formed in 1985, to participate in the *Jehad* against Soviet forces protecting the Communist regime in Afghanistan. It was formed by a group that walked out of another jehadi group, the Harkat-ul-Jihad-al-Islami (HuJI). With the Soviet withdrawal from Afghanistan in 1989, the outfit turned its attention to J&K, where terrorist violence had been unleashed by Pakistan supported outfits in 1988.

As the organisation chart shows, the Harkat-ul-Mujahideen merged with another terror outfit, the Harkat-ul-Jehad-al-Islami (HuJI), to form the Harkat-ul-Ansar (HuA) in 1993. This merger apparently failed to form an effective instrument for Pakistan's campaign in J&K as Indian security forces (SFs) arrested three of its top leaders in quick succession. First, Nasrullah Mansur Langrayal, chief of the former Harkat-ul Mujahideen was arrested in November 1993. Three months later, the HuA's General Secretary, Maulana Masood Azhar, and its J&K unit chief Sajjad Afghani were arrested in Srinagar.

The HuA made several attempts to obtain the release of the arrested leaders by abducting SF personnel and foreign tourists and using them as hostages. In the first attempt, made in January 1994, two SF personnel were abducted and subsequently killed when the government refused to release the leaders. A second attempt was made in June 1994 when two foreign tourists were abducted. Following local outcry against these abductions, the hostages were released without any success in their objective. In the third attempt made in October 1994, four foreign tourists were abducted in New Delhi and held in Uttar Pradesh and a demand was again made for the release of the arrested leaders. SFs however, ascertained the terrorist hideout and effected a successful rescue operation and also arrested the leader of the abductors, Umar Saeed Sheikh, a British student of Pakistani origin.

In the fourth attempt, made by a front outfit, Al-Faran in July 1995, six hostages were abducted from various locations. While one managed to escape, the body of the second was recovered in August 1995. The government refused to accept the demands of the abductors and since then there has been no news on the fate of the hostages. It is widely suspected that having failed in their mission, the abductors killed the hostages. These incidents as also reports that the outfit was linked to Osama bin Laden prompted the US government to declare the HuA as a terrorist outfit in 1997. To avoid the repercussions of the ban, the HuA decided to recast itself as the Harkat-ul-Mujahideen.

Meanwhile, Sajjad Afghani was killed during a jailbreak attempt in June 1999. Subsequently, suspected HuM terrorists, hijacked the Indian Airlines Flight IC 814 from Kathmandu, Nepal, forced the pilot to fly to Kandahar, Afghanistan and with the protection and support of the Taliban regime, successfully obtained the release of Maulana Masood Azhar, Umar Saeed Sheikh and Mushtak Ahmed Zargar, commander of the *Al Umar,* a militant group with a predominantly Kashmiri cadre base. The demand for the release of Zargar appeared to be a ploy to convey the impression that the hijacking was conducted for the sake of Kashmiris rather than foreign mercenaries. Certain news reports had speculated that Masood Azhar's brother led the hijackers and his father financed the whole operation.

As mentioned before, the 1993 merger of the Harkat-ul-Mujahideen and the HuJI was not a successful venture. SF sources in India have reported that terrorists claiming allegiance to the three outfits, HuJI, HuM and HuA, have been either arrested or killed throughout the 13-year insurgency in the State.

The HuM's operational capabilities had been severely curtailed by the formation of the Jaish-e-Mohammed (JeM) by Masood Azhar, immediately after his release. News reports from Pakistan suggested that the JeM had weaned away several HuM cadre and other resources. Subsequently, only isolated instances have been reported from J&K where cadre of the HuM have been involved.

## Al-Rashid Trust

The Karachi based Al-Rashid Trust (ART) is one of the 27 groups and organisations listed by the US State Department on September 22, 2001, for involvement in financing and supporting a network of international Islámist terrorist groups. In response, the trust, on October 4, 2001, said that it would challenge the US decision in the International Court of Justice (ICJ) at the Hague.

### Formation

Mufti Mohammed Rashid founded the Al-Rashid Trust (ART) on February 13, 1996, in Karachi. The Trust gradually grew to operate 21 branches across Pakistan. A day after the US announcement of the ban on the outfit, the State Bank of Pakistan issued a circular asking banks to freeze the accounts of Al-Rashid Trust.

### Objectives

Described as a 'welfare organization', one of its original charters was to carry out welfare projects within Pakistan, with financial resources provided by public donations. Overtime, the ART expanded its mandate to carry out 'relief activities' for Muslims in Chechnya, Kosovo and Afghanistan. The ART perceives the various non-governmental organisations (NGOs) currently working in Afghanistan as 'enemies of the Muslims' and media reports have indicated that one of the other significant objectives of the ART is to reportedly push Western NGOs out of Afghanistan. The ART subscribes to the Deobandi school of thought, a trait it shares with the Taliban. The trust also promotes the concept of *Jehad* among Muslims, especially at times and in places where it perceives the community of faithful is being 'oppressed'. One of the numerous ART booklets states, "the holy war is an essential element of Islam." "Any Moslem must carry the weapons, even with the mosque, if the need would be felt to make fire on a not-Moslem", states another work written by Mufti Rashid Ahmed, ART literature also denounces the United States for its policies toward Israel, Iraq and Saudi Arabia and praises Islamist terrorists. Among the other ART objectives is providing assistance to 'illegally jailed' Muslim prisoners, 'cleansing' the media of pornography and creating books "to promote in the people and the elite the fear of the Last [Judgment] Day."

## Leadership and Structure

Headquartered at Karachi, the ART has 21 branches in Pakistan. Mufti (religious leader) Mohammed Rashid is the amir (leader) of the trust. Rashid Ahmed teaches at a *madrassa* (religious seminary) - Darul Ifta-e-Wal Irshad - that he also runs. Maulvi Suleyman, an important functionary, is reported to be actually managing the ART affairs. Mufti Abu Lubaba is the ideologue, while Maulvi Sibghatullah of the Dar-ul-Uloom (religious school) in Karachi is the Director of ART in Kandahar, the southern Afghan city that served as the headquarters for the erstwhile Taliban regime. Only Mufti Rashid and Lubaba are reported to have had direct access to Osama bin Laden in Afghanistan. Abdul Hadi Mullakhel is the ART representative in Kabul.

It publishes an Urdu newspaper *Zarb-e-Momin* as well as an English paper, *Dharb-e-Momin,* and also runs a radio station out of Kabul. They carry reports on the *Jehadi* activities of the Taliban and the Pakistan-based terrorist outfit Jaish-e-Mohammed (JeM). Considered as one of the sectarian publications in Pakistan, *Dharb-e-Momin* is reported to contain anti-American and anti-Western propaganda. The newspaper has a web-site, which specifically endorses the Taliban's style of governance and is widely considered to be the mouthpiece of the Taliban. During his detention in Jammu and Kashmir (J&K), JeM chief Maulana Masood Azhar is reported to have sent articles clandestinely to the Al Rashid Trust and these were published in the *Dharb-e-Momin.* In one of these articles published on October 31, 1999, Azhar praised the services of Mufti Rashid Ahmed, opining that due to his services, "the Taliban gained strength and the long porous border of Pakistan became so safe that not a single army guard is needed there. If instead of the Taliban, Ahmad Shah Masood who is the enemy of Pakistan and ally of India had been the ruler of Afghanistan, Pakistan would have been surrounded by enemies on all four sides."

Among others, its offices in Pakistan are located at Lahore, Mansehra, Peshawar, Rawalpindi, and Mingora. ART operations in Afghanistan are located at Jalalabad, Kabul, Kandahar and Mazar-e-Sharif.

Al-Rashid documents indicate that the Trust secures most of its finances from *zakat* (annual alms) and overseas donations. However, the sources of donation are kept secret.

## Linkages

The Al-Rashid Trust is reported to be one of Osama bin Laden's many sources of income. It is closely linked with the Taliban as also with Jaish-e-Mohammed (JeM) and other terrorist outfits active in India's Jammu and Kashmir. The trust's formation coincided with the Taliban capture of Afghanistan in 1996. Some of its members are alleged to have secured military training in Afghanistan. The ART and JeM are reported to share office spaces across Pakistan with a certain overlapping of cadre strength. Maulana Masood Azhar, JeM chief is a regular writer in the *Zarb-e-Momin.* The trust is reportedly incharge of the foreign funds of JeM. Mufti Rashid Ahmed is also reported to have appointed Masood Azhar as the Amir of Taliban in Jammu and Kashmir. Mufti Rashid was also instrumental in setting up JeM's office near Usmani Masjid in Lahore and other places in Pakistan occupied Kashmir (PoK). The ART was initially linked with the Harkat-ul-Ansar (HUA) before the formation of JeM. It is also reported to be linked to the Pakistan-based Lashkar-e-Toiba (LeI). Al-Rashid is also suspected to have provided logistical support to the Taliban and the foreign mercenaries in Afghanistan.

The biggest source of funds for the Al-Rashid Trust is the Middle East and Pakistan. It also has a network in South Africa. Pakistani banks - consequent to the September 22, US State Department listing of ART as being involved in financing and supporting a network of international Islamist terrorist groups - froze Al-Rashid's bank accounts. In response, the Al Rashid Trust has said that that its activities, which include providing financial and legal support to jailed Muslim militants around the world, are purely humanitarian.

In year 2000, according to Pakistani media reports, Al-Rashid sent US $750,000 in cash to Chechnya after alleging that aid sent to Chechnya through the UN never reached the Chechen Muslims. The amount was reportedly handed over to the head of an unidentified religious party of Chechnya, headed by Sheikh Omer Bin Ismail Dawood and Zelim Khan, the former Chechen President. Al-Rashid is also reported to have sent Rs. 20 million in cash to the Taliban and Rs. 2.1 million to Kosovo.

## Activities

With charity and relief work as its professed goals, the Al-Rashid Trust says that its activities include providing financial and legal support to jailed Muslim militants around the world, and that all of its actions are purely humanitarian. Its most recent project was one to provide food for the poor in Afghanistan. The project was conceived following a conflict between the United Nations and the Taliban over the running of bakeries. Consequently, the ART set up its own bakeries in Kabul, Herat, Jalalabad, Kandahar and Mazar-e-Sharif. The trust also took over 155 bakeries vacated by the UN's World Food Program (WFP) when it pulled out following the September 11 terrorist attacks in the US. The annual budget for this program is approximately US$4 million. The ART plans to provide bread to 25,000 people, and it aims to set up bakeries in another 14 provinces in the near future. ART's Afghanistan operations became prominent when it began to operate a subsidised bakery project in Kabul, after that project was abandoned by the United Nations World Food Programme (UNWFP) over differences with the Taliban on employment of women for a survey.

The ART is reported to have many other functioning projects in Afghanistan. It reportedly sent 1,000 sewing machines to the country in June 2001 to help the 'widows of war', and it is scheduled to send another 1,000 for the same purpose.

According to ART sources, it sends more than US$1 million worth of goods, food, medicine and other relief items into Afghanistan on a weekly basis. It is reported to have sent more than 70 truckloads of relief goods up to November 2001. Al-Rashid also recently opened clinics in Kandahar, Kabul and Ghazni.

Al-Rashid Trust has been involved in the establishment of a network of *madrassas* in Afghanistan. It has also built many mosques across the country. Media reports indicated that prior to the US bombing of Afghanistan, it was building 20 mosques along the Kabul-Kandahar highway, and five mosques on the Kandahar-Chaman highway.

The trust runs many *madrassas* and mosques in Pakistan including the largest Arabia-Islamia, on the Karakoram Highway in Mansehra. The network of ART aided Deobandi *madrassas* in Pakistan reportedly act as recruiting centres for *Jehadis*. It also runs a hospital in Muzaffarabad in Pakistan occupied Kashmir (PoK) for the treatment of injured terrorists.

In Afghanistan, the Al-Rashid Trust coordinates its activities with an Arab NGO, Wafa Khairia, which was formed by Osama bin Laden and other Arab-Afghans as a reciprocal gesture for being provided hospitality in Afghanistan. The Wafa Khairia is reported to be largely funded by bin Laden.

The Al-Rashid Trust claims to be the first Muslim organisation in the world to send aid to the refugees and war-hit people of Chechnya. Furthermore, it is also reported to be carrying out 'welfare work' in Kashmir, Kosovo and the Central Asian states besides Afghanistan. It also accepts 'donations' for Kashmir *Jehad* and the *mujahideen* of Kashmir. It publishes advertisements in the Pakistani press soliciting funds for 'welfare work' in Kashmir, Chechnya, Kosovo etc, and also informs prospective donors that it will decide on the means of spending the money. Its advertisements reportedly list all its accounts with Karachi's Habib Bank, providing separate account numbers for donations received in dollars or pounds sterling.

The Al Rashid Trust said on October 4, 2001 that it would challenge the US decision in the International Court of Justice (ICJ) at Hague. Claiming that it has "no links with any sort of terrorism," the ART in-charge in Islamabad, Mohammed Arshad, said that his organisation has appealed to the Pakistan government to de-freeze its accounts and added that it planned to go to the ICJ to contest the US proscription. Despite the ban, media reports have indicated that it was still operating in Pakistan and all its offices were open. Pakistan's Foreign Office Spokesman Riaz Mohammad Khan said on October 3 that Islamabad would ask the US government to furnish details of the Trust's involvement in terrorist activities.

## Al-Akhtar Trust

The Karachi-based Al-Akhtar Trust (AAT) was on October 14, 2003, listed by the US Treasury Department as a Specially Designated Global Terrorist entity under Executive Order 13224 for its alleged involvement in financing and supporting a network of international Islamist terrorist groups, including the Al Qaeda.

## Formation and Objectives

The Al-Akhtar Trust was reportedly formed in November 2000 to provide financial assistance for Islamist extremists, including the Taliban and to feed, clothe and educate the children of religious "martyrs."

## Leadership and Headquarters

Mohammad Mazhar is the President of the Al-Akhtar Trust, which is headquartered in Karachi's Gulshan-e-Iqbal area.

## Linkages

The AAT is reportedly linked to the Al Qaeda network of Osama bin Laden. It has been accused by the US of being a terrorist financier, assisting the Al Qaeda and attempting to raise money for attacks in Iraq.

It is reportedly linked to the Jaish-e-Mohammed (JeM), a terrorist group which is active in the Indian State of Jammu and Kashmir (Jammu and Kashmir). According to the U.S. authorities, following the January 2002 house arrest of JeM chief Maulana Masood Azhar, the outfit's cadres set up two organizations registered in Pakistan as humanitarian aid agencies: the Al-Akhtar Trust and Alkhair Trust. JeM, it is alleged, hoped to give the impression that the two new organizations were separate entities and sought to use them as a way to deliver arms and ammunition to their cadres under the guise of providing humanitarian aid to refugees and other needy groups.

The Trust is also reportedly linked to another terrorist group active in J&K, the Harkat-ul-Mujahideen (HuM).

Among the other Pakistan-based groups, the AAT is linked to the Lashkar-e-Toiba (LeT) and the proscribed Sunni group Lashkar-e-Jhangvi (LeJ).

## Activities

The US Treasury Department in its fact sheet has alleged that the AAT clandestinely treated Al Qaeda terrorists injured during fighting in Afghanistan and Pakistan in year 2001. It is also accused of being involved in financing and supporting a network of international Islamist terrorist groups and bin Laden's followers in Afghanistan, raising money for Islamist extremists trying to infiltrate Iraq and maintaining links with an individual believed to have been involved in the abduction and murder of *Wall Street Journal* reporter Daniel Pearl.

The State Bank of Pakistan had frozen the bank accounts of the trust in May 2003 to which the trust has challenged in the High Court of Sindh.

The AAT, which runs medical centers in Karachi, Pakistan, and Spin Boldak in Afghanistan, has offices in Bawalnagar, Gilgit, Mirpur Khas, Islamabad and other Pakistani cities.

During a custodial interview in early 2003, according to the US Treasury Department, a senior Al Qaeda detainee related that the Al Akhtar Trust and Al-Rashid Trust were the primary relief agencies that Al Qaeda used to move supplies into Kandahar in Afghanistan. In 2002, the Al-Rashid Trust and Al Akhtar Trust decided to start a drive to collect donations from the business/ industrial circles of Pakistan. Mullah Izatullah, an Al Qaeda official living in Chaman, Pakistan, was associated with both Al-Rashid Trust and Al Akhtar Trust. Al-Rashid Trust was designated by the U.S. on September 23, 2001 and by the United Nations (UN) 1267 Sanctions Committee on October 6, 2001. The U.S. Government has indicated that, as of mid-March 2002, Al Akhtar Trust was conducting all activities of the Former Al-Rashid Trust.

According to the US Treasury Department, during a custodial interview in mid-April 2003, a senior Al Qaeda detainee stated that the Al-Rashid Trust and Al Akhtar Trust provided donations to Al Qaeda. While Al Qaeda was based in Kandahar, Afghanistan, these organizations provided donations in the form of blankets and clothing to Al Qaeda cadres. When Al Qaeda operatives fled from Kandahar in late 2001, these organizations provided the families of Al Qaeda operatives with financial assistance.

The Trust is accused of providing financial and logistical support as well as arranging travel for many Islamist extremists.

According to information available to the U.S. Government from March 2003, an associate of the AAT was attempting to raise funds in order to finance "obligatory jihad" in Iraq.

A financier of the Al-Akhtar Trust, identified as Al-Saud Memon, is also reported to be linked to the abduction and murder of Daniel Pearl. After the murder, Pakistani security agencies sealed Memon's home in Karachi. Memon remains one of the key figures still at large in the Daniel Pearl case.

## Rabita Trust

The US State Department on September 23, 2001 categorised the RT as an organisation linked to international terrorism. The US administration has pointed out that the Rabita Trust is part of a web of charities funding Islamist terrorist movements such as Osama bin Laden's Al Qaeda network.

### Formation

Rabita Trust (RT) was formed in 1988 during the term of the then President Ziaul Haq, who was its founding Chairman, with the aim of organising the repatriation and rehabilitation of stranded Pakistanis from Bangladesh.

### Objectives

The Rabita Trust describes itself as a "a popular, international, Islamic and non-governmental organization, at which Muslims from all over the world are represented." It is a charitable organization that assists Afghan refugees in Pakistan. The main objectives of the Rabita Trust are to disseminate Islamic *Dawah* (culture) and expound the teachings of Islam, and to 'defend' Islamic causes in a manner that safeguards the interests and aspirations of Muslims, solves their problems, refutes false allegations against Islam, and repels inimical trends and dogma which the enemies of Islam seek to exploit in order to destroy the unity of Muslims and to sow seeds of doubt in the Muslim brethren.

### Leadership and Structure

Jeddah-based Saudi businessman Wael Hamza Jalaidan is the Secretary-General of Rabita Trust. Jalaidan is reported to be a founding member of Osama bin Laden's Al Qaeda terrorist network and is also considered to be its chief of logistics and had fought along with bin Laden against the Soviet troops in Afghanistan. He was also temporarily head of the Saudi Red Crescent Society and the Muslim World League during his stay in Afghanistan. He reportedly developed strong linkages with leaders of the various Afghan factions, in his capacity as an official incharge of distributing large scale Saudi relief aid to Afghan refugees. He had also established linkages with the then Pakistani President Zia-ul-Haq and his successor former Prime Minister Nawaz Sharif. Jalaidan was one of the three persons during that period who represented Arabs assigned to Afghanistan and Pakistan. The other two were Abdullah Azzam and Osama Bin Laden. Jalaidan is considered to be an expert in arms transportation and distribution. Jalaidan left Afghanistan at the end of 1992 and thereafter settled in Saudi Arabia and is reported to have engaged in 'commercial activities'. He then joined the 'aid operations' to Bosnia, where he supervised temporarily the Saudi Aid Committee, the largest aid organization then in Bosnia. He also assumed the office of the supervisor of the Muslim World League endowments. Jalaidan is also reported to have lived in Arizona, USA, in the early 1980s and headed an Islamic centre there before joining bin Laden in the fight against the Soviets in Afghanistan.

President Pervez Musharraf was one of the patrons of Rabita Trust. Media reports quoting US sources have indicated that the US administration had warned the Pakistani President of the impending order against the Rabita Trust and encouraged him to disassociate himself from the trust. A Pakistani government spokesperson clarified on October 15 that the post of Chairman of the RT being an ex-officio position had been with the Prime Minister and after taking over as Chief Executive, General Pervez Musharraf became the Chairman, but never presided over any of the trust meetings. The spokesperson also said that the President had ordered an audit of the accounts of Rabita Trust by a private firm to ascertain whether its funds were used for any other purpose than the repatriation of stranded Pakistanis from Bangladesh. Simultaneously, the Auditor General of Pakistan is also reported to be carrying out an audit of the trust.

The members of the trust included Pakistan's ministers of finance and interior, Saudi Prince Talal ibn Abdul Aziz, secretary-generals of the Muslim World League and the International Islamic Relief Organization and President of the Council of Saudi Chamber of Commerce. The governing body of RT comprises an equal number of members from the Government of Pakistan and the Saudi-based Rabita Alam Al-Islami.

The RT secures its finances primarily from Saudi businessmen. Rabita Alam Al-Islami had contributed Rs. 50 million while the share of the Pakistan government was Rs. 250 million when the trust was established. The trust had constructed 1,000 houses in

Mian Channu, Punjab, during the early 1990s and it was the only expenditure incurred by the trust in this regard. The last meeting of the RT held in 1997 was presided over by the then Pakistani Premier Nawaz Sharif as Chairman. Currently, the secretary Cabinet Division holds the charge of Chairman of the trust.

### Linkages

Peshawar in Pakistan was the main depot for smuggling arms into Afghanistan and other bordering points and with the help of Azzam, Jalaidan was able to smuggle arms not only into central Afghanistan but further into the northern parts. Rabita Trust is affiliated with a Saudi-based Pan Islamic organisation Rabita Alam-e-Islami or the Muslim World League, which is known in different countries with different names. In Pakistan, they have links with the Jamaat-e-Islam (JeI).

The RT is also linked to the U.K. based International Islamic Relief Organisation (IIRO). Media reports indicate that Muhammad Jamal Khalifa, brother-in-law of Osama bin Laden, heads the IIRO branch office in Philippines. Khalifa is reported to be the intermediary between bin Laden and the Abu Sayaf terrorist groups.

## Ummah Tamir-e-Nau (Reconstruction of the Muslim Ummah)

### Formation

Dr. Sultan Bashiruddin Mahmood, former Director General of the Pakistan Atomic Energy Commission (PAEC), formed the Ummah Tamir-e-Nau (UTN) in March 2000 after his resignation from the PAEC in 1999. Bashiruddin Mahmood was arrested on October 23, 2001, from Islamabad along with his associate Abdul Majeed (arrested in Lahore) for their alleged links to Osama bin Laden's Al Qaeda network.

### Leadership, Structure and Overground Activities

Mahmood is the Chairman of UTN, which is registered as a non-governmental Afghan relief agency. Chaudhary Abdul Majeed, a former senior scientist at the PAEC, who also resigned in 1999, is a prominent member of the UTN. The UTN has seven Directors, Arshad Ali Chaudhary, a retired air force commander and Vice

President of the foundation; Humayun Niaz, a former naval officer and businessman with ties to the erstwhile Nawaz Sharif government and the foundation's Finance Director; retired Brig. Mohammed Hanif, a career army engineer; Mirza Baig, an industrialist with the biggest foundry in Pakistan; and Sheikh Mohammed Tufail, the owner of one of Pakistan's leading engineering companies.

Ummah Tamir-e-Nau calls itself "an organisation engaged in relief, rehabilitation and reconstruction activities". UTN refers to the greater Islamic community, transcending national boundaries. The declared objective of the UTN was to attract foreign investment, especially from Muslim countries, to Afghanistan for the rehabilitation of the war-ravaged country. It was involved in voluntary work including rebuilding schools, hospitals, and providing medical supplies, etc. Mahmood had been working recently on certain projects in Afghanistan including land development and education reforms. Among the humanitarian projects were the provision of mobile health units and primary school course books.

UTN has posted fliers in some Islamabad hospitals seeking volunteer doctors and paramedics for humanitarian work in Afghanistan. Bashiruddin Mahmood's son's phone number is reportedly given as a contact number.

Mahmood is reported to have travelled frequently to Afghanistan for 'land development research'. As poppy is no more being cultivated in Afghanistan, his efforts were reportedly directed towards substitute crops.

Mirza Baig also had extensive ties with the erstwhile Taliban regime and several contracts for building schools, hospitals, government buildings and a flourmill in Kandahar, the erstwhile Taliban stronghold in southern Afghanistan.

UTN was one of the few non-governmental groups permitted to function freely in Afghanistan and the Taliban gave Mahmood permission to conclude business agreements on their behalf. It also concentrated on commercial ties with Afghanistan with varied business interests, including mining ventures.

According to Asim Mahmood, son of Bashiruddin, Mahmood and Majeed donated their 1 million rupee ($14,000) retirement money from the PAEC to the UTN, and also used their prestige to pull in others to help Afghanistan. All seven of UTN's directors were detained on October 23, 2001.

## Subversive Activities and Linkages

The Ummah is affiliated with the now-proscribed Al Rashid Trust, which, in turn has links with the Al Qaeda network as also the Jaish-e-Mohammed (JeM). UTN also established links with the Al-Akhtar Trust. The Ummah, registered as a non-government organisation, is reported to have been floated at the behest of Osama bin Laden for 'development projects' in Afghanistan, and US and British intelligence agencies have confirmed that the UTN was directly linked to the Al Qaeda network. These Agencies have claimed that Mahmood's team was trying to develop nuclear technology for Laden. The UTN was said to be developing a nuclear program by smuggling nuclear materials from Russia and Central Asian States. U.S. intelligence agencies have suspected that Mahmood had provided nuclear information and assistance to the Taliban or bin Laden.

According to Pakistani intelligence officials, when UTN officials travelled to Afghanistan, their visas were sponsored by the Taliban's erstwhile Ministry for Mines and Industries, headed by Ahmed Jan. Jan has a long association with bin Laden—a relationship that dates to 1996 when the Taliban captured the eastern Afghan city of Jalalabad. Laden had already begun to set up his terrorist training camps and, intelligence sources say, Jan negotiated an extension of Laden's stay in Afghanistan— and his allegiance to the Taliban regime.

Reports quoting Pakistani investigators indicated on November 11 that Mahmood and Majeed had confessed about meeting Osama bin Laden at least twice this year. These meetings occurred when they were reportedly at Kandahar in connection with the construction of a flourmill.

Mahmood is also reported to have met Taliban supremo Mullah Mohammed Omar several times. Majeed has been associated with Pakistan's programme to exploit natural resources of uranium and plutonium.

One of the subjects on which the arrested scientists have been questioned is a complex of buildings outside Kandahar, which UTN helped to build. It has been described as a flourmill. The buildings were the targets of recent bombing raids but it is unclear what the buildings contained or whether any compromising installations might have been removed.

## Background

Although Pakistani media reports have indicated that both Mahmood and Majeed were handed over to a joint team of the Federal Bureau of Investigation (FBI) and Central Intelligence Agency (CIA), the government has denied these reports. Another former PAEC scientist Mirza Yousaf was also arrested for his alleged involvement with bin Laden. Mahmood was released on October 26 after being "cleared" by security agencies, but was arrested again after his release.

Mahmood was a project director when Pakistan conducted nuclear tests in May 1998 and won the prestigious Sitar-e-lmtiaz civil award for his work.

Dr. Bashiruddin Mahmood had resigned from the PAEC in protest following reports in 1999, that Pakistan would sign the Comprehensive Test Ban Treaty (CTBT). Such an action, he said, would wreck Pakistan's nuclear weapons programme. In an interview with *The Financial Times* in 2000, he expressed his opposition to the CTBT on the grounds that Pakistan needed to carry out test explosions to develop peaceful uses of atomic energy.

Mahmood had recently called for a cease-fire in the American-led attacks in Afghanistan.

Mahmood is described as an "extremely religious man," and is considered by authorities to be a vehement supporter of the Taliban. He is reported to have termed Pakistan's nuclear capability as "the property of the whole Ummah."

Mahmood is considered to be a founding father of Pakistan's nuclear weapons program, having headed, until 1999, the country's chief weapons-grade plutonium producer, the Khushab Nuclear Plant. Majeed was the technical director of the New Labs—Pakistan's main nuclear weapons design facility. The Khushab Plant is the country's chief producer of weapons-grade plutonium used in Pakistan's nuclear arsenal, which contains, according to U.S. intelligence officials estimates, 80 weapons.

The heavy-water moderated Khushab reactor which was designed and built with Chinese assistance, first went critical in early 1998. The reactor is rated at 40-50 MWth (megawatt thermal) but produces no electrical power. Mahmood himself explained in an article he co-authored in 1999 with another nuclear scientist, Muhammad Nasim, in opposition to the Nawaz Sharif government's moves to sign the CTBT, that the Khushab reactor was playing a critical role in the production of "boosted thermonuclear weapons and the hydrogen bomb". The plutonium and tritium produced at Khushab are also essential in the manufacture of compact nuclear warheads readily fitted onto even smaller ballistic missiles. The Khushab Plant also houses Pakistan's only heavy-water production plant. Mahmood then, rather than being just an ordinary nuclear scientist concerned with power production, was in fact one of the key Pakistani weapons scientists until his resignation from the PAEC in 1999. Prior to his role at Khushab, he had been in charge of the enriched-uranium production program at Pakistan's second weapons material reactor at Kahuta.

Mahmood is described as a bright student from a poor family of farmers. He finished first in Punjab in his final school exams. After studying electrical engineering in Lahore he spent seven years in Britain in the 1960s, taking masters degrees in control systems and nuclear engineering.

He is reported to have studied engineering in England, according to Dr. Zia Mian, a Pakistani physicist at Princeton's Woodrow Wilson School. He later acquired prominence as an engineer in the 1970's when he worked out a technique for detecting leaks in steam pipes at the Canadian-built reactor in the Karachi nuclear power plant. He patented this work later. He worked closely with Abdul Qadeer Khan, the man hailed as the father of Pakistan's bomb.

When his long career in Pakistan's secret nuclear program came to an abrupt end in 1999, family members and former colleagues say Bashiruddin Mahmood became more vocal in his beliefs—particularly his religious convictions. According to his son, since the UTN's founding in March 2000, Mahmood made "two or three" trips to Afghanistan, the last in May 2001. In Pakistan, Mahmood acted as a *de-facto* Taliban ambassador-at-large, praising Afghanistan's radical Islamic regime at various student rallies. Reports indicate the U.S.' Central Intelligence Agency (CIA) has given the government of Pakistan, a list of six more nuclear scientists who have to be investigated for their suspected links with bin Laden's al-Qaeda network as well as their association with

Mahmood and Majeed.

Earlier, in 1987, he published "Doomsday and Life after Death—The ultimate Fate of the Universe as seen through the Holy Quran," a 232-page treatise of theories based on 'Islamic teachings'. In one chapter, Mahmood theorizes that his "scientific mind can work backward and analyze the actual mechanism ... of the great upheaval before the Earth's Doomsday." He sought to explain how, through physics, the world would end. In the same year, he set up the Holy Koran Research Foundation in Islamabad as an Islamic study group.

He is a subscriber to a brand of what is known to practitioners as "Islamic science," which holds that the Koran is a fount of scientific knowledge. Bashiruddin Mahmood has published papers concerning *djinni,* which are described in the Koran as beings made of fire. He has proposed that these entities could be tapped to solve the energy crisis, and he has written on how to understand the mechanics of life after death. In an interview to *The Wall Street* Journal in 1998, he said, "I think that if we develop our souls, we can develop communication with them." He also added, "Every new idea has its opponents... But there is no reason for this controversy over Islam and science because there is no conflict between Islam and science."

Writing in *Yespakistan,* a Pakistani website, on the theme "Who are the Taliban?" Mahmood stated that the "Taliban are not people in power but upholders of a movement - the movement of the renaissance of Islam in the world. Simple proof of this is that all anti-Islamic forces are united in opposition to them. In the holy Koran, Allah has told us, 'All kufr [disbelief] will unite against the haq, the truth, of Islam'. Today the world is witness of this truth."

Described as a hard-line Islamist, his work was reportedly driven by an obsessive fear that Pakistan would one day be overshadowed by its rival on the subcontinent, India. Media reports indicate that after the May 18, 1974, Pokharan explosion, Mahmood is said to have sat in his room for two days and wept.

He wrote several books exploring his interest in life forces and doomsday scenarios. In one book, Cosmology and Human Destiny, written in 1999, he studied the peculiar impact of sunspots on daily life. Heavy sunspot activity, he argued, had coincided with the French Revolution, the American Declaration of Independence, the

Russian Revolution and both world wars. He concluded that governments across the world "are already being subjected to great emotional aggression under the catalytic effect of the abnormally high sunspot activity under which they are most likely to adopt aggression as the natural solution for their problems".

## References


1. Naunihal Singh (1989), p. 62.
2. Gozier (1972-73), pp. 18-19.
3. "Ulster : Politics and Terrorism, a study," Institute for Study of Conflict, London.
4. Washington Post, 5 October 1972, p. A-8.
5. N. 2, pp. 18-19.
6. Washington Post, 17 March 1973, p. A-6.
7. Gozier, (1972-73), pp. 15-17.
8. HCISC House Committee on International Security Report, "Gun-Barrel Politics : The Black Panther Party, 1966-71", H. Reht 92-470, 18 August 1971, p. 135.
9. Babylon, Somi monthly published in New York city by the Revolutionary People's Communications Network, 15 January, 1972.
10. Babylon, 15 December 1971, p. 19.
11. Washington Post, p. A-3; San Francisco Examiner; and Bakland Tribune—all of 6 February, 1974.
12. Washington Post : 25 March 1974, "stratregy of administration of the food programme," p. A-4.
13. Romerstein, Herbert, Minority Staff Chief Investigator, testimony, House Committee on Internal Security hearings, "The Theory and Practices of Communism, pt-3 (Expo-Cuba)", p. 2227.
14. Tricontinental News Service.
15. Workers World, 8 February 1974, p. 16.
16. Gozier, *op. cit.*, pp, 65-70; Guardian, 19-06-74, p. 13.
17. "Accessories to terror", pamphlet, Israeli Ministry of Foreign Affairs, July 1973.
18. For details, *see* New York Times, 12 April, 1974.
19. People's World, 12-5-73.
20. Gozier *op. cit.*, pp. 65-70.
21. Mark, *op. cit.*, pp. 13-15.

22. John, Gerassi, ed, "The coming of the New International, NY and Cleveland", p. 216.

23. New York Times, 1 January 1974, p. 1.

24. Washington Post, 1-6-72, p. A-11.

25. Edward Luttwak and Dan Horowitz, The Israeli Army, 1983.

26. Christine Fair and Peter Chalk, "United State's Internal Security Assistance to Pakistan", Small Wars and Insurgencies, 17(3), September, 2006.

27. Alan Kronstadt and Bruce Vaughn, "Terrorism in South Asia", Congressional Research Service (CRS) Report, Updated 31 August, 2005.

28. Praveen Swami and Mohd Shehzad, "Lashkar Raising Militants for Iraq", The Hindu, 13-6-04.

29. Luke Harding and Roise Cowan, "Pakistan Militants Linked to London Attacks", *The Guardian* (U.K.), 19-7-06, Occasional Report, The NEFA Foundation, August, 2006.

30. The Sunday Telegraph, cited *The Statesman*, 9-2-09.

# 5

# AL QAEDA AND TALIBAN

## Two Evils Threatening the World

Al Qaeda was and still is the most feared terrorist outfit. It announced its arrival on the world scene with a big bang : the most meticulously planned. and executed terror attack on US targets, including the Twin Towers and the Pentagon, which popularly Came to be known as Nine-Eleven. Its leader, Osama bin Laden, still remains the most wanted man in the world. Earlier President Bush and presently President Obama, would do anything to catch this big fish, which remain elusive till date, in the lad lands of FATA, according to most intelligence claims. Even if the outfit is believed to be outsourcing considerable of its destructive agenda, it still remains the biggest threat to the world order as it obtains today. Hence the reason to allot a separate chapter for its treatment.

As the Taliban during their half-a-decade rule hosted the al Qaeda in Afghanistan, the former too be discussed in this chapter.

Of late, the LeT is deemed the new Al Qaeda, it too has briefly been included in this chapter.

### THE AL-QAEDA

Al Qaeda is designated as a Foreign Terrorist Organisation (FTO) under the US law, while the Taliban are specially-Designated Global Terrorists.[1]

When Al Qaeda was expelled from Afghanistan in 2001 during Operation Enduring Freedom, some of its core elements relocated themselves in Pakistani cities of Karachi and Peshawar. Subsequently, some Al Qaeda members are known to have joined forces with Pakistani Sunni militant groups like LeT, JeM, SSP and Lashkar-e-Jahangir (LeJ), an FTO-designated offshoot of SSP that has close ties with Al Qaeda.

Al Qaeda is not known to have any significant physical infrastructure in Pakistan, but has perfected the art of getting its terrorist acts carried out through Pakistani outfits like LeT and HuM, in a process that can be called sub-contracting-outsourcing being the latest jargon. Reports indicate that the linkages between Al Qaeda and Pakistani militant groups are informal and extensive. So interestingly, despite Al Qaeda's reported linkages to several anti-Western attacks in Pakistan during 2002, the primary suspects in most attacks remained members of Pakistani groups.

Among the incidents in 2002 were: (1) the January kidnapping and murder of *Wall Street Journal* reporter Daniel Pearl; (2) the grenade attack on a Protestant Church in Islamabad in March that killed five, including a US Embassy employee; (3) a car bombing in May that killed 14 outside a Karachi hotel, including 11 French defence technicians; (4) A June car bombing outside the US Consulate in Karachi that killed 12 Pakistani nationals. The last outrage was also linked to the Al Qaeda.[2]

## Osama Bin-Laden

The wealthy Saudi-born bin-Laden was relatively unknown, shadowy figure till he moved to Afghanistan in the mid-1990s and helped bank roll the Mullah Omar's Taliban there. He reportedly married one of Omar's daughters to cement their alliance.

Whereabouts of Omar's ally and fellow fugitive have been matter of intense speculation in the world chancelleries and among the media Pundits ever since US-beacked forces ousted the Taliban from Afghanistan in late 2001. Mystery deepened in January 2007 when the reclusive, one-eyed Omar told the Reuter (3 January 2007) that he "has not seen him, nor made any effort to do so, but I pray for his health and safety."

A videotape of Osama was released late 2006, but it was identified as old footage, and the fifth anniversary of the 11 September, 2001 attacks on the US passed without any word from the Al Qaeda leader. For record, a half-dozen Audio-tapes of Osama were circulated during the first half of 2006, but the Al Qaeda leader last appeared on video-tape in late 2004, while tapes of his deputy, Ayman al-Zamahiri, have been issued regularly.

The best guess to Osama's whereabouts remains somewhere on the rugged border between Pakistan and Afghanistan, in the ethnic tribal lands where Omar's Taliban counts on support to fight an insurgency against US and NATO forces in Afghanistan and the Government of President Hamid Karzai.

## Al Qaeda No. 2 Escapes yet again

They missed him yet again on 31 October 2006. Al Qaeda No. 2 Ayman al Zawahiri was reportedly the target of pre-dawn US-Pakistan attack that day on a madrassa near Pak border with Afghanistan that killed 80 people and sparked off nation-wide outrage.

## Some Select Events Featuring Al Qaeda and Taliban

### October 2006 (7/7 Bombers Targets were Cricketers)

The 7/7 bombers were initially ordered to assassinate the English and Australian cricketers at the Ashes series second Test at Edgbaston during 2005. The plan fell because of differences among the bombers. It was then that Qaeda ordered Plan B of attacking London Underground that left over 50 dead and hundred injured (*Sunday Times*).

### 8 October 2006 (Al-Masri is Alive)

A statement on website known as a clearing-house for Al Qaeda material denied speculation that leader of the Qaeda in Iraq Abu-Ayub al-Masri was killed on the 3rd after a raid that killed four militants in the western Iraqi town of Hadetha.

Al-Masri is believed to have taken Qaeda in Iraq after Abu-Musab al-Zargawi was killed 7.6.06 in a US air strike. US and Iraqi officials said it did not appear that the slain militant, on whom they conducted a DNA test on the 5th, was Al-Masri, which is a pseudonym for Abu-Hamza al-Muhajer.

### October 2006 (Germany)

A suspected member of Qaeda network, Ibrahim R, 36, was detained near the Western German city of Osnabrueck, where he had been based since September 2005, prosecutors said. The Iraqi national is accused of having distributed video and audio recordings on the Internet from Osama bin Laden and other Qaeda members.

Suppterrorist groups is illegal under German law. Al Qaeda terrorists who carried out the 11 September 2001 attacks, were based in Germany for several years before moving to the US.

## October 2006

An Al Qaeda operative, Muhsin Musa Mat Walli Atwah, wanted in connection with the 1998 US embassy bombings has been killed in Pakistan, the Foreign office announced on the 25th. The FBI's most wanted Atwah was killed in April (2006) in North Waziristan during an airstrike by Pakistani force near the border with Afghanistan.[3]

## June 2009 Taliban bomb two schools

Suspected Taliban terrorists on 22 June blew up two schools in Pakistan's restive north-west region "Unknown militants planted explosive material in a girls' primary school in the Mashkagar area in Badhber", the police told Geo TV.

In another incident, extremists bombed a boys' primary school in Khar, the main town of the Bajaur Tribal Agency of the FATA, on the Afghan border.

## June 2009 US missile strikes Taliban base

A suspected US missile strike killed five people on 14 June 2009 in the tribal region of Dera Ismael Khan, where the intelligence believes Pakistan's top Taliban Commander is based.

The strike broke a lull in such attacks and posed a test for growing anti-Taliban sentiment in the country.

The Taliban has claimed responsibility for several recent attacks in Pakistan, including one that killed a moderate cleric, calling them revenge for the Pak Army's offensive in the North-West's Swat Valley. Such attacks are believed to have bolstered growing anti-Taliban sentiment in Pakistan, something the US hopes will translate into support for sustained military action against extremists who use Pakistani soil to plot attacks on Western troops in Afghanistan.

But US missile strikes could undermine that sentiment because they are deeply unpopular among Pakistanis. Islamabad has publicly protested such strikes.

## June 2009

'Rickshaw bomb' used to hit rush-hour crowd in market.

Dera Ismael Khan (DIK) is some 300 km. south of Peshawar, where a commando-style suicide gun and bomb attack killed nine people at the luxury Pearl Continental hotel on 9 June 2006. Three days later, on the 12th, there were twin bombings at mosques on Friday.

The Pak Taliban claimed responsibility for both the outrages to exact revenge for a 7-week military offensive against them across swathes of the NWFP, mainly centred in the one-time picturesque Swat Valley in the Malakand Division.

"The bombs were planted in a cycle-rickshaw and timed to explode at the rush hour in the bazaar, where-in were located the two mosques", said Syed Mohsin Shah, the top administrator of the DIK town.

## June 2009 Qaeda Financier held in Yemen

Yemeni authorities arrested the financier of al-Qaeda operations in the country and in neighbouring Saudi Arabia. An unnamed security official disclosed on the 14th that the arrested man Hassan Hussain bin Alwan, a Saudi national and he was the financier for the attacks launched in the two countries by the outfit. He is considered one of the most dangerous members of al-Qaeda.

In January 2009, the local al-Qaeda branch in Yemen announced in a video message hosted on the Internet the merging of the Saudi and Yemeni branches into "al-Qaeda in the Arabian Peninsula", led by a Yemeni, Nasser al-Wahaishi.

Yemen, the ancestra land of al-Qaeda leader Osama has witnessed a number of attacks claimed by the outfit in recent years against foreign missions, tourist sites and oil installations.

## July 2009 : Qaeda owns up Jakarta hotel blasts

An internet blog purportedly speaking on behalf of a group calling itself "al-Qaeda Organisation Indonesia" has claimed responsibility for the July 17 Jakarta bombings of two adjacent hotels, mainly run by and for the Americans. The entry was posted on the Google site blogspot. Come on the 26th but was discovered only on the 29th.

The message in Indonesian and Arabic was signed by "Abu Muawwidz Nur Din bin Mohd Top" and praised two "holy warrior brothers" who blew themselves up at the JW Marriott and Ritz-Carlton hotels in Jakarta.

The two human bombs killed seven people in the coordinated blasts at these two adjacent hotels.

## July 2009 : US man acts as Qaeda spy

An American man charged with giving al-Qaeda information on the New York transit system and attacking a US military base in Afghanistan has been a secret witness in the fight against terror, officials revealed on 23 July 2009. Court papers unsealed in federal court in Brooklyn identified the dependant as Bryant Neal Vinas, nicknamed "Ibrahim" or "Bashir-al-Ameriki", who grew up on Long Island. Court papers show he pleaded guilty in January in a sealed court room in Brooklyn and is in custody in New York.

## Al Qaeda Manual : To Guide the Terrorists

The 9-11 established Al Qaeda is the top most terror outfit. The thorough perfection it planned the attacks on the US mainland with got grudging praise even from its severest of critics. All aspects of the attack—concept, preparation and execution—were planned meticulously, leaving nothing to chance. It came as a no surprise when the Mancheter Metropolitan Police unearthed an Al Qaeda Manual during the search of a Qaeda operative's home in England. The Manual, found in a computer file, was then translated into English and subsequently introduced at the embassy bombing trial in New York early 2006. Billed as a useful instrument for terrorists who want to get away with their heinous crimes, the scary documents was brought to nation's notice by Mumbai police while charge sheeting the accused in the Ghatkopar bomb blast case of 2002.

Undoubtedly, Qaeda cadres have been making full use of this peace-destroyers' bible, when Mumbai was rocked by seven serial blast on 11 July 2006, the cadres were religiously translating into actions the instructions laid out in the manual. The systematic execution of the dastardly act, its timings and the advanced instruments used show how professional the perpetrators have become, thanks to the Manual which dilated upon the following subjects/aspects :

- How to recce a place before carrying out an act of terror and to assess the damage thereafter.
- Forging of documents, counterfeiting of currency, setting up the hide-outs, and access to and exit from there.
- Discreet ways of communication, unohtrusive modes of transport, use of weapons and the like.
- Legal recourse in the event of arrest.
- It elaborates on getting around investigations through abfuscation-levelling charges against the investigating officers.

There are empirical evidence/proofs that the terror outfits working by this near foolproof format render the detection tough. Casting aspercious on the investigation officers—a chapter in the Manual is a tool effectively employed by the accused in several cases against the Mumbai police. During the investigation (the first POTA case in India), of the Ghatkopar case by the Crime Branch one of the accused, Dr. Abdul Mateen, alleged that Khwaja Younus, the main accused, was beaten in custody that led to his death. The CID arrested five police officers after registering a case of murder. Eventually, the POTA Court acquitted all the eight accused in the blast case. Subsequently, the State Government moved the Bombay High Court against the acquital.

Through such allegations, the main case gets delayed, or at least, diluted. Ironically, while the CID was looking into Mateen's allegations, two units of the Crime Branch ran for cover, seeking anticipatory bail fearing arrests. The investigations got derailed. An officer, who was arrested following allegations, talked of political pressure as most of the arrested were from a minority community (read, Muslim) "For the sake of vote banks, the case was never investigated deeply",[4] he says. This boosted the morale of the terrorists, evident from the huge cache of arms seized in Aurangabad and Malegaon (Nashik) in May 2006.

Another officer, who ended up on the wrong side of the law, says "fundamentalists have managed to colour any arrests on religious lines. This is also preached in the Qaeda manual." When the Anti-Terrorist Squad of the Mumbai Police arrested Ghulam Elahi Yahya Baksh, *imam* of Haj House in Mumbai, an charges of harbouring LeT operatives early 2006, there was a public outcry.

Rohini Salian, Special Public Prosecutor, is certain that the Ghatkopar blast case accused were acting as per the manual. Saquib Nahan, ex-secretary, SIMI, had demanded that Salian be booked under POTA for falsely implicating him in the case. Nachan was later let off for lack of evidence although he continues to be an accused in the Mulund blash case of 13 March 2003. On moral grounds, Salian had then withdrawn from the case, but she was subsequently cleared by the trial court and the Bombay High Court.

If the Nine-Eleven established al-Qaeda as the top most terror outfit of 2001, it still holds the dubious distinction of being the most destructive terrorist organisation of the world of 2007 as determined by the US State Department's annual Country Reports on Terrorism States of that year. The (2007) Report staees: "Al-Qaeda and associated networks remained the greatest terrorist threat to the US and its partners in 2007." Al-Qaeda's psychological capacity for mass killing has been repeatedly demonstrated.

## Qaeda No. 3 : Iran Wants its Own Man

The Daily Telegraph reported on 14 November 2006 that the "Iranian are pushing for a pro-Iranian activist to be promoted within the Al Qaeda terror network's hierarchy. Intelligence inputs has Iranian President Mahmoud Ahmedinejad trying to persuade the Qaeda leadership to choose Saif al-Adel as its official No. 3, after Osama bin Laden and Ayman Al-Zawahiri.

A Western intelligence says : "This is an important power play by the Iranians and the prospect of Al Qaeda and Iran forging a close alliance is truly terrifying...They have had their differences in the past but with the survival of both Iran and Al Qaeda now at stake, they realise it is in both their interests to have closer ties.[5]

Egyptian-born Adel, 46, has reportedly been living under house-arrest in Tehran since fleeing there in late 2001 from Afghanistan following the US-led invasion of the country.

A former Colonel of the Egyptian special force, he joined Al Qaeda after fighting against the Soviets in Afghanistan in the 1980s. He was among the United States' FBI's 22 most wanted men, a list released after the 9/11 terrorist attacks.

The Telegraph says he has been living in a guest house in Tehran with two of Osama's sons, Saad and Mohammad.

Ahmadinejad has sanctioned Iran's bid to build stronger relations with Qaeda. If it agrees to appoint Adel as third-in-command, along with appointing other Qaeda figures presently in Iran to senior positions, the Iranians have apparently agreed to provide training facilities and equipment.

Iran has recently fallen foul of the West for refusing to stop its enrichment programme, which the latter suspect is for producing nuclear weapons while Tehran insists it is for peaceful purposes.

Meanwhile, British Foreign Office spokesperson said on 13 November that Al Qaeda is seeking to acquire technology that will enable it to carry out a nuclear attack on a western country. The two put together, West's—particularly, America's—paranoia about Iran's enrichment plans is understandable. He said the foreign did not believe that Al Qaeda had acquired such technology, even if he could not comment how far it had gone to get hold of that technology.

The Telegraph also reported that the Iranian Revolutionary Guards are training Al Qaeda fighters in techniques/subjects previously used by other Islamic militant groups, such as Shia militia Hezbollah—instructing them to carry out attacks against Western forces throughout the West Asia.

This report is bound to cause consternation among the Western powers/the US, and create suspicions about the future intentions of the Iranian leadership, in particular, of President Ahmadinejad.

## Ex-Laden aide held in Pakistan

Khalid Khawaja, a former close aide of Osama, who was also once a Squadron Leader in Pakistan Air Force (PAF) and has served in the all-powerful ISI during the 1980s was reportedly picked up by Pakistan's military intelligence on 26 January, 2007.

Khawaja is currently the Chief Coordinator of the Islamic Centre for Research and Defence of Human Rights, an organisation which campaigns on behalf of relatives of terrorism suspects who have disappeared. So far, it has negotiated the release of some 20 suspects.

Khawaja was a senior official of the ISI when it was fuelling Jihadi resistance movement against the Soviets in Afghanistan. After being forced to retire from the PAF and the ISI on the instructions of former dictator Gen. Zia ul-Haq, he went to Afghanistan and fought alongside with Osama bin-Laden.

"He went for this morning's prayers in (Islamabad) neighbourhood mosque and did not come back", his son Osama Khalid told a journalist. He said: "His disappearance is obviously a result of his role in the release of illegal detainers. Besides, he was active in talks between the people who were protesting against the demolition of mosques and the Islamabad administration. Thursday talks failed and this morning when my father went out to say his prayers in the nearby mosque he was presumably picked up."

Even after Khawaja was forced into retirement he was instrumental in many ISI operations, especially those in Kashmir and also in forging national political alliances. He admitted in many interviews that he allegedly secured funds from Osama and even arranged some meetings between former Pakistani Premier Nawaz Sharif and Osama in order to build a front against the secular Pakistan People's Party led by another former Prime Minister Benazir Bhutto.

Khawaja's name resurfaced when US reporter Daniel Pearl was abducted.[6]

## "Now, Al Qaeda in Algeria": 26 January, 2007

Algeria's main Islamist militant group, Salafist Group for Preaching and Combat (GSPC), has changed its name to Al Qaeda after getting the approval of Osama bin Laden, according to a statement posted on the Internet on 26 January, 2007. The move by the outfit marked the latest attempt by militants to exploit Al Qaeda's international "brand", following the establishment of regional branches in Saudi Arabia and Iraq.

The GSPC, which has led an insurgency against Algeria's secular government, said it was adopting the name Al Qaeda Organisation in the Islamic Maghreb. The statement signed by the GSPC and dated 24 January, 2007, said: "We had wished to do this from the first day we joined (Al Qaeda) but we wanted the permission of Sheikh Osama, may God protect him. This obstacle has now been removed."

The Group said in the statement that the name change was proof of "the sincerity of the ties between the Mujahideen in

Algeria and the rest of their brothers in Al Qaeda."

Some analysts believe the GSPC is trying to transform itself from a domestic movement into an international force capable of striking in Africa and in Europe.[7]

## They had Osama in their sights : 20 December 2006

Paris: A documentary, due to air in March 2007, says French Special Forces had Osama bin Laden in their sights twice during 2003 and 2004 but the US superiors never ordered them to fire. But the French military said the incident(s) never happened and the report was erroneous information.

The documentary, "Bin Laden, the failings of a man hunt" by journalists Emmanuel Razavi and Erie de Lavarence, and seen by the Reuters on the 19th, says the troops could have killed the Al Qaeda leaders in Afghanistan but the order to shoot never came, possibly because it took too long to request it.

The film quotes an anonymous French soldier (a sniper) saying : "In 2003 and 2004 we had Osama in our sights."

## Al-Qaeda, Taliban and Drugs

Concerns about the resurgence in Taliban activities raised questions about the sources of funding for the movement. Failure of the post-OEF reconstruction process and the obsence of an alternative livelihood programme in Afghanistan have resulted in a spike in Afghan opium production. This caused concerns of Afghanistan becoming a "narco-state", aiding terrorist groups in Afghanistan and Pakistan[8]. Afghanistan became the world's leading source of opiates, supplying the three quarters of the global markets. Nearly 80 per cent of the income from narcotics went not to farmers but to traffickers and processors, some of whose profits corrupts the government officials and support armed groups and war lords. Infact, reports indicate Taliban and Al Qaeda involvement higher up the drug trade chain, where profits are greater.[10]

There is congressional concern that heroin trafficking has become major source of funding for Al Qaeda. More details on the subject can be accessed from the following references :

- Christopher Blanchard, "Afghanistan: Narcotics and US Policy", *CRS Report*, Updated 25 January 06.

- Karen P. Tandy, "United States Policy Towards Narco-Terrorism in Afghanistan", DEA congressional Testimony, 12.2.04, at http://www.usdoj.gov/dea/pubs/engrtest/et021204.htm

Al Qaeda also benefits from drug trade in Afghanistan and Pakistan through networking. 70 per cent of narcotics produced in Afghanistan is trafficked through Pakistan. The drug trade nurtures a network of smugglers, traffickers, and terror groups in a "vicious cycle of conflict." The fugitive under world don Dawood Ibrahim, the mastermind behind the 1993 Mumbai blasts, has linkages with terror and Islamist extremist groups. India's claims pertaining to Dawood are largely shared by the US government. The US Treasury Department avers the Karachi—based criminal-Dawood Ibrahim—"has found common cause with Al Qaeda, sharing his smuggling routes with the terror syndicate and funding attacks by the Islamist extremists aimed at destabilising the Indian government."

## "Qaeda in Pak to plan next attack on US" : Febuary, 2007

Pakistan is home to top Al Qaeda leadership and the next terror attack on America could come from militant outfit based there, and not Iraq as popularly believed, a top US intelligence official said on 28 March, 2007.

The Al Qaeda leadership is trying to rebuild and establish training camps in Pakistan, the new Director, National Intelligence, USA, Adm. Mike McConnel said at a hearing of the Senate Armed Services Committee on Capitol Hill. He said this in reply to a question by Democratic Senator Jack Reed of Rhode Island, whether a new attack against the US would come from Iraq or Pakistan.

## Osama in control of Al-Qaeda again : Intelligence : Mid-Febuary, 2007

"Senior Leaders of Al Qaeda operating from Pakistan have reestablished significant control over their once-battered world-wide terror network and over the past year (2006) have set up a band of training camps and compounds in the tribal regions near the Afghan border". This is the assessment of American intelligence and counter-terrorism officials.

Osama and his deputy Ayman Al Zawahri have been steadily building an operation hub in the mountainous Pakistani tribal area of North Waziristan. Until recently, Washington had described Osama and Zawahri as detached from their followers and cut off from operational control of Al Qaeda.

There are several compounds in North Waziristan, including the one that trains operatives for strikes against targets, beyond Afghanistan in Western Countries. There compounds are functioning under a loose command structure and are operated by groups Arab, Pakistani and Afghan militants allied with Al Qaeda. They receive guidance from their commander and Zawahri, but Osama, who has long played less of an operational role, seems to have little direct involvement.

These camps have not reached the size and level of sophistication of the Qaeda camps established in Afghanistan under Taliban rule. Presently, groups of 10 to 20 are being trained in these camps.[11]

Earlier reports spoke about the growing capability of Taliban forces and Pakistani militants to launch attacks into Afghanistan.[12] New intelligence is focussed on Al Qaeda and sees the terrorist network gaining the strength and potential despite over five years of a sustained US-led campaign to marginalise it. The resurgence of Al Qaeda has been subject of intensive discussion among senior officials, reigniting debate about how to address Pakistan's role as a haven for militants without undermining the Musharraf Government.

"Last week, President Bush's senior Counter-terrorism adviser, Frances Fragos Townsend, went to Afghanistan during a West Asian trip to discuss with senior officials concerns about the resurgence of Al Qaeda in Afghanistan and Pakistan. This development is a major set-back to US efforts against Al Qaida since 2001.

A journalist said: "The intelligence and counter-terrorism officials would discuss the classified intelligence only on the condition of anonymity. They would not provide some of the evidence that led them to their assessments, saying that revealing the information would disclose too much about the sources and methods of intelligence collection."

There is a clear split over the strategy to be adopted. But debates within the administration are yet to yield any unanimous or workable solutions. Some within the Pentagon were advocating

American strikes against the camps but others felt any raids could cause civilian casualities. But State Department officials say increased US pressure could undermine Gen. Musharraf's military-led government.

John D Negroponte, the then Director, National Intelligence, told the Congress in January, 2007 : "Al Qaeda's core elements are resident, and the organisation was cultivating stronger operational connections and relationships that radiated outward from their leaders' secure hide-out in Pakistan to affiliates throughout West Asia, North Africa, and Europe."

As recently as 2005, American intelligence assessments described senior leaders of Al Qaeda as cut off from their foot soldiers and able only to provide inspiration for future attacks. But more recent intelligence describes the organisation's hierarchy as intact and strengthening.

One US official said : "The chain of command has been re-established. Qaeda leadership command and control is robust." A variety of factors in Pakistan had come together to allow "Core Al Qaeda"—a reference to Osama and his immediate circle—to regain some of its strength. The emergence of a relative haven in North Waziristan and the surrounding area has helped senior operatives communicate more effectively with the outside world via courier and the internet.

The investigations into the 2006 summer's failed plot to bomb airlines in London revealed "clear linkages" between the plotters and core Qaeda operatives in Pakistan. US analyst say that trials of terrorism suspects in Britain revealed that some of the defendants had been trained in Pakistan. In a 2006 videotape statement, Zawahri claimed responsibility for the July 2005 London suicide bombings. Included in the same tape was a statement by one of the London suicide bombers, pledging allegiance to Al Qaeda. Two of the four bombers traveled to Pakistan prior to the attack.

Bruce Hoffman, a terrorism expert at Georgetown University, told the House Armed Services Committee "last week (11-17 Febuary, 2007) that Al Qaeda in fact is now functioning exactly as its founder and leader, Osama bin Laden, envisioned it", because Qaeda leaders are now planning major attacks and inspiring militants to carry out attacks around the globe. Other experts questioned the seriousness of Pakistan's commitment. They argued that Pakistan's military still supported the Taliban and saw them as a valuable proxy to counter the rising influence of India, Pakistan's regional rival.

Since 2001, members of various militant groups in Pakistan have increased their cooperation with one another in the tribal areas, according to the US analysts the analysts posit that North Waziristan became a hub of militant activity in 2006, after Gen. Musharraf negotiated a treaty with tribal leaders in the area. He pledged to pull troops back to barracks in the area in exchange for tribal leaders' ending support for cross-border attacks into Afghanistan. But the officials in Islamabad and Washington concede the agreement has been a failure.

President Bush said at a press conference days before November 2006 elections : "Absolutely, we are winning in our compaign against Al Qaeda. Al Qaeda is on the run." But in a speech in January 2007, he pointed a more sober picture of Al Qaeda's current strength, especially inside Pakistan. Bush said : "Taliban and Al Qaeda figures do hide in remote regions of Pakistan. This is wild country; this is wilder than the Wild West. And these folk hide and recruit and launch attacks."

Intelligence services of the US and other countries collected enough evidence to conclude that at least one of the camps in Pakistan might be training operatives capable of striking Western targets. It is a matter of serious concern is that the camps are frequented by British citizens of Pakistani descent who travel to Pakistan on British passports. In a speech in November 2006, DG, MIS, British domestic intelligence agency, Dame Eliza Manningham-Buller, said that terrorist plots in Britain "often have links back to Al Qaeda in Pakistan". She said "through those links, Al Qaeda gives guidance and training to its largely British foot soldiers here on an extensive and growing scale."

The US still had little idea, the official said, where bin Laden and Zawahri had been hiding since 2001, but the two men were not believed to be present in the camps currently operating in North Waziristan.

It is likely that the two are ensconced in safe houses somewhere in Peshawar, as is believed by intelligence experts of India and some EU countries.

True to form, Pakistan on 20 Febuary, 2007 officially dismissed as "absurd" the US claims that Al Qaeda has established compounds in a remote tribal area (North Waziristan) to train small groups of operatives for possible attacks on the West.

## 29 Qaeda Members caught in Iraq

Iraq and US forces have captured 29 members of Al Qaeda, including a death squad leader, in a series of operations across Iraq, said Brig. Gen. Abdel Karim Khalaf, Director of Operations, Interior Ministry, on 5 March, 2007.

22 Qaeda members, including two brothers of Abu Omar al-Baghdadi, the leader of the Islamic State of Iran, were captured on 5 March at Baiji, 220 km. north of Baghdad.

The Islamic State of Iraq is an alliance of Sunni groups under the umbrella of Al Qaeda in Iraq, which said it had kidnapped and executed 14 Iraqi policemen on 2 March at Baquba, 60 km. north of Baghdad, to avenge the alleged rape of a Sunni women by Shia police.

Khalaf claimed to have arrested most dangerous man in northern Iraq, Fuad Ahmed-al-Mufraji, who is responsible for a number of assassinations. He was captured near Tikrit, 180 km north of the capital, also on the 5th.

On the 4th, the troops had captured a regional leader of Islamic State of Islam, Muharib Abdullah and five other Qaeda member in a raid at Dhuluiyah, 70 km. north of Baghdad.

## US-militants talks to isolate Al-Qaeda : March 2007

The outgoing US Ambassador to Iraq, Zalmay Khalilzad, admitted on 26 March 2007 that Americans had talked to militant linked groups to isolate Al-Qaeda and bring rebels into the political process to end Iraq's bloodshed. He told a farewell news conference after 21 months in Baghdad :

> "We have talked to groups who have not participated in the political process, who have ties with insurgent groups, who are reconciliable. There are groups who resisted the democratic change. It is our goal to reconcile and embrace the new Iraq."

His comments came amid continued violence, with six Iraqis reported dead in attacks in Baghdad while the US military announced the death of five more troops in roadside bombings, taking the military's losses since the 2003 invasion to 3,234.

He said "evolution" had been made following what he called some initial "unreasonable and unacceptable" demands from the groups concerned. Iraqi security forces on the 26th confirmed the arrest of an Al-Qaeda leader and two of his aides in Western Baghdad. A force from 3rd Brigade raided Abu Ghraib area and arrested Ahmad Farhan and his two close associates.

## "Al Qaeda expanding/regrouping in Pak : US : 10 May 2007

The Bush Administration says that despite three-quarters of Al Qaeda's known leadership having been either killed or captured, the terrorist outfit has actually expanded, and is regrouping in Western Pakistan.

In an obvious indictment of its ally in the 'war on terror', US Defence Secretary Robert Gates told a press briefing on 10 May that "within the last year (2006) or so, we have seen more defined training capabilities (of Al Qaeda) in Western Pakistan, alongwith Taliban safe haven there."

Gates earlier told a Senate Panel on Appropriations that going after Al Qaeda still priority. "They have established linkages now in North Africa. So Al Qaeda has actually expanded its organisation and capabilities."[13]

He directed intelligence agencies to analyse Al Qaeda's resurgence along these lines.

## Qaeda's minister (Nuclear) Designs

If it were in a position to do so, Al-Qaeda Pak nuclear weapons against the US. It was said in so many words by Mustafa Abu-al-Yazid, the leader of al-Qaeda in Afghanistan, in his interview with Al Jazeera Television on 21 June 2009.

Pakistan had been battling al-Qaeda's Taliban allies in the Swat Valley since April (2009) after their thrust into a regular/administered district (of the NWFP) 100 km. north-west of the capital, Islamabad, raised fears that the nuclear-armed country could slowly slip into the militants hands.

"God willing, the nuclear weapons will not fall into the hands of the Americans and the Mujahideen would take them and use them against the Americans", said the Egyptian terrorist leader. He was responding to a question about US safeguards to seize control over Pak nuclear weapons in case Islamist fighters came close to doing so.

He further added : "We expect that the Pak Army would be defeated (in Swat)...and that would be its end everywhere, God willing." Asked about the outfit's plans, he said: "Our strategy in the coming period is the same as in the previous period : to hit the head of the snake, the head of tyranny—the US .....That can be achieved through continued work on the open front and also by opening new fronts in a manner that achieves the interests of Islam and Muslims and by increasing military operations that drains the enemy financially."

The terrorist leader said al-Qaeda would be willing to accept a truce of about ten years with the US if Washington agreed to withdraw its troops from Muslim countries and stopped backing Israel and the pro-Western governments of Muslim nations.

## Qaeda leader asks Pakistanis to join anti-America jihad

The second-in-command of al-Qaeda, Ayman al-Zawahiri, accused the US of leading crusade to turn Pakistan from a Muslim nuclear power into a divided nation and urged Pakistanis to join jihad to resist that attempt. Zawahiri said in an audio-recording posted on an al-Qaeda-linked website in July 2009 :

"It is the individual duty of every Muslim in Pakistan to join the mujahedeen. The crusade aims at eradicating the growing jehad nucleus in order to break up this nuclear capable country, and transform it into tiny fragments, loyal to and dependent on the neo-crusaders.

"If we stand by passively without offering due support to the Mujahedeen, we shall not only contribute to the destruction of Pakistan and Afghanistan, but we shall always deserve the painful punishment of Allah."

"Militants are in a tug-of-war with the US—allied government as they push to make Pakistan a citadel of Islam in the Region."

He argued Pakistan was virtually occupied by the US through US-allied politicians and officers who are fighting the Islamists' plans "to establish Pakistan as a political entity standing as a citadel of Islam."

"The scholars of Islam have unanimously agreed that if the infidel enemy enters a Muslim country, it is the duty of all of its inhabitants, and whenever needed, their neighbour, to mobilise for jihad," he said.

The Egyptian militant—"terrorist" will be more appropriate term—leader described US' allies as a "clique of corrupt politicians and a junta of military officers who are fighting to remain on the US pay list by employing Pakistan's entire military and all its resources in the American crusade against Islam." He added: "Pakistan is involved in a fierce internal struggle between two forces (one representing Islamic values and the other being the US-led crusade) to neutralise fighters threatening Western interests."

## "Qaeda, Taliban trying to acquire Nukes": Mullen

Fears have persisted for long about possibility of some terrorist outfit gaining access to nuclear weapons, with the al-Qaeda leading the field. Such a possibility has been voiced by no less a person than Adm. Mike Mullen, Chairman, Joint Chiefs of Staff of the US in his address to the junior statesman summer school programme on 24 July 2009. He says :

> "Terrorist organizations, al-Qaeda in particular, have been very open and direct about their desire to get a nuclear and continue to terrorise people in accordance with their strategic approach, killing as many Americans and Westerners as they possibly can, with a device like this.
>
> "So, it is very dangerous time. Those are very dangerous weapons. And we would like to contain them and see them over time reduced as much as possible.
>
> "It becomes all the more important to make sure no new countries are able to acquire it."

## "Osama's Son may have been Killed" : A Report

"One of the sons of Osama bin Laden is said to have been killed by a US missile attack in Pakistan earlier this year (2009)", said a media report 23 July 2009, datelined Washington. Saad bin Laden, Osama's third son, might have been killed by hellfire missiles fired from a US Predator drone "sometime this year", National Public Radios reported quoting unnamed officials.

However, Saad in his late 20s was not a major al-Qaeda player. A US counter-terrorism official said Saad was simply "in the wrong place at the wrong time", and was not important enough to be targeted. Another source said that without a body to conduct DNA test it is "hard to be completely sure" if he is really dead. "But he characterised US spy agencies being 80 to 85 per cent certain that Saad is dead."

It was not known whether Saad was close to the location of his father, who is said to be hiding in the rugged mountainous tribal belt along the Afghanistan-Pakistan border, when he died.

Saad reportedly spent years under house arrest in Iran before traveling in 2008 to Pakistan, according to former National Intelligence Director Mike McConnell.

## Qaeda Training Techniques Revealed

Bryant Neal Vinas, who journeyed from long Island to Pakistan to join al-Qaeda, agreed to carry out a suicide bomb attack in 2008. While there, Vinas, who went by the name of Bashir al-Ameriki, made side trips to search for a wife. It was in Peshawar that he was captured by Pak agents in November, 2008.

Chapters in Vinas's Odyssey, replete with details on how al-Qaeda uses applications and written evaluations of students, directs terrorist camp life, and trains recruits to handle silencers and build suicide bomb vests, are found in a Belgian defence lawyer's transcription of an official summary of parts of Vinas' FBI interrogation.

In January 2009, Vinas, 26, stood up at a sealed hearing in a Brooklyn court and pleaded guilty to the charges—admitting to receiving Qaeda training and providing terror leaders with information that might result in an attack on the Long Island Rail Road.

The summary offers a rare window into the life and training of al-Qaeda recruits living in Western Pakistan.

The document details Vinas' apparent quick acceptance into the ranks of a terrorist training class just weeks after arriving in Pakistan, his education in explosives and the written evaluations that recruits received after their 'course work'.

Vinas converted to Islam in 2004 and considers himself a member of the Salafi sect, a rigorously fundamentalist strain of Sunni Islam. Until 2007, he attended services at the Islamic Association of Long Island.

On 10 September 2007, he boarded a flight to Lahore. He says he placed a call to a different New Yorker, who eventually led him to the Qaeda training camps.

He went across the border into Afghanistan's Kunar province. Upon returning to Pakistan, Vinas was asked to join a unit that carried out suicide bomb attacks. He agreed but al-Qaeda leaders, said he needed further religious indoctrination.

In Waziristan, between March and July 2008, he underwent education. There were three basic courses, each with 10 to 20 students. Details follow :

- The first : an introduction to AK-47, machine gun and pistol.
- Then came a class in explosives. This 15-day course taught students to manufacture suicide belts, how to tuck the belts around their waists, and how to test the battery and voltmeters.
- The third offered an introduction to rocket-propelled grenades (other classes offered instruction in forgery, poison and advanced bombs).

"Soon after Vinas had completed the courses ... Students under Went a written evaluation of their performance during the courses", the interrogation summary notes.

He remained on the Afghan border until October 2008. At this point, he decided to return to Peshawar to find himself a wife. He was arrested by Pakistani agents.

"I consulted with a senior al-Qaeda leader and provided detailed information about the operation of the Long Island Rail Road system which I knew because I had ridden the railroad on many occasions", he said, reading from a prepared statement. "The purpose of providing this information was to help plan a bomb attack of the Long Island Rail Road System."

(Michael Powell, New York Times, 24 July 2009; cited Indian Express, 25 July 2009)

## THE TALIBAN

Pakistan is guilty of original sin: creating, training, equipping and arming these *madrassa* "students" to help it to oust the Soviets from Afghanistan. In a moment of strategic delusion, they helped these "students" to take over Afghanistan, and in the process, aimed at gaining strategic depth for Pakistan in their ever-lasting 'confrontation' with India.

During their rule over Afghanistan, the Taliban practised the most extremist form of Islamic tenets—going beyond even the much-maligned ultra hard-line Wahabbism. Worse than their oppression of women and denial of civil rights to their 'subjects', was the destruction of the Bomian Buddhas—with the world standing by as helpless, mute witness. Even more horrendous than the daily death dance and never-ending destruction of Afghan life and property was their hosting of Osama bin Laden who subsequently grew into a monster, the Satan personified.

But for the American action subsequent to the 26/11 enormity, the Taliban would have been still ruling that hoapless nation, Afghanistan. Ousted from Afghanistan, their leadership took shelter in the major cities of the NWFP and the cadres—the fighters/terrorists—got ensconced in the fastness of the Bad Lands, officially known as the FATA.

Under the US pressure, consequent to the 26/11, Pakistani government has been acting against the Taliban in a manner most people dul as "half hearted", a put on, a pantomime, meant to waggle the cash and weapons from the US. Islamabad became serious only when the Taliban became an existential threat to Pakistan itself. Passing through a variety of shenanigans—understandings, agreements, peace deals and the works with "good" Taliban—Islamabad finally launched an offensive against them in Swat Valley in mid-April 2009. The going was tough.

Duly chastened and shaken by now, Pak President Asif Ali Zardari wrote in the *Washington Post* of 22 June, 2009 :

"The Taliban and the al-Qaeda could spread in the other parts of the world if they were not defeated in Pakistan and Afghanistan.

"Pakistan and the world community cannot afford defeat in the war against terror.

The international community must render urgent assistance to Pakistan to fight these outfits.

The world should rally in support of Pakistani democracy.

"We need immediate assistance, Pakistan paid a heavy price, more than US and NATO in the anti-terror war."

This loud cry of despair and despondency notwithstanding, majority of the world opinion feel that the ISI, the Army and the strategic community of Pakistan still look at the Afghan Taliban as a strategic asset for furthering their national agenda. The Americans—and the NATO—are not going to stay in Afghanistan beyond a time—so goes the logic. Once the foreigners upstick and leave, the country will fall to the Taliban like the nine pins. Even today, the South and East are practically under their control what Pakistanis do not realise is that the Taliban are not going to remain content with the smaller booty. Their eyes are already fixed on the "nuclear weapons" of an unstable, rickety nation.

This part discusses some aspects of Taliban reality, their strengths and frailities us the Pakistani polity.

Pakistani Army has been periodically claiming since end-June 2009 that its operations "are nearly over in Swat". Presently, end-July 2009, it is all set to beard the lion in its own lair, South Waziristan. Knowing the reality of Swat, South Waziristan is going to be a tough call. For its own sake, and the world beyond it, Pakistan must succeed. The world will be watching with not a little anxiety the outcome of this combat—which presently lie in the womb of the future.

These introductory remarks are followed by some important incidents, happenings and prognosis.

## The Taliban : Sure of their Strength

If there is one entity sure of success at the terrorism stakes, it is the Taliban. Their apparent defeat at the hands of the mighty US in Afghanistan did not decimate them. After that strategic withdrawal, they are back at the prowel. The strategy reworked by the new US President Barack Obama, including his 'surge', does not seem to be yielding long-term prospects of victory, some small day-to-day gains in the field notwithstanding! Each summer, they come out with the renewed energy and strength. Senior US and Western analysts are already talking about Afghanistan as America's second Vietnam. Obama is already under pressure to hasten the exit dates from Afghan imbroglio.

Having seen the discomfiture and failure of Pakistan at striking peace deals with their Taliban, there is inexplicable talk of US and UK planning similar peace deals with the Afghan Taliban. Surely, the Taliban are well aware of these peace overtures : Their adversaries cannot take the heat in the kitchen!

## Extremist Foreign Fighters Bolster Taliban: October, 2007

Afghan police officers working a highway check point noticed something odd recently about a passenger in a red pick up truck. Through covered head-to-toe in a burqa she was unusually tall for a women. When the police asked her questions, she refused to answer. When the veil was eventually removed, the police found not a women at all, but Andre Vladimirovich Bataloff, a 27-year-old man from Siberia with a flowing red beard, pasty skin and piercing blue eyes. Inside the truck was 1,000 pounds of explosives.

This is opening paragraph of a 31 October, 2007 story, accompanied by a picture of the said Siberian (suicide) bomber, in an Indian daily.[14]

This is indicative of a more serious threat to Afghanistan from the terrorists from foreign lands. Afghan and American officials say the Siberian intended to be a suicide bomber, one of the several hundred militants who have grauitated to the region to fight alongside the Taliban this—2007—year, the largest influx since 2001. The officials on either side of the Afghan-Pakistan warn that these foreign fighters are not only holstering the ranks of the insurgents, they are also more violent, uncontrollable and extreme than even their locally bred allies, the Taliban. More important, they are changing the face of the Taliban from a movement of hard-line Afghan religious students into a loose network that now includes a growing number of foreign militants as well as disgruntled Afghans and drug traffickers.

Foreign fighters are coming from Pakistan, Uzbekistan, Chechniya, various Arab countries and perhaps also Turkey and Western China, officials say.

Their growing numbers are indicative of the worsening problem of lawlessness in Pakistan's travel areas, which they use as a base to train alongside militants from Al Qaeda who have carried out terrorist attacks in Afghanistan, Pakistan and Europe, according to Western diplomats. Maj. Gen. Bernard S. Champoux, deputy Commander for security of the NATO-led International Security Assistance Force, said: "We have seen an unprecedented level of reports of foreign-fighter involvement. They will threatened people if they do not provide meals and support."

In southern and eastern Afghanistan, local officials and village elders also told the journalists that they have seen more foreigners fighting alongside the Taliban than in any year since the American-led invasion in 2001. In Afghanistan, the foreigners serve as mid-level commanders and train and finance local fighters.

Determining the exact number of Taliban and foreign fighters in Afghanistan is difficult. The Analysts say, at any given time, the Taliban can field upto 10,000 fighters, of which only 2,000 to 3,000 are highly motivated, full-time insurgents. The rest are part-time fighters, young Afghan men who have been alienated by government corruption, who are angry at civilian deaths caused by American bombing raids, or who are simply in search of cash, the officials said.

Five to ten per cent of full-time insurgents—about 100 to 300 combatants—are believed to be foreigners.

The foreigners are also increasingly financing younger Taliban leaders in Pakistan's tribal areas who maintain closer ties to Al Qaeda, like Sirajuddin Haqqani and Anwar-ul-Haq Mujahed. The influence of the older, more traditional Taliban leaders based in Quetta, Pakistan, is diminishing.

Afghan Education Minister Hanif Atmar said threats from foreign Taliban have closed 40 per cent of the schools in southern Afghanistan. "He said many local Taliban oppose the practice, but foreign Taliban use brutality and cash to their benefit."

## Taliban terror reign returns: December, 2008

By December, 2001 the Taliban had been routed and an army of international donors had promised a new era in the mountainous district of Jaghatu, some three hour drive from Kabul en route to the southern city of Kandhar. This environ of hope and expectations was created by the defeat of the Taliban consequent to the US led "allied" invasion post 9/11. This story of one single district is true, more or less, of entire Afghanistan—barring some northern areas.

Leaders of the Taliban fled, most of them to Pakistan or Iran. Others from the atrocious and repressive movement, which ruled Afghanistan from 1996 until (December) 2001 and sheltered Osama, slipped into the shadows and into obscurity.

This is the story of a district as narrated by two of its inhabitant : Mohd Naim and Mohd. Arif, but it is equally pertinent to the rest of Afghanistan beyond the boundaries of Jaghatu. Like many other inhabitants of the district, Naim and Arif were full of hope at the end of 2001. The enormity and calamity known as Taliban had disappeared, or expelled by the US arms. But seven years, something once deemed impossible had happened. The Taliban had returned, swept along by a catalogue of failures committed by the US and the Afghan Government created and nurtured by it. Growing public rancour fuelled by ineffective and corrupt Karzai Government and the incorrigible local war lords.

The Taliban were so weak that the American did not pay any attention to them, says Naim, who was head of the local district Government from late 2002 until late 2008. But as the years passed by, the militants gained confidence, because there was no official or public entity to stem their growing influence. The writ of the Karzai Government did not go beyond Kabul, the national capital.

"The Taliban networks were reconstituted in Pakistan", says Arif, another district representative, who like Naim has taken refuge in Kabul. "Those who stayed behind started to lead pinpointed and effective attacks."

As time passed, the people of Jaghatu saw initial hopes of a better future, built on the back of international aid, dissolve because they instead became collateral damage amid anti-militant operations by foreigns troops.

For seven years, most people went to school and had access to health care. But no economic development had taken place, there was no jobs, which led to frustration among the people. The roads were worse than before, the prices higher, and what is worse, there was hardly any security worth the name.

Given all this, it should be no surprise of some people yearned for the order under the Taliban, even if they committed worst excesses under their version of the *Shariah*. The situation will only be worse once the foreign troop withdrew and the local/regional war-lords started getting at each 'others' throats.

Will the Afghan Government be able to control the situation? The answer lies in the future.

## Taliban : "Enforce Shariah throughout Pakistan"

The Taliban showed their hand brazenly when its spokesman Muslim Khan, in an interview told the *Dawn News* on 20 April 2009 that they want *Shariah* (for Shariah-e-Muhammadi) to be enforced not only in Malakand Division, which include the valley of Swat, but throughout Pakistan. The Shariah or Islamic law regime approved recently was to be in force in Malakand, one of the terms of peace deal with the Taliban. But Khan ruled out the possibility of laying down arms, the other important part of the deal.

Religious hardliner Sufi Mohd had negotiated the deal with the Taliban on behalf of the Government. Commenting upon the resurgent Taliban's refusal to go by Sufi's assurance that they will surrender their weapons, US special envoy for Af-Pak said on the 20 April: "What happened in Swat is a huge wake-up call for Pakistan. It is in a dangerous situation. Swat is not in the tribal areas. It is 100 miles (160 km) from Islamabad...for it to fall under such murderous people. Hate philosophy is really extraordinary.."

Muslim Khan said Pakistani Taliban wanted all Muslims to work for the creation of a "caliphate" comprising of all Islamic nations in the region, with one army, one Shariah-e-Muhammadi and one currency.

Taliban fighters led by Maulana Fazlullah, the son-in-law of Sufi Mohd, now controls most parts of Swat, which till two years ago was a popular tourist destination.

In another serious development, Pak jets and helicopter gun-ships killed 20 militants, residents on 20 April (2009) in an attack on a Taliban commander, "who claimed responsibility for a bombing last week". Escalating militant violence has raised fears that nuclear-armed Pakistan, a US ally whose cooperation is vital to fight militants in Afghanistan, and al-Qaeda remnants in the FATA, including Osama, will fail to stop the spread of the Taliban and al-Qaeda in the Af-Pak region.

## UK, US ready for talks with Afghan Taliban

In significant change in tactics in Afghanistan, envoys from US and UK have started a concerted effort to start unprecedented talks with Taliban, the Guardian reported on 28 July 2009.

Senior ministers and commanders on the ground believe they have created the right conditions to open up a dialogue with "second-tier" local leaders now that the Taliban have been forced back in a swath of Helmand province.

The second tier of the insurgency is regarded as crucial because they control large number of Taliban fighters in Pustuh - dominated southern Afghanistan.

## 200 Child Fidayeen rescued from Swat

About 200 boys, some as young as six years, were rescued by Pakistani security forces from Taliban camps in the lawless Swat valley, where they were being "brain-washed" and trained to become suicide bombers. The 28 July 2009 reports disclosed that the Army kept the children in Mardan area where they would go through "mental rehabilitation" with the help of psychiatrists so that they can return to normal life.

The boys, all between 6 and 13 years, have been so thoroughly brain washed that consider all others as "infidels", NWFP minister Bashir Bilour told the *Geo News* Channel. "They were brain washed in a way that now they want to kill their own parents", Bilour said.

Several would be suicide bombers had been rescued from the captivity of militants, Mingora commander Brig. Tahir Hameed told the media. "We are trying to bring them back on track", he said, adding, "They will be enrolled in the schools with free boarding and lodging, and given monthly scholarships. He said the Taliban turned to children for using them as suicide bombers since they were easily influenced and less likely to be caught while undertaking an operation. "They are told that the Pakistani army has become an enemy of Islam, as it is fighting for Christians and Jews", said a senior officer involved in the interrogation of potential suicide bombers who have been captured.

## Reclaiming Swat from Taliban

Here is brief narrative of the Swat Valley. Pakistan's effort to buy peace here through an agreement with Taliban came a cropper when the latter refused to lay down weapons under its terms. By end 2008, Swat was under the Taliban control Pakistan was forced to march its army into this valley to free it from occupation. The operation started mid-April 2009 and by end-June, Pakistan announced "operations will soon be over". Still some incidents were reported in July 2009 also some select details/information follow.

## How 'Pakistan's Switzerland' became Taliban Land

By January 2009, Swat became the most threatened area of Pakistan. The picturesque valley in the Malakand Division of Pakistani province of the NWFP was once bustling tourist hule before Taliban overran the area. Unlike the proxy wars raging in the fringes of Pakistani territory, Swat is much closer to country's heartland—a mere 100 miles from Islamabad and three-hour drive. Radical cleric Maulana Fazlullah's band of foot soldiers have made sure that the place once called 'Pakistan's Switzerland' is now a valley marked by death and destruction.

## The History

A princely state in NWFP until it was dissolved in 1969, Swat was a famous centre of Buddhism during the Mauryan period. By December 2008, most of this area was captured by Taliban insurgents headed by Maulana Fazlullah and his outfit Tehreek-e-Nafaz-e-Shariat-Muhammadi (TNSM). In most places, they had established a parallel government with their own code of law based on *Shariat*.

Traditionally, area has been a stronghold of the Pakistan People's Party (PPP) and the Awami National Party (ANP), but the militants are trying to eliminate their supporters. Nearly a third of Swat's 1.5 million people have migrated due to the fighting.

## The Present (January 2009)

The area has been under indefinite curfew since January 26. So effeetive is Fazlullah's army of 10,000 that the government's influence is now largely confined to just 36 sq. km. of territory in and around Mingora, Swat's main town. His feared—and well-equipped—rebel army reportedly takes its cue from the Tehrik-e-Taliban Pakistan (TTP), an extremist outfit led by Baitullah Masud—the man believed to have orchestrated the assassination of Benazir Bhutto. The two (Fazlullah and Masud) came together in the aftermath of a sweeping military operation in 2007 at the Red Mosque in Islamabad that killed many seminary students and clerics.

On 24 December 2008, the militants asked all governments and private schools to close down girl's classes by 15 January. Education for girls was banned and more than 172 schools were bombed or torched. Some 400 schools discontinued girl's classes, affecting some 40,000 students. Additionally, "84,248 girl students of state-run institutions are unlikely to attend school fearing the militants, despite the resolve of the local administration to reopen schools on 1 March" (*Indian Express*, 2 February, 2009).

CD shops and barber shops have also faced the militants' wrath. The Pak Army says armed groups have so far blown up or torched 80 video shops, 22 barber shops, and destroyed 20 bridges.

Some recent incidents :

- On 2 January 2009, a resident of Swat, Shabana, who sang in weddings and other functions to earn a living was shot through the head by Taliban militants. Her "last wish was granted": they did not slit her throat.
- One of the region's busiest squares is now infamously called "Khooni Chowk". Everyday, decapitated bodies can be seen there hanging from poles and trees.
- A report in *The News* said a school teacher, who worked to support her children, was labeled a prostitute by the Taliban, which forced her to wear *ghungroos,* demeaned her and then killed her.

## Fazlullah's Voice

In speeches on his personal radio station—hence his appellation : Radio Mullah—Fazlullah propagates his teachings and beliefs. "Recently, he released the names of 40 people, including that of provincial ministers, MPs and local government officials, "wanted" by the Taliban.

## The Government's Intervention : Long last (End January, 2009)

There have been numerous reports of indiscriminate firing by the Army, resulting in the deaths of many innocents. It claims to have killed 784 extremists, while losing 189 of its men since the launch of military operations. Recently, the Pakistani Parliament passed a resolution rejecting the boan on female education. Troops have also moved into numerous schools. The Army, which has four brigades in Swat, says it is considering retrieving the situation by securing the main supply routes. However, scepticism abounds. (As mentioned above, Pak Army launched well-planned operations in mid-April 2009 only).

## "Fazlullah Cornered" : Pak Minister

Some 30 militants (Taliban) and two women were killed in attacks by fighter jets on 22 June 2009 in the restive areas of Swat and South and North Waziristan. These attacks were carried out after the Taliban struck out four military bases overnight.

Pak Interior Minister Rehman Malik gave this information to *Geo News* channel, and further added : "There are reports that Fazlullah has been injured. He has been spotted and would not escape. But nothing could be confirmed without seeing (Fazlullah's) body". Members of his family were detained in Haripur.

The Army sought to play down the issue, with Chief Military spokesman Maj. Gen. Athar Abbas saying there was no confirmation about Fazlullah's whereabouts. He added : "The military was engaged in positioning forces and preparatory manoeuvres before launching an operation in (South) Waziristan again Mehsud and his network... In Swat, troops were in the final phase of eliminating terrorist hideouts and camps. Bihar valley, the last stronghold of Taliban in northern Swat has been fully secured and Shamozae in the west is being cleared.

Prime Minister Yousaf Raza Gilani said that the Taliban's "first, second and third tier leadership in Swat has been killed."

An official said on 22 June that up to 45,000 people have left their homes, fearing a military offensive against Mehsud in Waziristan.

## Fleeing Taliban a threat to Tajukistan

A secretive military operation by Tajik authorities has raised fears that Islamist fighters fleeing Pakistan and Afghanistan may be shipping into Tajikistan, threatening a fragile peace in this sensitive ex-Soviet state.

Since May 2009, Tajik security forces have set up a tight security cordon and engaged in gun battles with armed groups close to the Afghan border. Officials term it counter-narcotics operation, but the diplomats fear the government has been battling insurgents, possibly fighters linked to the Taliban.

Fighting between Taliban militants and Pak Army in Swat Valley had already raised concerns that militants with ethnic ties to Tajikistan could seek refuge inside Tajikistan.

## Fresh fighting in Swat frightens refugees

Fresh fighting broke out 15 July 2009 between Taliban fighters and security forces at three places in Swat valley, in which 13 militants and one soldier were killed. Details below :

| *Place* | *Killed Militant / Soldier* | *Details* |
|---|---|---|
| Kabul | 5/1 and two foreigners | Kabul was a militant stronghold for long and has witnessed furious fighting between two sides for months in the recent times |
| Raema | 4/0 | The encounter was triggered during a search operation in the area. A huge cache of ammunition including explosives and detonators besides foreign currency and Fazlullah's audio tapes were recovered from the site. |
| Peochar | 1/0 | Troops raided a militant hideout in the area and killed a militant leader Abu Laith. The Swat Taliban HQ was located in Peochar area and they used to run their courts and jails here. |
| Gol Sakhra | — | Another militant commander Ismael surrendered to the Army here. |

This is an interesting development—rather surprising—since the Army had started saying mid-June 2009 onwards that the operations in Swat are "nearly over". Three encounters taking place on 15 July are inexplicable. Two fears expressed earlier by the military analysts are turning out right. One Pak Army failed to kill or capture most of the militants, who obviously fled to neighbouring countries like Tajikistan and Afghanistan to regroup and fight another day. Two: A number of the militants simply went up the hill slopes to surprise the troops as and when required.

This violent eruption could discourage the displaced people from returning to their homes in Swat Valley. Thousands of people displaced by military offensive had started returning to Swat and other parts of Malakand in batches since 13 July when the government began the repatriation process (An official said 15 July "about 2700 displaced families have so far returned to Swat and Buner"). The Swat residents are apprehensive of the Taliban resurgence as the Army has failed to kill any top Taliban Commanders including its Swat Chief Fazlullah.

A concerned local resident Noor Mohd. put it straight : "The militants hiding in the mountains can regroup as long as their leadership is not eliminated. The government can restore the people's confidence only by capturing or killing them."

## Kudos for Pak Army Operations in Swat : Analyst

> "Long reviled for their reluctance to fight the Islamist militancy that they themselves helped unleash, Pak generals have a reare victory to bost. In a 3-month offensive against the Taliban in NWFP, the Army has regained control of the lofty Malakand region, killing hundreds of militants. This has done less damage to civilian life and property than two previous failed offensives in Malakand. The local Pushtoons, over 2 million of whom were displaced by the fighting, are returning home. They mostly support the army's efforts."
>
> This is a teribute to Pak Army operations in Swat Valley, and surrounding Malakand Divisions. One may not agree with all the Kudos showered on Pak Army, but it must be accepted that the praise is largely well-deserved, knowing the rugged and mountainous terrain it had to operate through and in.

It is easy to fathom the success. The Taliban's take over in Malakand and the consequent cruelties, atrocities and criminal enormities, expectedly caused an outcry not only in Washington DC, but also in Pakistan and its media. Many blamed it on the army, which had made many truces with the Taliban militants in Malakand. Gaded thus, the top brass launched an unusually serious offensive in Swat with three divisions, against one in previous two failed offenses in the past six years. Not allowing an orderly withdrawal, the Army chased the militants into Malakand's hills.

There is much to celebrate in this success, not least a hope that it will bost army morale. During the course of a hopless six-year campaign in the north-western Pakistan, "the ideological a version many Pak soldiers initially felt to killing their Muslim compatriots has often ceded to despair at their poor progress. Some 1900 Pak soldiers have been killed and hundreds taken hostage, as the Taliban's influence spread." (*The Economist,* cited *Indian Express,* 25.7.09). For this very reason, it is imperative that these gains are not lost by a hasty withdrawal of troops from the area as it happened in the past two offensives. The generals seem to appreciate it as they plan for the troops to stay put for a year. In this period, the local police must be retrained and enlarged to replace the army in due course. The refugees too must be repatriated to their homes. It is all a tall order for the NWFP Government. But if it fails, grievances will fester that the Taliban will certainly exploit.

But there is tougher fight ahead. Compared to Swat, it will be much more difficult to take on the Taliban in their larger den, the South Waziristan Tribal Agency—the most powerful among the near—autonomous seven tribal agencies of the FATA. Not to forget, the Pak Taliban leader, Baitullah Mehsud has his fief here. It is public demand that Islamabad acts again Mehsud. It is he who is chiefly responsible for the series of suicide blasts that have ripped through Pakistan's main cities in recent years, terrorising Pakistanis and banishing foreign investors. He is widely believed to the behind Benazir Bhutto's assassination. Eliminating him, therefore, is essential, though decidedly hard. With the backing of his bellicose tribe, in remote terrain, Mehsud is a more formidable challenge than his counterpart in Swat, Fazlullah. Yet, for the first time, it seems likely to happen. After all, the Army is already positioning its troops for the purpose, as mentioned above.

This resolve is welcome. But it is too soon to see the light at the end of the tunnel. Pakistan's fallering campaign against militants in the fastness of FATA does not have a credible history. If Pakistan is serious about defeating Taliban, it must not only put all in its battle against them, but as a long time measure, it must tame its tribal areas—the collectivity that goes by the name of FATA. For success against Mehsud, the Army will hake to secure the supply lines in the area. For that, it will have to buy the support of two rival commanders of Mehsud. It is no surprise that analysts see the impending operation against Mehsud as a joint operation with his rival commanders. If media reports are to be believed, GHQ has already completed the home work. The names of the two rivals are already a common knowledge. Islamabad should not repeat the error of pulling back the troops from South Waziristan.

In facts, observers aver that not only should army stay put in the region, but Islamabad must tame the tribal areas initially by force and subsequently, as a long-term measure, by extending the regular administration into these wild, bad lands—a la India.

Now to a broader objective. The Pak Army troops in tribal areas must not only tame these areas, but must also prevent and quel jihadist raids into Afghanistan. It is not an easy proposition, since several Pakistani militant leaders—including the two rival commanders of Mehsud—dedicate their forces to such jaunts into Afghanistan. The Army has not made much effort to stop them. The ostensible excuse—that it is unable to do so given the rugged and inhospitable terrain in question—seems less tenable now since it has achieved some military successes against Taliban in Swat.

But there is larger reason behind this inability to stem the flow of Taliban depredators across the border into Afghanistan. Islamabad—read the ISI and the Pak Army—has not ceased looking at the anti-Afghanistan Taliban as a strategic asset. To the Islamised section of the Army, which is in majority post-Zia-ul-Haq, India is a bigger threat than the Taliban, LeT, al-Qaeda put together. The recent noises notwithstanding, Afghanistan still remains a strategic backyard for larger goals of Pakistani establishment. For the same reason, Pakistan can never reconcile to the Indian presence in Afghanistan.

The truth to be told, Pakistan is only waiting for the US withdrawal—or retreat—from Afghanistan. It has successfully and intelligently fooled America in its cooperation in that nations GWOT. It takes some ostensible—if token—anti-terrorist measures during or on the eve of visit to the region by US leaders, and for the rest of time, it is business as usual—playing footsie with the terrorists. It has been hoodwinking Americans for long years on this front. The US may not be a foolish nation, but in the given circumstances, to eliminate Islamist terrorists from FATA and Afghanistan, which pose potential threat to their mainland,

Washington has no choice but to accept whatever Pakistan gives by way of cooperation in counter-terrorist operations. In the bargain, Pakistan obtains substantial US financial aid, as also much desired arms to fight terrorists, which it eventually earmarks for use against India.

It should be no surprise if some Pak generals want Afghanistan's government to fail. There is method behind the recent madness: Pakistan moaning that the American-led surge in Afghanistan may drive militants over the border. If they indeed want, the Pak generals can stop this Afghan influx of terrorist into its territory. The moaning only indicates that many generals are loath to help their neighbour. After all, the same militants will be helpful against the Afghan government in the Pakistani strategic game for the region.

But how short sighted! If, as Pakistan's generals also like to complain, their Taliban insurgency is largely consequence of the *Jihad* next door, is not it in their interest to try harder to help US, NATO and the Afghan government to end it? Would not that be a watershed in the counter-terrorism war in the region? Admittedly, it is the ploy of the Pak Army to keep the pot boiling to retain its relevance to that nation. But the tragedy runs deeper. The inability of the civilian leaders to put up a united front to call the Army's bluff—and vacuousness. The game goes on!

Again, a word on the Pak Army's ability to defeat Taliban terrorism and Baluch insurgency. It has till date only fought classical set-piece battles against it 'pet' enemy, Indian Army, and that too, mostly of its own making. Not to extend the story too far, for the rest of its time, it has stayed in its barracks, with its officer class governing the country and enjoying the accompany perks and privileges—for more than half of the life of its nation. For obvious reasons, it cannot have a stomach for hard-fought guerrilla wars, a sine quo non to defeat the Taliban and Baluch rebels. No wonder, of late, the US Army has undertaken the job teaching counter-terrorist tactics to Pak Army personnel.

For the time being, the world will have to wait and watch its performance in the life-and-death battle against Mehsud's fanatical militants, including his suicide bombers, in South Waziristan.

Let the last word on Swat operation remain with Richard Holbrooke, US Special Envoy, Af-Pak :

"The test of this (Swat) operation is, of course, when the refugees return. Can they go home? Are they safe? We have to wait and see." (31.7.2009)

## Cleric who brokered Swat Peace arrested

Pro-Taliban cleric, Sufi Mohd, who brokered the now defunct peace deal between the government and Taliban militants in the Swat Valley, was arrested 26 July 2009 in the City Town area of Peshawar for his links to militants and his role in fomenting unrest in the region.

Sufi, who heads the now—banned TSNM, was arrested during a raid with his sons Ziaullah and Rizwanullah and an accomplice. The four were whisked away to an unknown location.

The influential cleric brokered a controversial peace deal between the Taliban fighters led by his son-in-law Fazlullah and the NWFP Government in February 2009. Under the deal, the authorities agreed to set up Islamic Courts in Swat in exchange for the militants laying down their arms.

The NWFP Information Minister Mian Iftikhar Hussain told reporters that Sufi was arrested for speaking against the government and encouraging terrorism in Malakind division, which embraces Swat. Moreover, he never cooperated with the government to restore law and order, and went underground to avoid dialogue on crucial occasions and declared democracy and judiciary "un-Islamic".

Taking advantage of the peace deal, the Taliban in Swat extended their influence to nearby Buner and Dir districts. The last straw was the refusal of Taliban to lay down arms. Consequently, the Federal Government scrapped the deal in May 2009 and launched major military offensive in Swat and nearby Buner and Dir.

Over 1700 militants and nearly 170 soldiers have so far died in the fighting. One of Sufi's son was killed in a military operation in Dir.

Earlier on the 26 July, media reported that Sufi, who had disappeared after a military operation in Swat, had resurfaced in Peshawar in a new look to hide his identity. A private TV channel caught him during his outfits meeting on the 25th "Sufi left the meeting after he spotted the camera", the channel reported. A

TNSM supporter told the *Daily Times* that Sufi had "trimmed and dyed his beard red to keep his identity secret."

There were reports of locals mobilising themselves in certain areas of the NWFP to fight the Taliban. Some dailies carried a photo of a youngster carrying a rifle on 25 July 2009, with this caption below it: "Javed Khan, 13, at the headquarters of a 'lashkar' or local citizens' militia to fight against Taliban in their area in Sultanmas village, in Pakistan's Buner district."

## Taliban supporter ex-MP held for Murder

A former parliamentarian, once a member of the National Assembly, Shah Abdul Aziz was arrested by Pak authorities on the suspicion of involvement in the kidnapping and execution of a Polish engineer, Piotr Stanczak, by the Taliban.

Aziz, who is affiliated to the Muttahida Majlis-e-Amal (MMA) was handed over to the police in attack on 25 July 2009 on a 2-day physical remand for alleged involvement in the abduction and killing of the Polish national.

Aziz and another suspect in the murder case, Attaullah, were brought to the court in an armoured vehicle.

## LET Emerging as new al-Qaeda

The Lashkar-e-Tayyaba is already the strongest and most heinous terrorist outfit in Pakistan. Its founder-leader, Hafiz Mohd. Saeed, is presently putative head of a charity organisation, and is most 'popular' and powerful terror chief in the country. He, in fact, is so powerful that the federal government in chary of arresting him even when he has been declared an international terrorist by the UN Security Council and India has sent convincing documents to Islamabad regarding his being the mastermind behind the 26/11.

He indeed was arrested on India's insistence for being involved in the 26/11. But the Lahore High Court set him free for lack of substantive evidence. Islamabad went on appeal, essentially under the Indian pressure, against the High Court order but the Supreme Court refused to over rule the order of the High Court and set a date for hearing the case. Consequently, Saeed walked out as a free man—cocking a snook at the prosecution, and more importantly, at India.

The Al-Qaeda is already known to outsource its violent chores to the LeT, and the outfit is already busy spreading its wings beyond the Pak border. What follows should suffice to show how and why it is emerging as the new Qaeda.

## Dubai new LeT Base?

Any move by the outfit to expand its boundaries should be a cause of serious concern to India, as almost all terrorist attacks on this country have been perpetrated by it; and at the very least, it is the prime mover through its acolytes and cells. So New Delhi is obviously concerned by the news of purported plans of the LeT to move its base to Dubai.

Given below is the opening paragraph of a news story in a daily of 22 June 2009 :

> "The LeT is reinventing itself and exploring alternative routes to wreak havoc. The move follows Islamabad's crackdown on Pak terrorist groups as it buckled under the intense global pressure in the aftermath of 26/11."

The arrest of key LeT operative Mohd. Umer Madni earlier June 2009 and ongoing investigations against Pak-based groups have revealed some startling facts :

> Sources in New Delhi said the proscribed outfit and its Pak mentors are working on a new strategy that involves using Dubai as the centre of planning for future strikes against India and recruiting locals for the job.
>
> It is well known that Dubai had earlier come into limelight subsequent to the 1993 Mumbai serial blasts. This followed understandably from the fact of Mumbai emerging in the 1990s as a centre of anti-India activities led by mafiadon Dawood, Ibrahim. Fortunately, close security cooperation between India and the UAE in the past decade has kept the terror network in Dubai under check. But, of late, India feels efforts are afoot to revive it.
>
> Bangladesh, which has been on the radar of the LeT for the past few years, can again be used to target Indian cities. The ISI is known to use that country for sending its operatives into India by air and land routes.

The *modus operandi* is simple : when more and more attacks are planned and hatched outside Pakistan, it would be difficult for India to directly accuse Islamabad of abetting terror against it. Still better way to deflect attention from Pakistan is to make greater use of locals in India to carry out terror strikes there. The LeT already has a network of sleeper cells, created and maintained over the years assiduously, in Delhi, Jharkhand and Bihar. This network can be expanded, as the LeT is planning, by recruiting graduates from different Indian states. This will enable the outfit to employ more sophisticated devices, based on the greater technological know—how available to these men entrants to the sleeper cell strength. Earlier, sleeper cells provided logistical and monetary support to its men—all potential terrorists—who sneaked either through LoC in Kashmir or the porous Indo-Nepal and/or Indo-Bangladesh borders. Now they can also enhance the technological skills of the incoming operatives.

Keeping the above in mind, India must improve its internal security apparatus under the guidance of the new incumbent in its Home Ministry. All possible loopholes must be plugged.

The 26/11 Mumbai attack was the most sinister so far and it exposed the vulnerability of India's coast line, which obviously had been neglected. Even when a lot of attention has been bestowed on this aspect, there are still gaps, particularly in the ships, radar coverage and skilled manpower. But the adversary is already one step ahead, if we are to go by available reports. It is learnt that the outfit is now planning to transfer arms to Indian ships and vessels to be delivered to the sleeper cells or the incoming terrorists on the coast or within India. "Vessels arranged by the LeT's contacts in India can enter Indian waters without much difficulty. This reduces the risks attendant on smuggling or transferring arms through the territorial route", said a source (Mail Today, 22.6.09).

Another cause of concern for the Indian security is the reports of Gulf money flowing into Nepali *madrassas* along the Indian border. The money could easily be channelised for training and providing logistic support to jihadi outfits which are trying to set up bases in the Himalayan nation.

## "Al-Qaeda supported LeT in Mumbai Train Bombings" : US

The US and UN Security Council have said that al-Qaeda provided support to the LeT to carry out the July 2006 train bombings in Mumbai and the February 2007 Samjhauta Express blasts in Panipat.

If correct, this would be the first-ever confirmation that an international jihadi outfit like al-Qaeda was directly involved in aiding and abetting major terrorist attacks in India.

The revelation came when the US and Security Council proscribed on 29 June 2009 four men, all residents of Pakistan and belonging to the LeT. They are :

Fazeel-at-ul-Shaykh Abu Mohd. Ameen Al-Peshawari.

Arif Qasmani

Mohd. Yahya Mujahid

Nasir Javaid

The US and the UN said that Qasmani is the Chief Coordinator for LeT dealings with outside organizations and has provided significant support for LeT terrorist operations.

## LeT Fast Emerging as New Al-Qaeda

"The evidence is tumbling out of the closet. Pakistan's creation LeT is not merely allied to al-Qaeda but can now be described as the new al-Qaeda." This is the assertion made by the analysts consequent to the Security Council proscribing four men belonging to this outfit as internationalist terrorists under its resolution dated 29 June 2009. The resolution rips the veil off Pakistan's terror claim. The four LeT men banned under the resolution are not mere foot soldiers of the outfit. In fact, the resolution establishes their importance for the LeT and al-Qaeda.

It says: "Arif Qasmani has worked with LeT to facilitate terrorist attacks including the July 2006 train bombings in Mumbai and the February 2007 Samjhauta Express bombing in Panipat, India. Qasmani utilised the money that he received from Dawood Ibrahim to facilitate the July 2006 train bombings in Mumbai, India."

The most dangerous part in all this is that while the US and Pak armies are targeting the Taliban, the ISI continues to shelter the LeT—a greater threat to India and the world. It is openly acknowledged in the counter-terrorism circles that 26/11 attacks in Mumbai were masterminded by the ISI and executed with Commando precision by the LeT. Increasingly, the LeT is emerging as more than a mere Pakistani terror outfit. It is now revealed to have connections with al-Qaeda and globally at par with it.

The primary target of LeT continues to be India, aimed at weakening it and establishing a caliphate here. It is for this mission that the LeT receives the bulk of its funding from ISI and is so close to the Pak army that some of its retired officers are the Chief Combat trainers for the LeT, which has, in turn, training Taliban-Qaeda fighters.

Over the years, al-Qaeda has found great use for the extensive work of the LeT—its charitable arm, JKD, is an effective front for its terror activities. Several years ago, ISI brought the LeT and Dawood's organised crime network together.

Recently, Bruce Riedel, former CIA officer who is in charge of Obama's Af-Pak strategy review, was quoted as saying: "I think we have to regard the LeT as much a threat to us as any other part of the al-Qaeda system."

## LeT's Greater Idea : Creation of an Islamic Caliphate

Like ISI earlier, the security experts say, LeT essentially runs a state within a state inside Pakistan, and its greater idea is to create an Islamic caliphate. In a 1999 document, "Why we are fighting jihad?" Saeed said: "Muslims ruled Andalusia for 800 years but they were finished to the last man. Christians now rule Spain, and we must wrest it back from them." It further adds more menacingly :

> "All of India, including Kashmir, Hyderabad, Assam, Nepal, Burma, Bihar and Junagarh were parts of the Muslim empire that was lost because Muslims gave up Jihad. Palestine is occupied by the Jews. The Holy Qilla-e-Awwal in Jerusalem is under Jewish control. Several countries such as Bulgaria, Hungary, Cyprus, Sicily, Ethiopia, Russian Turkistan and Chinese Turkistan were Muslim lands and it is our duty to get it back from unbelievers."

India should feel warned!

## References

1. *See* the US Treasury Department's master list at http:/ www.ustreas.gov/offices/eotffc/ofac/sdn/index.html

2. "Pakistan : 2002 Overview", at http://www.tkbe.org/more Patterns.jsp? Country Cd/Pk & Year = 2002.
3. No reasons are available for such a delayed disclosure of his death.
4. Rahul Mahajani, The Week, 23.7.06.
5. AFP, cited The Asian Age, 15.11.06.
6. Syed Saleem Shahzad, AKI, cited Asian Age, 27 January, 2007.
7. Reuters, *Times of India*, 28 January, 2007.
8. "Afghanistan as a Narco State", *Christian Science Monitor*, 8.3.05; Paul Geitner, "UN: Afghanistan Sees Increase in Opium", *Associated Press Online*, 19 November, 04.
9. Carlotta Gall, "Afghan Poppy Growing Reaches Record Level, UN Says", *New York Times*, 19.11.04.
10. Tim Mcgirk, "Terrorism's Harvest", 2 August 04, at http://www.time.com/time/asia/magazine/printout/0,13675, 501040809-674806,00.html
11. Mark Mazzetti and David Rohde, *New York Times*, cited, Asian Age, *Hindustan Times and Indian Express*, all 20 Febuary, 2007.
12. Experts are sanguine about Taliban launching a summer offensive in 2007.
13. Sridhar Krishnaswami, Washington, *The Pioneer*, 11 May, 2007.
14. David Rohde, Gardez (Afghanistan), NYT, in Exp., 31 October, 07.

# 6
# COMBATING TERRORISM

Presently, the international terrorism is at its virulent worst—particularly of the Islamist genre, fired by fundamentalist fanatics and heaven-seeking "human-bombs."

Each nation facing the terrorist depradation and murderous enormities is individually devising ways to counter it, and collectivity of nations suffering from the scourge are finding solutions under U.N. aegis.

The enormity of the evil visitation can be judged by the casualties over the past decades.

Rising trends in casualties in acts of terrorism

| *Period* | *Terrorists Incidents* | *Deaths* | *Injuries* |
|---|---|---|---|
| 1970s | 8,114 | 44,798 | 6,902 |
| 1980s | 31,426 | 70,859 | 47,849 |
| 1990-96 | 27,087 | 51,797 | 58,814 |

The number of casualties in acts of terrorism varies from year to year but the trend is clearly increasing. Between 1970 and 1995, on an average, each year brought 206 more incidents and 441 more fatalities.[1] The death toll from acts of terrorism rose from 163 in 1995 to 311 in 1996, as the trend continues towards more ruthless attacks on mass civilian target and the use of more powerful weapons. In 1996, the number of international incidents declined, but "while terrorists were becoming less active, they were also becoming more lethal". The new statistics show that terrorist strikes against non-military targets world wide remain virtually unchanged in 2007 from 2006, at roughly 14,500 attacks, but the number of death increased to 22,685 from 20,872, according to the statistics compiled by National Counterterrorism Centre.

## From Statistics to the Narrative

## Fighting terrorism the World Over

There was time when the terrorism was known to Eurasian, African and South American countries only. Even if some European countries were victims of the home grown variety, it was free from the menace as the world knows it today. In a manner of speaking, the so-called West (Europe and the U.S.) was largely free from it and proudly and loudly made it a point to maintain its liberal laws and traditions as a show piece of its democratic freedoms. But it took one 9/11 to change it all. Islamist terrorism was unlike any other, in its viciousness and sweep. Consequently, the West, including the U.S. and the U.K., enacted laws, unprecedented harsh, to deal with this variety of terrorism. As the curse of terrorism prevails the world over and more than a hundred nations are its victims, the international community must find ways, institute laws under the U.N. auspices and stand united to fight this unprecedented threat not only to the world order as it stands today but to its very existence. Therefore, any nation fighting terrorism within its borders must be deemed as a part of the international effort against the curse.

### India is fighting for the entire World

There is variety of answers to the terrorism imperiling the entire world. For one, and most important of it all, there is the need for a very powerful, not only domestic but also international cooperation in the field of intelligence sharing in real time context. The intelligence agencies of all the countries must forge, at first instance, a national grid and subsequently, its international variant.

The starting point, of course, is with the intelligence on the terrorists involved in the violent incidents and it must extend to all the suspects, their accomplices and over ground sympathisers. It is essential that intelligencies gather information about their sinister plans in advance as only then can the latter abort them, saving so many innocent lives as a result of this pro-active approach. The best instance of an alert intelligence acting before the perpetrators could kill the innocent people is the success of the British intelligence recently (April 2007) uncovering a terrorist plot to explode mid-air several—U.S.A. flights. All the terrorists involved the deadly conspiracy were nabbed.

As the terrorists never proclaim warnings about their evil plans, the targets are taken by surprise. Hence the need for effective, real time sharing of intelligence on the terrorists and their activities. It is also obvious that understandably, it is not an easy to achieve this cooperative framework. But once it is understood by all concerned that the only alternative to this cooperative agreement is surrendering ground to the terror leaders, creating such a cooperative regime should not be an unsurmountable task.

## Security Regime

Another important counter-terrorism requirement is to have an effective, strong security regime to keep a track on the movements and activities of the known terrorists and the suspects. Finally what is needed is an efficient, effective legal regime to deal with the culprits once they are arrested.

## Legal Regime

Most countries have instituted strong legal regimes to counter the menace. The U.S. and the U.K. are two countries among some others to have put on the statute tough counter-terrorism legislation. Consequently, strong legal regimes the world over have provided enough ground to several organizations to actually start complaining that some provision of this legislation are too harsh, and some NGOs, expectedly, use the term 'draconian'. It needs to be raid that certain anti-terrorism laws enacted by the U.S. after 9/11 and by the U.K. after the metro blasts are tougher than ours like the TADA, which in any case is defunct consequent to a decision by the UPA Government in 2004. But there are no two opinions among the legal community and geo-strategic fraternity that some of the so-called harsh provisions are indeed necessary if we are to fight the terrorism.

First and foremost, we must have a clear-cut definition of terrorism and a very harsh punishment for it. Funding of terrorism must be an offence such funds must be confiscated. It must be understood that when funds used to be passed on the same organization earlier, it could well have been offences under much softer laws like FERA or now FEMA. But once such transfers are established as funding of terrorism and gets identified as a terrorist act itself, that would be a major deterrent action against terrorism.

That, in fact, is the reason why one of the major demands that countries which were victims of terrorism, made to several other nations, which were the source of funding, to block such recognised sources.

The next ingredient of a strong anti-terrorist legal regime, related to the preceding one, has to be that profits of terrorism, which then provide an infrastructure to terrorism itself, should be confiscated. It is a rule of law in any civilized society that no person can be allowed to retain to himself profits of crime. In fact, 35 years ago India legislated a law where profits of smuggling under SAFEMA (Smugglers and Foreign Exchange Manipulators [for feature of property] Act) are to be confiscated. No man can enrich himself with profits of crime. Gun running, drugs, narcotics, arms presently provide rich avenues of illegal profits. No organised so city can allow the culprits to enrich themselves with such profits. Therefore, one important component of anti-terrorist legal regime has to be this : What even is earned through blackmail or loot, whatever properties it is converted into, whatever bank accounts or liquid cash it is converted into, the same does not belong to the person who converts and the same is liable to be confiscated.

## International Scene : Post 9/11

Before the tragic 9/11, there was hardly any hope of the affluent West understanding the ravages of terrorism countries like India were subjected to. It was galling, and even patronising to hear the U.S. President and his officials sermonising India on the virtues of avoiding over-reaction to a serious terrorist incident killing scores of Indians and injuring hundreds. We were advised against rash and intemperate response to such terrorist depredations.

All this changed after the cataclysmic 9/11. It is not that Indians were gleeful seeing this tragic attack on the "fortress America". May be, some Indians saw the hands of destiny in this ghastly terrorist attack. Before the 9/11, the Americans were smug about the security of the mainland, considered a fortressed hemmed in and guarded by two largest oceans of the world. It needed a 9/11 jolt to shake Americans out of this complacency. It was like the Indians waking up one morning in October 1962 to find that the Himalayas were not that impregnable defenders of India's borders as the Chinese pierced them to inflict a humiliating blow at its international image and standing built so assiduously by that man called Jawahar Lal Nehru who thought he was among the towering leaders, nay statesmen, of the world. Mao had undone him physically, mentally and politically with that one stroke. Nehru's image lay in the dust, after strutting on the world stage for 15 years! The 9/11 attack undid the U.S. in somewhat same way. No wonder its President said "we are under attack" and declared a "War on Terror". Another important decision was to create the Department of Homeland Security.

As for the international counter-terrorism regime, it has been slowly building up over the last few years. After the 9/11, hopes were really raised that the international regime against terrorism is actually going to be very powerful and strong. Indian Home Minister L.K. Advani expressed certain relevant views on the issue on 1 August 2002 in Parliament : "There was one definite impression of the world during the cold war regime. There were identified groups, identified poles with which smaller nations had their respective friendships ; so their stands of the latter were known in advance. But once the world started moving towards being transformed into a unipolar world (after the demise of the Soviet Union), coupled with the new terrorist threat, the world has started actually having a new methodology—an attitude or disposition—of looking at all things".[2]

In this context when the Indians met their U.S. friends after 9/11, say in 2002 or even in 2003, they expressed surprise at the practice or proclivity of certain countries, including the U.S., obviously, for maintaining and following two different standards on dealing with the terrorist organizations, or on dealing with the democracies the world over. Therefore, when an effort is made to give at least some more time, if not benefit of the doubt, to the nations which are responsible for sponsoring terrorism in India's neighbourhood and destabilise the region, it is not easily understandable, much less appreciable, particularly after 9/11. India's war against terrorism did not begin on 9/11. We have been fighting it since the long decades, and its more vicious form since 1989—12 years before the West's defining date, which in a macabre may woke the West to the sinister dimensions of the terrorism and its world wide sweep.

If 3,000 American lives persuaded their President to declare that America is at war, can India, having suffered 81,000 deaths, view it any differently, or less seriously? Thus, India's fight against the terrorism on its own soil cannot be taken as an ordinary war, and the leaders of the global alliance should avoid the earlier patronising temptation to merely advise restraint. They have a responsibility to be on the fore-front of fighting this war against terrorism. Country's cannot fight terrorism selectively because it is one, indivisible global war.

## Banning Terrorist Outfits

Banning is the preferred method of dealing with more dangerous and more potent of the terrorist organizations. The ban outlaws the outfit and makes its membership and activity an offense. The ban has several consequences.

Way was India expecting—and perhaps insisting that—the U.S. to ban the H.M. or LeT? Why were they first to ban the Al Qaeda? When an outfit is banned in one part of the world, consequences flow from that. Therefore, one (civilized) nation expects another as part of the global alliance to start banning terrorist groups.

One of the two most important instruments in law which have been used against terrorists and hardened criminals world over have been the use of modern technology. After all, terrorists no longer operate in the forests. They are no longer desperados who live away from the mankind.

They may be living in the buildings or apartments next to our house. One of the methodologies by which police has been able to track down hardened criminals is the use of modern technology : intercept. In the good old days of 1970s and 1980s whenever there was move to grant police the powers to intercept communications, a liberal society stood up and said in horror : "A Big Brother keeping a watch on us? Not done. It is not conducive to liberal ethos".

In this situation what does an investigator do? What does an anti-insurgent force do? After all, terrorists do not announce their targets of attack. It is part of the police training on intelligence gathering that they must obtain in advance (all) necessary information about the plans of the terrorists and their next targets. Earlier human intelligence was the most effective tool in their hands : the informers and plants. But presently, intercept is the most effective instrument for the purpose, and most reliable. In fact, in most of the cases where the Mumbai Police has been able to achieve success was through intercept which was allowed under MACOCA. It must be recorded that Maharashtra's MACOCA was the first law in India which allowed intercept to a police. Intercepts the world over—the British Law now allows it, the American Law allows it—have become important instruments in not only intelligence gathering but also in securing conviction.

Ordinarily, denials will have to be proved in a normal court of law, because the policeman is at odds to prove various facts and the accused is entitled to benefits of doubt and many others. But when faced with his own voice, not many are able to deny and wriggle out of what their real intent was. But there should be no scope of lawful intercepts being misused by anyone, under any circumstances. There should be safeguards regime in place, listing people who can be intercepted. The intercepts must be approved in a post-decisional hearing by a specialized review committee. Special rules of evidence and special rules of trial are required in such cases.

The U.S. has gone to the extent of setting up secret military tribunals. One reason for this decision is that large number of ordinary citizens are not prepared to come and depose in the open trails against the hardened criminals. Some other important legal instruments of a powerful anti-terrorist regime are : (1) The kind of protection to be given to the witnesses. (2) The more difficult bail provisions.

In this context, a little deeper analysis of the issues involved is required here than the surface reactions to the changes made in the relevant law. Three examples should suffice : two comparatively recent ones and third a well-known illustration. When the Parliament was attacked on 13 December 2001 all the five terrorists were killed in the ensuing fire fight with the security forces guarding the premises. In every suicide attack, getting a *fidayeen* alive is rather difficult. They either kill the security people and escape or get killed themselves. So one can get no evidence from the dead. In such cases, how does an investigator move under the normal Law? He has to find out who were the people behind these five who provided them logistical support to execute the dastardly act?

At one stage, a particular clue leads to the first person, then to second person, third person and to the fourth. In due course, somebody breaks down and says : "We were all brought into the picture. Money was given to us by some one hiding in the hills at Pahalgam called Gazi Baba." Another one says he gave us the money that came from across the border. It was learnt that they were taken across the border several times to receive necessary training for the tasks allotted to each of them. They were members of a banned organization.

The most important pieces of evidence are not going to come from the ordinary eye witnesses who were present in the Parliament that day like some MPs and officials, because eye evidence can only be against the five who are no more alive. But to get behind those who were behind the five, police has to crack up one of the former. And that leads from one to another. Therefore, the traditional rule of confessional statement not being admissible is one procedural aspect that needed to be changed. This has indeed been changed in anti-terrorist laws in various parts of the world.

But for that component, the amendment worked into the law of evidence, how does the police establish the entire chain? A major case comes to mind when one of the leaders of the separatist organizations in Kashmir was arrested for having received huge funds from abroad (in 2001). How do the investigators get the first clue about the source of these funds? It came from the intercepts. Intercepts of messages exchanged between the international funding groups and recipients on the other ends. But when you demand repatriation or extradition of the people from foreign countries who have sent funds, they require evidence. In the present days, but for the intercepts made possible by the modern technology and rules as permissible, and yet again, but for the confessional statements with safeguards being made admissible, it will be very difficult to go behind these conspiracies.

There was a significant case when TADA was still in force. Incidentally, the campaign against TADA had started because of its misuse after the Mumbai blast cases. But when Rajiv Gandhi was assassinated in 1991, TADA was still in force. The people who killed Rajiv Gandhi died on the spot. When the special Investigation Team started investigating all those who were behind the conspiracy, all that they could find in terms of evidence—about such details as who gave the money, who gave the weapons, who provided the inspiration, who provided them shelter, who provide them with vehicles, etc—were their own statements. A careful study of the judgment of the Supreme Court in the Rajiv Gandhi assassination case revealed that TADA had a similar provision, a much tougher provision for recording confessional statement, and admitting them. The difference between TADA and POTA was that under TADA it could be recorded before a senior police officer and that was enough but under POTA it was to be recorded before a police officer but within 24 hours ratified before a judge. So there is a safeguard one had to first do it before a police officer and then go before a judge. We take those four or five statements which these people had made against themselves out. But for it, there was no other admissible evidence.

So we would actually have had situation where a former Prime Minister gets assassinated before a crowed of several thousand people and assailants die on the spot. But for the fact that a special rule of evidence did exist, there was no other way where evidence against them would have been forth coming. The establishment of a strong anti-terrorist legal regime is one of the very important aspects of fight against terrorism. When nations establish strong regimes against terrorism, whether it is security regime or a legal regime, and puts in place best kind of safeguards, human rights groups the world over complain that some form of aberrations or violations of human rights may take place.

## Human Rights Groups : Are they all Genuine?

It is important to ensure that when this anti-terrorist legal regime is being implemented, a democratic society must never lose sight of the fact that to fight terrorism it does not give such powers to police that it can actually go and haul up innocent citizens with no legal remedy available to them. Such concerns are justified, and must be appreciated. Hence the importance of safeguards against such arbitrary exercise of power by police or any other authority of the State.

There are large number of human rights groups, citizen groups, political groups, state human rights mechanism which in the given situation have a very important role to play. As responsible organization they have to watch out that no innocent people become a victim of a tough regime but that is as far as human rights groups genuinely concerned with human rights go. But then there is a second category of human rights groups also which has emerged. The aim of this second type seem to be to malign the governments, the security forces and intelligence agencies.

It should not come as a surprise if some analysts believe the second category of human rights groups to be the over-ground face of the underground. It is a known fact that every underground insurgent movement has its over ground sympathisers generally organized as a human rights organization. These are to be seen in contra-distinction with some of the statutory ones and other genuine ones. A major Object of such organizations is to actually continuously carry on a campaign which indirectly helps the cause of terrorists. So every time the PWG in Andhra Pradesh attacked an industrial establishment during early years of 2000s decade, one would have found same old faces coming up and saying "we are fighting the repressive machinery of the state". "They are always silent about what the PWG has done to the people of Andhra Pradesh or to the economy of the State or the industrial establishment or the innocent persons it is trying to target", one finds similar campaigns presently carried out in Chhattisgarh, Bihar or Jharkhand. Essential aim is to support the insurgents and malign and weaken the counter-terrorism agencies.

Therefore, as a mature democracy, a responsible society, the civil society must be very watchful and wary of this second category of human rights organizations, which, by now experience has taught us, have actually become the over ground supporters of which otherwise is a banned, an insurgent or a terrorist activity in itself.

So these are the challenges which a mature society has to face. Terrorism's capacity to destroy life, to destroy economy, to destroy sovereignty of the countries is tremendous. Likewise, its ability to devalue democratic tradition is also tremendous. Externally-sponsored insurgency also gains support when they are given refuge from segments of the democratic society. So maturity of the Indian society is always on trial when the country is under threat from these disruptive and subversive forces in the guise of terrorists and insurgents. It is a war India just cannot afford to lose. It is a war which has to be fought through the instrument of intelligence and through a determined effort to eliminate some of the social discontent which in some areas does help or cause terrorism. It is one of the major challenges as far as the Indian polity is concerned.

## Nations Handling Terrorism : A Comparative Study

Political assassination has a hoary history. But here, only some recent examples are cited, starting with Prime Minister Indira Gandhi who was assassinated on 31 October 1984 by her own guards at her official New Delhi residence. Sant Harchand Singh Longowal, President of the Akali Dal, was felled down by the militant Sikhs for concluding an accord with Prime Minister Rajiv

Gandhi to resolve the Panjab imbroglio in July 1985. The latter himself fell to the LTTE human bomb on 21 May 1991. In the spring of 1981, President Reagan was shot in the chest as he left the Hilton Hotel in Washington, by a young man. On 13 May 1981, Pope John Paul II, blessing the crowds in St. Peters Square, Rome, was hit in the stomach with bullet fired by a Turk from the Grey Wolf terrorist group. The Provisional IRA detonated a bomb at Sullom Voe Oil terminal in the Shetlands while Queen Elizabeth was inaugurating it. Then, as she was riding at the head of a Sovereign's Escort of Household Cavalry, her ceremonial bodyguard, to the Trooping of the Colour in London, a 17-year-old boy fired a shot at close range from a replica Colt revolver. Had the bullets been real, she would have died. On 30 August 1981, President Mohammad Ali Rajai of Iran and his Prime Minister were killed by a terrorist bomb in Tehran. Only weeks later, a terrorist in the Egyptian Army Uniform murdered President Anwar Sadaat on 6 October 1981 with burst of Kalashnikov fire while he was reviewing a ceremonial parade.

So, once again the terrorists had turned to assassination as a tactic to draw public attention. The 1981 CIA report on international terrorism had confirmed the trend : "The number of terrorist incidents apparently aimed at causing casualties". More notably, assassination attempts had increased in the 1980s. Growing international cooperation, changes in the law, improved security and police methods, and creation of the special anti-terrorist forces rendered the terrorists' task more difficult in many fields. But it is an accepted fact that statesmen, religious leaders, members of Royalty, because of their positions, cannot be fully protected. The very nature of their jobs and offices they hold demand their appearance in public, and in particular for the politicians, it is unavoidable not to come in close contact with the people they serve and represent.

Then there were certain international conventions and practices that affected certain counter-terrorist measures for reasons of human dignity, human freedom, and needs to guarantee minimum human rights. Post-World War II, the United Nations, through the Universal Declaration of Human Rights, made references to the need for guaranteeing the right to life and security of the person. In another covenant, it was recommended that no one shall be orbitrarily deprived of his life. Other U.N.

declarations mandated that every state had a duty to refrain from forcible actions which deprived people of their right to self-determination. All these are desirable aims, but collectively, all such declarations have restricted the powers of nation-state, to certain extent, to defend their integrity and sovereignty.

A Declaration of Principles of International Law stated : "In their actions against and resistance to such forcible action in pursuit of the right to self-determination, such people are entitled to receive support". Hence it is easy for an out-of-job international lawyer to use any such declaration as justification for any kind of murderous activity undertaken in the pursuit of securing the 'sacred' right of self-determination! Of course, self-determination is an acceptable, even noble idea, were it not for some ugly campaigns which sometimes secured it theoretically in the Third World, bringing to power a gang of political thugs who would then ensure that the unfortunate people under their control would never again have the opportunity to exercise it. One cynic, but perhaps a realist, asserted that it was the ploy of former colonial powers to keep their erstwhile colonies in turmoil. India is still suffering the consequences of pledge of self-determination for the Kashmir is given through the U.N. by its then idealistic Prime Minister yet again, some European nations who gave shelter to all kinds of revolutionaries, from Marx through Lenin to Khomenei and working against their own nations, in the name of preversation of individual freedom have changed tack after the 9/11 and 7/7. Forgetting the lofty idealism they flaunted enthusiastically before the world, these very nation have legislated laws that curb that very individual freedoms and institute discriminatory practices against their own non-white citizens.

Consequently, the United Nations is a helpless spectator, unable to act as a body against the terrorist desperados. Its only achievement was instituting legal measures dealing with certain specific forms of terrorism. The General Assembly did adopt a convention on the prevention and punishment of crimes against the international, protected persons, including the agents. It was ratified by the requisite number of member-states for it to come into effect.

As early as 1963, the Tokyo Convention set down legal principles for dealing with the offences aboard aircraft, and instituted rules to ensure the return of hijacked aircraft and their passengers. But due to certain dissensions, it did not come into force till 1969, by which time individual countries were already taking their own measures to tighten aircraft security. Again, the Hague Convention on hijacking was signed in 1970, and came into force the next year. It required contracting states either to permit extradition of highjackers to country of origin, or to prosecute them under the legal code of the state where they were arrested. The Convention also recommended acceptance of the principle that it is a crime for any person to board an aircraft and to seize it in flight, or to gain control over it by force of arms or threats.

After the Hague Convention came another in 1971 in Montreal, where on international quorum extended the scope of international to include attacks on airports and grounded aircrafts. AI also instituted the principle of awarding severe penalties for such offences. Seven years later came the Bonn Summit (July 1978) attended by the government heads of Canada, France, Italy, Japan, the U.K., the U.S. and West Germany. They decided to apply sanctions against states which aided and abetted the hijacking of aircraft. It did contribute to making the world airlines safer for passengers and the crew. Analysts saw that "even Arab hard line members of the terrorist supporters' club were shy of continuing with their aid if the price of it meant disconnecting their airline communications with the world beyond theirs".

As in personal affairs, so in the international sphere, a good argument or a virtuous principle can always be put on its head by clever saphists. So it came as no surprise when the supporters of the terror trade tried to use the Geneva Convention in a self-serving way—never intended by the original formulation. They pleaded that terrorists who are arrested be treated as prisoners of war, and not as common criminals ; as after all, the terrorist outfits like to keep their men in pay play even after they have been captured. Next ploy is to rouse public opinion by claiming that they be given the special status of political prisoners.[3] For sure, the tactic works as the argument would find favour with certain category of countries and NGOs.

In early 1970s' organization of American States (OAS) formulated a convention to Prevent and Punish Acts of Terrorism taking the form of crimes against persons and the related extortion which has international significance. But as the Latin American States have traditionally believed that the principle of political asylum as inviolate, the legal apposition to the new measures slowed down its ratification and implementations. It is obvious that there have been attempts at controlling certain aspects of terrorism at the regional levels but these were rendered ineffectual, and even were aborted, in the face of certain ground realities.

The Interpol (International Criminal Police Organizations), with its headquarters just outside Paris, insists that it should restricts its activities to dealing with crime, but unfortunately, not all the governments, who contributed/enrolled their police personnel into the Interpol, were convinced that terrorism was a crime. This, undoubtedly, hampered its counter-terrorism—ender vour. Even then, Interpol has its uses as a line of communications between different police forces the world over. To wit, the Athens's police were able to identify the West German terrorist, and to detain him.

Apposed to the unhappy Latin American experience, its European version has proved a success. Since 1977, a permanent structure of police cooperation, TREVI (= Terrorism, Radicalism and Violence International), has been operating from its headquarters, 'secretly' located near the Champs Elysees. In U.K., it works from New Scotland Yard under the title of European Liaison section of the Special Branch. The Republic of Ireland (Eire) was the only EEC country not represented in TREVI. On the other hand, it has two non-EEC members (Israel and Switzerland). Its top secret sessions held in Switzerland go under the ruberic of the Club of Berne.

On its part, the NATO (North Atlantic Treaty Organization) set up a useful system for exchange of information on terrorists, their organizations, techniques, and their weapon-holdings. Joint training visits and exchanges of security people among NATO nations as also among those of the EEC became a regular feature.

Most important development in the field of counter-terrorism till then was the initiative by the Council of Europe to formulate a Convention on the Suppression of Terrorism, signed in January 1977 by 17 of its 19 member-states. The Republic of Ireland and Malta Chose to stay out. The Convention aimed at persuading European states to treat all acts of terrorism as criminal. Such acts embraced assassinations, kidnapping, hostage-taking, bomb attacks including grenades and rockets, and hijacking.

In dealing with such attacks, the signatories were urged to include even those arrested under the 'political offence' clauses which, in the past, had been used to justify refusal to permit extradition. Austria, Denmark, Sweden, the U.K. and West Germany readily agreed to this proviso. But Belgium and France were reluctant to ratify, declaring that their Constitutions enshrined the principle of political asylum. (It needs to be said that it was late 1970s, two and half decade's before 9/11, and U.S. attacks in Afghanistan and Iraq. Things have changed since. Today, most European nations, led by U.K., France, and Germany have in place stringent anti-terrorist legislations).

Canada was the first victim of native terrorist campaign. In the late 1960s, French Canadian separatists in Quebec led by the Front du Liberation du Quebec (FLQ) launched a series of violent attacks, culminating in the kidnapping of the British Trade Commissioner for Quebec James cross in October 1970. Adopting a firm line, Prime Minister Trudeau refused to yield to their demand for a $500,000 ransom, and release of an FLQ terrorist already in prison. The FLQ then seized Pierre Laports, Minister of Labour is the Quebec Provincial Government. As Canada refused to budge, the Minister was murdered. After Trudeau agreed to a deal under which three of the kidnappers and four of their relations were flown to Cuba in a Canadian military aircraft, the FLQ freed James Cross.

Even if Ottawa did make a partial surrender, the incident is of great significance in the annals of counter-assaults on terrorism, because, thereafter, Prime Minister Trudeau made a firm commitment to rid Canada of the FLQ, deploying all means at his disposal. But India did not show similar firmness after Prime Minister Indira Gandhi was gunned down by her own guards, instigated by Sikh terrorists/separatist. Young Rajiv Gandhi, her son and successor 'surrendered' to the terrorists by ordering release of the detained Sikhs, under false notions of political accommodations. He himself was felled in May 1991 and after a long trial, her assassin, a female "human bomb", was handed down death sentence. His wife, Sonia Gandhi, publicly pardoned the criminal, but she is yet awaiting the gallows. When Prime Minister Rajiv Gandhi promised to be sympathetic towards the "wanted" Sikh terrorists, a prominent Sikh leader dubbed the move as a fraud.

But the Sikh extremists continued on the terror track. Ottawa again invited adverse attention when within hours two terrorist crimes were perpetrated at places separated by thousands of miles. The crash of an Air India flight coming from Canada off the coast of Ireland, killing all its passengers as also a bomb explosion at the Narita Airport in Tokyo involving the baggage unloded from a C.P. Airflight from Canada that killed two Japanese workers, were both ascribed to the Sikh terrorists. But misplaced concern for civil liberties come in the way of out right and strident condemnation of such barbaric crimes. Here is David Barrett, head of the opposition New Democratic Party, addressing an international conference on the subject : "The scar on Canada's record of civil liberties which occurred ten years ago is a classic illustration of how the State in an attempt to combat terrorism, over stepped its boundaries and threatened its own citizens".

As a cynic put, these are the pitfalls of democratic governance. Even in the face of such horrific human tragedy, which dispatched hundreds of innocent persons to their watery graves, the opposition leader has to lament the "threats" to civil liberties, forgetting the mass murders! Democratic governments, by definition, cannot legitimately establish consent for the use of force. Even a country like India, which has suffered the ravages of terrorism for nearly half a century and has seldom demonstrated firm resolve to defeat terrorism by adoption of draconian measures, has been accused by the international community of using excessive force and "trampling" over the human rights of the terrorists who are bent upon inflicting death and destruction in Jammu and Kashmir and are keen to see it as a part of Pakistan. One cannot blame some concerned Indians if they dub such attitude as travesty of truth—a perversity unimaginable.

But when the U.K. faced similar threat to its peace and integrity, the western media was not as loud in its condemnation, which it had earlier heaped on India, but some NGOs were. It was in 1969 when the Provisional IRA unleashed a new campaign of terrorism. The British Army was called in, both to fight the terrorists and to protect the Catholics from the volatile Protestants. The Westminster Parliament the Northern Ireland (Emergency Provisions) Act 1973. The measure was dubbed "draconian" as it made it possible to try those charged with terrorist offences by a judge sitting without a jury. This Act informed the legal basis for all security activity in Northern Ireland. But the IRA then spread its terror tentacles to the British mainland. After a particularly vicious bomb attack on two pubs in Birmingham in 1974, which killed 21 people and roused strong public emotion, the Labour Government brought in the Prevention of Terrorism (Temporary Provisions) Act.

The Act gave the Home Secretary the power to expel from the U.K. persons concerned in commission, preparation, or instigation of acts of terrorism. The court procedure were dispensed with on grounds that the decision was taken usually on intelligence information which could not be disclosed in the court. The second major power given to him allowed the Minister to detain a suspect terrorist upto seven days without bringing him before the court after his arrest by policemen without a warrant. It also provided for the proscription in Great Britain of organizations considered to be concerned with terrorism. The Act has proved effective against international as well as Irish terrorists.

These two Acts show how far a democratic state was prepared to go in combating terrorism. Successive British governments have been conscious of the conflict between such provisions and the preservation of civil rights. But in times of emergency/crisis, extreme measures have to be resorted to.

It is worth mentioning that post 9/11 and 7/7, London has legislated for harsher measures than those detailed above. These will be discussed a little later in the text.

Different countries have different modalities to deal with emergent situations of similar natures. The Republic of Ireland has even harsher laws against the IRA than the British. Analysts assert that anti-terrorist legislation in the Republic of Ireland is probably a greater infrigement of civil rights than tolerated in any other Western democracy.

In the same context, although a law like the Britain's anti anti-terrorist legislation should be imposed in the United States too, but theoretically that would be ruled out by the 5th Amendment which specifies that no one shall be deprived of liberty without due process of law, and that the accused shall enjoy right to trial by an impartial jury. But then the U.S. Supreme Court has never treated the commands and prohibitions of the Bill of Rights as categorical. After all, Abraham Lincoln suspended *habeas corpus* intended for those suspected of being confederate sympathisers, and tried people by non-jury Military Commissions without interference from the courts. Even more, he defended his action by claiming that no government, however liberal and democratic, could be expected to stand by and see itself destroyed by the lawless who place no restriction on their own violence.

Even if 140 years intervene between Lincoln and the current incumbent Bush, with an approval rating hovering about 30 per cent (June 2006), the latter seems to be well emulating the record of the Great Lincoln in ignoring the Bill of Rights, and without annoying the courts. But the squeamish may carp that Bush is facing no civil war! But there has been worldwide criticism, even condemnation, of the U.S. treatment of Iraqi prisoners inside Iraq post-U.S. attack, and of the terror suspects, stationed at Guantanmo Bay in Cuba and others transported to foreign soils post-Afghanistan and 9/11.

The U.S. Supreme Court has given a critical ruling in July 2006. Its details and action by the Bush Administration in consequence of that ruling, will be studied in a latter chapter of this work.

The anti-terrorist forces of some other countries are mentioned below briefly :

1. France : GIGN. Raised in 1974, it is based in Maisons Alfort, near Paris.
2. West Germany : GSG9. It is believed to have undergone five years of intensive training before taking the field.
3. Soviet Union : Spetsnaz. It is well trained for sensitive missions, including action overseas. Spetsnaz and KGB are reported to have figured in the assassination of Afghan President Hafizullah Amin before the Soviet troops moved into Kabul. Even during the World War II, Spetsnaz units operated behind the enemy lines. Organised in two brigades, they are trained in radio and weapons operations, infiltration tactics, sabotage, explosive and incendiaries, hand-to-hand combat and silent killing techniques. A feature of Spetsnaz is that some of its personnel are strong women, outstanding athletes, with ability to handle most weapons.

## Terrorism and its Motivation : U.S.—CIA View

After President Reagan declared/dubbed the Soviet Union "an evil empire", there was a manifest Proclivity in the U.S. academia to blame most of the ills the world war heir to at the door of the latter. Scholars and analysts were liberally helped by the CIA. One of the scholars, Miles Copeland wrote in 1975 : The current wave of terrorism which is mostly of an extreme leftist variety, is harder to contain than terrorism by nationalist rightist extremists because many leftist militants "have decided that anyone or anything that aids 'capitation' or 'imperialism' is a legitimate target. The rightist extremists are generally more selective and hence, it is easier to protect against their attacks".[4]

To paraphrase Copeland : "There is sizeable case in thc nations today of the New Left-type extremists and their supporters determined to use violence, if necessary, to destroy our basic institutions. What motivates these young people, many of whom come from affluent homes and are well-educated? What is the cause of their desire to destroy social institutions; their behaviour that violence is justified; their alienation from democratic values? Why have many of them categorically rejected their families and the institutions—schools, home, religion—in their early years? Many of them have shut themselves off completely from contact with their parents and former friends, and live almost completely in the radical youth culture."

These are difficult questions. The answer might lie in the inner motivating principle which could be called "a morality of revolutionary radicalism" a "code" of ethics" that not only sanctions and justifies violent actions against society, but also may on occasions, by creating personal feelings of 'guilt', encourage or trigger unlawful acts. Copeland feels, to understand this dangerous phenomenon of new left extremism and its appeal to sections of youth, we must know more about the strange 'Morality' that provides a false spiritual underpinning and motivation for violence. Taking the case of USA, the American discusses some aspects of New Leftist "Morality of revolutionary radicalism".

1. "They believe this nation (USA) is a modern day 'Babylon' (a world used in the New Left literature) characterized slavery, fear, exploitation and repression, sans any freedom of any kind. Its institutions—economic, political, social, religious—are permeated with evil. Democratic government Judeo-Christian values are mere delusions.
2. "The way to meet evil (Babylon,' read USA) is not simply to reform or change it but to totally destroy existing institutions." 'In death-directed America', reads a message from some radical bombers, there is only one way to a life of save and freedom : to attack and destroy the forces of death and exploitation and to build a just society-revolution.' (The phraseology is a direct import from

Marxist-Leninist tracts). Violent destruction is the creed. A weatherman leader said, 'we have to tear down this country using bombs, guns, fire bombs, anything and everything.

3. "In their destructive zeal, they do not realize or even care that though the violence they advocate, people might be injured, the rights of others violated, and injustice committed. The fanatic devotion to their cause overrides reason, compassion and even common sense. One of their leaflets starts : 'Until a student is willing to destroy totally and joyfully...his student movement will be just that, never truly revolutionary... The building are yours for burning for until they are destroyed, along with civilization and its death, you with not live.'

4. "For him the use of violence is defensive. He has 'moral' compunction to obliterate through violence what we regarded as evil... His justification : 'was not the Government on evil and demonic institution already perpetrating violence'. By this reasoning, violence is seen as constructive, creative, an agent of freedom and justice!

5. "The New Left Morality" is elitist, discriminatory, and unidimensional. 'Justice' becomes what it says it is! It selectively creates its 'Martyrs' and 'victims'. It is indifferent to injustice suffered by its victims. Its sympathies and animus are programmed; they can be turned off and on at will.

6. "The New Left Morality is expressed in bitter polemical terms that choke off reason, respect for the other person, and rational debate. All too often these young people feel they are the sole custodians of virtue, knowledge, and truth. They pour out a continuous stream of vituperative outpourings, often laced with abuse and even obscenity, against the 'enemy'. Where is the chance for an honest discourse?

7. "The New Left Morality seeks and depends upon a scapegoat, which conveniently is 'America', 'the imperialist United States', and 'bourgeoise'. All the ills of the society are heaped onto this scapegoat, with no attempt to analyse or understand historical or other reasons. In this way they absolve themselves of any responsibility to work out

possible alternatives or seek solutions to the problem they rail against so passionately.

8. "The Morality of the New Left espouses freedom from personal responsibility which in essence, means anarchy. 'We are outlaws, we are free', proclaims Bernardine Dohrn, a key healherman leader in a communiqué from the underground. He rejects any concept of law unless he makes it himself. In his eyes violence is not a crime, though violent act of a person he does not like is a 'crime' without question.
9. "In their morality play, the inherent dignity of a man, who is God's creation, is moched. These revolutionaries do not trust man to exercise his faculties—his judgment, his understanding of the past, his vision of the future. For they look upon him as a piece of matter to be manipulated".

"Let us not lose faith in our young people. Both clergymen and lay people have been doing tremendous work in bringing the 'world of God' to these misguided and spiritually hungry young men and women". This scholar seems to be giving too much credit to God and spiritualism to change the minds of these "Misguided youths". "Undoubtedly, the current decline of militancy on campuses is due in part to the efforts of dedicated religious people working among the extremists. The excitement of knowing God have given many former militants a new adventure of the spirit. They have been transformed from extremist revolutionaries to religious revolutionaries." He feels religion has a key role in meeting revolutionary violence. "Personal evangelism, carried out with understanding, compassion and love." It is construed that lives changes for religion lead to a changed society and changed world."

This 1975 Copeland analysis has been quoted in extensor advisedly as it lends itself to some apt observations in 2006 :

1. 30 years back, terrorism of the New Left was harder to contain as compared to the one by nationalist right extremist. In the 1990s, and particularly the-post-Nine-Eleven, the world seems to find no ways of dealing with the violence unleashed by the men blinded by fanatic beliefs or fired by ideological zealotry.
2. Osama's message may not be in florid prose, but it is as powerful as those of the New Left, and perhaps even more so, as he quotes the Quran to the faithful.

3. There is no scope or hope for a dialogue with today's terrorist groups.
4. It seems so easy to transform a terrorist into a 'human bomb' with the promise of heaven and 74 virgins.
5. The terrorists today too have their scapegoats for the ills of the world-everyone else but for themselves.
6. Three great evils, or satans, presently are the USA, Israel and India.
7. Copeland invoking evangelical solution to the terrorism problems of 1975 sounds so much like Bush 2004-06 invoking God in his public pronouncement and advocating evangelism in public.

Let it be acknowledged that terrorism post Nine-Eleven and post-Iraq is of for more lethal variety than ever seen earlier presently, terrorism is the function of the "fanatical few."

## Power of the Fanatic

One of the paradoxes of our advanced high-tech world is the "power of the fanatical few"; that is, as our society becomes more urban, industrial, complex and inter-related, the greater becomes the power of the fanatical minority—sometimes only one or two individuals, or a small handful if it so desires, to disrupt, subvert, destroy, and endanger the rights, lives, and property of others. Perhaps the most demonstrative and sensational aspect of this "power of the fanatical few" is reflected in the cases of the aircraft hijacking. Here just one person takes total control of the aircraft, jeopardising the lives of hundreds of passengers and crew members not to speak of concern and anxiety of their relatives, and friends of those aboard.

For law enforcement agencies of nations concerned, the crescendo of bombing, hijackings, sabotage, and assault on police and military personnel have posed serious problems law enforcement is the first line of defence of democratic societies. The police officer, on guard duty 24 hrs. a day, is the protector of the rights, lives and property of the citizens. But then, has not the law enforcement always faced the destructive and criminal law? What is so different about these bombings and hijackings? Simply put, law enforcement has always faced hoodlum-type criminals—the bank robbers, kidnapper, the thief and he is still there. But the new type of *criminal* is qualitatively different—trained, skilled and highly motivated.

The old line, a hoodlum's hatred of society usually stemmed from personal and selfish reasons; and could not be bothered about society as a whole or moved by any greater causes or moral impulses. If he needs money or an automobile, he steals. If anything or anyone comes in his way, he destroys and kills. Nothing pleases him more than anonymity and non-interference. His hope is to rob a bank or kidnap a victim and make a clean break, without being identified. He does not seek out the policeman for the purpose of inflicting injury.

The revolutionary guerrilla or a terrorist today is highly motivated, ideologically fired up, and trained to kill for effect. He deliberately attacks the police, bombs police stations, kills officers and public figures, and taunts and harasses the symbols of law and social order. His violence is offensive, designed to tear down society as a whole. The destructive and destabilising potential of the terrorist is on the increase since the 1980s, and achieved new heights on Nine-Eleven—with the use of advanced technology and well-honed and coordination skills.

## Fighting Terrorism : Simplistic Solutions

How should the world act effectively against Terrorism? Having identified the essential nature of terrorism, some suggest it be treated as a *crime* and its perpetrators as *criminals*. They feel that the fact of the terrorist being politically motivated does not move them any different from the common criminal. It should provide clues for their apprehension, the rest is irrelevant. It is argued that no special legal powers be given to the Governments beyond those which already exist to combat organised crime of the Mafia variety. This obviously is simplistic. As recent experience shows, special laws are needed to combat the menace. Infact even before Nine-Eleven, most states facing this threat had equipped themselves with special powers to deal with it. In India's case it was POTA (Prevention of Terrorism Act), passed by the NDA Government (1998-2004). But the UPA Government removed it from the Statute Book in 2004, as some State Governments were deemed to have misused its draconian provisions against the Minority community (read Muslims).

Next it is suggested that a terrorist must never be allowed to feel safe anywhere in the world. A terrorist kept constantly on the defensive is an ineffectual terrorist. It again is being idealistic, a mere desideratum. Given the state of the world, to expect all the states to act in unison against terrorists is asking for the Moon! The U.N. would be the ideal body to deal with international terrorism, but it has failed to agree on the term. It has passed an international Convention on Terrorism, but that has proved of little use in dealing with the evil. There are insuperable problems in the way. To wit, the al Qaeda and Taliban terrorists creating havoc in Afghanistan find ready shelter in the border areas of Pakistan, particularly in Waziristan. Nearer home, Islamic terrorists chased by the Indian military escape into their safe haven in Pakistan Occupied Kashmir (POK). Pakistan has brazenly acknowledged its moral, political and diplomatic support to Muslim extremists creating Murder and Mayhem in Indian Kashmir. It trains, equips and arms them in the camps located in POK and Punjab but again brazenly denies their existence for form.

There are other states sponsoring and nurturing terrorism to destabilize its adversaries or neighbours. President Bush's "Axis of Evil" has three states : Iran, Iraq and North Korea. A look back at an earlier period tells us that China gave shelter, training, and material and financial help to the Indian insurgents to enable them to carry out their terrorist acts on the Indian soil. They were, to name the names, Nagas, Mizos and Manipuri groups in the 1950s, 1960s, and even the 1960s. Then Pakistan and later Bangladesh entered the field to keep the Indian terrorism's pot boiling. The Nagas in particular, were always comfortable with their ethnic brethren in Burma, now Myanmar just across the border. If the Myanmar ethnic rebels on its eastern and western areas found shelter in Thailand and India when ever under pressure from its military, its Muslim recalcitrant in the south-west often flee to Bangladesh just across the Chittagang Hill Tracts (CHT) border. Bangladesh blames India for sheltering its Chakma rebels, forgetting that these hapless Chakmas were pushed out to Indian border states as a consequence to policy measure by various East Pakistan and Bangladeshi Governments post-1947; viz, the settling of Muslims from the surrounding plains in the CHT inhabited by the former. If Sri Lanka accused India of running training camps for Tamil rebels in South India, Pakistan blamed it for extending helping hand to the MQM fomenting anti-Pakistan sentiments in Sindh in the past, and to the Baluchi rebels presently (2004-05).

So it is, obvious that the inter-state dynamics of terrorism in South and South-East Asia presents a pretty messy picture. Moving north, the Soviet Union in its hey day trained guerrillas and subversives from many nations to destabilize their Governments. It was openly exporting revolution and communism to the foreign shores. From the preceding, it is obvious that there was hardly any chance of the international community acting in concert against terrorism, some shrill noises on the issue not withstanding.

Some unknown hands seem to be dealing justice to the states that earlier wantonly spread the cancer through their policy measures. All these states are themselves facing serious terrorist violence, espousing secessionism ; viz Baluchistan in Pakistan and NWFP (Waziristan), China in Sinkiang, and Russia in Chechniya and Ossetia. The fires they lit for others have reached home! But the best case in the genre pertains to U.S. and Pakistan which jointly nurtured the mouster called Al Qaeda with men, money, and material, in Afghanistan to ouster Russia from there. Today, the monster is feeding on its foster parents. Some natural justice, this!

Libya under *Khadafi/Ghaddafi/Gaddafi* had earned notoriety with its open and well-publicised help to various terrorist outfits, including the IRA, President Reagan's attack on Tripoli in Mid-1980s sobered the flamboyant Dictator! His instantaneous public repudiation of the subsequent Pam Am hijacking in Pakistan drew world-wide attention, for changed stance of that nation in such incidents. The U.S. raid did have some effect on the maverick. There was sudden drop in Libyan-inspired terrorist acts in the wave of the U.S. raid on Tripoli. We can imagine the effects of more nations adopting firm, uncompromising policy stance on the scourge. But that is easier said than done as will be seen presently, because of the turns and twists the international policy of various players engaged in the Great Game of controlling the Frankenstein's monster in the form of mindless terrorism spawned by its perpetrators.

Some western analysts were fond of asking the all-important question in the 1970s and the 1980s : "why have not the civilized powers moved against this new barbarism?" The question was spawned by the superiority complex the West nurtured vis-à-vis the Communist nations led by the Soviet Union. The 'civilised powers' obviously were the US—led West. It was certainly a battle they could win, if they really wanted to.

The hesitancy of some of the governments could be ascribed to the success of the terrorist propagandists and to the influence of the media and many revered and influential public figures who conferred political and moral respectability on the terrorist leaders and their cause.

This analyst could not understand why the murderous policies of the Arafat's of this world are regarded with anything but loathing. He is obviously a die-hard anti-communist of the McCarthy School, as his analysis below shows :

Why have not other writers addressed this critical issue? If they do so, they do not resolve it, but they hint at the answer—the moral self-doubt. This is because the west has lost confidence in its ethnical foundations. And so it has conceded some legitimacy to the goals of today's (1970s and 1980s) terrorists, and has therefore disarmed itself.

The clearest evidence of this can be seen in the fact of our granting moral recognition to the Soviet Union and the people's Republic of China where—as is characteristic of terrorist organizations—the human life is summarily decimated when the needs of some faceless collectinist cause demands it. The significance of the people gunned down periodically on the West's airports or blown up in its shopping centers pales before the fact of the millions cold-bloodedly killed by the buthers of totalitarianism. If Communist States are treated as respectable members of the comity of civilized people, why should not the PLO welcome too?

The cause of this disabling moral relativism is not some terrorist publicity coup; it is rather our own schools and universities, which have stained man's minss for generations with a steady diet of pragmatism, whih holds that there are no moral absolutes could lead ven to believe that "one man's" civilisation is another's Black Hob of Culture."

Communism and terrorism are inned not only in theory but also in blood-stained practice. Without Soviet support international terrorism would revert to its earlier localised manifestations before the 1960s and would hardly dominate the global scene. Over a thousand killers have been trained for the PLO in the Soviet Union above. All of the major terrorist organisations have benefitted from the military instruction in the Soviet Union and in such satelites as Cuba, South Yemen, and North Korea. The Soviet Union documented in 'Claire Sterlidgs'. *The Terror Network*, is a natural co-conspirator in terrorism since it istelf is a totalitarian State, the goal of all terrorist groups. It is no coincidence that there have been no reports of terrorist bombings in Moscow, Peking, or Havana; totalitarian states permit no competition for power in conquered lands. No Libyan assassination teams or IRA dynamite squads will ever strike in those capitals.

What terrorists desire is the imposition of tyronny. It is certainly not the rights they wish to establish, but the obliteration of rights. Their action and their words covey this over and over. We should believe then, and respond in kind.

If the free world ever finds the moral rectitide to take terrorism seriously enough to act as suggested above, it must ultimately reconsider its relationship with the other totalitarian Governments. The logic of self preservation must apply to all instances of criminality. It does not allow an individual or a nation to stamp out one gang while attempting to live in "peaceful coexistence" with another. It requires honesty to see the absence of any fundamental difference among the Weatherman, the Mafia, the PLO and the Soviet Government. All exist via the barrel of gun, and seek power for power's sake—whether over a city street or over a continent. We are targets.

Guns qalore, there are, smoking or not and the total framework of the Soviet support of international terrorism is surely beyond reasonable questioning.

The above is an attempt to provide badly needed public account of a systematic political and moral challenge to the way of life in the pluralistic societies.

The analyst at the end is bold enough to say (late 1980's) that in his opinion his formulations are based on information contained in the restricted intelligence files of governments, and perhaps not even there. For all his claims of intense research and sincerity of purpose, the above averment is likely to be dismissed by the Russophiles and even liberal Americans as fulminations of a fervid mind of a rabid anti-communist pseudo-intellectual. Even then certain observations should be in order to put the issues in perspective :

1. The above was written in the 1980s, during the Cold War, on between the two blocks. President Reagan had designated the Soviet system as the 'Evil Empire', and worked hard for its dissolution.
2. At the time, a majority of terrorism had been spawned by communist states against liberal democracies. This generally remained time till the collapse of the Soviet Union.
3. China had started being seen as a threat to the west.
4. After the Soviet collapse, and particularly post Nine-Eleven, the face of international terror has changed. Besides an old exception, it is generally inspired by Muslim fundamentalist ideology. Expectedly, a scholar has talked of 'clash of civilizations'.

One observation made in this analysis remains as valid today as it was 20 years back : A state cannot act against one set of terrorists and sup with another. Pakistan cannot continue to attack and eliminate the terrorists threatening its own integrity and simultaneously train and equip another set to bleed India with a thousand cuts.

## Panel wants hi-tech tools to counter terror

The Administrative Reforms Commission (ARC) is going to recommend to the government a total technological overhaul of the anti-terror machinery and streamlining of the intelligence network to make anti-terrorism a success, sources disclosed on 31 October 2006.

Based on the inputs from IB, RAW, and studies conducted conducted by experts abroad, the reports calls for stringently containing activities like drung trafficking, money boundering and cycler crimes, as there are clear linkages between terrorism and these crimes.

The report's major postulation, however, is that terrorism stems out of conflict resolution failures. It favours concerted efforts by the administration to resolve conflicts without allowing them to prolong. A conflict situation arising out of local discontent tends to be exploited by hostile foreign elements. It refers to lingering conflicts in the North-East and suggests how inimical forces take advantage of such situations. Referring to the links between terror and festering conflict situations, it argues that the best pre-emptive measures against the ultras would be speedy resolution of such conflicts. Inimical foreign serces have made use of such situation to unleash aggression against the country.

The ARC calls for efforts to involve civil society in the anti-terror campaign suggesting that an exclusive police approach is unlikely to yield much success.[5]

However, the report is equally emphatic that in the coming days technology is going to play a big role in chasing the terrorists.

## Anti-Terrorism Coordination: World-wide

It is for note that in this period, mid 1980s hijacking was the main threat. Four Chairmen of the US House Committees wrote to President Ronald Reagan proposing an international treaty requiring all member nations to treat all terrorists as criminals and to impose economic sanctions against countries that offered sanctuaries to the hijackers. They said: "The accords and organizing conventions should include the nations of Europe and the NAM to avoid turning the agreement into a pro or anti-American Statement."

This joint proposal from the four came in the wake of a spate of recent terrorist depredations, including the hijacking of a TWA Flt. 847 and taking of 39 American hostages, and loss of 329 lives off the Irish coast as a result of the bombing of Air India flight 182 from Montreal to India. A congressional Staff aide noted that condemnation of the hijacking of TWA Jetliner by Indian Prime Minister Rajiv Gandhi and his call for the immediate release of all American hostages "is very positive". India, *under* attack by terrorism itself, can contribute much to the success of such an international convention, particularly in its role as chairman of the NAM".

In a report from New Delhi late in June 1985 the *Washington Post* said: "With terrorist forces now threatening at home and overseas, India has turned full circle from its previously passive attitude towards acts of violence by extremist groups." *The Post* quoted an Embassy official as saying: "We were pleasantly surprised by it (Rajiv Gandhi's call) you know they usually do not do that". It said New Delhi's posture "came as international terrorism has been brought forcefully to the Indian nation with a series of assassinations, including the 31st October 1984 slaying of Indira Gandhi mother of Rajiv Gandhi....."

After Rajiv Gandhi's visit to US, in a joint communiqué "the Prime Minister and the President noted with concern the emergence of organised terrorism as a threat to peace and democracy". It noted that Gandhi had "welcomed the President's, desire for continued consultation and close cooperation's with the Indian Government on the international dimensions of terrorist violence in India."

The 7th UN Congress held in **Milano** (Italy) on 7th September 1984, its concluding day, adopted a 15-nation resolution on terrorism calling upon member nations to rationalize their extradition procedures and practices" and also make anti-terrorist laws. It expressed grave concern at the human, social and economic cost of such attacks to normal international intercourse in the areas of travel, commerce and diplomatic relations. It also request the Committee on Crime Prevention and Control to consider development of international measures aimed at strengthening of extradition procedures and other allied measures.

The resolution apparently fell short of the expectations of the NAM members. After protracted discussion the operative paragraph had to be dropped. The observers felt if this contentious paragraph had been endorsed, it would have had damaging implications for the liberation movements, fight against apartheid, colonialism, imperialism, etc.

The scope of final resolution is limited, as it confirms itself mainly to hijacking and does not even remotely touch the causes of terrorism. Still, even in its limited scope, most of the delegates welcomed it.

One of the delegates advised India to learn from experience and performance of Britain, Israel, the US etc., and create specialized anti-terrorist force "the nucleus of could be trained in Britain by that Country's crack anti-terrorist force, SAS which has been in the field since World War II, and has fought terrorism in several countries, including Malaya, Oman and Kenya, with outstaying and gratifying results. "Other countries have their specialized anti-terrorist forces, but none has quite equalled the professional standards of the SAS". Comprising of carefully selected and trained 1000 men; it is pressed into action when the normal police force finds the situation beyond its ken. So specialized and professional is the SAS that its men are always on a three-minute standby. It is headquartered at Hereford, England. The Delta force, US version of the SAS, is based at Fort Bragg.

## Canada's Stance on India-related Terrorism

Two aviation incidents, their origins traced to the Canadian Airports, caused considerable embarrassment to the nation and its Government: (1) Crash of an Air India flight originating in Canada off Ireland's west coast with the death of all 329 of its passengers (2) Bomb explosion on Tokyo's Narita Airport involving baggage unloaded from a CP Air Flight from Canada that killed two Japanese workers. Apart from the beating its anti terrorist stance received, Canada had reason to worry about its bilateral relations with India which may perceive it as a breeding ground for Sikh Terrorism against it.

Ignoring for the time being all its concern about the balance between the imperatives of free speech and association and the need to contain potential terrorists, it launched a vigorous drive to control Sikh extremism. Its security agencies, particularly the RCMP and the newly autonomous Canadian Security Intelligence Services (CSIS) mounted full time surveillance of Khalistani groups. They even began security checks of Canadians of Punjabi origin to "penetrate" extremist groups. There was an understanding with India to share anti-terrorist intelligence to deal with the Sikh terrorists active in Canada, US, Britain, West Germany and India.

The arrest of Rajinder Singh Purewal, caught smuggling parts of an Israeli Uzi submachine gun in Vancouver, was an evidence of Canada's serious resolve. Another person caught by British officials trying to bring in from Canada the other parts of the same gun was repatriated to Canada. This resolve showed Canada's commitment to combat international terrorism as a signatory to the Bonn Economic Summit Declaration on International Terrorism.

In addition, Canada relied on diplomacy based on personal contact between the two neophytes on the world scene, Prime Ministers Mulroney and Rajiv Gandhi, to right an uneven India - Canada relationship.

India, under attacked by terrorism itself, can contribute much to the counter-terrorism laws and efforts are watched and evaluated constantly and globally, so that every mistake and false move is broadcast immediately, and constant difficulty is experienced in distinguishing minor tactical success from major strategic advances. But they might also conclude that this reinforces the lessons of past conflicts, that acquiring or retaining the trust and confidence of populations requires sensitivity to their concerns and treating them with respect.

Although irregular warfare has caused the west considerable problems in recent years it is important not to be too despondent about our capacity to deal with it as a military problem. The key point however is that military strategy must be integrated with political strategy. If the side we are supporting is weak it is probably because it lacks a strong political base and is prone to division. If the enemy is weak it will be for similar reasons. The side with the strongest political foundations should prevail militarily, following Mao's dictum: "respect the enemy tactically but despise him strategically".

## Strategies Employed for Violent Social Change

An earlier theory had a group out of power wanting to effect violent social change employing four strategies. The table were sketches out the characteristics of these four strategies.

**Strategies of Violent Social Change**

| *Strategy* | *Time taken* | *Relationship with existing armed forces* | *Status of old regime* |
|---|---|---|---|
| Coup d'etat | Short | Won Over | Ousted |
| Insurrections | Short | Defeated | Ousted |
| Guerrilla War | Long | Defeated | Ousted |
| Terrorism | Long | Evaded | Ousted |

The said theory is only of academic interest in today's context. All four strategies are essentially a function of mindless violence. Presently, nations and societies are faced with violence perpetrated by the non-state entities. The state-sponsored violence is not a serious problem ; and whenever it is seen, it can be dealth with by regional groups like NATO, ASEAN etc.; or by the UN in the last resort.

The major problem in dealing with terrorism is the inability of the nation to agree on its definition. Let us first delineate the issues complicating the effort at defining international terrorism. Two of the major controversies in the earlier decade were :

1. Did the acts of violence committed by some natives or Africans in the Portuguese colonies of Angola, Mozambique etc constitute international terrorism? To the African it was a struggle to liberate the colonies and Portugal thought otherwise, as these territories were its overseas provinces, as they had earlier claimed in case of Goa. This is the case pertaining to one colonial power. There are/were others too. So we revert to the cliche-one man's terrorist is another's freedom fighter. This is the conundrum facing India in Kashmir were terrorism has the support of neighbours.
2. Presently, foreigners in the field of terrorism are a subject of contention. Arabs often claim that the Palestinian Arabs carrying out acts of violence in Israel are not foreigners attacking citizens of another State but rather legitimate Palestinians returning to fight for their homeland.

## U.N. Fighting Terrorism

As a representative body of the nation states of the world, the UN has been alive to its responsibilities in fighting terrorism, by passing resolutions and providing guidelines to its members on the subject.

The first accord on the subject of hijacking was passed at Tokyo in 1963. The other accords and resolutions passed by the UNO are given on the following pages.

It also needs to be said that the most detailed resolution against terrorism was passed only after 9/11 attack on the U.S. mainland. It bears emphasis in this regard that a draft comprehensive convention on terrorism, sponsored by India years ago, has not yet been passed due to a variety of reasons.

## Anti Hijacking Accords

Three multinational anti-hijacking accords were negotiated :

1. Tokyo, 1963
2. The Hague, 1970
3. Montreal, 1971.

All the three had ratifications by the requisite number of states, and consequently the accords have come into effect. As a result, the airport and airline security and screening procedures were considerably tightened up. It shows the serious assigned to the subject by the international community, that two states USA and Cuba, not having diplomatic relations and glaring at each other perched on two opposite ideological poles, set aside their mutual hostility and signed an anti-hijacking bilateral accord in February 1973. Consequent to the world uniting in its resolve to face the common danger, the phenomenon of hijacking which during 1969-1971 seemed to have posed a mortal threat to civil aviation, had largely been brought under control by 1975.

Thus when it perceived serious threat to its interests, the world community acted purposefully to contain certain manifestations of terrorism. But that was not destined to be a happy ending. A quater century later, these very aeroplanes, whose security and safety were meant to be foolproofed through these anti-hijacking accords were used as missiles to enact the horrors of Nine-Eleven. But this is jumping the narration.

## UN and Terrorism : International Law

The seventh UN congress on its concluding day on 7th September 1985 at Milan, Italy, adopted the critical resolution on terrorism calling upon the member nations "to rationalise their extradition procedures and practices" and "also make their laws against persons committing terrorist acts." The 15 nation resolution expressed grave concern at the human, social, and economic costs of such violent attacks against innocent persons and national assets and institutions. Such attacks seriously impaired freedom and political stability of communities.

The resolution called upon the nations to take necessary measures as recommended by the International Civil Aviation Organization to prevent violent attacks and to ensure strict compliance of air security conventions. After long discussions one operative paragraph, which if passed would have had damaging implications on the liberation movements, fight against apartheid, colonialism, imperialism, etc, was dropped. The ambit of the resolution was limited as it mainly confined itself to hijacking and does not even touch upon the cause of terrorism.

UN Resolution 1373 of 28 September 2001 Full text of the resolution follows.

**UN RESOLUTION 1373**

Security Council
4385th Meeting (Night)

**Security Council Unanimously Adopts Wide-ranging Anti-Terrorism Resolution:**

**Calls For Suppressing Financing, Improving International Cooperation**

## Resolution 1373 (2001) Also Creates Committee to Monitor Implementation

Reaffirming its unequivocal condemnation of the terrorist acts that took place in New York, Washington, D.C., and Pennsylvania on 11 September, the Security Council this evening unanimously adopted a wide-ranging, comprehensive resolution with steps and strategies to combat international terrorism.

By resolution 1373 (2001) the Council also established a Committee of the Council to monitor the resolution's implementation and called on all States to report on actions they had taken to that end no later than 90 days from today.

Under terms of the text, the Council decided that all States should prevent and suppress the financing of terrorism, as well as criminalize the wilful provision or collection of funds for such acts. The funds, financial assets and economic resources of those who commit or attempt to commit terrorist acts or participate in or facilitate the commission of terrorist acts and of persons and entities acting on behalf of terrorists should also be frozen without delay.

The Council also decided that States should prohibit their nationals or persons or entities in their territories from making funds, financial assets, economic resources, financial or other related services available to persons who commit or attempt to commit, facilitate or participate in the commission of terrorist acts.

States should also refrain from providing any form of support to entities or persons involved in terrorist acts; take the necessary steps to prevent the commission of terrorist acts; deny safe haven to those who finance, plan, support, commit terrorist acts and provide safe havens as well.

By other terms, the Council decided that all States should prevent those who finance, plan, facilitate or commit terrorist acts from using their respective territories for those purposes against other countries and their citizens. States should also ensure that anyone who has participated in the financing planning, preparation or perpetration of terrorist acts or in supporting terrorist acts is brought to justice. They should also ensure that terrorist acts are established as serious criminal offences in domestic laws and regulations and that the seriousness of such acts is duly reflected in sentences served.

By further terms, the Council decided that States should afford one another the greatest measure of assistance for criminal investigations or criminal proceedings relating to the financing or support of terrorist acts. States should also prevent the movement of terrorists or their groups by effective border controls as well.

Also by the text, the Council called on all States to intensify and accelerate the exchange of information regarding terrorist actions or movements; forged or falsified documents; traffic in arms and sensitive material; use of communications and technologies by terrorist groups; and the threat posed by the possession of weapons of mass destruction.

States were also called on to exchange information and cooperate to prevent and suppress terrorist acts and to take action against the perpetrators of such acts. States should become parties to, and fully implement as soon as possible, the relevant international conventions and protocols to combat terrorism.

By the text, before granting refugee status, all States should take appropriate measures to ensure that the asylum seekers had not planned, facilitated or participated in terrorist acts. Further, States should ensure that refugee status was not abused by the perpetrators, organizers or facilitators of terrorist acts, and that claims of political motivation were not recognized as grounds for refusing requests for the extradition of alleged terrorists.

The Council noted with concern the close connection between international terrorism and transnational organized crime, illicit drugs, money laundering and illegal movement of nuclear, chemical, biological and other deadly materials. In that regard, it emphasized the need to enhance the coordination of national, subregional, regional and international efforts to strengthen a global response to that threat to international security.

Reaffirming the need to combat by all means, in accordance with the Charter, threats to international peace and security caused by terrorist acts, the Council expressed its determination to take all necessary steps to fully implement the current resolution.

The meeting, which began at 10:50 p.m., adjourned at 10:53 p.m.

## Resolution

The full text of resolution 1373 (2001) reads as follows :

*"The Security Council,*

*"Reaffirming* its resolutions 1269 (1999) of 19 October 1999 and 1368 (2001) of 12 September 2001,

*"Reaffirming also* its unequivocal condemnation of the terrorist attacks which took place in New York, Washington, D.C., and Pennsylvania on 11 September 2001, and expressing its determination to prevent all such acts,

*"Reaffirming further* that such acts, like any act of international terrorism, constitute a threat to international peace and security,

*"Reaffirming* the inherent right of individual or collective self-defence as recognized by the Charter of the United Nations as reiterated in resolution 1368 (2001),

*"Reaffirming* the need to combat by all means, in accordance with the Charter of the United Nations, threats to international peace and security caused by terrorist acts,

*"Deeply concerned* by the increase, in various regions of the world, of acts of terrorism motivated by intolerance or extremism,

*"Calling* on States to work together urgently to prevent and suppress terrorist acts, including through increased cooperation and full implementation of the relevant international conventions relating to terrorism,

*"Recognizing* the need for States to complement international cooperation by taking additional measures to prevent and suppress,

in their territories through all lawful means, the financing and preparation of any acts of terrorism,

"*Reaffirming* the principle established by the General Assembly in its declaration of October 1970 (resolution 2625 (XXV)) and reiterated by the Security Council in its resolution 1189 (1998) of 13 August 1998, namely that every State has the duty to refrain from organizing, instigating, assisting or participating in terrorist acts in another State or acquiescing in organized activities within its territory directed towards the commission of such acts,

"*Acting* under Chapter VII of the Charter of the United Nations,

"1. *Decides* that all States shall:

"(*a*) Prevent and suppress the financing of terrorist acts;

"(*b*) Criminalize the wilful provision or collection, by any means, directly or indirectly, of funds by their nationals or in their territories with the intention that the funds should be used, or in the knowledge that they are to be used, in order to carry out terrorist acts;

"(*c*) Freeze without delay funds and other financial assets or economic resources of persons who commit, or attempt to commit, terrorist acts or participate in or facilitate the commission of terrorist acts; of entities owned or controlled directly or indirectly by such persons; and of persons and entities acting on behalf of, or at the direction of such persons and entities, including funds derived or generated from property owned or controlled directly or indirectly by such persons and associated persons and entities;

"(*d*) Prohibit their nationals or any persons and entities within their territories from making any funds, financial assets or economic resources or financial or other related services available, directly or indirectly, for the benefit of persons who commit or attempt to commit or facilitate or participate in the commission of terrorist acts, of entities owned or controlled, directly or indirectly, by such persons and of persons and entities acting on behalf of or at the direction of such persons;

"2. *Decides also* that all States shall :

"(*a*) Refrain from providing any form of support, active or passive, to entities or persons involved in terrorist acts, including by suppressing recruitment of members of terrorist groups and eliminating the supply of weapons to terrorists;

"(*b*) Take the necessary steps to prevent the commission of terrorist acts, including by provision of early warning to other States by exchange of information;

"(*c*) Deny safe haven to those who finance, plan, support, or commit terrorist acts, or provide safe havens;

"(*d*) Prevent those who finance, plan, facilitate or commit terrorist acts from using their respective territories for those purposes against other States or their citizens;

"(*e*) Ensure that any person who participates in the financing, planning, preparation or perpetration of terrorist acts or in supporting terrorist acts is brought to justice and ensure that, in addition to any other measures against them, such terrorist acts are established as serious criminal offences in domestic laws and regulations and that the punishment duly reflects the seriousness of such terrorist acts;

"(*f*) Afford one another the greatest measure of assistance in connection with criminal investigations or criminal proceedings relating to the financing or support of terrorist acts, including assistance in obtaining evidence in their possession necessary for the proceedings;

"(*g*) Prevent the movement of terrorists or terrorist groups by effective border contects and controls on issuance of identity papers and travel documents, and through measures for preventing counterfeiting, forgery or fraudulent use of identity papers and travel documents;

"3. Calls *upon* all States to :

"(*a*) Find ways of intensifying and accelerating the exchange of operational information, especially regarding actions or movements of terrorist persons or networks; forged or falsified travel documents; traffic in arms, explosives or sensitive materials; use of communications technologies by terrorist groups; and the threat posed by the possession of weapons of mass destruction by terrorist groups;

"(*b*) Exchange information in accordance with international and domestic law and cooperate on administrative and judicial matters to prevent the commission of terrorist acts;

"(*c*) Cooperate, particularly through bilateral and multilateral arrangements and agreements, to prevent and suppress terrorist attacks and take action against perpetrators of such acts;

"(*d*) Become parties as soon as possible to the relevant international conventions and protocols relating to terrorism, including the International Convention for the Suppression of the Financing of Terrorism of 9 December 1999;

"(*e*) Increase cooperation and fully implement the relevant international conventions and protocols relating to terrorism and Security Council resolutions 1269 (1999) and 1368 (2001);

"(*f*) Take appropriate measures in conformity with the relevant provisions of national and international law, including international standards of human rights, before granting refugee status, for the purpose of ensuring that the asylum seeker has not planned, facilitated or participated in the commission of terrorist acts;

"(*g*) Ensure, in conformity with international law, that refugee status is not abused by the perpetrators, organizers or facilitators of terrorist acts, and that claims of political motivation are not recognized as grounds for refusing requests for the extradition of alleged terrorists;

"4. *Notes* with concern the close connection between international terrorism and transnational organized crime, illicit drugs, money-laundering, illegal arms-trafficking, and illegal movement of nuclear, chemical, biological and other potentially deadly materials, and in this regard *emphasizes* the need to enhance coordination of efforts on national, subregional, regional and international levels in order to strengthen a global response to this serious challenge and threat to international security;

"5. *Declares* that acts, methods, and practices of terrorism are contrary to the purposes and principles of the United Nations and that knowingly financing, planning and inciting terrorist acts are also contrary to the purposes and principles of the United Nations;

"6. *Decides* to establish, in accordance with rule 28 of its provisional rules of procedure, a Committee of the Security Council, consisting of all the members of the Council, to monitor implementation of this resolution, with the assistance of appropriate expertise, and calls upon all States to report to the Committee, no later than 90 days from the date of adoption of this resolution and thereafter according to a timetable to be proposed by the Committee, on the steps they have taken to implement this resolution;

"7. *Directs* the Committee to delineate its tasks, submit a work programme within 30 days of the adoption of this resolution, and to consider the support it requires, in consultation with the Secretary-General;

"8. *Expresses* its determination to take all necessary steps in order to ensure the full implementation of this resolution, in accordance with its responsibilities under the Charter;

"9. *Decides* to remain seized of this matter."

## TERRORISM

*"Terrorism is a global threat with global effects; ... its consequences affect every aspect of the United Nations agenda from development to peace to human rights and the rule of law. By its very nature, terrorism is an assault on the fundamental principles of law, order, human rights, and the peaceful settlement of disputes upon which the United Nations is established. The United Nations has an indispensable role to play in providing the legal and organizational framework within which the international campaign against terrorism can unfold".*

Kofi Annan
UN Secretary-General
4 October, 2002

### Implementing International Action Against Terrorism

Terrorism has been of concern to the international community since 1937 when the League of Nations elaborated the Convention for the Prevention and Punishment of Terrorism. Subsequently, the United Nations and regional inter-governmental organizations have dealt with terrorism from a legal and political perspective. Since 1963, the international community has elaborated *universal legal instruments* related to the prevention and suppression of international terrorism. The most recent, the International Convention for the Suppression of Acts of Nuclear Terrorism, opens for signature on 14 September, 2005.

In addition, the United Nations General Assembly and Security Council have adopted several resolutions pertaining to terrorism. In particular, and in response to the attacks of 11 September 2001, the *Security Council adopted resolution 1373 (2001)* on 28 September (2001) which declared that :

> "...acts, methods and practices of terrorism are contrary to the purposes and principles of the United Nations". It called upon Member States to "become parties as soon as possible to the relevant international conventions and protocols" and "to increase cooperation and fully implement the relevant international conventions and protocols".

This resolution also established the *Counter-Terrorism Committee* (*CTC*) to monitor the implementation of the resolution by all States and increase the capability of States to fight terrorism, including bringing Member States to an acceptable level of compliance with the terrorism-related conventions and protocols. The CTC has since become the United Nations' leading body to promote collective action against international terrorism. In restructuring the CTC, the Counter-Terrorism Executive Directorate (CTED) has been established as a special political mission for an initial period ending on 31 December, 2007. It is headed by an Executive Director, Ambassador Javier Ruperez, appointed by the Secretary-General of the United Nations.

## The Role of UNODC in the Prevention of Terrorism

In the context of the UN's efforts to prevent and combat terrorism, the United Nations Office on Drugs and Crime Unodc has an expanded programme of work for technical assistance to counter terrorism that is based on mandates recommended by the *UN Commission on Crime Prevention and Criminal Justice* and approved by the General Assembly. These mandates, carried out by UNODC's Terrorism Prevention Branch TPB within the Division *for Treaty Affairs (DTA),* include the provision of technical assistance and advisory services to countries in their fight against terrorism. As a consequence, UNODC's operational activities focus on strengthening the legal regime against terrorism. This involves providing legislative assistance to countries, which enables them to become parties to, and implement, the universal anti-terrorism conventions and protocols and Security Council resolution 1373 (2001).

A detailed description of UNODC's activities may be found in the Report of the Secretary-General "Strengthening international cooperation and technical assistance in promoting the implementation of the universal conventions and protocols related to terrorism within the framework of the activities of the United Nations Office on Drugs and Crime" submitted to the Commission on Crime Prevention and Criminal Justice at its fourteenth session ( **E/CN.15/2005/13** available in *English, French, Spanish, Russian, Chinese and Arabic).* Overall then, UNODC aims at responding promptly and efficiently to requests for counter-terrorism assistance, in accordance with the priorities set by the Commission on Crime Prevention and Criminal Justice and the CTC by:

- Reviewing domestic legislation and providing advice on drafting new laws;
- Providing in-depth assistance on the ratification and implementation of new legislation against terrorism through a mentorship programme or other follow-up action; and
- Facilitating and providing training to national criminal justice systems with regard to the practical implementation of the universal instruments against terrorism.

## The CTC and UNODC

In carrying out its activities, UNODC works closely with the CTC and in so doing a complementary and synergistic relationship between the two has developed. While the CTC analyses the reports received from Member States and facilitates the provision of technical assistance to requesting States, UNODC, with its substantive expertise, delivers such assistance. Regular working contacts with the CTC are maintained, in particular through the sharing of mission reports with the CTC and by identifying with the CTC countries in priority need of legislative assistance. In this regard, the CTC directs requests for assistance from countries to UNODC.

An example of the close ties between CTC and UNODC was the, bi-annual special meeting of the CTC, with 40 regional and other organizations, which was hosted jointly by the Organization for Security and Co-operation in Europe (OSCE) and UNODC in March 2004. This resulted in the Vienna Declaration (S/2004/276), in which the representatives of the participating organizations agreed - inter alia - to seek ways to coordinate and exchange information with the CTC and one another, as well as to further improve cooperation and coordination, including where appropriate, by conducting joint technical assistance programmes or joint visits to requesting States.

## UNODC's Technical Assistance Activities

UNODC's legislative technical assistance activities for the implementation of the universal anti-terrorism instruments are based on Security Council resolution 1373, as well as the more recent General Assembly resolutions ( 59/153, 58/81, 58/136 and 58/140) and ECOSOC Resolution 2005/19. UNODC conducts these activities within the framework of its project on "strengthening the legal regime against terrorism", which focuses on the provision of direct legal advisory services to requesting States for incorporating the relevant provisions contained in the 12 universal anti-terrorism conventions and protocols into national legislation. Generous contributions to this work have been made by Austria, Canada, Denmark, France, Germany, Italy, Japan, Netherlands, Norway, Spain, Sweden, Turkey, the United Kingdom (funds have been pledged), and the United States. In kind contributions have been received from Argentina, Belgium and Portugal.

Through the project, over 600 national officials have been provided with substantial briefings or training on the ratification and implementation requirements, between October 2002 and March 2005.

Specific national action plans have also been developed jointly with Governments and legislative drafting committees have been established to study the provisions of the instruments and to make recommendations to ministers regarding ratification, as well as implementation of the legislation, including the provisions of the 12 universal legal instruments relating to terrorism and the requirements of Security Council resolution 1373 (2001). As of March 2005, this direct country-specific assistance has been delivered to more than 60 countries.

In addition, *regional and sub-regional workshops* have been held that have allowed countries from the same region to compare progress, learn from each other and harmonize legislative efforts. These workshops have produced final documents focusing on the follow-up technical assistance needs of participating States with regard to the ratification and implementation of the universal anti-terrorism instruments.

In some cases, UNODC staff have also provided States with the elements needed to complete reports to the Counter-Terrorism Committee in response to Security Council resolution 1373 (2001). The Office has also strategically placed terrorism prevention experts in a number of regions to support and follow up assistance activities.

In the future and in line with the priorities of the Counter-Terrorism Committee, UNODC will orient its activities towards in-depth, qualitative follow-up aid to requesting countries for the implementation of the instruments. It will also broaden the scope of its assistance. Focus will be on strengthening institutional structures and mechanisms to enable States to implement the relevant international instruments, providing online advice on extradition and mutual legal assistance requests and advising on international cooperation mechanisms through mentorship programmes - thus working towards the full implementation of the international instruments. UNODC will work in this direction while continuing to promote the universal anti-terrorism instruments. Through both the sub-regional and regional activities, as well as the direct assistance provided bilaterally, 109 States received assistance from TPB between October 2002 and March 2005.

In order to further assist UNODC in providing technical assistance to Member States as per its mandate, UNODC has developed a number of technical assistance tools, such as the Legislative Guide to the universal anti-terrorism conventions and protocols, checklists for the universal anti-terrorism conventions and Security Council resolution 1373 (2001), and a Guide for the legislative incorporation and implementation of the universal anti-terrorism instruments. (See *technical assistance tools*).

## Building Partnerships

Given that a number of relevant organizations and entities both internal and external to the United Nations are involved in the prevention and combat of terrorism, an integrated and coordinated response to terrorism will serve to increase complementarities, avoid duplication of efforts and resources, increase cost effectiveness, and broaden the audience that each entity can reach individually. As a result, the Terrorism Prevention Branch is committed to building partnerships with relevant entities on a number of levels.

The work of the Programme is guided by policy decisions made by the Counter Terrorism Committee and as such the TPB's activities are coordinated with the CTC. In addition, the *Office of Legal Affairs* is also consulted on relevant matters.

Where possible, activities draw on existing UNODC in-house expertise, such as that in *Anti-Money Laundering, Organized Crime and Corruption*, as well as in the *Legal Advisory Section*.

Exchange of expertise and information with other international and regional organizations and national institutions is emphasized. Moreover, where appropriate, the TPB works with other international organizations, as well as with regional and sub-regional organizations, such as the Council of Europe, the Intergovernmental Authority on Development, the International Monetary Fund, the Office of the High Commissioner for Human Rights, the Organization of American States and the Organisation for Security and Cooperation in Europe.

UNODC plans to expand its partnerships with relevant organizations in order to enhance a complementary and synergistic approach and facilitate an efficient response to the needs and requests of Member States in their terrorism prevention activities.

**Contact us :**

Terrorism Prevention Branch (TPB)
United Nations Office on Drugs and Crime (UNODC)
Vienna International Centre
P.O. Box 500
A-1400 Vienna
Austria
Tel.: +43 1 26060 5604
Fax: +43 1 26060 5968
E-mail: Terrorism Prevention Branch

## Rules to deal with the hostage takers : 18 April, 2007

UN Secretary General Ban Ki-Moon said on 18 April, 2007 that he supports international rules living drawn up to deal with hostage crises such as that ended Italy freeing jailed Taliban in a move that angered the United States.

## UN watchdog is active on Anti-terrorism Policies

A working committee of the UN Security Council was constituted to oversee implementation of resolution 1373 : (1) to scrutinize whether every country was following the guidelines laid down post-9/11 to crackdown on terrorists as well as their finances, and (2) to share intelligence on terrorism. The Committee found India amiss in compliance of the standards and responsibilities enjoined by the UN Security Council.

Notwithstanding the increasing threat of jihadi terrorism to India's security and integrity, the country still does not have coherent strategy to deal with the menace. After one serious terrorist after another, the governing authorities from the Prime Minister downwards come out with hackneyed statements like the following :

- We will not be cowed down.
- We condemn all acts of violence and appeal to the people to remain calm.
- Terrorists want to fomment communal riots but people must not let them succeed in their vicious designs.
- The culprits will be arrested and punished.

If such 'pious' assertions could defeat hardened criminals, that is what terrorists are, India would have been a land of peace and honey many years ago. Alas it has not. The soft-pedaling by the Indian Government, particularly since the UPA took over in 2004, has only further emboldened the ultras of Islamist variety. Due to whatever reasons—analysts opine it is because of its vote-bank policies—the Congress-led UPA Government has come to create an image of India as a 'soft state'. Inane, toothless statements will not curb the terrorism. All this government does is to repeat such meaningless statements after every violent, gruesome act of terrorism.

Incident after incident has proved Government's ineffectual anti-terrorism policies : Delhi, Mumbai, Varanasi, Hyderabad, Ludhiana and the latest, Dargah Sharif in Ajmer. It is but obvious that India's response to terror lacks teeth—'political will' is more accurate term. It is time that the Government realise that its defeatist attitude and soft poling are encouraging terrorist outfits to carry on enacting their death dances least concerned with any effective counter-action by the Government. It has also exposed the UPA's inadequacy and helplessness in protecting the lives of average citizens—a constitutional responsibility devolved on a country's government. In the UPA's case, the Government responsibility ends with its naming after every act of mindless terrorism some foreign terrorist outfits like JeM, LeT, HuJi etc. There is seldom a serious effort to follow up such inane 'naming' exercise by a serious investigation to nab the culprits. There has been instances of the Governments of concerned states asking the police to go slow when members of a particular community come under its scanner. There is no official explanation about failure of authorities to detect and arrest the culprit terrorists in most cases of terrorist strikes. In some cases where certain suspects are arrested, there is a hue and cry from the community the arrested suspects belong to : "They are not the terrorists. Police have arrested them on planted evidence".

The most important "anti-terrorism" measure adopted by the UPA Government on coming to power, as a cynic put it, was to rescind the Prevention of Terrorism Act (POTA), because it was presumed to have been misused against a particular community by its predecessor, NDA. The right course was to amend the act to ensure that it was not misused. Instead of enacting tough anti-terror laws, as most democracies did in the West, the UPA threw away the only instrumentality available to it to fight terror. The consequences were on the expected lines—one serious terrorist strike after another. More than 3,674 people have been killed in terrorist attacks in Jammu and Kashmir, North-East and in Maoist violence between 2004 and October, 2007.[6]

That India has the unique capacity of remaining 'calm' even when subjected to most atrocious of terrorist excesses is stating the obvious. But tolerance is not the virtue the criminally-inclined terrorist would appreciate. They would take it as weakness. This astounding tolerance—and accommodation-shown to the terrorists only prove that the Government of India does not consider securing the life and liberty and liberty of its citizens a priority.

It should come as no surprise, in view of the foregoing, that the working committee of the UN Security Council, referred to earlier, has "accused India of failing miserably on counter-terrorism measures, including breaching the *hawala* network".[7] India must rise to the challenge forth with.

## Indian Position on Terrorism at the UNO

Some references on the subject are given at the Appendix that follows.

> "Our message is loud and clear: The life of every Indian citizen under our dispensation is precious. In our fight against

terrorism, we will be guided by the principle of 'Zero Tolerance'."
Prime Minister Atal Bihari Vajpayee, October 16,1999

## INDIA AT UN : GLOBAL TERRORISM

### Attack on Democratic Societies

*India's position on Terrorism :* Statement by Mr. V. K. Nambiar, Permanent Representative, on Threats to international peace and security caused by terrorist acts at the Security Council - March 04, 2004.

*Hijacking of Indian Airlines Flight IC-814 :* Statement by Mr. K. Kalavenkata Rao, Member of Parliament and member of the Indian delegation—Measures to Eliminate International Terrorism at the Sixth Committee of the 58th session of the UN General Assembly—October 15, 2003.

*India's Contribution in Combating Terrorism :* Joint Statement of the India-US Joint Working Group on Counterterrorism—July 12, 2002.

Recent terrorist attacks in Jammu & Kashmir.

*On Global Terrorism Terrorist* attack on Indian Parliament

The Prevention of Terrorism Ordinance, 2001.

Working document submitted to UN by India on the draft comprehensive convention on international terrorism.

Information and Press Releases on terrorist attacks on World Trade Center and Pentagon.

Prime Minister Vajpayee's address to the nation on terrorist attacks on America—September 14, 2001.

Prime Minister's letter to U.S. President Bush on terrorist attacks on America—September 11, 2001.

India condemns terrorist attacks on World Trade Center, New York and Pentagon, Washington, DC - September 11, 2001.

Joint U.S.—India Statement on Counter-terrorism Working Group—June 26, 2001.

External Affairs Minister Jaswant Singh's statement in Parliament on Taliban's cultural vandalism - March 02, 2001.

Resolution adopted by both Houses of Indian Parliament on Taliban's decree to destroy all religious statues in Afghanistan - March 02, 2001.

India - U.S. Statement on Joint Working Group on Counter Terrorism - September 26, 2000.

Statement by the Home Minister L. K. Advani on situation in Jammu & Kashmir in Parliament - August 9, 2000.

**The Education of a Holy Warrior -** New York Times,

June 25, 2000

In a Pakistani religious school called the Haqqania madrasa, Osama bin Laden is a hero, the Taliban's leaders are famous alumni and the next generation of mujahedeen is being militantly groomed. (Complete text).

Countering the changing threat of International Terrorism - US National Commission on Terrorism Report - June 5, 2000

Patterns of Global Terrorism: 1999 (South Asia Region) - U.S. State Department Report - May 1, 2000.

## Joint U.S.-India Statement on Counter-terrorism Working Group

February 8, 2000

India and the United States have a shared interest in strengthening a regime to counter international terrorism. This working group is intended to enhance the effectiveness of our efforts to counter international terrorism worldwide. (Complete text).

## India identifies all five hijackers of Indian Airlines flight IC-814 -

January 6, 2000

L.K. Advani, Union Home Minister, while addressing a press conference has said that the Mumbai Police have arrested four Pakistani intelligence operatives based in Mumbai, who assisted the five hijackers of the Indian Airlines plane. He further added that during interrogation of these four operatives, they have confirmed that the Indian Airlines hijack was a Pakistani intelligence operation executed with the assistance of Harkat-ul-Ansar. All five hijackers are Pakistani nationals. (Complete text).

Measures to eliminate international terrorism - Statement by Mr. Kamalesh Sharma, Permanent Representative to the United Nations on November 16, 1999.

## Press Release on Pakistan's support of cross border Terrorism

November 10, 1999

India once again called upon the Pakistan to abandon their irresponsible support of cross-border terrorism. (Text)

## UN Security Council Resolution 1269

The Security Council unanimously adopted a resolution on October 19, 1999 unequivocally condemning all acts, methods, and practices of terrorism and calling on states to strengthen international cooperation in fighting terrorism and bringing terrorists to justice. (Complete text)

Working Group on International Terrorism: Adoption of Convention on Financing of Terrorism - Statement by India to the United Nations in New York on October 6, 1999

Working Group on International Terrorism - Statement by India to the United Nations in New York on September 27, 1999.

## Statement by Jaswant Singh, External Affairs Minister in the UN General Assembly - September 22, 1999

"Terrorism is a menace to which open societies are vulnerable; it becomes particularly difficult for democracies to counter when terrorists are armed, financed and backed by governments or their agencies, and benefit from the protection of state power. Cross-border terrorism, sponsored from across our borders, has taken the lives of thousands of our citizens, and ruined, those of countless others. We will counter it, as we have done over the past decades, using the methods available to a democracy. India will defeat such forces. That is both our duty and our obligation to our citizens." (Complete text).

## India signs the International Convention for the Suppression of Terrorist Bombings, 1997 - September 17, 1999

The Convention which was adopted by resolution 52/164 of the General Assembly on December 15, 1997 requires States to either prosecute or extradite those accused of terrorist bombings within their territory (Complete text).

External Affairs Minister writes to Russian Foreign Minister on terrorist activities in Dagestan - September 13, 1999.

External Affairs Minister writes to the Minister of Foreign Affairs of Kyrgyz Republic, Mr. Muratbek Emanahiere on recent terrorist activities in that region-September 01, 1999.

## Prime Minister Vajpayee writes a letter to the President of Afghanistan—August 25,1999

Prime Minister condemned the brutal massacre of innocent people, torching of houses, use of incendiary bombs, destruction of crops and deliberate displacement of women and children perpetrated by the Taliban forces backed by Pakistan on the people and to all Afghans. (Text of letter)

The Union Cabinet approves signing and ratification of the international convention for the Suppression of Terrorist Bombings - August 5, 1999.

We must join hands to fight terrorism - Speech by Mrs. Vasundhara Raje, Minister of State for External Affairs, at the International Conference "Terrorism: Threat to the 21st Century", January 11, 1999.

Measures to eliminate international terrorism - Statement by Mr. Rup Chand Pal, Member of Parliament at the United Nations Sixth Committee, November 12, 1998.

## UN for Global Decree on Hostages : 18 April, 2007

UN secretary Ban Ki-Moon said on 18 April, 2007 that he "supports international rules being drawn up to deal with hostage crisis such as that ended Italy freeing jailed Taliban in a move that angered the US."

Ban, in comments published before he met Italy's Foreign Minister Massimo D'Alema on the 18th, declined to say whether he agreed with the release of the five Taliban in return for Italian reporter Daniele Mastrogiacomo. Taliban beheaded the Italian's two Afghan colleagues.

"It is not up to me to say what was done was right or wrong", he said. "To address the issue of kidnappings, common rules are needed, and the UN is the right place to put them forward. I invite all states, including Italy, to present such proposals."

Critics of the Taliban-hostage deal said it encouraged kidnapping and endangered NATO troops by returning jailed guerrillas to the battle field.

NATO Secretary-General Jaap de Hoop Schaffer has agreed to "initiate a debate" on whether to have a policy on kidnappings.[8]

Italian Foreign Minister D'Alema said "last week that the UN and NATO should consider guidelines about appropriate ways to respond to kidnappings". At the same time, he ruled out a blanket no-negotiations rule that would "deny all countries their sovereign prerogative."

The debate comes after a string of high-profile kidnappings of Western reporters, including BBC journalist Alan Johnston, kidnapped in Gaza over a month ago.

## Tracking down the Terrorists : New tools : November 2007

Anti-terrorism war is entering new, unconventional fields. New tools are required to detect the terror merchants on the web. Arizona team's persistentence and doggedness seem to be succeeding.

Here is a webb page depicting horror from *A guide to kill American in Saudi Arabia*, with hatred oozing from the text :

> The quivering images and militant writings are frightening : an exploding Humvee blankets passing cars with dust; a lab technician makes explosives, step by step-pure hate.

Tens of thousands of web pages are now devoted to terrorist propaganda designed to attract followers. Interestingly, on the surface, the messages and videos reveal little about their creators. But the programmers and writers leave digital clues : the greetings and other words they choose; their punctuation and syntax; and the way they code multimedia attachments and web links.[9]

Researchers at the University of Arizona are developing a tool that uses these clues to. automate the analysis of online jihadism.

The Dark web project aims to scour Web sites, forums and chat-rooms to find the Internet's most prolific and influential jihadists and learn how they reel in adherents.

Lab Director Hsinchun Chen hopes Dark Web will crimp what he calls "al Qaeda University on the Web", the mass of websites where potential terrorists learn their trade, from making explosives to planning attacks.

There are different opinions about the success of the project. Experts admit that they are not aware of any comparable effort, though some opined that the project may have only limited applications.

## India Pitches for pact against Terror

India's External Affairs Minister Pranab Mukherjee made strong pitch at the 15th Non-Aligned Movement at Tehran on 29 July, 2008 for early adoption of a convention mooted by it over a decade ago to tackle the menace of terrorism, days after its two key cities were rocked by serial blasts, leaving more than 50 people dead.

"I would particularly underline the need for concerted efforts by all of us to work towards early finalisation and adoption of a Comprehensive Convention on International Terrorism, a draft for which was presented by India at the UNO as far back as 1996", urged the Minister.

Referring to the recent serial blasts in Bangalore and Ahmedabad and the terror attack at the Indian embassy in Kabul, he said the terrorists' intention, quite clearly, is to repture India's resilient social fabric.

He said : "We shall be remiss in over commitment to the theme of this Conference if we do not send a strong message that our movement stands resolutely for international cooperation in bringing the perpetrators, organisers, financiers, and sponsors of all acts of terrorism to justice."

## India continues pressing for early adoption of convention

Speaking at the ministerial segment of the 15th NAM summit on 13 July, 2009 at Sharm el-Sheikh in Egypt, India's External Affairs Minister S.M. Krishna called for an early adoption of comprehensive convention on International Terrorism under discussion at the UN for over a decade.

Again, during the visit of U.S. Secretary of State Hillary Rodham Clinton to India, She and her counter part SM Krishna reaffiermed their commitment to an early adoption of a UN Comprehensive Convention against International Terrorism, draft of which was sponsored by India in 1996.

## How individual Countries Perform

Post 9/11, the Western World, and in particular the U.S., became painfully aware of terrorism and its potential as a threat to international peace and stability. Starkly sure of its 'sole superpower' status and drunk on its infallibility, in a gut reaction, the U.S. attacked the Taliban-ruled Afghanistan. Soon it had the Taliban on the run, and eventually overthrow its government. In another impetuous decision, and without completing the task of 'total extermination' of evil—fanatical extremism linked to puritanical Islamic ideology—in Afghanistan, it opened second front by attacking the Saddam-ruled Iraq.

By late 2005, the analysts were concluding that the U.S.-led coalition was not mining the war are openly asserting that the U.S. has lost the war not only Iraq but also in Afghanistan. Presently, the situation in the world—in regard to spread of, and violence caused by, the terrorist outfits led by Osama's International Islamic Front (IIF)—is not only back to the pre-9/11 one, but is decidedly worse than that. A brief survey of the present picture of international (situation of) terrorism follows. It is universally accepted that the most serious threat to the world order today is posed by Islamist terrorism' and its potent weapon of late is turning out to be "suicide terrorism."

## Afghanistan

The country, which witnessed fairly peaceful Presidential elections in October 2004, had started sliding slowly back into its traditional anarchy about mid-2005. The remnants of the Taliban and the Al Qaeda, which had been driven out of Afghanistan by the US-led coalition, are back in a reinforced *avatar* in the Pashtun-majority areas of Southern and Eastern parts of the country. Others have joined such as Gulbuddin Hekmatyar's Hizb-e-Islami (HEI), the Hizb-ul-Tehrir (HUT) and the Islamic Movement of Uzbekistan (IUM). And what should be the greater cause of concern to the international community, the Taliban-Al Qaeda duo is getting the open support from the fundamentalist political coalition of

Pakistan, Muttahida Majlis-e-Amal (MMA) which is ruling the NWFP and is a member of the ruling coalition in Baluchistan. The MMA's support for the terrorist outfits/elements was corroborated by none other than Lt. Gen. Syed Safdar Hussain, the Pakistani Corps Commander at Peshawar.

The ideological stance of the MMA should be clear from the Taliban-style legislation it has enacted in NWFP, over which the Federal Government is sitting apprehensive of adverse reaction in the international community.

Suicide terrorism which had disappeared from terrorist landscape of Afghanistan, has made its reappearance after three years in 2005. Following allegations of the desecration of the Holy Quran by the U.S. troops at the Guantanamo Bay detention centre in Cuba, the Islamic world witnessed wide-spread anti-U.S. demonstrations, but these were largely peaceful bar in Afghanistan, which experienced serious anti-U.S. violence. Through out 2006, hardly a day passed without clashes, raids, be headings etc by the terrorist combine in Afghanistan. A U.S. helicopter was shot down in 2005 killing all its 17 occupants, including three members of U.S. Special Force Unit. In July, 2005, when the U.S. troops chased a raiding party, it crossed over into Waziristan area of Pakistan's NWFP. For the first time since the beginning of "Operation Enduring Freedom (OEF), the U.S. troops exercised the right of hot pussuit and killed all the members of the raiding party on the Pakistani soil. This has been stated not only by outside observers, but also by prestigious sections of Pakistani media such as the *Herald*, the monthly published from Karachi by the well-known *Dawn* group of publishers. There was no Pakistani protest over this "transgression of that country's sovereignty".

The jihadi terrorist training infrastructure which had been destroyed by the U.S. in airstrike during the course of OEF, had been fully restored by mid-2005—this time in Pakistani territory contiguous to near the Afghan border. By early 2006, this infrastructure was set up in the Taliban controlled areas in Eastern and Southern Afghanistan too, which facilitated the launching of cross-border terrorist attacks from the Waziristan areas of NWFP in Pakistan. Just for information, it is apt to mention here that Musharraf's Pakistan has signed "peace pacts" with pro-Taliban tribals in North and South Waziristan agencies of the FATA.

Ironically, the ostensible aim of these so-called 'peace pacts' was to deny access to the area of the Taliban and establish permanent peace there surprisingly, the West seems to have accepted this ingenuous interpretation of the "peace pact" with the Taliban, at least there has been no public protest by the U.S./ the EU countries. On the contrary and in a credulous display of its naivete, the NATO British commander in Afghanistan flattered Islamabad by emulation : signing a similar 'peace pact' with Taliban in one district of Southern Province of Helmand.

## Pakistan

The jihadi training centre have been functioning once again in different parts of Pakistan. Having lied low for a couple of years after 9/11, Pakistan has reverted to its duplicitous ways fighting terrorism within its borders—hunting with the hounds and running with the rabbits!

Pakistan continues to be the most important hub of jihadi terrorism in the world. It is a veritable warren of jihadi terrorists of various hues, generations, vintages and nationalities. There were 220 references to Pakistan in the report of the U.S. National Commission on 91/11, which was released in 2004. Pakistan has 'impeccable' credentials in the field of international terrorism. Since the attempt to blow up the New York World Trade Centre in March 1993, there have been very few international terrorist strikes during the investigation of which Pakistan and Pakistanis have not figured in some way or the other.

In clear violation of the promises repeatedly made by Gen. Musharraf to the U.S., Pakistan has not taken any action against the Pakistan—based jihadi terrorist training infrastructure directed against India. Equally surprisingly, the General has also not proceeded against Taliban leaders and cadres indulging in terrorist acts against Afghan and U.S./NATO troops in Afghanistan from their bases on Pakistani soil. The only limited action Musharraf has taken is against some cadres and operatives of the Al Qaeda who pose a direct threat to U.S. interests and its nationals. Even that anti-terrorist 'drive' by Pakistan has not lead to the arrest or killing of Osama bin-Laden and his Deputy, Ayman al-Zawahiri, who continue to operate from the tribal regions straddling the Pak-Afghan border and periodically disseminate video/audio recorded statements from the Al Jazeera network, inciting the faithful in different countries to step up jihad. Incidentally, another such tape was broadcast from Al Jazeera in December 2006, the eleventh this year.

In his televised address to the nation on 21 July, 2005 in the wake of the London explosions, Musharraf called upon his security forces to crack down on the extremists operating from Pakistani territory. He was not taken seriously by large sections of his own people, who loved upon that crack-down—third in a row ordered by him since 9/11—which had reportedly led to arrests of hundreds of terrorists/extremists, as another eye-wash and another instance of shadow-boxing. The eminent journalist Ayaz Amir of the repted *Dawn* asks, Longue-in-Check : "How many crack-downs make a genuine crack-down?" When his own people ask such cynical questions, indicative of certain lack of belief in what he says, how does one explain or understand American's expressing repeated public faith in Musharraf's policies and his words? May be, that is for public consumption. Things are more blunt and direct in private or, may be, they have no choice or second option. They have to make do with him.

There are credible reports of Pakistan's ISI arranging terrorist training for ultras of South Thailand. To wit, here is what a prestigious daily of Lahore, the *Daily Times*, says on 18 July, 2005 : "Jihadis from Southern Thailand continue to come to Pakistan for training and the plan for the jihad in Southern Thailand was finalised at a clandestined meeting of the jihadi leaders in Lahore."

## Bangladesh

As if Pakistan to its West was not enough of a 'headache' for India's security and national interests, Bangladesh to its east has emerged as the second major hub of jihadi terrorism in the Asian region. The terrorist training camps of the Harkat-ul-jihad-al-Islami (HUJI), a member of bin Laden's International Islamic Front (IIF), located in Bangladesh territory have been training jihadi terrorists from South Thailand. Bangladesh continues to provide safe sanctuaries, funds, arms and ammunition, explosives et al to various anti-Indian terrorist groups—jihadi as well as non-jihadi.

Bangladesh's exertion for spread of jihadi terrorism has not gone waste. Southern Thailand has joined Southern Philippines and Indonesia as another favourite playground for jihadi terrorists in South-East Asia. Since the beginning of 2004, more than 8,000 persons have been killed there—suspected terrorists as well as innocent civilians. Explosions using mobile phones, assassinations of officials at point-blank range and beheadings of not only Buddhists, but also Muslims suspected of cooperating with the authorities—these are the terrorist repertoire taught at training camps/centres in Bangladesh.

## Iraq

Beyond India's immediate neighbourhood, Iraq is the first country that grabs our attention. Today (January 2007) it is on the verge of a civil war. The U.S.—installed government has been unable to exercise control on the country's sectarian Sunni Vs Shia violence, and Saddam's hanging, in indecent haste, has only worsened the civil strife. Analysts fear the situation could spin out of control, leading to a civil war—until saner elements come to the fore to lead the Sunni and Shia communities. Here are a frightening set of statistics :

- There have been more acts of suicide terrorism in Iraq alone during the last two years than during the previous two decades in the entire world.
- More innocent civilians and government workers have been killed in Iraq by terrorists in the last two years than in the entire world during the last two decades.
- In July 2005 alone, there were 55 attacks of suicide terrorism in Iraq's Sunni Triangle.
- There has been an unending flow of volunteers for suicide terrorism in Iraq-about two-thirds of them from Saudi Arabia alone, and the rest from Syria, Kuwait, Pakistan and some other Muslim countries.

## Saudi Arabia

The country continues to bleed despite the ruthless measures taken by the security forces to eliminate the Al Qaeda from its territory. Unfortunately for Government, its suspected complicity of sections of intelligence and security agencies of the country with the terrorist have made the task more intractable. The energy security of many countries, including India, could be jeopardised if Saudi Arabia goes under, overwhelmed by the terrorism.

## Jihadi Terrorism has spread

Of late, jihadi terrorism had made even larger gains in Kenya, Morocco, Turkey, Spain and the U.K., and has reappeared in Egypt from where it had disappeared since 1997.

## EU Countries

Suicide terrorism has claimed its first victims in the UK. The Muslim immigrant communities in the EU countries are emerging to become the Western hub of the international Jihadi terrorism. The largest number of terrorist suspects detained for questioning in the EU countries after the Madrid blasts in March 2004, were Moroccans and Pakistanis or people of Moroccan and Pakistani origin. The Saudis, the Egyptians, the Moroccans and the Pakistanis constitute the driving force of Jihadi terrorism today, be it in the East or the West.

## Vintage and Character Traits of Terrorists

The Jihadi terrorists of three different vintages are operating in different parts of the world.

- Those of the Afghan vintage are now in their late 30's or 40's.
- Those of the Bosnian vintage are now in their late 20's or 30's.
- Those of the Iraqi vintage are in their 20's. Importantly, they do not all belong to the Al Qaeda or any other single organization. They, in fact, belong to different organizations, divided into a number of small cells, which have learnt to operate autonomously even in the absence of or without the need for a central command and control.[10]

No single organization or a single individual leader or even a single united front like Osama's International Islamic Front (IIF) unites the Muslims world over. The *Ummah*—the Muslim term for the international Muslim community or 'nation of Islam' the world over—is united today, particularly after the U.S. attack's on Afghanistan and Iraq, by a widely shared anger against the U.S. and those perceived to the cooperating with it. Another reason for the anger against the U.S. is its influence on the ruling classes of most Islamic countries. The *Ummah* sees the U.S. in particular and the West in general, as the main hurdle in the way of its ultimate objectives : the restoration of the Islamic Caliphate. The U.S. occupation of Iraq and its robust and stringent counter-terrorist methods, with their emphasis on the use of the military approach, have considerably contributed to this anger. But surely that is not the only reason behind the anger. The clerics teach establishment of the world purified of all the infidels (=non-Muslims) and the U.S., the role of super power of the day, is the only power capable of standing in their way and frustrating their designs of achieving an Islamic Caliphate.

## The Causes, the Lessons and Root Causes

This chapter has discussed earlier the causes of terrorism as expounded by some earlier theorists, academics and scholars. The reasons were attributed to an unjust social order, economic deprivation and/or political discrinimation. All such theoretical postulations stand rejected today. It is universally accepted today that cold-blooded murder of innocent persons, hapless women and children has simply no place in any civilized community. Nothing can justify despicable actions of inhuman desperados like beheading and senseless blood-letting.

Much of conventional wisdom regarding terrorism have been proved misplaced. Deprivation and poverty cannot be the cause of the terrorist anger as many of these terrorists are the children of well-to-do, and some even from affluent families. Osama, of course, stands out as an illustration of the latter class. Lack of education and the consequent un-employment are not the cause of their anger either. Many of them are university graduates—having studied science and technology. Not all of them are the products of the *Madrassas*. Some of them are the products of reputed secular educational institutions. Neither all of them are the products of jihadi terrorist training Camps. Many are self-taught in the fabrication and use of explosives/IEDs.

Many of them are graduates of the ubiquitous Internet, an alma mater of sorts for them. They have converted the Internet into a veritable global madrassa and a virtual global training centre. As far as mastering the use of the innovations of science and technology are concerned, they have beaten the intelligence and security agencies of the nations. They always seem to be one step ahead of the latter. As Dr. Mare Sageman, a former CIA operative, has remarked, the international network of jihadi terrorists has grown organically. It has grown like the Internet. In the case of internet, it would be very difficult to trace its stupendous growth, through a process evolution as also to delineate various stages of its growth. Even more so will be the case with the growth and expansion of the international jihadi terrorist network.

This is the intricate nature and magnitude of the threat the international community faces today and will face for another decade or so. How does it face this threat? What are the post-9/11 Lessons? What are the lessons to be learnt from Ayodhya, London and Sharm-el-Sheikh? How to deal with these terrorist network effectively and make them wither away?

An effective counter-terrorist and counter-terrorism doctrines must start with a lucid analysis and assessment. The counter-terrorist doctrine focuses on the terrorist organisations and their networks. It treats terrorism as a modus operandi and as a crime, that has to be eradicated. The counter-terrorism doctrine treats terrorism as a phenomenon, which has non-security related aspects, requiring equal and simultaneous attention. The counter-terrorism doctrine seeks to provide a humane corrective to an exclusively security-driven approach to terrorism.

Analysts have drawn certain lessons from the 9/11 attacks. The first and foremost lesson is that terrorism is an absolute evil and cannot be justified by any cause. Even Musharraf had to admit this in his televised address to the Pakistani people on 22 January 2002. No one has unlined this more eloquently than UN Secretary-General Kofi Annan. In his address on 10 March 2005 to the four-day international summit on "Democracy, Terrorism and Security", held at Madrid to coincide with the first anniversary of the Madrid blasts, Annan said :

> "We cannot, and need not, redress all the grievances that terrorists claim to be advancing. But we must convince all those who may be temped to support terrorism that it is neither an acceptable nor an effective may to advance their cause. It should be clearly stated, by all possible moral and political authorities, that terrorism is unacceptable under any circumstances, and in any culture."

This lesson; about the unacceptability in a civilised world of a terrorism as a means to articulate grievances—real or imagined—has been learnt at what cost? The following points need to be made here itself :

- Any angry Indian may be appreciated if he asks why these lessons were not learnt before 9/11? 70,000 or more Indians had fallen to terrorist bullets and IEDs by that date.
- Why was world so upset when a single 9/11, a single series of London blasts, and the Madrid blasts happened? Is it because the affluent nations were attacked? Do we have two standards to mourn the deaths of individuals in Asian countries and the West?
- Why was the world summit not deemed necessary before 9/11?
- Will the West take the terrorism-related killings in Asia and Africa as seriously as it wants them to take the deaths in their backyard?

After this discordant note, let us resume the narration. The single, most important reasons that explains the spread of terrorism is the lack of unity of action by the international community against the terrorists. This is in glaring contrast to the unity of action displayed by the terrorists against the civilised world. Until the two match, the innocent of the world will continue to be killed by the terrorist—abominable and merciless.

One example that illustrates the lack of unity in counter-terrorism war is the hairsplitting arguments over the definition of terrorism and the root causes of terrorism. This lack of political will is unpardonable as far as the relatives of thousands of victims of terrorist attacks are concerned. They are simply being told that these lives could not be saved because the UN could not define the term 'terrorism'. This would be sidiculous if it was not so tragic.

Even meanest intellect knows what terrorism is Hijacking an aircraft is terrorism, for whatever reasons or objectives. Planting explosives in trains, buses and airplane is terrorism. Throwing grenades at civilians is terrorism. Planting explosives in public places is terrorism. Targeted assassination of individuals is terrorism. Any organization, which indulges in these acts is a terrorist organisation, and any state, which supports or assists such organisations, is a state-sponsor of terrorism.

The second lesson is that we must make a clear distinction between the root causes of anger in an aggrieved community, which are exploited by terrorists. "We have allowed terrorists and dubious human rights organisations to define what are the root causes of terrorism, thereby playing into the hand of terrorists.

A root cause of terrorism is what facilitates the murderous acts of the terrorists and helps them to go unpunished. Kofi Annan introduces a healthy balance in this debate on the so-called root causes and removing any confusion. Told the 10 March 2005 Madrid Summit :

> "Groups use terrorist tactics because they think they tactics are effective, and that people, or at least those in whose name they claim to act, will approve. Such beliefs are the true "root cause" of terrorism. Our job is to show unequivocally that they are wrong".

The conventional wisdom that lack of development is the root cause of terrorism has been proved wrong in Pakistan, Saudi Arabia, Turkey, Spain and England. There has been an impressive growth in the Pakistani economy since 9/11. This has had no impact on the growth of terrorism from its territory.

B Raman[11] cities five root causes of continuing and thriving terrorism.

The first and foremost root cause is the failure of international community and the individual victim—States to make it clear to the terrorists that terrorism does not and will not play. A soft state will always be a victim, because of its failure to deal with terrorism effectively. India surrendered when terrorists kidnapped the daughter of the Union Home Minister in 1989. It has failed to shed its image of a soft state ever since. The action of Government of India in December 1999 in releasing some of the terrorists from Indian jails to meet the demands of some Pakistani Jihadi hijackers paved the may for the attack on Jammu and Kashmir Legislative Assembly in October 2001, the attack on Indian Parliament in December 2001, and kidnapping and murder of Daniel Pearl, the American Journalist, in Karachi in Jan.-Feb. 2002. The withdrawal of the Spanish troops from Iraq soon after the Madrid blasts paved the way for the subsequent London explosions.

- The failure of the international community to act firmly against the State-sponsors of international jihadi terrorism. The collapse of the USSR and other Communist States of East Europe brought about the collapse of the Red Army Faction of Germany the group led by Carlos and other ideological outfits because they all were dependent upon the support of the Communist States for their existence. The jihadi terrorist are able to survive because of the support and complicity of states such as Pakistan and Bangladesh. Certain Charities in Saudi Arabia are known to divert funds to the Islamist terror outfits and some of these have been named/banned by the U.S. administrations. Post-9/11, there is less talk about one nation's terrorists being another's freedom fighters. But, one still finds that one nation's (India's) state-sponsor of terrorism (Pakistan) is another nation's (US') stalwart ally against terrorism.

- Double standards adopted by certain nations in their attitude towards terrorism. India has been a victim of double standards by the U.S. and other Western countries. Things have not changed even after 9/11. Pakistan's complicity with anti-Indian terrorists is not viewed with the same glasses as its complicity with the anti-US terrorists. More galling than this should be the advice—"Please show restraint while dealing with Pakistan on issue of cross-border terrorism—India frequently receives from them.
- The unsatisfactory implementation of the UN Security Council UNSE Resolution No. 1373 by many states, particularly Pakistan, and the failure of the international community to act against them. Pakistan has avoided the arrest of 20 terrorists figuring in the INTERPOL's Red Corner Notices, who are wanted in India for indulging in acts of terrorism. It has also avoided freezing the bank accounts of many jihadi terrorist leaders and organizations and Dawood Ibrahim, the notorious mafia leader, who was declared by the U.S. Treasury Department as an international terrorist in October 2003. The U.S. had requested the UNSE to move for the freezing of his bank accounts. Pakistan has chosen to ignore this all.
- The fifth and last root cause of thriving terrorism is to be found in India's civil society, and not in those of others. That is the opposition of India's liberal elite and vociferous Human Rights groups to the legal empowerment of the police and other security agencies to enable them to perform effectively their counter-terrorist responsibilities. Indira Gandhi and Rajiv Gandhi were in the forefront of the national and global battle against terrorism and both

fell to the scourge. Both never hesitated to give to the police and other agencies the required capabilities. Ironic then that their own Congress Party has rescinded anti-terrorist legislation (POTA) from the statute.

## Doctrines : Counter-terrorist and Counter-terrorism

A satisfactory counter-terrorist doctrine that provides for effective action to remove the above-mentioned five root causes of terrorism, will help to bring terrorism under control but it will not help to eradicate terrorism unless it is combined with an effective counter-terrorism doctrine. The counter-terrorist doctrine, meant to deal with terrorism as a crime, seeks to neutralise the existing terrorist leaders, their followers and their organizations. The counter-terrorism doctrine seeks to prevent the flow of new volunteers to the terrorist organizations. For this purpose, it pays attention to the grievances of the community from which the terrorist organization draw their volunteers, in order to deny these organization the opportunity to exploit those grievances for keeping terrorism alive.

While the counter-terrorist doctrine seeks to remove the root causes of terrorism, which acts as its oxygen, the counter-terrorism doctrine seeks to address the root causes of the grievances or anger nursed by the community. Among such root causes of grievances or anger, one could mention perceptions of injustice to the community, perceived violations of its human rights, a perceived insensitivity to their problems and difficulties, overreaction of the security forces in terrorist—related situations, disproportionate use of force while implementing the counter-terrorist methods, bad governance, poor political leadership, the absence of a grievances monitoring and redressal machinery, the political grievances related to various issues.

Any state has to address the legitimate root causes of grievances and anger if it has to stop the flow of new volunteers to the terrorist outfits. The success of counter-terrorist policies depends on the national will and international cooperation. The success of counter-terrorism policies depends purely on the national will.

## Indian Muslims are different

India is an oasis in the world devastated by jihadi terrorism of the Al Qaeda variety. Indian Muslims whether in Jammu and Kashmir or in Gujarat or elsewhere in the country, have had reasons for angers. Some of them have even taken to terrorism to give vent to their anger as one had seen in Jammu and Kashmir, Mumbai and Tamil Nadu. But their anger, however intense and however justified, has not diluted their patriotism and their sense of values. India's Muslim community, the second largest in the World, has kept away from Al Qaeda and its creation, IIF. It does not support pan-Islamic ideas of an Islamic Caliphate. About a dozen Indian Muslims went to the Pakistan-Afghan border regions in 1980s to be trained in the jihadi training camps, but they never joined the Muslims from other nations in their jihad against the Soviet troops.

The Americans did not capture a single Indian Muslim in Afghanistan. One Indian Muslim living in Saudi Arabia participated in the jihad against the Serbs in Bosnia. No Indians Muslim has gone to Iraq to join the jihad there.

The U.S. National commission on 9/11 contains 220 references to Pakistan, but just one reference to India, which is about a visit to India by Khalid Sheikh Mohd for unknown reasons. There is one confirmed instance of a Hindu convert to Islam from East Africa living in the UK helping the Al Qaeda. Another instance has come from Mumbai. There is an as yet unconfirmed instance of a Gujarati Muslim living in the UK being in touch with the Al Qaeda and having played a role in the recent London explosions.

These are exceptions which proves the general rule that the Al Qaeda and the IIF have so far had no major base of support in India or amongst Muslims of Indian origin living abroad. This speaks highly of Indian Muslims Community, Indian political leadership and policy-makers, and its security bureaucracy. The world has much to learn from India. The important question for India and Indian leadership is this : How to ensure that the country continues to remain such an oasis ? While drawing lessons for the future and framing our counter-terrorism policy, this is the all important lesson we must address.

It is worth recording that President Bush during his March 2006, visit to India specifically drew attention to this fact of Indian Muslims not succumbing to the lure of Al Qaeda's repeated calls for the Muslims' to join jihad. The Union Home Minister and his Secretary as recently as December 2006, publicly saying that there is no evidence as yet of any Al Qaeda presence in India.

But all this should not bull Indians and the Government into complacency that India does not—and cannot—provide a fertile soil for the Al Qaeda. There are reasons for this warning : Al Qaeda is not known to give up easily and will continue to strive to enlist the Indian Muslims into its IIF ; there are many Al Qaedas working in the field today and Osama's Al Qaeda is certainly not the apex body of the world's jihadi campaign even if it could be the leading one; even if the Al Qaeda may not be active in India, but many of the Pakistani members of the IIF are and could be trusted to be working overtime to persuade, lure or coerce their Indian "brethren" into the "Holy Mission"; and finally alongwith these Pakistani members of the IIF, the outfits like the LeT, JeM etc could turn out to be the Trojan Horse of the Al Qaeda. All this bears remembering again and again as India is too much of an attractive prize to lose for want of striving for the Islamist jihadis!

## Combating terrorism : Media can be an Asset

Media, especially television channels, plays an important part in any crisis situation—be it floods and famine, earthquakes or typhoons, or a terrorist strike killing/injuring large number of victims. If it is not always mis-reporting or reporting out of context—as officials and politicians usually blame it for—it also cannot be denied that some channels (like some newspapers) indulge in competitive sensationalism to enhance their TRP.

Between the print and visual media, the latter need to be more circumspect and balanced because of its real time reach to the target audience, and right upto their bedrooms. An irresponsible coverage can do more harm to the national cause than any other agency or group of people.

The governments should not make the mistake of thinking that the answer lies in curtailing coverage by restricting access, or issuing "guidelines" aimed at blocking out inconvenient truths. If ever the authorities try to do that, the media will go all out either to ferret out the truth through their own sources, and failing that, it will invent or broadcast its own truth.

Speakingly specifically of 26/11 of Mumbai, officialdom went initially into overdrive slamming the media coverage of the tragedy. Later realising that some of the blame lies within, the Home Ministry issued a missive to the states on how to interact with the media during crisis situations. It is a good development that the Ministry, instead of taking recourse to a kneejerk reaction, held internal deliberations on the subject. Controlling or restricting the information channels can bring no credit or credibility to a democratic polity like India's, nor is this the solution to some channels going out of the way to sensationalising the situation. So, the Ministry's call to quickly inform the media of a strike, and to follow that up with a supply of authentic information from an easily accessible source is a reasonable solution to a sensitive problem, and more importantly, an acceptance of the reality that the media does have a role to play-even if, as some cynic may say, that of a necessary evil.

It is a fact of life that media plays an important part in all walks of life—and particularly so in a crisis situation like a terrorist strike. Of course, there is a real possibility of media going on an overdrive, and government must devise ways of controlling that. It should not be forgotten that the terrorism and its perpetrators seek publicity for themselves. It is oxygen for their outfits. It must be denied to them. Banning all news cannot be the solution. The then British Prime Minister Margaret Thatcher banned the media—print and visual—from publishing any pictures of the North Irish 'nationalist' terrorists!

To strike a balance, if the government must resist the temptation to put any curves on the media coverage of terrorist strikes, the lather too should act responsibly while covering these events.

## Intelligence : Strengths and Infirmities

Whenever there are systemic failures at tactical, strategic or national level, it is usually ascribed to 'intelligence failure' at respective levels, in the first instance. Be it the 1962 national humiliation at the Chinese hands, the discomfiture of the Indian peace-keeping force against the determined LTTE in Sri Lanka in the 1980s, or the Kargil imbroglio of 1999, it is the 'intelligence failure' to blame! Some feel people who fail to perform their duties subsequently take shelter behind the much—misused phrase when things go wrong.

*As flies to Wanton boys*
*Are we to terrorists*
*They kill us for sport*

Playing on the poet's lines, an analyst[11] painted a macabre scenario, realistic if frightening. It also stresses the need to have professionally efficient intelligence agencies to unobtrusively keep a tab on the activities of potential evil doers to rescue the country from sabotage, subversion and espionage.

Some specialists found the intelligence apparatus failing to measure upto its responsibilities. But first the book at the organizational set-up. Besides the Intelligence Bureau (IB) at the centre, which is the nodal agency for counter intelligence operations, there are various other actors in the field like anti-terrorist cells and intelligence arms of various forces to ensure the safety of citizens and nation's assets. But the sophisticated terror network often succeeding in weaking death and destruction on an unwary population, the task becomes tougher for the genies. Add to that their systemic infirmities, and the intelligence outfits, however well-equipped, are often rendered hapless witnesses to the terrorist depredations.

A terrorist act often is followed by the authorities blaming 'intelligence failure' for it and the intelligence agencies claiming that prior inputs had been given to the former. In case of 11/7 Mumbai, an intelligence officer did admit that lack of 'specific intelligence' was the cause of terrorist success. But more often it is the delay in acting on the 'specific intelligence' that results in unfortunate tragedies. The reason for it is not far to see. Barring the Special Operations Groups (SOG) in Jammu and Kashmir, leaving the onus of cracking down on suspects on the entities like Anti-Terrorist squads, special cells, Central forces like the NSG or the local police.

Another major flaw is lack of coordination among the multiplicity of intelligence agencies. Even when we have Joint Intelligence Committee in place at the Centre, coordination at the middle or lower level is poor, nearly abysmal one-upmanship lies behind this flaw. There is no mechanism worth the name to mark or trail resident agents who build up sleeper cells for terrorist outfits in a city like Mumbai. The fact that its population is in a state of constant influx further adds to the complexities of the task in hand. It is a tough call indeed. But that is exactly where the assistance of local police is warranted

The mismatch between the sophisticated global terrorist and an ill-equipped intelligence operative working within a cumberous bureaucratic set-up also adds to our woes in our combat to defeat the terror machine. Is not it appalling that a sizeable number of sbuths in the IB are from state or central forces or from other Central services. They indeed get basic training on induction, but would they be effective in defeating the innovative moves and fanatical determination of a modern terrorist? To wit, critics cite the case of an officer from the Army Veterinary Corps[12] (AVC) who got inducted into the IB as in charge of technical communications in the highly volatile Jammu region.

It is an axiom repeated endlessly in the intelligence community that "late intelligence is no intelligence". It is worse than the units and field formation of the Army failing to take timely action on the 'actionable intelligence' sent to them by the intelligence agencies. As of today, a foolproof intelligence apparatus is a far cry, as was shown up by the 1993 Mumbai serial blasts, and yet again by the July 2006, serial train blasts. This is perhaps even more unfortunate when certain recommendations, made by the Kargil Review Committee and accepted by the Group of Ministers, have been acted upon, particularly with the creation of certain additional headquarters to ensure better coordination between a variety of intelligence agencies.

> A senior policeman blames government : "Terrorist struck Mumbai in 1993 and at the Gateway of India in 2003. Now they have struck once again in July 2006. The strikes of 2003 and 2006 suggest that the Centre and State had done nothing worthwhile since 1993 to protect the citizens of Mumbai one can excuse the government for their failure to prevent the 1993 blasts, citing surprise element, but there can be no excuse for their failure to prevent the July 2006."

This is Dr. S. Subramanian, former DG, CRPF and NSG and Founder-Director, SPG speaking to a weekly.[13] He also made the following additional points :

- Experts over that to survive a State should have an efficient intelligence apparatus. The sickening regularity with which the terrorists are attacking targets in different parts of our country, and the case with which "unfriendly" and "too friendly" powers are infiltrating our defence establishment and stealing our secrets prove that India lacks this very intelligence apparatus. Even our efficient Army and paramilitary need precise intelligence to neutralise the enemy.

- The centre must bear responsibility to protect the country from external threats. Since terrorists are trained, equipped and sent to India by Pakistan and from Bangladesh, they constitute an external threat. The IB should be solely responsible for locating infiltrators and their cells, and neutralizing them.
- Do we need intelligence agencies to tell us that terrorists are likely to strike at the VVIPs on national days or important Hindu shrines? Any one can predict that. This type of frequent, inane alerts affect the credibility of the Centre and field officers tend to ignore them.
- Infiltrators/terrorists can't operate successfully without the support of sympathisers among the local population. State intelligence and local police should work with the IB to identify such elements and take action against them.
- Why has the centre taken no action to protect the Hindu shrines?
- It is apparent that the events of 11-7 were not anticipated. A commission should go into this failure and recommend measures to improve our intelligence apparatus (particularly at state level).
- It is time to create a Ministry of Internal Security under a young and knowledgeable minister.

After making the above points, Dr. Subramanian sounds a dire warning : "If we do not eliminate terrorism soon, it will eliminate our identity as a nation."

The observations made by this senior retired police officer are valid and unexceptionable and generally well known. The flows mentioned by him are not of recent origin but have adversely affected our intelligence apparatus since our Independence. The pertinent question is : did Dr. Subramanian and other retired police officer initiate measures to improve the things when they were in service and holding senior posts in the hierarchy. Majority of them must have had a stint in the IB too. After all, most of the senior positions till date are held by the IPS officers. Or is it a case of being wise after retirement?

## Intelligence

Intelligence is critical input in effective counter terrorism plans. It is necessary that the state, where terrorist acts are likely to occur or whose citizens and property are to be their victims, have timely warning to prepare themselves and others. Advance warning of terrorists' movements and plans and other information—sharing arrangements are of great value and very helpful. But information—sharing, while desirable in theory, raises some legal and moral questions that would need serious thinking if an effective intelligence-sharing system was to be put in place. After all, the identification and tagging of citizens or resident foreigners to keep track of individuals, seen by police as potential terrorists, can be used for a variety of unsavoury purposes relating to local political disaffection but bear little relationship to international terrorism.

Intelligence sharing arrangements among the like-minded governments pertaining to terrorists and their mode of operation should be related to acceptable parameters such as identification, extradition, and prosecution. Agreements relating to extraditions and prosecution must strike a delicate balance between encouraging nations to cooperate and actively resist terrorist threats and allowing sufficient space for tactical maneuvering during crisis situations.

## Counter-terrorism Aspects of Arms Control Regimes

Some of the arms control measures are devised to counter and thwart terrorism. The arms control regions aim to establish political and strategic stability and prevent proliferation of nuclear weapons. Stability problems are highlighted when so many nations are aspiring to join the nuclear club, giving impetus to arms race in their respective regions. But what is even more unsettling is the potential of some sub-national groups to brandish their atom bombs.

In specific terms, an arms control initiative should be in place dealing with the sale and transfer of portable anti-tank weapons and surface-to-air rockets/missiles. These and other weapons should be strictly controlled. There would be little loss of completive edge if the suppliers would unilaterally, voluntarily forego the sale or transfer of such weapons. Of course, multilateral agreements would be preferable. But in the real world of commerce and profits are rarely taken—and this world is certainly not populated by the angels.

## Agreements : Desirables and Possibles

Formal agreements to counter terrorism are difficult to obtain. In all likelihood, an informal arrangement could prevail. "As the severity of the terrorist problem increases" so will the proclivity for international cooperation. Some observers hoped that an 'Old Boys' network would be formed, just as the police, military, and intelligence communities did long ago one could say. But all this prognosis is, rather was true, till the 1990s. As the terrorism did not impinge the western and rich nations, they hardly took any serious notice of it. So far the victims were countries like India in South Asia, and some impoverished ones in West Asia, the rich North contented themselves with sermons and advice to end the causes of terrorism. But since the late 1990s, when the conflagration engulfed the large parts of the world, the problem assumed an urgency and immediacy which were absent earlier, when various think tanks and institutions of academic excellence thought their part was over after producing learned monographs on the subject.

But situation changed drastically when the Muslim world 'united in hatred' against the U.S. intervention in Afghanistan and Iraq. The 9/11, and later the 7/7, shook the West out of their smugness if not somnambulism. During the last decade (1995-2005), there has been flurry of bilateral counter-terrorism agreements and accords between most nation of the world. Then most regional groupings—SAARC, ASEAN, NATO, etc—have resolved to fight the terrorism. But an international agreement on the subject still eludes the world, not only because of definitional difficulties, briefly discussed above, but also other reasons of politics and differing perceptions of the problems. President Bush's enthusiasm and zeal in an all-out war against terrorism and use of terms like 'crusade' has made the Islamic world wary of his motives. An earlier prophesy by Huntington about "Clash of Civilizations" had added unnecessary stridency in the argument between the Islamic world and the Christian west. Majority of Muslims the world over consider Bush-led America as an enemy of the Muslim world, eyeing their rich resources, particularly the oil. The U.S. support of Israel in any situation, including its disproportionate use of military force against Hezbollah and Lebanon (August 2006) has only deepened the Muslim distrust of America. Even an atheist scholar like Tariq Ali has blamed the "American Imperialism" for all the trouble and turmoil in the Muslim world.

Given the above ground realities, there is no hope of any universal action-plan against the prevalent terrorism, mostly perpetrated by the Muslims trained at the *madrasas* by the overzealous clerics bent upon seeking revenge against the *kafirs*, led by the U.S., Israel, and India in the same order.

## Any Justification for Terrorism is Ingenuous

The human rights activists and bleeding heart liberals often cite 'plausible' causes behind people taking to violence for redressal of their grievances. It is rather unconvincing—this 'fact' of social and political injustice behind the violence unleashed by the underclass—when people try to justify killing innocent civilians, including children and women by the hardened criminals masquerading as Bodo rebels or Leftist Maoists. Most of the 'rebels' or 'revolutionaries' end up as people kidnapping, killing or torturing the innocent for dirty lucre.

The following pages examine this proposition in some details.

## Terrorism : Its Semantics and Justification

Employing terrorism to gain strategic and tactical aims has been a subject of controversy, essentially concerning its effectiveness and morality. Karl Marx and Fredrich Engels had somewhat mixed is not contradictory feeling about terrorism. On the one hand, they were suspicious of many 19th century terrorist movements because they felt their leaders erroneously believed that a conspiracy of a few individuals could overthrow a government, but on the other they greatly admired the *Narodniki*, the 19th century Russian terrorists who assassinated Czar Alexander II in 1881.

But Lenin and Leon Trotsky both attacked their rival Social Revolutionary for espousing terrorism. Lenin argued against individual terrorism for two reasons. One strategy of terrorism distracted desperately - needed personal from the main task of a Revolutionary movement; viz. organization of the working class. Terrorism as such was not linked to working among the masses. Two, individual terrorist acts were a submission to what he called "spontaneity" rather than to "consciousness".

Che Guevara condemned[14] the use of terrorism in his book, arguing that terrorism was generally ineffective and that it destroyed many lives that could be useful to revolution.[15] Following the Lenin line, Soviet Union supported guerrilla movements in Angola, Mozambique, Guinea-Bassau, Zimbabwe (Rhodesia), and

Namibia; pro-communist movements in Indo-China ; and the Greek Communist guerrillas during the Civil War in Greece after World War II. But on several occasions, they condemned some of the more spectacular and indiscriminate act of terrorism committed by militant revolutionaries in the contemporary world *Pravda* condemned the "killing of one Belgian and two U.S. diplomats in Kharfouni by Black September terrorists." The Soviet Press indirectly criticized the incident at Ma'alot by reporting that "world public opinion" condemned the killing of Israeli children by Arab *fedayeen*.

During July-August 1974, *Isvestia* sharply condemned the tactics of the Black September Palestinian group, claiming that its action such as plane hijacking, letter bombs, and the killing of Israeli athletes at Munich Olympics were doing great harm to the reputation of the Palestinian Resistance Movement. An article in the Soviet Weekly *New Times* sharply criticized the Italian Red Brigade for assassinating the former Italian Premier Aldo Moro, dubbing it as "Psuedo-revolutionaries" lacking any real proletarian consciousness.[16]

The Soviet Union was particularly critical of George Habash, leader of PELP, which had carried a series of hijackings in September 1970 in which a TWA 707, a Swiss Air DC-8 and BOAC VC- 10 were hijacked to Dawson airfield in northern Jordan while a Pan Air 747 was hijacked to Cairo. Habash was criticized for "irresponsible acts" and Maoist demagoguism."[17]

What are the objectives and the aims the terrorists want to achieve from violent acts :

1. A major goal is publicity for their cause, seeking to influence their own constituents whose battle they claim to be fighting, and the international community.
2. To force the polarisation of society.
3. To aggravate relations between States to serve their own interests. In 1918, The Russian Social Revolutionaries assassinated the German Ambassdor in Moscow and the German Governor General in the occupied Ukraine, hoping to sabotage the peace settlement earlier reached between Lenin's Bolsheviks and the German Government.[18]
4. To free the prisoners and secure monetary ransoms. Lenin authorized bank robberies to secure funds for the Bolshevik movement.[19] Menachem Begin organized a daring assault

on the British prison at Acre to free captured members of the Irgun.

## Causes of Terrorism

Various scholars have studies the subject and found varieties of causes underlying the phenomenon of terrorism. Some of these are discussed here.

It may be a fallacy to believe that terrorism is of recent origin. Violence has been used in different forms fairly early in history. We start with some instances in 20th Century. Robert Ted Gurr (1971) argues that political violence is a consequence of a significant gap developing between the value expectations of a given group of people and the value capabilities of the group. He discussed three possible patterns of relative deprivations.

1. "Decremental deprivation" occurs when the value capabilities of a given population decline due to one or several national disasters. Gurr argues that the success of the Bolsheviks in seizing power in Russia in 1917 was due in large part to decremental deprivation : the enormous material and human sacrifices of the Russian people World war I had created wide-spread discontent, and the failure of Kerensky government to terminate Russian involvement in the war led to a swing in popular sentiment to the one group that promised immediate peace, namely Lenin and his party.
2. "Aspirational deprivations" occurs when the value capabilities of a group remain constant while its value expectations increase. Gurr points to the violence by the black Americans in the 1960s as an example of violence caused by inspirational deprivation. Black demands for immediate equality had come up against the realities of continuing discrimination and prejudice, resulting in wide-spread dissatisfaction and frustration.
3. "Progressive Deprivation" occurs when value capabilities stabilise or decline after a period when value capabilities and value expectations have increased together. As an example of progressive deprivation Gurr notes the waves of rioting in colonies when liberalising tendencies and reforms did not result in prompt independence.

## Modernisation

The process of modernisation (in 1970s-80s) invariably leads to widespread feeling of relative deprivation. Samuel P. Huntington has argued that, during modernisation, isolation of various ethnic groups from each other breaks down. The new contact between the groups enable them to compare unfavourably their share in values such as health, power, and knowledge with those of other groups. Huntington argues that Modernisation also produces feelings of relative deprivation by changing the relationship between communal groups in different societies : a previously dominant group may find its position threatened by another group that is better able to take advantage of the social and political changes taking place.[20] After the American intervention (2004), the Sunnis have lost their dominant position in the polity, and hence the violence against the Shias.

Besides deprivation, there are other factors that add to the current wave of terrorism. These are discussed in the succeeding text.

## Ethnicity

The second factor that contributed considerably to the growth of terrorism in that period can be called the "ethnicity explosion." Rapid socio-economic change generally leaves the ethnic minorities in margins, endangering their personal security. This insecurity leads them to a search for an identity in the political field, as the economy has left them untouched. In the 1960s, violence amongst the ethnic, religious and social groups achieved an upward swing that continued in the 1970s and the 1980s. The main manifestation of this violence occurred in places which were the meeting places of major cultures or races. Here are some relevant examples in this field. A number of terrorist and guerrilla movements of the period grew out of these clashes across the "demographic fault lines of human civilization." The Palestinian *fedayeen* grew out of the conflict between Jews and Arabs over the possession of Palestine. The Front de Liberation du Quebeck (FLQ) emanated from tensions between the French and English speaking Canada. The birth of the Eritrean Liberation Front can be attributed to the Christian - Muslim conflict in Ethiopia. Religion was behind the rise of violence for a Sikh homeland in India in the 1980s. The florescence of ethnic aspirations in India's North-East in the 1950s and subsequent decades gave rise to long years of violent movement of secessionism and autonomy by the Nagas, Mizos, Bodos, Manipuris, Tripuris, and sections of the Assamese.

## Violence *qua* Violence

Frantz Fanon is the prophet of this postulation—"Violence for save of violence." He was the leading theorist and scholar of this period (1960-80s). He influenced FLQ, Tupamoro guerrillas in Uruguay in 1971, and later the Palestinian movement. Holden Roberto, the founder of the Fronte National de Liberatacao de Angola (National Front for Liberation of Angola-NFLA) was in turn heavily influenced both by Fanon's writing and his personality.

Undoubtedly, Fanon[21] had a deep impact on the contemporary revolutionary ideology and literature. He argues that violence *qa* violence is useful and productive, regardless of whether violence actually moves the revolutionary movement any closer to its goals. Why is violence constructive for oppressed people? At the individual level he avers, violence is a cleansing force that frees the native from his inferiority complex and turns him fearless. A people who had taken part in a violent war of national liberation would jealously guard the results of their action and refuse to allows their destiny to be placed in the hands of the "liberators." Again at the level of community, he argues, violence has a positive impact because it raises national consciousness. Its practice mobilises an oppressed people and binds them together into a new nation. He seriously advocates mindless violence, which might have convinced theoretician and his admirers, but at this stage of governments commanding vest logistical and technological resources, it is a self defeating philosophy.

## Anti-colonial Struggles

Wars of independence against the colonial countries and masters involved use of violence by the freedom fighters. This lent certain respectability to the violence and its practitioners. The terrorist of the British period, like Bhagat Singh and Chandrashekhar Azad, are national icons of free India. Seg and Alder argued that the reason why many Governments rather took an indulgent stance towards terrorism was frequently seen as a manifestation of political and ideological struggles against imperialism and colonialism.[22] The two contend that the result of this sympathy is that punishment for terrorists has been lenient for the most part. A Rand Corparation Study of 63 Major hostage-taking incidents during 1968-74 supports this contention. This study found that in these situations there was a 79 percent chance that all members of the terrorist team would escape punishment or death.[23] This governmental tolerance towards terrorism, Segre and Alder argue, "has created an international climate conducive to terrorist activities."

I Bowyer Bell (1971)[24] says the "myth of the guerrilla" helps the cause of the terrorists. The myth has it that any movement that employes the strategies and tactics of guerrilla warfare and/or terrorism is fairly assured of success. After all, so many guerrilla movements have indeed been successful—viz. Mao Zedong in China, the FLN in Algeria, Ho Chi Minh and Viet Minh in Indo—China, EOKA in Cyprus, and Zionist Underground in Palestine. In the move recent times, the Taliban Guerrilla generously helped by U.S. and Pakistan, routed and ousted the mighty Soviet army out of Afghanistan. Then there were guerrilla leaders who became legends in their own lives : Moshe Dayan (1915-81) was a legendry guerrilla leader before he became famous as a General who twice led Israel to dramatic victories over its Arab neighbours. Che Guevera (1928-67) who outshone even Castro as a guerrilla leader in Latin America.

### Che Guevara

Pen picture of the iconic guerrilla leader is given below.

## Guerrilla Leader

An Argentine revolutionary and guerrilla leader, Che Guevara's tragic early death in Bolivia created a legend that still lives. He once said that "the true revolutionary is guided by a great feeling of love", but he also wrote influential works of guerrilla warfare.

His execution in Vallegrande at the age of 39 only enhanced Guevara's mythical stature. Guevara's full name was Ernesto 'Che' Rafael Guevara de la Serna.

He was born in 1928 in Rosario, Argentina into a middle-class family of Spanish-Irish descent. Celia de la Sernay Llosa, his mother, had lost her parents while she was still a child. Celia was raised by her religious aunt and her older sister, Carmen de la Serna, who married in 1928 the Communist poet Cayetano Cdrdova Iturburu. Guevara's family was liberal, anti-Nazi and anti-Peronist, and not very religious. With Gelia's fortune, the family lived comfortably, although Ernerto Guevara Lynch, Ernesto's father, managed to spend much of it in his unlucky business ventures. In his youth Guevara read widely and among his reading list in the 1940s were Sartre, Pablo Neruda, Giro Alegria, and Karl Marx's Das Kapital. He also kept a philosophical diary and in Africa in 1965, Guevara planned to write a biography of Marx.

In 1953 Guevara graduated from the University of Buenos Aires, where he was trained as a doctor. During these years, Guevara read Stalin and Mussolini but did not join radical student organizations. He made long travels in Argentina and in other Latin America countries. At the same time, his critical views about the expanding economic influence of the United States deepened.

After witnessing American intervention in Guatemala in 1954, Guevara radicalised and become convinced that the only way to bring about change was by violent revolution.

## The Warrior

- 'Che' variously translates as "Hey, you...", or 'Chum', or 'Buddy', or 'Pal', or 'Dude', or 'The Kid'.
- The nickname "Che" was derived from Guevara's habit of punctuating his speech with the interjection che, a common Argentine expression for a friend.
- In Guatemala Guevara met Hilda Gadea. They married in 1955 and had one child. Guevara was arrested with Fidel Castro in Mexico for a short time.
- He had joined Castro's revolutionaries to overthrow the Batista government.
- In the areas controlled by the guerrillas, Guevara started land reform and socializing process.
- In spite of his chronic asthma, Guevara enjoyed the hard conditions and war.
- In the mountains Guevara met Aleida March in 1958, a 24-year-old revolutionary fighter, and she became Guevara's second wife in 1959.
- A selection of Guevara's articles, which he wrote between 1959 and 1964, was published in 1963 as 'Pasajes De La Guerra Revolucionaria'.
- For the media, Cuba was a hot subject. New York Times, Paris Match and Latin American papers sent reporters to the mountains to make stories of the revolutionaries.

- At the same time when Guevara was in the mountains, his uncle was Ambassador to Cuba.
- After the conquest of power in January 1959, Guevara gained fame as the leading figure in Castro's government. He argued strongly for centralised planning, and emphasised creation of the 'new socialist man'.
- In 1959, Guevara adopted formally the nickname Che and was granted honorary Cuban citizenship.
- The most famous picture of Guevara was taken by Alberto Diaz Gutierrez, known professionally as Korda. He declined to take royalties when the picture became a worldwide icon.
- From 1961 to 1965 Guevara was minister for industries, and director of the national bank, signing the bank notes simply 'Che'.
- Guevara was shot in a schoolhouse in La Higuera on 9 October, 1967, by warrant officer Mario Teran of the Bolivian Rangers at the request of Colonel Zenteno.

## Revolutionary Movements

Strictly speaking, revolutionary Movements is not the subject of this book but as some terrorist activities get elevated to such movements, and violence is their chief weapon, a brief word on it should be in order. There pre-conditions are pre-requisites for the success of revolutionary movements.

1. There must be a valid cause to attract a core of militants without alienating the populace. The public must perceive the cause as legitimates
2. The revolutionary movement must have some legitimacy in the eyes of the opposition also, thought this pre-requisite becomes redundant if the movement achieves a military victory, because then the perception of the insurgents in the eyes of the status quo forces is irrelevant.
3. The revolutionary forces must be able' to raise the price of the continuing struggle to a point at which those resisting the change will no longer be willing to pay and ultimately give in.[25]

## Reasons for Failures

Theoretical postulations and belief in the "myth of guerrillas" do not always translate into success. Following the success of Castro's revolutionaries in Cuba in the early 1960s, there were euphoric expectations about the wave of rural-based insurgencies spreading revolution all over Latin America. With the death of its Chief Che Guevara in 1967, half the battle was lost and within a decade or so thereafter, it was all over for the rural-based revolution, bar the analysis of reasons for the hope gone awry. These revolutions were defeated because of increased governmental counter-insurgency tactics and techniques, internal splits and infighting among the revolutionary movements, and inability and unwillingness of the largely middle-class and city bred revolutionaries to relate to the peasantry.

The success met by the Arafat - led Palestinian movement through ostensible use of terrorism was bankrolled by the oil-rich Arab States. But this success cannot gross over the hostility of many Arab autocracies and monarchies led by Jordan towards the "Socialist Palestine" of Arafat's dream! But contrast the success of Palestine Authority (PA) in attaining international recognition including a seat at the CIN with the plight of Kurds suffering repression for the last six decades at the hands of three governments. At the point seemingly so close to its destination, we should be well-aware of the hurdles it faces with the Hamas winning its first national elections in 2006 and the Hamas-Fatah cadres attacking each other. The last mile seems to be the toughest for PA, especially with death removing Arafat from the scene.

The Kurds might have gained a little with the American intervention in Iraq, but they are far from their goal of having a unified Kurdistan, which perhaps is best explained by an old Kurdish saying : "Kurds have no friends."

## Technology has helped Terrorists

Terrorist groups have skillfully exploited the technological advances in the areas of transportation and communication. The worldwide airways network has provided terrorists with vast avenues of opportunities to ply their trade. A single terrorist can seize/hijack an airliner, and the life of hundreds of hostages at his/her mercy. The hijached airlines also provides a means of escape for the terrorist to a country of his choice-willing to provide sanctuary to the criminal. The air travel facility has enabled various terrorist groups to develop on international network of contacts. Unfortunately, the obsession for one-upmanship and urge to win the TRP war, and the ability of the news agencies to broadcast live around the world scenes from a terrorist incident—an armed hoodlum, with face covered, threatening to shoot the cowering hostages at point blank range, negotiators entering and exiting the airliner, emotional scenes of relatives of the hijached passengers wailing and crying loudly outside the Prime Ministers house, demanding that the government yield to the terrorists terms, the terrorists throwing the bodies/body of hastage/s out of the airline, and worst, the terrorists killing a hostage to pressurise the Government into surrender/accepting their demands—via radio and television, have given the terrorists a means of attaining a larger than life image, immediate publicity and recognition they crave for. And so it happenned when TWA airliner was hijacked from Athens to Beirut and the Americans were taken hostage by the Lebanese terrorists in July 1985.

## Noting can and no one should justify terrorism

Any one condoning terrorism not to speak of legitimizing it through espousal, terrorism can be said to be a fellow-traller! A prominent American, David Patrick Moyni, who contributed a chapter *Terrorism : How the West can Win*? to the book Benjamin Netanyahu : Ferrar, Straus, and Girouse, 1986), says : "I understand that no one genuinely opposes real (or even imagined) injustices by committing, even worse atrocities. I wish to make it clear that the meaning of terrorism's political ends is simply totalitarian power disguised in a separatist, liberationist, or other pseudo-plausible rationale...Terrorism when successful, ends in totalitarianism. The totalitarian state is terrorism to come in power."

Terrorism today is the most serious issue confronting the world. Unless handled effectively and promptly, it has the potential to destabilise the existing world order. What, when, is the way to act against the scourge? It is generally accepted that terrorism is a crime and must be see as such. Its practitioners are simply criminals, and must be treated as such. A terrorist kept constantly on the defensive is an ineffectual terrorist. Analysts of this like are rather sure, too sure, perhaps, that "no special powers need be given a government beyond those which already exist to combat organised crime of the Mafia variety." Such simplistic solutions are the result of academia skimming the surface of the issues involved. They urge that terrorist must never be allowed to feel safe anywhere in the world. A western analyst rails against the UN : "It is doubtful if it can play any role for the simple reason that terrorist states are among its honoured members...what should be our policy towards the governments of such countries as Iran, Syria, and Libya, which regularly strike at the world and, in particular, at the west through their terrorist praxis?"

We are living in an age of excessive usage of clichés in any given situation! "The force alone cannot solve the problem of terrorism," is the one cliché often mouthed by some scholars at the seminar circuit on the issue of terrorism. It will be more true to say that the terrorism cannot be defeated without employing force. It is only when a wrong doer, be he a terrorist or a common criminal, is convinced that he cannot face the determined state that he deems it necessary to mend his ways and come to the negotiating table. The Chambal dacoits found it convenient to take advantage of the Saintly Vinoba's call to lay down arms in the 1950's and 1960s when they found the heat flowing from the government's anti-dacoits measures unbearable! How come Osama could not play his trade in his own country Saudi Arabia? It is difficult to imagine the havoc the terrorists can perpetrate on the nations and their law-abiding citizens if they did not have the fear of the states' determination to administer their own medicine to them. What applies to individual desparados is also true of the nations. The world did not fail to notice the cessation of Libyan inspired terrorist acts since U.S. President Reagan ordered raids on Tripoli. Consequently, its President, Kadafy, publicly and instantaneously repudiated "the recent Plane hijacking in Pakistan". While these raids could be condemned as being against the international law, even then this slap on the face alarmed the Dictator enough to mend his ways. Imagine the pleasant and unexpectedly quick results if the international community could unite to craft a truly firm, uncompromising and rational policy on terrorism.

But that is easier pronounced than accomplished. Perceived national interests of various countries would be seen to be adversely impinged upon by certain aspects of a universally binding, UN-approved action plan against the terrorism. Why go for, the nation have failed so far to come to even an agreed definition of terrorism. So it is no surprise that 'civilised' nations have failed so far the confront this 'modern' barbaric practice. Some would say it is certainly a battle they could win, 'if they really wanted to'. No, they all 'want' to win this battle but do not know how to go round the obstacles - religious, national, racial, or ethnic-blocking their way. Some of government's reluctance to face the terrorism squarely can, at least, in part be ascribed to the success of the terrorist propaganda barrage, the influence of the media, both press and television, and many public figures—all bestowing certain political and moral respectability upon the terrorist leaders and their cause.

But those who nurture no such moral compunctions fail to understand "why the policies of the Arafats, or for that matter, of the erstwhile Soviet Union and People's Republic of China should get moral recognition?" To all the three entities, the life of an individual has hardly any sanctity. If demanded by a collective cause or their perceived interests, it can be exterminated summarily. We have the long-serving Soviet Foreign Minister, the late Andrei Vishinsky, saying plainly : "When it is a question of annihilating the 'enemy', we can just as well do without a trial". This is where the issues are joined. The western scholars accuse the Communist States of Messacring the 'heretics' without caring for human life. Thus goes the reasoning : "The significance of the people gunned down periodically in the West's airports or blown in its shopping centres pales the fact of the million cold-bloodedly killed by the butchers of the totalitarianism". Then follows the rhetorical flourish : "If communist states are treated as respectable members of the community of civilised people, why should not the PLO be welcome, too?" Well, ironically, the PLO has been admitted to the UN even before it achieved its desideratum of statehood for itself. Even more ironically, after the death of its mentor, Arafat, the PLO has lost on violence stakes to its more violent and less politically accommodating Hamas. After losing the democratic vote to the latter early 2006, Palestinian President, Arafat's successor, is pitted against the Hamas Prime Minister—both trying to rule over their yet-to-be born nation in their own respective lights!

The above is detailed to show how the 'moderates' are losing ground to their more volatile counterparts in the field of terrorism. More importantly, it is also meant to show why the Communist East (and also the Muslim World) can never come to craft a mutually-agreed definition of the term 'terrorism' even when it is posing the potent threat to the world peace and stability.

Reverting to the 'morality' question, do the terrorists have any morality quotient attached to their wanton acts of destruction? If it is there, as indeed is seen by some sections of educated class, the analysts believe it is the product of 'liberalist' trend in the educational field encouraged by certain western tradition. This disabling moral relativism has not been caused or promoted by some clever terrorist propaganda play. "It is rather our schools and universities which have stunted men', minds for generations with a steady diet of pragmatism," pasits a western scholar. It is only this pragmatism, which holds that there are no moral absolutes, that could lead men to believe that one man's civilization is another's 'Black Hole' of Kolkata. To this line of thinking, the matter of moral self-doubt is a transient problem, which will vanish once the nature and purpose of terrorism are grasped by the victims—individuals or nations. But this belief itself seem untrue to some Indian analysts who are cominced that the West has lost confidence in its ethical foundation and so has conceded some legitimacy to the goals of today's terrorists—consequently disarming itself.

The western scholars are quick in returning the compliments. If Indians have retained their ethical values, how come they have suffered the ravages of terrorism in terms of time and the grievous death and destruction. If the Europe has experienced the pain only in the recent years, the U.S. suffered it on its soil only after the 9/11, where as India has been its victim since its independence itself. So the debate continues.

## Funding and Financing Terrorism

It is obvious that the terror outfits are seldom short of funds. They have found out various ways of keeping their coffers overflowing. Illegal narco money was known to fund terror outfits for long time. Of late, many more ways of funding these outfits have come to light : diverting charity funds, ransoms for kidnapping, extracting money from government and public officers, hawala transactions et al.

Several Islamic Charities are known to divert funds to terrorist outfits, as explained hereafter. But the latest to come to light is the case of the JuD, the public face of the LeT, diverting funds into the coffers of its terror twin.

The creation and (mis) use of the fake currency by the masterminds behind the terrorist operations is another.

## 'Tsunami Funds in Terror Hands'

Tsunami donations post-December 2004 may have been diverted to terror modules across the world believe some U.S. terrorism experts.

Prof. Jimmy Gurule, former Assistant Attarney General of the U.S. and an expert on the terrorist funding network, says the U.S. government has identified around 48 charities which directly or indirectly fund terrorist organizations. He said : "some percentage of the multi-billion dollars donated by the international community towards tsunami rehabilitation were diverted to terrorist groups like Al Qaeda...While U.S. Treasury and State Departments are currently looking into the matter, some money might also have made its way to LeT, outfit behind the 11-7 Mumbai blasts."

Gurule, who was also Under Secretary for Enforcement, U.S. Treasury Department, 2001-03, said that his government has come out with a guideline in September 2006, meant for the international community, suggesting the charities which are genuine as also the necessary cheeks and balances about donating money.

In Saudi Arabia alone, some of these organizations collected as *Zakaat* (= religious donation) around U.S. $10 billion. "Around one to four per cent of these funds are diverted for purposes of terror. Saudi-based International Islamic Relief Organization is one such entity with offices in 20 countries and it has been found that the Organization has close ties with Al Qaeda," he explained.

*Hawala*, largely practised in the sub-continent, was another efficient way of funding the terrorist outfits. The system is used to transfer money globally, without any bounds and legal system must be put into place to plug this loophole. Although the system of verification of new customers by banks has been put into place, financial institutions need to be sensitised.

Gurule, a professor of criminal law at University of Notre Dame, U.S., is presently on a visit to India, to meet policy makers, in New Delhi, Mumbai and Pune to discuss know how on financing of terrorism.

Indians were aware of the LeT diverting large amount of funds when it was practically the only entity doing rescue and rehabilitation work after the 2005 earthquake in PoK. It was happening at local level. That it has also been happening at the international level is what has been confirmed by Prof. Gurule.

## Hawala deals financing terror" : U.S. Report

Cautioning that the hawala money in India is directly linked to terrorist financing, the U.S. has suggested to New Delhi to strengthen its anti-money laundering and counter-terrorism-finance legislations.

A U.S. State Department report, released 27 February 2009, finding chinks in India's efforts to combat money-laundering and financial crimes, has sought greater participation of its enforcement agencies in bringing transparency in foreign trade as the latter has often been used as the "back door channel to underground financial system" or hawala.

The report talks about the hawala transaction in financing terrorism and magnitude of illegal money transfers in India. The report estimates such money transfers in the region of $ 13-17 billion annually.

It specifically talks about alleged abuses in the diamond trade while urging India to join the Financial Action Task Force (FATF), an inter-governmental body based in Paris. A senior official with an enforcement agency said : "By joining the FATF, it will become binding on India to share information relating to a financial crime registered by any member country in any jurisdiction even when the inquiry relates to a country's VIP".

All the FATF members have the obligation to not only share information relating to an accused, but the law provides for attachment of property and arrest of an accused anywhere across national boundaries.

However the U.S. report—pointing that foreign trade channels had been used by some to finance terrorism—is a big blow to the credibility of the entire system that has failed to curb the menace despite repeated terror attacks across the country.

India's own Financial Intelligence Unit (FIU) in its 2008 report found the number of suspicious transaction through banking channels having escalated two-fold in a year. It had found at least 130 suspect cases relating to terror financing. In 500 cases, the FIU had found that the banks and other institutions were not aware of the identity of the clients or their background. These accounts had been opened by fictitious entities based on forged documents.

Now, with Parliament having passed the Prevention of Money Laundering (PML) Bill, India is set to become a full time member of the FATF which meets every four months while the FATF is headquartered in France, its regional outfits, the Asia Pacific Group, is based in Australia.

With the recent amendments, the Enforcement Directorate (ED), the prosecuting agency for all PMLA cases, gets power to register cases at the time of filing of complaint by the police.

Things should, indeed, improve with India joining the world body.

## Shady Transaction Point to Terror Funds

"In what could probably throw light on funding of terror modules, the Financial Intelligence Unit (FIU) has detected around 200 suspicious transactions worth Rs. 2,000 crore in the country", said a report 3 March, 2009. The exercise to trace suspicious transactions started in the aftermath of 9/11 terror strikes.

Though the origin of these funds is being ascertained, the cash transaction report show that investments in India were routed through Mauritius, Bahamas, Cook Island and Gulf.

The FIU has forwarded these suspicious transaction reports to investigative and enforcement agencies, including the IB and Income Tax department.

A request for facilitating assistance in probing the accounts has been sent to almost 30 countries in 2008-09 so that international networks financing terror networks in the country could be exposed, sources in FIU said.

## Cost of Combating Terrorism

The cost of countering and combating terrorist 'death and destruction' dance is huge in terms of resources energy and time spent by the official and non-official agencies. But the psychological scars and trauma and mental distress suffered by the world is incalculable, indeed.

While the heaven-seeking perpetrators of the crime feel blessed in death, the victims who survive the carnage face living-death experience—seeing the sufferings of the near and dear ones.

The costs of terrorism to the individuals are discussed in the next pages.

No attempt has been made to quantify the expenditure involved in raising new departments and intelligence, as by the U.S., and in creating new infrastructures and units/special forces to counter the future attacks, as raised by India. Hundreds of thousands of lives have been lost over the past half century or so. Can one put value on the trauma and agony of their living relatives?

"The U.S. would be spending a massive $ 110 billion next year 2007 in Iraq."

Prof. Alpha Oumar Konare, Chairman, Commission of African Union, speaking at International Council of World Affairs (KWA), New Delhi on 20 December, 2006.

## Mounting Costs of The Financial War Against Terrorism

## December 20, 2001 Printer-Friendly Version

U.S. and international moves to block terrorist funds since September 11 have been extraordinarily swift. Over $61 million in Taliban and *al Qaeda* assets have been frozen worldwide, with additional tens of millions of dollars in other terrorist money also frozen.

The administration of U.S. President George W. Bush in October dubbed its financial anti-terror strategy Operation Green Quest, reflecting its recognition that denying terrorists of funding is as crucial an element in the anti-terrorism war as the military campaign under Operation Enduring Freedom. "Those who do business with terrorists will do no business with the United States," Bush recently reiterated.

However, military and financial strategies parallel one another not only in their import and apparent success, but also in the complexity of their impacts on countries around the world. Examining some of the political, economic and social costs of the financial war on terrorism shows that U.S. ability to deal with its indirect consequences will be increasingly linked with its ability to keep the international coalition intact.

## Political Cost: Tensions with the Arab World

A recent asset freeze order from Bush demonstrates the far-reaching political effect of a single step in the counter-terrorism campaign. On December 4, 2001, the Bush administration ordered the freezing of assets of three financial groups it accused of financing Hamas, a militant Palestinian organization designated as terrorist by the United States, and which claimed responsibility for the recent suicide bombings in Israel that killed 25 people. Soon after Bush's announcement, eight American Muslim organizations responded with an outcry, claiming that the administration was again manifesting its pro-Israel proclivity and asking Bush to retract the order. The Holy Land Foundation for Relief and Development, one of the three groups targeted and the largest Muslim charity in the United States, denied any link to Hamas and stressed that the foundation is strictly humanitarian in its mission.

Commotions were far greater in the Middle East, where Beit El-Mal Holdings and al Aqsa Islamic Bank, the other two suspect organizations, are located. The asset freeze order intensified the already heavy diplomatic pressure the United States has been exerting on Yasser Arafat to crack down on militant groups responsible for acts of terrorism in Israel. Arafat thus responded two days after Bush's order by placing Sheik Ahmed Yassin, the spiritual leader of Hamas, under house arrest - a move that led to violent clashes between Palestinian security forces and the hoard of Hamas supporters that gathered in protest.

Arafat now confronts enormous risk and uncertainty as Washington extends the war on terror - at least on the financial front - beyond Afghanistan. Despite Arafat's rhetorical commitment to counter-terrorism and his expressed desire for a settlement to the bloody 15 month-old Israeli-Palestinian conflict, the Palestinian populace remains largely sympathetic to Hamas's causes and actions, which to them are legitimate responses to Israel's brutal occupation of their territory. While the United States calls for an end to extremist militancy as part of the global anti-terrorism campaign, recent counter-terrorism efforts, including moves related to terrorist assets, have thus added another dimension - and more violence - to the thorny Middle East conflict.

On an even broader scale, the series of asset freeze orders from the Bush administration is deepening the sense of unease and ambivalence about U.S.-led campaign in the entire Arab region. While Arab nations have voiced their unequivocal support for counter-terrorism, they remain wary of many of the U.S. approaches in the war, not the least in the matter of terrorist finances. From the start of the campaign, countries such as Saudi Arabia, Egypt, Jordan and Syria have urged Bush to focus narrowly on blocking off Osama bin Laden's financial network rather than simultaneously targeting other terrorist groups. After freezing the assets of the three organizations related to Hamas, Arab governments warned Bush that the order may help undermine his administration's efforts to maintain the anti-terrorism coalition. Aversion to U.S. unilateralism is pervasive in the region, with Arab countries persistently calling for any action to be taken under UN auspices. Egypt's foreign minister, for instance, declared that the United States alone is bound by the asset freeze lists it generates, and that Egypt is committed only to UN resolutions.

Since September 11, the Israeli-Palestinian conflict has become intertwined with the anti-terrorism war. Middle East countries are simultaneously home to some the most wanted of terrorist entities and to the most vital U.S. supporters in the current campaign. The administration will thus need to consider how further counter-terrorism measures will affect its allies in the Middle East and, given the set of U.S. priorities, carefully weigh out the costs and benefits of the measures.

## Economic Cost: The Collapsing Somali Economy

Not unlike Afghanistan, today's Somalia is a country that has been devastated and impoverished by a decade of factional wars, severe drought, hyperinflation, a livestock export ban, lack of central government, lawlessness, and a dearth of foreign aid. On November 7, when the U.S. Treasury Department accused al Barakaat, a major banking and remittance transfer company, of funneling money to *al Qaeda* and ordered its assets to be frozen, many Somalis saw themselves suddenly bereft of their only form of sustenance, leaving them with little or no income for the time being.

According to UN officials, the largest source of income for Somalia is money sent from relatives abroad. Known as one of the largest companies in Somalia, al Barakaat served as the predominant money transfer medium for Somali people, sending about $140 million a year in remittances. Those who depended on the company for receiving income from abroad numbered in the hundreds of thousands, and another several thousands worked for the company in Somalia. The closing of the bank, together with the enduring problems of the failed state, recently led UN officials to project for Somalia a rare and disturbing future—the collapse of the entire national economy.

Further exacerbating the situation is speculation that the country may become a target if the U.S.-led war moves beyond Afghanistan. In preparation for any anti-terrorism operation there, both the United Nations and the European Union have reduced the desperately needed relief flights to the country since September 11. With the U.S. Embassy in Mogadishu closed for over a decade, Somalia has alarming resemblances to the political, economic and humanitarian state of affairs of post-Soviet Afghanistan.

Aware of what such resemblances may portend, UN and U.S. AID officials have met in Somalia since the censure of al Barakaat to examine the conditions there. The United Nations is seeking $250,000 to set up an alternative money transfer system, and is seeking other ways to counter the effects of the company's closure. Such aid is needed not only for the Somalis in dire situations, but also for retaining the cooperation of Somali leader Abdiqassim Salad Hassan who, having promised Bush his full support, is now expecting the United States to take more than an arms-length approach toward Somalia. As Bush takes further strides in choking off terrorist funds, he may increasingly find that economic and social assistance to countries affected by the anti-terrorism war is key for winning their political allegiance.

## Social Cost: The Fate of Islamic Charities

Some of the social consequences of financial crackdowns on terrorists derive from a bizarre conceptual irony of this aspect of counter-terrorism: dozens of entities on Bush's asset freeze list claim that, far from violence and terrorism, they in fact promote welfare and humanitarian relief. Many even claim to be providing financial assistance to the very people affected by the current war.

The chief executive of the recently-targeted Holy Land Foundation, for instance, claims that the charity raised $13 million from American Muslims last year, which it spent on humanitarian causes in the West Bank and Gaza, as well as on earthquake victims in Turkey, refugees in Kosovo, Chechnya, Jordan and Lebanon, food pantries across the United States, and in setting up a fund for families of victims of the September 11 attacks. Its mission statement declares that the organization seeks to "find and implement practical solutions for human suffering through humanitarian programs that impact the lives of the disadvantaged, disinherited, and displaced peoples."

In mid-December, the U.S. Treasury Department ordered the raiding of two more Muslim charity organizations in the Chicago suburbs. Like Holy Land Foundation, both groups immediately denied having any ties to terrorists, with one of them stating that the raids are "a terrible, terrible, terrible, tragic mistake" on the part of the U.S. government.

Nevertheless, the United States asserts that it has grounded evidence that the targeted organizations are linked to bin Laden or other terrorist organizations. The U.S. government claims, for example, that the money raised by the Holy Land Foundation is eventually used by Hamas to support schools that encourage children to become suicide bombers. Just how much evidence the Bush administration shares with its allies is unknown, although the Saudi government has often complained that asset freeze orders are not accompanied by sufficient proof. The legitimacy of U.S. crackdowns on these charities aside, in the global alert for suspect Islamic organizations, two sensitive and potentially explosive issues rise to the surface.

The first is that for many Muslims, donating to Islamic charities is a fundamental practice in their faith. The Koran stipulates that Muslims must give zakat, or charitable donations, calculated at 2.5 percent of a person's income. In this light, the reason for the outrage resulting from the Treasury's raiding of the largest Islamic foundation in the United States is obvious - the move touches on the sensitivities of Muslims who had dutifully given their zakat to the foundation. The Treasury's intensification of the financial attacks on terrorism during Ramadan, furthermore, was seen by many Muslims as a highly provocative decision. In the spirit of devotion, purity and charity, Muslims customarily donate more than the usual amount during the Muslim holy month. The recent crackdowns have thus led leaders of Islamic organizations around the world to argue that targeting Islamic charities will only fuel the perception that the U.S.-led war is a war against Islam.

Secondly, many of the charity organizations currently under scrutiny do in fact accomplish their stated humanitarian missions.

The Saudi-based International Islamic Relief Organization, despite being accused of having past links to bin Laden and Filipino Muslim extremists, still operates an orphanage in the southern Philippines. The recently raided Global Relief Foundation, which raised about $5 million last year, sends contributions to clinics in Israeli-occupied territories and refugee camps in Kosovo. In Southeast Asia, charities are credited with having played a vital social role since 1997, when the financial crisis crippled effective governmental action in Asian societies. In fact, in corruption-ridden Indonesia, many people are said to give more credibility to charities than to the government for the provision of social safety nets.

Because many Muslims remain wary of orders from Washington, success in U.S. efforts to disrupt terrorist funds will depend significantly on Bush's ability to persuade cooperating governments to take their own initiatives to monitor suspect charities and other organizations. Thus far, the Bush administration has been able to secure worldwide cooperation in this regard, receiving support even from governments that remain cautious about their role in the anti-terrorism war. The government of Kuwait has agreed to invite international auditors to oversee finances of Islamic charities in the country. Saudi Arabia, despite experiencing tensions with the United States over financial aspects of anti-terrorism, allowed an American delegation in charge of establishing mechanisms to oversee charities into the country in early December. It also established a Self-Supervisory Committee to coordinate the financial counter-terrorism efforts. Washington's diplomacy with its allies appears to have paid off so far, and will remain essential for maintaining the global coalition in the months ahead.

## Conclusion

Denying existing terrorists of funds is a core part of the anti-terrorism campaign. And the operation is as difficult and complex-with broad implications for countries around the world—as it is indispensable. Measures taken in the past three months have already affected large segments of people from Somalia to Southeast Asia to Saudi Arabia.

The Bush administration is well aware that it cannot take the support of foreign governments for granted, and that continued support is crucial for combating global terrorism. With this awareness, the degree of consideration the U.S. leadership affords to religious and cultural sensitivities, ally governments' exhortations, and to the war's impact on ordinary citizens, will greatly determine whether the United States can keep this campaign a global effort—as it must be to attain its goals—or will increasingly have to do it alone. But the United States also knows that solutions to global problems must come from global sources. As air strikes in Afghanistan were accompanied by humanitarian food drops, so the financial strikes on terrorist assets will increasingly require political and economic accompaniments for people who are negatively affected—before they become disaffected with the war.

*By Reyko Huang*
*CDI Research Assistant*

**Source :** Center for Defense Information
1779 Massachusetts Ave, NW, Washinton, DC 20036-2109
Ph : (202) 332-0600 : (202) 462-4559
info@cdi.org

## Crippling Cost of Iraq War for the U.S.

The U.S. invaded Iraq in 2003 since in its perception that country was aiding and abetting the international terrorism. After toppling of Saddam Hussain, it became the objective of the U.S. to control and eliminate a variety of sectarian militants/terrorists operating on the Iraqi soil before planning the exit from there.

The main reason, the analyst to feel, why there has not been a grounds well of disapproval and dissent in matters relating to the proposed 'surge' in troops to be ordered to Iraq (Frontline, 6.4.07) is the shroud around the full costs as estimated by independent economists. Many analysts have asserted that the U.S. invasion of Iraq and continued war there for over six years have 'created' more terrorists than the U.S. would ever care to admit. "The hostilities have created and sustained a political ambience in Iraq that achieves the terrorists' and Jihadist's objectives than those of the anti-war pacifists.

The prediction, made three months before the war began in 2003, by the National Intelligence Estimate of the 16 security agencies, that terrorists would gain the upper hand in the case of a U.S. intervention/invasion, has proved unerringly accurate.

Even before the war, in 2002, William D. Nordhaus, Sterling Professor of Economics at Yale University, estimated the Iraq war costs to the U.S. alone at between $ 100 billion and $ 1.9 trillion over a 10 year period (2003-2012). This study took into account the costs of (a) occupation and construction, (b) humanitarian assistance, (c) impact on oil imports, and price shocks and (d) the macro-economic impact.

Earlier, Larry Lindsey, a White House official, had noted that the costs of an Iraq war would be between $ 100 billion and $ 200 billion or about 1 to 2 percent of the UDP of the U.S. The Lindsey estimate was dismissed by other officials as an overestimate. In fact, this and other estimate made around 2002, with the exception of Nordhaus, were serious miscalculation, intentional or otherwise, that took the war impact on the budget and economy too lightly. The fact is acknowledged widely, and today the Congressional Budget Office talks about $ 500 billion or more for this hasty adventure.

Some gullible in the media accept the figures trotted by the U.S. Administration, such as $ 300 billion so far (till March 2007), without grasping that this is just the lowball budget cost. The media also continue to reiterate uncritically the budget figures, such as the monthly cost was $ 4.4 billion ($ 52.8 billion annually in 2003 and now it is $ 8.4 billion ($ 100.8 billion annually) in 2007.

### Total Cost of Iraq War

| | *Conservative* | *Moderate* |
|---|---|---|
| Direct Costs | $ 839 billion | $ 1,189 billion |
| Macro-economic costs | $ 187 billion | $ 1,050 billion |
| Total costs | $ 1,026 billion | $ 2,239 billion |

*Source :* Linda Blimes and Joseph Stiglitz (2006) *The Economic Costs of the Iraq War*, An Appraisal Three year after the beginning of the conflict, paper presented at the annual meetings of the ASSA, Boston, January 2006.

## References

1. Jessica Stern, The Ultimate Terrorist, Harvard University Press, Cambridge, MA, 2000, p. 6.
2. Cited, Arun Jaitley, in his 2 August, 2002, lecture.
3. The author is reminded of the days when his unit was guarding the Pakistani Prisoners of War (PoW) in the PoW camps in a

cantonment in Eastern India. They claimed they were not PSoW but political prisoners as they were forced to lay down arms as a result of a political decision. It was amusing to hear their phony if passionate argument : "We would have continued fight till the last man only if...."

4. Coapeland, 1975, pp. 82-83. Copeland has been a long time associate of many of the top people in the American Intelligence community.
5. *The Times of India*, 1.11.06.
6. Sunita Vakil, *Pioneer,* 27 October, 2007.
7. Pioneer, 27 October, 2007.
8. Philstewart, Reuters, Cited *Hindustan Times*, 19.4.07.
9. Arthur H. Rostein, IE, 14.11.07.
10. B. Raman, a terrorism specialist, at the Round Table on "Ayodhya and London : Lessons for the Future", hosted by the International Terrorism Walch Project of Observer Research Foundation (ORF), New Delhi, 29 July, 2006.
11. B. Raman is Additional Secretary (Retd.), Cabinet Secretariat, Government, of India, New Delhi and, presently, Director, Institute for Topical Studies, Chennai, and Distinguished Fellow and Convener, Observer Research Foundation (ORF), Chennai Chapter. E-Mail : itschen36@gamil.com.

11A. Anandan 5, The week, 23-7-06.

12. This perhaps is a case of over blowing the criticism for sake of criticism, perhaps handed out to the press by the IB officer's whose career promotion was adversely affected. Army officers are well-rounded enough to take on, after a capsule course, any job in the IB, forget about the communecations branch for which in any case this AVC officer was well-qualified.
13. *The Week,* 23.7.06.
14. Lenin (1902), pp. 470-72.
15. Che Guevara (1968), pp. 15-16.
16. Freedman (1976) p. 133, Levi Tolokonov, Izvestia 31-7-74.
17. The Journal of Palestinian Studies, Vol. IV, No. 1, (Autumn 1974) pp. 168-169.
18. Ienkins and Johnson (1975), p. 23.
19. For details of several such robberies, *see* Lenin (1948) by David Shulnu.
20. Huntington (1971), pp. 11-12.
21. Fanon, 1966, pp. 73-75.
22. Serge and Alder, 1973, p. 179.
23. CIA, 1976, p. 22 1976.
24. Bell, 1971, p. 114.
25. *Ibid.,* passim.
26. Cited Drimi Chaudhuri, *The Hindustan Times*, 19.10.06.

# 7
# PAKISTAN : THE WAR WITHIN

The country is being called a failing state, a nation in denial, the most dangerous place on earth and a volcano waiting to erupt.

What is a greater cause of anxiety for the world is that the Islamist extremists, led by al Qaeda and Taliban, are extending their influence beyond the land bands of North western region, especially the Federally Administered Tribal Area (FATA). The well-regarded Pakistani Army took months to retake a small regularly-administered district of Swat from the Taliban. How will it fare in retrieving the virtually autonomous seven tribal agencies that presently comprise FATA from the Islamist militants is yet to be seen. The nightmare feared most by the West led by the U.S. is this nuclear—armed country going under, and its nuclear weapons falling too the Islamist terrorist! Such a catastrophe may not happen soon, but it cannot be ruled out altogether. Hence the jitters.

Pakistan is an unfortunate country. It lost half of its territory to Bangladesh before completing 25 years of its existence. The rump itself is not sure of remaining one united entity. Besides terrorism of virulent kind, the country also is facing a long-running Baluchi rebellion.

Pakistan can be torn as under if its leaders do not face upto the current crisis. Unfortunately, for more than half of its time since it came into existence, it has been ruled by the military dictators. Consequently democracy never found feet in the country. Ostensibly, it may be presently under a civilian rule, but Army rules the roost for all practical purpose—being the only cohesive entity. All democratic institutions have been destroyed by the Army, often helped by the divided self-serving politicians.

Before the faultlines are discussed in detail, some essential information on the country follow.

## Pakistan

| Islamic Republic of Pakistan | |
|---|---|
| Area | 803,940 sq km |
| Population | 148,166,000 |
| Capital | Islamabad |
| Official Religion | Islam |
| Official Language | Urdu |
| **Ethnic Composition** | |
| Punjabi | 48.2 % |
| Pashto | 13.1 % |
| Sindhi | 11.8 % |
| Saraiki (A Punjabi Variant) | 9.8% |
| Mohajirs | 7.57% |
| Baluchi | 3.57% |
| Others | 5.43 |
| **Religious affiliations** | |
| Muslims (Sunni 76%, Shia 20.7.) | 96.7% |
| Christian | 1.6% |
| Hindus | 1.5% |
| Others | 0.2% |

## Key Historical Events

The Muslim state that was created by partitioning India in 1947 included two wings : West Pakistan and East Pakistan. For nine years, Pakistan remained a Dominion of the British Empire. It was proclaimed an Islamic Republic on 23 March 1956. A federal parliamentary system functioned until Gen. (later Field Marshal) Ayub Khan seized power in a coup in October 1958. Eversince, Pakistan has been under military rule, interspersed by spells of civilian rule :

| | |
|---|---|
| Gen. Mohd Ayub Khan | October 1958—March 1969 |
| Gen. Yahiya Khan | March 1969—December 1971 |
| Gen. Zia-ul-Haq | July 1977—17 August 1988 |
| Gen. Pervez Musharraf | 12 October 1999-till date |

In the first free elections in December 1970, Zulfikar Ali Bhutto's Pakistan People's Party won a majority in the board in the West, while Sheikh Mujibur Rahman's Awami League swept the East, winning 160 of the 102 seats. In totality, Mujib won majority of seats in Pakistani parliament. In the natural course of things he should have been the Prime Minister. That honour was denied to him due to Bhutto's over weaning ambitions.

Subsequently, East Pakistan proclaimed sovereignty and formed the People's Republic of Bangladesh on 26 March 1971. Civil war followed after Yahya, supported—some would say, egged on—by Bhutto ordered troops to arrest Mujib and put down the Bengali uprising. It was genocide of Bengali population. The freedom fighters, helped by Indian Army, defeated the Pakistani troops and Bangladesh was free of the Pakistani yoke on 17 December, 1971.

To cut to the recent past, the Pakistani polity experienced its 4th coup when Gen. Musharraf seized power and the then Prime Minister, Nawaz Sharif and his predecessor, Benazir Bhutto have been residing in foreign countries ever since.

A milestone in Indo-Pak relations was much-publicized Prime Minister Vajpayee's bus ride to Lahore in February, 1999.

Presently, Indo-Pak peace process has entered an interesting phase, with President Musharraf and Prime Minister Manmohan Singh agreeing on a joint anti-terrorism drive during their Havana meeting.

The contentious issue of Kashmir is also seeing interesting development with Huryat's Umar Farooq pleading for peaceful solution as militancy has only been creating more and more graveyards. He said this in Pakistan (January 2007).

Some more important events/incidents in the recent past are mentioned here :

- In January 2006, upto 18 people were killed in a U.S. missile strike, apparently targeting senior Al Qaeda figures on a border village in the north.

- More than 30 people were killed in a suspected suicide bomb attack and ensuing violence at a Shia Muslim procession in the north-west.
- In April 2006, a suspected double suicide bombing killed at least 57 people at a Sunni Muslim Ceremony in Karachi.

Finally, it will be fair to accept that Pakistan is also on the receiving end of terrorist rage, as is India, but the intensity and viciousness of the visitation in its case is nowhere near the enormity India has been subjected to since the late 1970s by the terrorism, nurtured and sponsored by Pakistan. In Pakistan's case, to put it simply if bluntly, it is a self-inflicted injury. The terrorists now turning their guns on Pakistan have been recruited trained and equipped for the "battle" in Pakistani *madrassas* and terror training camps run by the extremists and the jihadis. Of course, they had been put through their paces, including guerrilla warfare course, to train their guns on India. They obviously had forgotten VK Krishna Menon's blithering riposte that he was yet to come across a gun which fires in one direction only, when the Indian Defence Minister was informed of Pakistani pledge in 1950s to the American authorities that it "will never use the U.S.—supplied weaponry against India." Unmindful of the Menon repartee, Pakistan had been turning out militants, including suicide bombers, from its 'factories' located in the PoK and hilly regions bordering Afghanistan. Having realized the futility of its terrorism enterprise, it offered joint fight against the curse, which the Indian leadership gracefully accepted.

Of course, it must be said here and now that Pakistan's sincerity to its pledge for joint counter-terrorism strategy with India is yet to be tested. The first meeting of Indo-Pak officials on the subject is scheduled for February, 2007.

## Pakistan Backgrounder

All developing societies confront the problem of accommodating a variety of groups that owe allegiance to - often ideologically - conflicting views and Pakistan is no exception. What distinguishes Pakistan from other South Asian countries, however, is the easy and abundant availability of weapons, the control of the state largely by a Punjabi-Mohajir elite in the earlier phase that led to ethnic tensions with other provinces. The failure of economic growth strategy made the state more dependant on Islam as a binding force for society and polity. This increased ethnic tensions as regional groups began to assert their cultural and nationalist agendas. The movements in Baluchistan and Rural Sindh were the result of provincial demands. Failure of successive regimes in fulfilling any of their stated developmental agendas led to a basic legitimisation crisis and all regimes, beginning Bhutto's, began to promote Islam in the affairs of the State. General Zia took this policy further when he began promoting Islamists in the Pakistani Army, which was never done before as it was sought to be a relatively secular institution.

The process of Islamisation of the State and the Afghan war were turning points in the role of Islamic orthodoxy in Pakistan. This also brought into Pakistan a more codified and strict Wahabi Islam from Saudi Arabia. The role of Pakistan as frontline state, serving American interests in the war against Communist Soviet Union, led to a major fall out for Pakistan and its society. America stopped its campaign to check the growth and export of heroin in the wake of larger strategic interests, which had a catastrophic impact on Pakistani society. The number of drug users in Pakistan today stands at 3.2 million. This was one of the major offshoots of active involvement in the Afghan crisis and the state's decision, in the early eighties, to be a conduit for Western weapons bound for the war in Afghanistan.

There have been a number of consequences of this involvement in Afghanistan, and many of these have fostered violent internal conflicts in Pakistan. They include:

- The migration of Afghan refugee groups to major urban regions of Pakistan added to antagonisms within the Pakistani society, especially in Karachi where ethnic strife increased.
- The shift in the Afghan movement where Pakistan began backing rabidly pro-Islamic elements after the Afghan movement had failed to arrive at a pro-Pakistan and pro-Saudi solution gave a fillip to Islamists in Pakistan.
- The establishment of a powerful network of militant madarssas, originally set up to train volunteer 'students' - Taliban - for the war in Afghanistan. These madarsas combined weapons training with a fundamentalist and violent interpretation of Islam. The 'Victory' of the Taliban in Afghanistan has freed substantial numbers of these

'students', as well as their motivators and mentors; who are now progressively turning their attention to other areas of conflict, including Pakistan itself.

- Drug trafficking which was encouraged for the short-term motive of financing the Afghan resistance movement and which, now, is the most important source of finance for most militant groups.

State support of these militant groups who were meant for external threats is likely to endanger the Pakistani establishment, as they seem to have acquired a relative autonomy over the years.

The authoritarian character of the state whose formation and later development has led to the control of the institutions of the state in the hands of a select elite, where all dissent meets with violent suppression, have further fuelled violence in society. It is significant that Pakistan has spent nearly half of its 52 years of independence under military dictatorships.

The crushing of the Baluch insurrection in 1973, with the use of overwhelming force, is a dramatic example of this military response. In this case, an estimated 55,000 tribal guerrillas were met with about 70,000 troops from the Pakistan Army before the revolt was quelled. The Air Force was used in these operations for bombing a large number of villages. These operations were also backed up by the bombing of villages in Baluchistan by the Iranian Air Force, ordered by the Shah of Iran. About 3,000 were killed on both sides in this civil war. Small groups of tribal guerrillas continue to operate from mountain bases in this province and frequent military expeditions are sent to quell these guerrilla groups.

## Sources of Major Ongoing Conflicts

**Sectarian Strife :** The roots of the conflict can be traced to the use of religion by General Zia-ul-Haq (1977-88) as a tool for regime legitimisation. Devoid of a democratic constituency, Gen. Zia turned to the right wing Islamic elements for support. His attempt to create an Islamic polity and society was an attempt to gain legitimacy. These goals subsequently coalesced with the national security goal of building close linkages with the Afghan Mujahideen after the Soviet intervention in Afghanistan in 1979. During the eighties, consequently, a complex network developed between the Afghan mujahideen, domestic religious groups in

Pakistan, and the Pakistani State, with a generous supply of weapons from the US. The combination of easy availability of arms and a growing motivated cadre resulted in the rapid spread of violence from Afghanistan to Pakistan itself. Religious scholars in Pakistan say militancy among the rival extremist groups intensified with shift from a board support of Afghan groups fighting the Soviets to specific support of hard-line Islamic groups who were supported in the later phase after the Soviet withdrawal. The training camps established for training Afghan guerrillas underwent a change. Establishment of just training centres gave way to growth of religious schools training students in Islamic ideology.

Pakistan - particularly central and southern Punjab - served as the ground where young freedom fighters were trained; in Punjab, especially Southern Punjab, there have been problems because of Siraki language. Therefore this area provided even recruits for Islamic militancy. Almost the entire leadership of the militant Sunni outfit, the Lashkar-e-Jhangvi, is made up of people who fought in Afghanistan.

The conflict within Pakistan began in the 1980s, when a group of Deobandi militants formed the Anjuman Sipa-Sahaba (ASS) to wage war against the Shia landlords of the Jhang. This organisation was later rechristened as the **Sipah-e-Sahaba Pakistan (SSP).** The Shias formed the Sipah-e-Muhhamad (SMP) to counter the threat from Sunni militant Groups (1993).

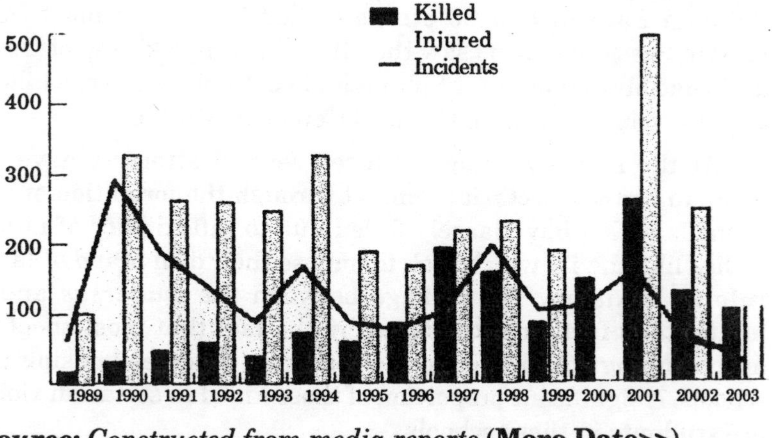


***Source:** Constructed from media reports* **(More Date>>)**

An attempt was made in 1995 by moderate leaders to procure peace between these violent groups through the Milli Yakjehti Council (MYC), which brought about a temporary lull in violence. The respite was brief, as the SSP and the SMP failed to co-operate with the peace effort. However, the SSP's leadership had joined the political mainstream, making an overt adherence to violence difficult. The extremist elements within the SSP, consequently, organised under the leadership of Riaz Basra to form the Lashkar-e-Jhangvi (LeJ). There are also a number of other splinter groups engaged in this strife. These splinter groups formed alliances with other extremists and were supported by a large numbers of *madarsas* (religious schools or seminaries) across the country.

In 1957, there were just about 150 such schools functioning in the country. The number now exceeds 5,500, with nearly 4,500 having come into existence after 1980. Half of these *madarsas* are in the Punjab. In May 1998, the Federal Cabinet was informed by the then Prime Minister, Nawaz Sharief, that about 100 *madarsas* were imparting military training. Press reports, however, suggest that over 750 *madarsas* were directly or indirectly connected with sectarian violence, and 810 of students of various *madarsas* were wanted in cases of terrorism. Patterns of retaliatory killings suggest some involvement of the Iranian establishment in the conflict, in solidarity and support of the Shia minority. Iranian diplomat Sadiq Ganji was gunned down in Lahore following the assassination of SSP founder Haq Nawaz Jhangvi in March 1990. Similarly the 1997 assassination of Jhangvi's successor Zia-ur-Rehman Farooqi and 26 others (killed in a bomb blast in the Lahore Sessions Court) saw the alleged revenge killing of Iranian diplomat Muhammad Ali Rahimi and six locals who were killed in an attack on the Iranian Cultural Centre in Multan.

At the non-governmental level, several attempts have been made to end the sectarian conflict through the formation of peace councils which have largely failed due to inflexibility of militant bodies like the LJ which seek to impose their own brand of Islamic rule in Pakistan. The linkage between the *madarsas* and the militants is further established by the fact that most shoot-outs and bombings originate from or occur at mosques housing these schools. A significant proportion of those killed in sectarian violence are students in these schools.

The provincial government in Punjab has had to face the main burden in dealing with this strife. Two major campaigns were initiated to round up suspects since the problem began. In February 1994, the Manzoor Wattoo government arrested over 200 suspects, but almost all were released on MYC's plea. A fresh initiative was undertakén by the Shahbaz Sharief administration when an estimated 700 suspects from all over the province were arrested. The erstwhile Nawaz Sharief government agreed upon a code of ethics on May 5 with most of the religious and sectarian groups. But the government failed to rope in the Lashkar-i-Jhangvi and the newly formed SMP, the real actors in the ongoing conflict. The move to call out the Pakistan Rangers and the Frontier Constabulary and banning pillion-riding once again were purely administrative steps which failed to yield desirable results. It now remains to be seen how the military administration deals with the situation.

## Ethnic Strife

The roots of ethnic conflict in Pakistan, primarily concentrated in Karachi and other urban regions of Sindh, lie in the concentration of *mohajirs* (refugees) within a province where a common religion is too weak to build bonds with other population groups who were injected into the area at the time of Partition. Refugees from the Indian Punjab have been successfully integrated into Pakistani Punjab, owing to a common language and culture. (The term *'mohajir'* refers to refugees who arrived in Pakistan from the areas that fell within the newly constituted India, in the aftermath of Partition. It derives its origin from the term Hijr, the flight of the prophet from Mecca to Medina, a journey that was undertaken to escape persecution due to religious beliefs). Refugees from other parts of India, however, did not undergo any comparable process of assimilation and were initially concentrated in Karachi, though they later moved to other urban provinces of Sindh, such as Hyderabad and Latifabad, as well. These refugees spoke Urdu and had a set of cultural and social values different from the native Sindhis. Unlike the Sindhis, the new *mohajir* society did not suffer from the restrictions imposed by a feudal order and hence adapted to modern education. Being in the forefront of the struggle for Pakistan, they were naturally in a dominant position and were ardent supporters of Pakistani nationalism, as opposed to the regional identities professed by the Sindhis, Pathans and Punjabis.

*Mohajir* dominance in Pakistan's politics was gradually eroded by the Punjabi bureaucratic-military clique, and Federal power gradually shifted to Punjab. This was followed by instances of Sindhi assertiveness, particularly provincial government initiatives, such as imposition of the Sindhi language in education and the adoption of the Sindh (Teaching, Promotion and Use of Sindhi Language) Act in 1972. These actions led to the first violent clashes involving *mohajir* groups. In 1985, when a *mohajir* girl was crushed to death under a bus, a fresh round of violence involving the *mohajirs* and Pathans began, since the latter were perceived to control the urban transport business. Subsequent police intervention led, for the first time, to clashes between the state and *mohajir* groups, a common occurrence since then.

Until this time, ethnic clashes in Sindh were marked by animosity between Mohajirs on the one side and other ethnic minorities (Sindhis, Pathans) on the other. In 1986, Mohajir Quami Movement (MQM) leader Altaf Hussain provided a new direction to the ethnic strife. The agenda of MQM has been to get a better deal for the Mohajirs from the Punjabi centre and from the Sindhi provincial government, which it sees as oppressive. One of its important demands has been the change in quota policy which it feels is inimical to Mohajir interests. It has not been able to wrest substantive concessions despite using coercion, violence and terror tactics. But some of its demands that Mohajirs be declared as the fifth nationality have not been well received. It has managed to cut across red tape and solve some of the housing problems in the city of Karachi. Its support base is the lower middle class and it has been financed by middle class Mohajirs.

Rather than targeting any specific minority group, the Punjabi dominated state bodies in Sindh were exclusively targeted by the Mohajirs. After this point, ethnic strife in Pakistan has largely involved the Mohajirs and state law enforcement agencies, including the army. As a consequence of disagreement between Afaq Ahmed and Altaf Hussain (the former being a close confidante of the latter) ostensibly on the issue of renaming the organisation, the movement split into two. The new faction which later on came to be identified with its proximity to the army was called the MQM(H). There have been a series of incidents of violence between the two factions in the past couple of years. Whenever there has been a killing, MQM (Altaf) has often accused its rival organisation of masterminding the killings.

Several bouts of violence have occurred after 1986, when Altaf Hussain first gave the call for a movement against the Punjabi dominated state. These include the reported spate of reprisal killings by drug barons in Karachi, where over one hundred persons lost their lives and several hundred were injured. Several connected instances of attacks on Sindhis and Mohajirs sparked riots in 1988, with Hyderabad bearing the brunt. According to a report, the "streets of Hyderabad were littered with bodies right from Hirabad to Latifabad". The riots claimed over 60 dead in just one day, and more than 250 deaths in this phase of rioting. In a backlash, more than 60 Sindhi speaking people were gunned down in Karachi.

These killings provoked a massive police operation in the city, where over 4,000 policemen, according to press reports, and two thousand according to official sources, from all over the province surrounded the Pucca Qila locality and "fired at the house. This was for the first time in Pakistan's history that an operation been launched where thousands of people were besieged, and water and electric supply was disconnected. Appeals were made from mosques and newspapers offices were flooded with complaints, but nobody could move out as curfew had been imposed in the city". Failing to curb the protests, the police were removed and the army was called in. According to the list provided by a medical superintendent of Bhittai Hospital (Karachi), Dr. Shaiq Ali, 62 dead and 117 injured had been brought to the hospital. The dead also included women. Dr. Shaiq Ali was later murdered at his private clinic on Khai Road.

The most tragic off-shoot of the Pacca Qilla operation is that, notwithstanding the marriage of convenience between the Jeay Sindh Qaumi Mahaz (JSQM) and the Muttahida Qaumi Movement (MQM), a clear divide had taken place between the Urdu and Sindhi speaking people. There was only a trickle of internal migrations before the operation, but the operation triggered a mass exodus of population. The *mohajirs* migrated *en masse* from Qasimabad and the interior of Sindh into Hyderabad. Similarly, the Sindhis people moved to Qasimabad from Hyderabad and Latifabad.

While dismissing the government of Benazir Bhutto in 1990, president Ghulam Ishaq Khan had charged that just in seven months from January to July, 1,187 people had been killed and 2,491 injured in Sindh against 99 killed and 166 injured in the other three provinces of Pakistan. This is indicative of the threat to stable regimes from unsettled political issues and extremist agendas. Moreover the ethnic violence has become a feature of the political life of Sindh in particular where the rural urban divide and MQM's control of the urban constituency has alienated them from the Sindhis who speak the Sindhi language and have different cultural practices from the settlers in urban Sindh. Efforts to bring about even a common political agenda in rural Sindh amongst groups demanding separation has not borne fruit in concrete terms. The socio-economic agenda of the Jeay Sindh movement which has demanded a separation of Sindh at various points has been unclear though it does gravitate towards separation.

In Pakistan one can easily say that religious and ethnic organisations representing their respective communities are increasingly using violent methods including terrorism and even democratic and legal tools to achieve the ends that they have set for themselves thereby resulting in increasing incidents of violence and terrorism the last decade. In the past ten years another important factor in the internal strife in Pakistan has been the impact of Afghan war in South Asia. Its ramifications include the growth of various Islamic groups that have been implicated in the running feuds between the Sunni and Shia organisations, and the drug Mafia operating in Pakistan which poses a threat to state security in the long run.

## Faultlines : Is the Country Falling Apart?

Pakistan is not so much a nation-state as an unwieldy collection of competing ethnic groups, tribes, castes and interest. And each of the four ethnic groups—Punjabi, Sindhi, Baluch and Pashtun—has its own interests.

## The Turbulent North-West

Punjab, most populous of the four provinces, may be ruling Pakistan, but most troublesome is its wild North-West. From the hijacked planes that flattened the Twin Towers to mass murder on trains in London, a trail of carnage leads to the al-Qaeda network—and increasingly to a remote corner of Pakistan.

Pakistan's rugged tribal areas along the Afghan border have been pinpointed by the U.S. and other countries as the base for Osama. Pakistan government blamed al Qaeda, and its ally, the Taliban behind the assassination of Benazir Bhutto, on 27 December, 2007.

If so, the outfit's culpability merely highlights the country's inability to drive out al-Qaeda militants and their pro-Taliban allies from the forbidden border regions.

History has shown that the tribal zone—a region of seven semi-autonomous "agencies" under loose (rather, no) government control (and collectively called FATA)—has resulted in bloody noses for a succession of outsiders down through the centuries. Britain and Russia are the last two to have learnt the bitter truth, at heavy costs.

In 1893, the Raj declared the hostile North West an independent tribal territory. Pakistan followed suit after its creation in 1947, naming seven so-called federally administered tribal areas.

The latest round of trouble began after 9/11 when hundreds of Islamist rebels fled across the border after U.S.-led forces ousted the hard-line Taliban. There they sought refuge with same tribesmen who once backed the Jihad against the Red Army in Afghanistan in the 1980s.

Pervez Musharraf joined the U.S.-led war on terror after 9/11, and in 2003 launched military operations in the tribal areas that left 1,000 soldiers and many more rebels dead till December 2007. "Pakistan still has some 90,000 troops in the area, but has failed to quell the unrest in a belt where tribesmen do not even pay lip service to the control of Islamabad", said an analyst in December, 2007.

At its heart is a nexus between mainly Arab Al-Qaeda agents and local tribesmen who either support the Taliban or directly take part in attacks on security forces in both Afghanistan and Pakistan.

Pakistan's support for the Taliban between 1996 and 2001 has led to allegations, especially from Afghanistan, that its intelligence services are still involved with the tribal belt's holy warriors.

Controversial peace deals between Islamabad and militants in 2005, 2006, and the latest in 2009 broke down leading to a surge in violence—which had aggravated since a government raid on the Al-Qaeda-linked Red Mosque in Islamabad in July 2007.

Time and again Al-Qaeda has been linked to international attacks, most notably to the 7 July 2005, London bombings that killed 52 people. At least, one of the attackers visited the area, where he met Osama's deputy, Ayman al-Zawahiri.

In 2007, officials claimed they had traced most of the record 40-plus suicide bombings to militants in the region—latest of which accounted for the extremist's most valuable target yet on 27 December 2007. (Post-2007 violence in the region, especially the Army offensive in Swat against the Taliban in May-July 2009, is covered in the next Chapter).

## Punjab : The Centre of Power and Jealousy

Punjab is home to some half of the Pakistanis. Its capital, Lahore, is country's thriving second city (next only to Karachi) and its cultural heart. Punjabis dominate not only the federal machinery but also the Army, much to the chagrin of Pakistan's other ethnic groups, all minorities.

Lahore sits not far from the Indian (Punjab's) border—the only land bridge across the border is a 30-minutes drive away—and it is poised to benefit from the gradual opening of trade between the two countries. Like the rest of Pakistan's major cities, it is booming, with an independent news media and an lite and highly educated upper class.

The growing urban middle class prospered under Musharraf. Rural Punjab, by contrast, is largely poor and agricultural. Southern Punjab produces most of the country's economically critical cotton crop. Here, especially, feudal arrangements persist.

All the other three provinces are resentful of Punjab's domination in all spheres of nation's life. Baluchis, in particular, complain that their mineral resources are mainly exploited for the benefit of the Punjab.

Punjabis enjoy being the ruling class of Pakistan. They feel the rivalry with India particularly strongly. Urban elites were impatient for democracy and openly hostile to the U.S. after its invasion of Iraq. Musharraf was popular in the province for initial years, but lost his appeal in 2007 and 2008 which added to anti-American feelings. The lawyers movement, which overthrew him in the end, was essentially started and fuelled by Punjabis.

## Sindh : In Punjab's Shadow

Largely rural and agricultural, Sindh is Bhuttos' power base. The farm areas are dominated by wealthy feudal families—like the Bhuttos—who employ the impoverished local Sindhis. New York Times, cited, *Hindustan Times*, 29 December, 2007.

But Karachi, Pakistan largest city and commercial capital, is a polyglot megapolis dominated by a different group, Mohajirs—Muslims, many of them civil servants, who migrated/fled from India in 1947.

Sindhis chafe at the Punjabi-dominated central government and army, convinced that their province is being short-changed in respect and government largesse.

## Baluchistan : Restive and Remote

Largest province of Pakistan is sparsely settled. It is natural gas—rich region with a clan—based population of ethnic Baluchis and Pashtuns. It is badly lacking in mater and good roads.

It borders both Afghanistan and Iran and has extensive smuggling, mostly of heroin, with both the countries. Its capital, Quetta, has become a refuge for Taliban fighters. The leader of Afghan Taliban, one-eyed cleric Omer, is believed to be based in Quetta, which is also the site for a command council, or *Shura*, that directs attacks in southern Afghanistan.

Baluchi grievances are largely economic : They want higher royalties for their natural gas and a larger share of government resources.

These fault lines notwithstanding, some analysts feel it is unfair to call Pakistan 'failed' state. Will it be fair to dub it as failing or collapsing state? Even that may be a hasty averment, some Pakistani watchers assert. There seem to be some kind of consensus that the country indeed is imploding.

Having said it all, let it be known that there is one authoritative journal which has recently (2009) placed Pakistan among the 10 failed states.

## Pakistan among top 10 Failed States

Pakistan, split in the middle with terrorist attacks and facing an economic crisis, remains among the top 10 failed states, says an index prepared by the renowned Foreign Policy journal.

The country placed 9th among all countries last year in terms of its over all achievement, has improved its position only by a notch—it is placed 10th in the index for 2009 published in the July-August issue of the journal.

The annual exercise, now in its fifth year, is carried out by the journal and Fund for Peace, an independent research organisation. The ranking is done on the basis of the following factors :

- Demographic Pressure
- Refugees/internally displaced persons
- Group grievance
- Uneven development
- Economic decline
- Delegitimisation of the state
- Public service
- Human rights
- Factionalised elites
- External intervention

The top 10 failed states in the latest list are :

1. Somalia
2. Zimbabwe
3. Sudan
4. Chad
5. Democratic Republic of Congo
6. Iraq
7. Afghanistan
8. Central African Republic
9. Guinea
10. Pakistan

India is placed 87th among the 177 countries under study, with its score showing an improvement over the previous year.

**Foreign Policy :** Noted that it is "a sobering time" for the world's most fragile countries, what with the global financial meltdown, natural disasters, and government collapse.

## Pak President : "Extremists were Created and Nurtured"

President Asif Ali Zardari coming clean on Pak terrorist said 8 July, 2009 religious extremists "were deliberately created and nurtured as a policy to achieve some short term tactical objectives". Zardari's remarks, delivered when he spoke in a consultative session with former civil servants on issues confronting Islamabad, seem to have given an official seal of endorsement to something which was widely known to strategic community : Policy-makers in Pakistan, especially among the military and intelligence agencies, regarded Islamic militant groups as strategic assets required to be protected and patronised to expand Pakistan's interests, especially in Afghanistan and Kashmir. Even if Zardari did not elaborate what the objective of the "policy" of creating and nurturing extremists was, his somewhat elusive reference is unmistakable - as stated above.

Zardari's remarks, candidly admitting something no Pakistani ruler has done earlier, is also indicative of his country's changed stance towards militant and extremist groups operating within and from his country. They are increasingly being seen for what they are—terrorists—instead of being regarded as strategic tools helping the state advance and achieve its strategic objectives.

Even if not spelled in so many words, this—regarding these terror merchants as national/strategic assets—has been the de facto policy of all the governments in Pakistan since late 1970s. But then, as Zardari said in the meeting, "9/11 occurred and they (the militant groups) began to haunt us as well."

He said Pakistan had now become a frontline state in the war against terrorism. "I have taken the charge at a difficult time and will come up to the challenges the country is facing", official news agency, the Associated Press of Pakistan, quoted him as saying. Badar Alam in Lahore, Mail Today, 9.7.09.

It is a well-accepted proposition that major impetus to involve religious extremists in the conflict/contest with India come from Pakistan's external intelligence agency, the ISI. It all started with General Akhtar Abdul Rehman's tenure as the ISI chief. The organisation practiced and perfected the ways and techniques of using the religious fundamentalists to harass, fight and oust the Soviets from Afghanistan. The success of the experiment elated and emboldened them. It was only understandable that when the Pakistan-incited/fuelled unrest—"revolt" is the term preferred by

Islamabad—broke out in 1989-90, the ISI decided to enlist the services of the extremists and hard-line Islamist fundamentalists to push Pakistan's cause in the valley.

Pakistan and its sword-arm, the ISI, have not looked back ever since. Gen. Akhtar died in the same plane crash as Gen. Zia-ul-Hoque in 1988, but his successors at the ISI (Lt Gens. Hamid Gul. and Javid Nasir, had not only proved equal to the task but brought greater enthusiasm and progressive perfection to it. At the strategic level, the ISI, provider and sustainer of the terrorist outfits active against India, also know which extremist organisation was to be weakened and emaciated through denial of the where withals. It was not a difficult task. The JEI (Jamaat-e-Islami), Pakistan and its counter part in the Valley were both for the accession of Jammu and Kashmir to Pakistan. But the uprising was led by the JKLF, a secular formation which sought independence for the state. As a natural corollary, from 1990-91 onwards, the ISI systematically starved the JKLF of funds and built up the HM (Hizb-ul-Mujahideen), a militant group created by the JI. To enhance the combat efficiency of the group, its members were trained alongside the Afghan Mujahideen owing allegiance to another ISI client, the Hizb-e-Islami of Gulbuddin Hekmatyar.

In 1993-94, the Indian Army's tough response resulted in the great setback to the H.M. and the ISI began to explore other option. Principal among these were two outfits who had been involved in the Afghan jihad : Harkat-ul-Jehad-i-Islami International (HUJI) and its splinter, the Harkat-ul-Mujahideen (HUM). Their support base lay among the Punjabi business community with Jamaat-ul-Ulemah-e-Islami (JUUI or JUI) and Tablighi Jamaat affiliations. Earlier in 1991 itself, the ISI had pushed the Deobandi ulemas of Karachi to get the two Harkats to reunite so as to prosecute the Kashmir jehad more effectively. As a result of these exertions, the Harkat-ul-Ansar (HUA) was born in October, 1993.

The general secretary of this new outfit HUA, Mohd Masood Azhar, was sent to India on a Portuguese passport, but was arrested soon after arrival there. The effort to free him virtually broke the back of the HUA (His release consequent to the 1999 hijack of an Indian airliner and his raising a new terror outfit in Pakistan, JEM, is another story to be detailed elsewhere).

But by that time (late 1993), the ISI had another pan-Islamic groups, the Markaz Dawa-ul-Irshad (MDI) and its military wing, the Lashkar-e-Tayyaba (LeT), ready to do its bidding. Unlike the Harkats, LeT has been uniquely focused on India. When Musharraf was forced to ban the militant outfits in January 2002, consequent to 9/11, the LeT was allowed to relocate its camps and operations in Azad Kashmir (PoK, for India), where they have remained till date.

An important development took place post 9/11. Many of the groups took different trajectories. While the LeT remained loyal to the Pakistani state apparatus, the Harkats and the JeM forged collaboration with the al-Qaeda and the Taliban.

"There is a growing evidence that strong ideological, organizational and operational links exist among the al-Qaeda, the Taliban and several sectarian and religious militant outfits in Pakistan", expanded a Zardari aide. He further clarified, adding what Zardari had refrained from : "Without breaking this nexus, we cannot succeed in the war against terrorism and this cannot happen if we continued with the old policies towards these militant groups."

It needs to be noted that Pak had taken a U-turn into policy of fuelling fires in India through its loyal terrorist outfits in 2002 under Musharraf, but it took a Zardari seven years to make public confession of the fact of nurturing anti-India outfits. Unfortunately, the wisdom dawned on Islamabad only when the fire reached home and started singeing the nation itself. Some analysts believe Pakistan action of proceeding against these terror-monger came too late. Presently, these terror outfits are not only threatening the very integrity and sovereignty of Pakistan, but also seem to be defying the writ of state not only in semi-autonomous FATA regions but also in major town and cities of the country.

Another important thing need to be watched along the line : will Zardari continue to follow the Musharraf line of 2002 when the latter did not proceed against anti-India outfits like the LeT allowing it to shift base to the PoK region? Will he also be harsh on the anti-Pakistan and anti-U.S. outfits only for obvious reasons—giving kid-gloves treatment to anti-India ones? After all, a powerful section of the ISI, that has played footsie with the latter outfits, is still ruling the roost! We have to wait and watch the Pak stance on the issue after Zardari's 'bold' confession.

Pakistan, as the rest of the world, knows that one day the U.S. and NATO troops would pack their bags and depart from Afghanistan. It is then that the need for a Pakistani strategic backyard in Afghanistan will be revived and "good" Afghani Taliban and loyal anti-India outfits would prove handy for the purpose. It is doubtful if Islamabad, goaded by the Army/ISI, ever decimate the outfits that have been regarded as national assets against India for its aims in Kashmir!

## Pakistan Internal Strife and Terrorist Outfits

Pakistan has faced internal strife from the day one of its creation. Large number of Muslims who migrated from India could not become part of the Pakistani society for long years to come. Even today, they are known somewhat pejoratively as 'mohaijirs'. Baluchistan was not part of Pakistan for months after 14 August 1947. Then there were Sunni-Shia rivalry, often leading to violence. Ahmadiyahs then became the target of the Sunni Muslims in the 1950s and subsequently the Ahmadiya sect was declared non-Muslim.

The internal strife has continued eversince under one pretext or the other. Identified as a key ally in Global War on Terrorism (GWOT), Pakistan however continues to experience severe internal strife and instability under the present military (Musharraf) regime. Sectarian violence, terrorism, internal discord, narco-traffecking, organised crime and corruption continue to wrack Pakistan. The military regime has been playing footsie with the extremist religious parties—6-party MMA, in this instance—to stay in power, after 'marginalising the mainline political parties.

It is known that Pakistan is extending total support to certain anti-India and anti-Afghanistan terrorist organisation while fighting those which are banned by the U.S. and certain others which are active within Pakistan.

There are large number of terrorist outfits in Pakistan, nourished by the ISI, which are avowedly anti-Indian and functioning openly in Islamabad, Lahore, and Karachi. They are popularly and commonly known as *jihadist tanzeems*.[1] They advertise for recruits and funds to "wage holywar against Hindu India". Representatives from PoK, who had come for a seminar 18-19 May 2006 at Manesa (Haryana), 42 km from Delhi, discussed the subject openly with Indian analysts. These outfits, with an agenda on Jammu and Kashmir, have been fortifying their activities.[2] So it is abvious that Musharraf's Pakistan is fighting terrorism selectively with an eye on the U.S. dollars and American masters, and for the rest it is business as usual.

The sectarian strife carried out by *Sipah-e-Sahaba* Pakistan (SSP) and Lashkar-e-Jhangvi (LeJ) on the Sunni side and the Tehrik-e-Jafaria Pakistan (TJP) and its militant arm Sipah-e-Muhammed Pakistan (SMP) on the Shia side has plagued Pakistani society for years.[3] As the International Crisis Group's (ICG) report on Asia observed in 2005, the sectarian conflict "is the direct consequence of state policies of Islamisation and marginalisation of secular democratic forces", and the manner in which successive military governments in Islamabad have manipulated Sunni orthodoxy and militancy as an instrument of control and subjugation. Gen. Musharraf has continued the (military) tradition of his predecessors of making alliances with *mullahs* at the expense of moderate political forces.[4] A well-known Pakistani commentator and academic has written extensively on the subject.[5]

On going strife in Baluchistan against Pak Army is also an expression of internal strife. The province, bordering Afghanistan, has witnessed serious violence since 2004. Groups like Baluch Liberation Army (BLA), the Baluch People's Liberation Army (BPLA), and Baluch Liberation Front (BLF) have been locked in deadly combat against military regime for a greater share of returns from its natural resources, in particular oil and gas, to address the province's under development. The 26 August 2006 killing of Nawab Bugti by the Pak Army and the violent protests that followed portends a worsening of the Baluch discontent. Interestingly, the weapons used in killing of Bugti were of the U.S. origin supplied to Pakistan for fighting terrorism. No wonder, Akbar Mengal (a member of the Provincial Assembly from Baluchistan Nationalist Party), reacting strongly to the killing, drew attention to the ironic fact that "all these weapons that U.S. has given to Pakistan to fight Al Qaeda and the Taliban, the Pakistan Army is using against the nationalists in Baluchistan."[6] U.S. officials have conceded to the media that it cannot always control how the Pakistani Army uses its weapons.

Military repression of Baluchistan is reminiscent of Yahya's ruthless, strong-arm suppression of Bangladeshi nationalism, leading to East Pakistan emerging as Bangladesh. Islamabad should worry about history repeating itself. The ICG report of September 2006 has made some disturbing observation on the situation which Pakistan must take a serious note of : "By using indiscriminate force, the military government is perpetuating this conflict and the reliance on Pashtun religious parties to counter Baluch opposition (nationalism) has strengthened Pashtun Islamist forces at cost of the moderates in Baluchistan. With their Chief Pakistani patron (MMA) running the Baluchistan government in alliance with Musharraf's Muslim League—PML (Q)—a reinvigorated Afghan and Pakistani Taliban are attacking international forces across Baluchistan's border with Afghanistan."[7]

Following Al Qaeda's expulsion from Afghanistan in 2001 during Operation Enduring Freedom (OEF) and ensuing relocation of some core elements in Pakistani cities of Karachi and Peshawar, a number of Al Qaeda militants are known to have joined forces with Pak Sunni militant groups, including LeT, JeM, SSP, and LeJ—an FTO—designated offshoot of the SSP that has close ties with the Al Qaeda.

In January 2002, Pakistan banned five extremist groups, including LeT, JeM, and SSP. It is common knowledge that in spite of this ban, it is a business as usual for these outfits which continue to operate al be it under different/changed names, with the connivance of Pak authorities.

But situation in Pakistan vis-à-vis Al Qaeda has changed since 2005 or so. Taliban-Al Qaeda combine have found refuge and been able to regroup in Pakistani cities and more particularly, in the rugged terrain of the Pak-Afghan border region, which is inhabited by the ethnic Pashtuns long-time, enthusiastic supporters of Taliban. It is time the world, India and U.S. in particular, take note of the growing influence of the Taliban in North and South Waziristan as well as the rest of the NWFP, and the radicalisation of the Pakistani society.[8] There are obvious reasons for it. The MMA is not only supporting the central government of Musharraf, but is also ruling party in NWFP and a member of the ruling coalition with Musharraf's party in Baluchistan. The following reported facts about the presence of Taliban—Al Qaeda combine should be enough to create disquiet among the analysts and countries who believe in sincerity of Pakistan's counter-terrorism war :

- The Taliban's most important leadership council, the Quetta Shura, is based in the capital of Pakistan's Baluchistan province.

- The Peshawar Shura is based in the eponymous town of Pakistan's NWFP province.
- Gulbuddin Hekmatyar, is operating in the two tribal agencies in FATA—Dir and Bajaur.
- Haqqani is based in Waziristan.
- Al Qaeda has a presence in Waziristan and Chitral (Northern Areas), the areas of Pakistan contiguous to Afghan[9] border.
- Taliban are busy in recruiting and training in Pakistan for combat in Afghanistan.
- Al Qaeda has its camps near the Pak-Afghan border.[10]

Al Qaeda reportedly forged alliance with Pakistani terrorist outfits like JEM (proscribed in 2002 and now operates under the banner Jammat-ul-Furqan), HUJI, and HUM[11]—all three being implicated in both anti-Western attacks in Pakistan and terrorism in Jammu and Kashmir, exploiting the prevailing anti-American sentiment in the country. These groups combining with Al Qaeda have become a lethal force with over lapping linkages, membership and ideologies, signifying serious implications for stability of Pakistan and peace in India. The situation becomes more dangerous with growing evidence of relocation of forcing extremists, linked to the Al Qaeda, in FATA in Pakistan's NWFP, leading to revived offensive in Afghanistan and their spread even into Iraq. Adoption of lethal technique by the resurgent Taliban in terms of suicide and road side bombings is indicative of "Iraqisation of the conflict".

Pakistani officials, including Gen. Musharraf deny the presence of Al Qaeda leadership in the country but U.S. and others are not convinced. In late 2004, then Secretary of State Colin Powell, a top U.S. military commander in Afghanistan and a member of the 9/11 Commission, in separate statements suggested that Osama was in Pakistan's tribal area.[12]

The U.S. policy makers, growing frustration due to lack of progress in nabbing "high value targets" (HVT), privately acknowledge that parts of the Pakistani state may not be fully on board. But given Musharraf's vulnerability, Washington has hardly an option but to stick to a policy of "public support and private pressure", so as not to destabilise his regime. In June 2005, former Director of Central Intelligence Porter Goss made an explicit statement : "We have an excellent idea of where bin Laden is—in sanctuaries in sovereign states, and our sense of international obligations present obstacles to his capture.[13]

Gen. Musharraff himself has been vague and issuing contradictory statements on Osama's whereabout. In December 2004, he claimed that Osama's trail had gone cold. But in June 2005, he thought Osama was alive, living near the Afghan border, "where it is very easy for a person to hide." Henry Crumpton, U.S. Ambassador in charge of counter-terrorism, directly contradicting Musharraf about Osama possibly being in Afghanistan, stated explicitly that parts of Pakistan are a "safe haven" for militants and that Osama was more likely to be hiding there than in Afghanistan.[14] An Indian analyst further quotes Crumpton as saying: "Pakistan is not doing enough to root out Al Qaeda and Taliban leaders who have found a safe haven on its soil. The two were stepping up violence in Southern and Eastern provinces of Afghanistan bordering Pakistan". Presently (November 2006), nearly half of Afghanistan is reeling under the impact of resurgence of the Taliban.

## Pakistan : The most dangerous place on Earth

There is hardly any doubt about the fact that Pakistan is the epicenter of international terrorist attacks, particularly its lawless tribal was over in its north-west. It is for this reason that U.S. poured military and financial aid into Pakistan to enlist its cooperation in the global war on terrorism.

If the world is wary of terrorist attacks originating from Pakistan, the country itself finds itself unequal to control the terror within its boundaries.

## Is the Army serious in fighting Terror within the Country

This can best be seen and discussed by analysing the events and situation that followed the terrorist attack on Sri Lankan cricket team in Lahore on 3 March 2009, which left six policemen dead and shook the cricketing world.

After the dastardly attack, Pak army chief presided over the corps commanders conference to review the situation in the country. As things stood, it was review the situation in the country. As things stood, it was not an enviable one. Terrorists seemed to be making advances all over the country by means of attacks or signing peace deals with the authorities. Making things worse, there was political chaos because of a dispute between the ruling PPP and the opposition PML (N) led by Sharief, whose "upcoming long march to Islamabad" did not bade well for a country facing a major terrorist from within. There is much to criticise about the inability of political leaders to work together after the civil society restored the democracy after fourth spill of military dictatorship, but the bigger concern must be about the Pak Army's perception of the prevailing situation. Is it serious to continue with its so-called 'war on terror' ?

Till then, the armed forces gave the impression that they were silent spectators, quietly playing along with the decision of civilian government. Army Chief Gen. Ashfaq Pervez Kiyani keenly marketed the Swat peace deal—essentially brokered by the federal PPP and the provincial ANP governments—during his recent visit to the U.S. Many believed the agreement under which the NWFP (now Pashtunkhwa) government acceded the Taliban demand for implementing Sharia law in Swat in exchange for peace, will only strengthen the terrorist outfit. (After all, this was the result of similar deals in 2005 and 2006). Moreover, the deal sets a dangerous precedent of the state giving in to a brute force. It was no secret that the security forces were finding the going tough in Swat until they agreed to sign the peace deal. While the authorities justified the deal as a move that benefits the locals (by way of faster justice), it served to expose the military's inability to fight the war against terrorists. After all, this had been proved in a recent development.

Army had abandoned its plans to jam Taliban leader Fazlullah's radio due to alleged lack of equipment—and proposed a counter programming in stead. But not many bought this argument. Technical experts asserted that jamming a radio station is not a difficult task for the army.

If taking on the militants is held up because of so simple a matter as lack of technical capability, why does the Pak army not allow American drone attacks on its western borders? In the past, the army chief vociferously condemned the U.S. drone attacks, making people wonder about the real reasons for such confrontional statements, especially when Pakistan has allowed its air forces bases in NWFP and Baluchistan to be used by American drones and other purposes. But senior commanders have never admitted to having such intensive military links with Washington.

The bottom line is that both the government and the military had been sending confusing signals at that point in time about their stand on the war on terror. While the army had been fighting the Taliban in Bajaur in FATA, NWF, and seemed to have made some headway against militant groups including the TSNM, the government had signed peace deal with the very same outfit in Swat!

This was Swat. There is South Waziristan as well, where Baitullah Mehsud is the overlord who "recently formed a partnership with Maulana Nazeer, earlier supporter by the army. Another one of Mehsud's partner is Maulana Masood Azhar of Punjab's JEM." Interestingly "little is being done to uproot Punjab—based militant outfits. The editor of the Daily Times, Najam Sethi, believes this inaction stems from Army's fear that any adverse action against these outfits will have severe repercussion." If true, it is tantamount to an admission that the writ of the state does not run even in the mainland Pakistan, his is not the opinion of outsiders but of two Pakistanis, well-respected in their country. Najem Sethi, a brave anti-establishment journalist and Ayesh Siddiqa, author of an authoritative book on Pak military. "Clearly the military does not have a clear strategy for fighting terrorism in its back yard." Ayesha Siddiqa, author of "Military Inc : Inside Pakistan Military Economy."

True to their, the Taliban went back on their commitment under the peace deal—handing over their weapons to the government. Consequently, the Army had to push in more than four Infantry divisions to retrieve Swat from their strangle hold. More worrying is the fact that they fled into surrounding jungles and districts to fight on another day. This was in April-July 2009. Now the Army is preparing for a tougher job—to win back Waziristan from the Taliban under Baitullah Mehsud.

Now follow some terror incidents. It is only a selection, not an exhaustive one.

## Shelter to dangerous Extremists

Pakistan always seems to be ready to provide succour and shelter to most dangerous of the terrorists, without any questions being asked. To wit, longtime Pakistani terrorist chief Fazlur Rehman Khalil, the Harkat-ul-Mujahideen leader who cosigned Osama bin Laden's 1998 edict declaring it a Muslim's duty to kill Americans and Jews, has been living openly in Rawalpindi, not far from Pakistan's Army General Headquarters.

This is the averment made by two senior journalist in January 2004.

## Majority in Pakistan back Army Rule, says a Study : 25 December, 2006

Islamabad : Even as the movement by the Opposition to oust the military regime is gathering steam in Pakistan, a recent study claims a majority of its population back army rule in the predominantly Muslim nation, with Bangladesh being the only other South-Asian country to follow the trend. "The idea that the country should be governed by the Army was endorsed by six out of every ten responses in Pakistan and Bangladesh", said the "State of Democracy in South Asia" report of 25.12.2006, adding that about half the Pakistanis opined both the democratic or non-democratic forms of government made no difference to them.

The least support for Army rule is in India. The support for the Army rule diminishes in the countries which are educationally forefront. But overall the South-Asian overwhelmingly support democracy, with Sri Lanka emerging as the country where democracy was most popular, while India was placed third in terms of the percentage of people expressing support for the democratic system.

## LET 'all-India Commander' killed in Kashmir : 18 July, 2007

Security forces on 18 July, 2007 claimed to have killed LET's all-India coordinator and architect of suicide attacks in the Valley Khalid-ul-Rehman alias Abu Umer after an encounter. The operation was jointly conducted by the Jammu and Kashmir Police, Special Cell of the Delhi Police, and Rashtriya Rifles (RR) in Bhaderwah town of hilly Doda district in the wee hours. Bhaderwah is the Assembly constituency of Chief Minister Ghulam Nabi Azad.

The killed militant, a resident of Railway Colony at Bahawalpur in Pakistan, had been a LeT coordinator for carrying out major strikes all over the country, including Delhi. He also used to get militants in through sea routes.

The police had been on the trail of Umer for more than a month after he killed state police's ace shooter and Special Operations Group's, Dy SP, Shaily Singh in Bhaderwah on 31 May.

His name cropped up during interrogation of three terrorists arrested by Delhi Police at Dilli Haat in the last week of April

(2007). He had asked these three to carry out blasts at Delhi, informed Karnail Singh of Special Cell, Delhi Police.

Umer, who was active in the valley for the past one decade, had engineered the first fidayeen attack in the Valley on a para-military force headquarters at Bandepore resulting in the killing of six personnel, including a DIG, in July 1999.

Thereafter he planned similar fidayeen attacks on a number of civilian and military installations in the valley, before shifting to Doda districts in 2005. He was also behind a failed plan to attack Chief Minister Azad at a rally in Ramban in connection with the grant of district status to the area in April. Three persons, including a couple, who were arrested in that connection, were in fact sent by Umer, the police said.

Meanwhile, the police took in custody Bashir Ahmed Ganai in whose house Umer had stayed for the night.

## "Qaeda may be linked" : Pakistan : October, 2007

Pakistan police said on 31 October, 2007 that Osama bin Ladin's Al Qaeda network and the Taliban are likely lined to the suicide attack near [Pakistan] President Musharraf's Army office that killed seven people.

30 October blast in the garrison town of Rawalpindi may also be a reaction to an ongoing government crackdown on militants in northwest Pakistan and a raid on the hardline Lal Masjid in Islamabad in July (2007), the city's police chief said. "Taliban and Al Qaeda elements are there. Most probably they could be instrumental in this attack", said Saud Aziz, police chief of Rawalpindi.

Aziz said police has found the disfigured head of the bomber, who is believed to be about 23 year old and who blew himself up when the police stopped him at a check point guarding a high security area. "A plastic surgeon has reconstructed the face of the bomber. The police also found three of his fingers and have sent to the national registration office for identification", he said.

The police was also carrying out DNA tests on the attackers' remains.

The attack raised further fears for the safety of President Musharraf, a key U.S. ally in the "war on terror" who has survived at least three assassination attempts by Islamists who detest his ties to Washington. Aziz also said investigators suspected there could be a link between the 30 October explosion and the Army's storming of the pro-Taliban Lal Masjid in which scores of people were killed. The blast happened directly outside the house of a senior general who was reportedly one of the key planners of the operation against militants who had infiltrated the Lal Masjid.

Aziz said there could also be connections to operations against a hardline Taliban-style cleric in north western Swat Valley and clashes with rebels in Pakistan's troubled tribal areas bordering Afghanistan. Pakistan has fought bloody battles in the tribal belt with insurgents.

## 8.10.06 (PoK and NWFP)

Gen. Musharraf visited PoK on the first anniversary of 2005 earthquake 8.15 AM that killed over 73,000 and rendered over 3 million survivors homeless. He announced measures aimed at easing the sufferings of the survivors as they build their homes and lives. He further said : "80 per cent reconstruction work in quake ravaged areas would be completed in 3 years—by 2009—while major projects may take upto 5 years to complete. Against on earlier estimate of 400,000 houses, government will now have to build 600,000 houses, all of which would be completed by December, 2008."

International aid agency Oxfam said in a report last week that 1.8 million people would spend the approaching winter, the second after the quake, without proper shelters—an assessment contested by Musharraf. Oxfam also said red-tape and corruption had showed down recovery in the quake hit areas.

*At Muzaffarabad* stadium, Musharraf asked people to vote for his supporters in the elections due in 2007 so that he could continue to do good work.

After PoK, NWFP took the brunt of earth quake fury which caused wide-spread loss of life and destruction of property in Mansehra, Balakot and Abbatabad. The General asked people to reject extremists and sought support against foreign militants. The NWFP being a sensitive area in the "war on terror", he stressed the importance of stopping "those foreigners who are committing terrorism in Pakistan or outside its borders". He also added : "We should reject extremism and terrorism within our society. Those who are spreading extremism or inciting people towards terrorism must be stopped."[1]

Some comments on the preceding two paragraphs :

- In PoK, he sought people's votes but did not ask them to shun extremism or terrorism nor to stop foreign terrorists.
- In the NWFP, he asked the people to stop foreign terrorists, meaning terrorists from other Muslim countries and especially from Afghanistan; and did not seek their votes—may be, he does not expect many after Army brutalities in Waziristan.
- By "foreign terrorists...committing terrorism in Pakistan or outside its borders" he mean just this : "if any terrorists are crossing into India to create trouble, they are foreign ones."

## Blast near Gen. Musharraf's Residence : 10 October, 2006

Three cadres of a banned militant outfit were arrested in connection with a blast during the night 4/5 October at the Ayub park, close to Gen. Musharraf's Army House residence in Rawalpindi and subsequent recovery of rockets near Parliament and ISI Headquarters, English daily the *Post* reported. But online news agency said only one person, Natleem, a 4th year student of a local college and resident of Miran Jaffer, was arrested by security forces in connection with the incident. The police recovered a briefcase and some important material from him. Federal minister of Interior Ahmad Khan Sherpao talked about "an important development" taking place in the probe but refused to give details.

It was not yet clear if the suspected banned militant group has any links to the Al Qaeda, which Musharraf has accused of engineering two close attempts on his life in December, 2004.

## 6 February, 2007, Islamabad (Pakistan)

A suicide bomber blew himself up in the car park at Islamabad airport. Four policemen were wounded. Two accomplices of the bomber were arrested.

This is the second suicide bombing attack in Islamabad since 26 January, 2007 when a bomber killed himself and a guard while trying to rush into one of Islamabad's top hotels, where Indian High Commissioner was to host the Republic Day celebrations a few hours later.

These bombings are bound to raise fears that Pakistan's war

against Islamist militants in remote mountains on the Afghan border has spread to the relatively peaceful capital.

"This is a pure act of terrorism", said Brig. (Retd.) Javed Iqbal Cheema, head of Crisis Management Section, Interior Ministry.

The wave of bombings followed a Pakistani military air strike on an Islamist military camp in the South Waziristan region on the Afghan border in mid-January 2007 that killed up to 20 people. Analysts have speculated the blasts have been revenge for the air strike.

## Jihadis kill 3 abducted Pak soldiers : November, 2007

Pro-Taliban militants killed three Pakistani paramilitary soldiers on 8 November, 2007—two days after they were abducted from a restive tribal area bordering Afghanistan. The kidnapped soldiers were executed by a militant firing squad and their bodies were dumped near military check post close to the town of Razmak in North Waziristan, early on the 8th. "We strongly suspect involvement of the Taliban in the murders", security official said at Miransh, main town of North Waziristan, on 8 November.

Insurgents abducted four paramilitary soldiers from Razmak on 6 November as they headed home on leave in a privately hired car, local officials informed. The fate of the fourth trooper was not yet known.

Separately, the Army said it had killed five pro-Taliban militants in the same region, the semi-autonomous North Waziristan, after a bomb blast struck a security forces convoy near the town of Spinwam on 7 November. In retaliatory counter-attacked, not only killed five ultras, but also captured one rocket launcher.

U.S. officials hold Al Qaeda and Taliban who infiltrated Pakistan's tribal belt after the fall of the Taliban in Afghanistan in late 2001, have regrouped in the area.

Pakistan, a key U.S. ally in the "war on terror" that is currently under a state of emergency, has around 90,000 troops in the tribal zones but it has failed to quell the unrest.

## Pakistan "has more terrorists per Square Mile"

There is sharp contrast in the Obama administration handling war on terror in Pakistan and Afghanistan.

The deeper Pakistan has dug itself into Jihadist dungeon over the past decade and more, the more the U.S. has gotten involved in that country, including in propping up its tottering economy through generous aid, macro-managing Pakistani politics and mollycoddling the powerful military. This political approach contrasts sharply with the current stepped-up U.S. military approach in Afghanistan, exemplified by a troop "surge".

The above sums up the analysis of a perceptive mind in an article in May 2009. Brahma Chellaney, Professor of Strategic Studies, Centre for Policy Research, New Delhi, Asian Age, 27.5.09.

By fighting the wrong war, the U.S. risks losing the battle against Islamists and transnational terrorists. The real war needs to be fought in Pakistan.

The 2001 U.S. military intervention in Afghanistan was intended to deny that landlocked country's lawless regions as a base for transnational terrorists. To a large extent, that goal has been realised, despite the threat from a resurgent Taliban, who get their sustenance to a large measure from their sanctuaries in border areas and FATA of Pakistan.

Today, the main global-terrorist base is not Afghanistan but Pakistan, which according to the co-author of President Obama's 'Af-Pak' strategy review Bruce Riedel, "has more terrorists per square mile than any place else on earth" and a nuclear armoury "growing faster than any place else on earth."

Still while reviving up its war machine in Afghanistan, America pursues a delicious political strategy in Pakistan, best illustrated by its new $10.5 billion aid package to win hearts and minds in a country that resembles a Molotov Cocktail waiting for a match. Even as the U.S. seeks to bribe the Pak military to stop providing succour and sanctuary to militants along the Afghan frontier, the major terrorist safe havens remain deep inside Pakistan, not at its borders. While it frets over the Pakistan, not at its borders. While if frets over the Pakistani Taliban, the scourge of Pakistani-terrorism still emanates from military generals who reared the forces of jihad.

Munificent U.S. aid, in fact, is allowing Pakistan to divert more of its scarce resources to expand its WMD capability. Pakistan's success in employing blackmail to extort ever more ransom money is a precedent to be followed by the then President Bush's "Rouge States"—North Korea and Iran. Have not the two countries watched carefully that Islamabad can play nuclear poker to shield its export of terrorism and still get rewarded with $23.6 billion in international aid commitments in the first half of 2009.

Actually, Obama is replicating the past failed approach on a bigger scale. His administration has even managed to dissuade the Congress thus far not to impose any rigid conditions on the unprecedented, $10.5 billion aid for Pakistan—the first $2 billion tranche of which has already been cleared for release. Obama has followed the flawed policy of his predecessor : Throwing more money at Islamabad, pampering the Pak army and intelligence and undermining Pakistan's elected leaders. He publicly excoriated President Zardari's fledgling government as "very fragile", ineffectual and unable "to gain the support of the Pakistani people. This is indeed a strange way to build up democracies, knowing that the U.S. has created an international organization to encourage democratic regimes the world over.

Today, no country challenges international security like Pakistan. Osama can not secure an honorable exit from Afghanistan without dismantling the Pakistani military's sanctuaries and sustenance infrastructure for Afghan militants. As Stephen Hadley pointed out just before leaving office as the U.S. national security adviser : "you can't really solve Afghanistan without solving Pakistan". It is not surprising that it has been suggested that it should be Pak-Af, not Af-Pak, policy.

Yet Obama has no real strategy to uproot Pakistan's terror complex other than to entice the Pakistani military establishment with larger funds and more weapon transfers—inducements that it will gladly grasp only to continue aiding extremists. Pakistan army has practised this art of blackmail to perfection over the years.

As long as the army continues to hold the real power and the rogue ISI remains unreformed, Pakistan is likely to stay a common thread in the investigations of most acts of international terrorism. Yet the Obama strategy relies on these very entities for gains on the Afghan battle field. Yet, by publicising his intent to exit Afghanistan, Obama has undercut his own objective. Now the Pakistani military and its progeny, the Taliban, will prefer to just wait out the Americans to reclaim Afghanistan.

The right course for the U.S. is to cut the Pakistani military establishment down to size by actively assisting the country's elected leaders to undo policies and mindsets implanted by a succession of army rulers. Ironically, the civilians in office today take all the blame but do not have the power to deliver. The emergence of a fully empowered civilian government and robust civil society will foster democracy, marginalise radicals and bring Pakistan back from the brink. Is it too much to hope in the given circumstances?

## "Qaeda fighters leaving Pakistan for Somalia, Yemen"

U.S. officials told the press in June 2009 that "they are seeing the first evidence that dozens of fighters al-Qaeda, and a small handful of the terrorist groups' leaders, are moving to Somalia and Yemen from their main haven in Pakistan's tribal areas." This is clear from the monitoring of increased communications among the terrorist groups in the three locations, by the officials at the Pentagon, White House and the CIA.

Some attribute the moves to pressure from intensified drone attacks against Qaeda operations in Pakistan, after years of unsuccessful American efforts to dislodge the terror outfit from their have there. But there are other possible explanations, chief among them being the growth of the Jihadist campaign in both Somalia and Yemen.

Somalia is now a failed state that bears some resemblance to Afghanistan before the 9/11 attacks, while Yemen's weak government is ineffectually trying to combat the militants.

The shift of fighters is still small, perhaps a few dozens, and there is no evidence that the top leaders—Osama and Ayman al-Zawahiri—are considering a move from their refuge in FATA areas.

Most officials would not comment on the record on the details of what they are seeing, because of the sensitivity of the intelligence information they are gathering.

CIA Director Leon E. Panetta said in remarks in Washington on 11 June, 2009 that the U.S. must prevent al-Qaeda from creating a new sanctuary in Yemen or Somalia.

The steady trickle of fighters from Pakistan could worsen the chaos in Somalia, where an Islamic militant group, the Shabab, has attracted hundreds of foreign jihadists in its quest to topple the weak moderate Islamist Government in Mogadishu.

Adm Mike Mullen, the Chairman of the Joint Chiefs of Staff, said in remarks at the Brookings in Washington on 18 May : "I am very worried about growing safe havens in both Somalia and Yemen, specifically because we have seen al-Qaeda leadership, some leaders, start to flow to Yemen."

## "42 terror-training camps still functional in Pakistan"

When Prime Minister Manmohan Singh talked tough with Pakistan President Asif Ali Zardari at Yekaterinburg on 16 June, 2009—"My only mandate is to tell Pakistan to take action against the culprits of 26/11—in the full glare of TV cameras, he had reasons enough to do so."

"There are still 42 terror-training camps directed against India, alive and kicking in Pakistan and PoK," as assessed by the Multi-Agency Centre (MAC), the nodal agency for all terror-related intelligence under the Home Ministry of India.

Giving a break down, the MCA says there are 34 'active' and eight 'holding' camps operating across the border in Pakistan. The PoK and Northern Areas account for 17 'active' and four 'holding or dormant' camps.

The MAC assessment is based on inputs from the RAW, IB, Military Intelligence (MI) and National Technical Research Organization (NTRO), among others. Around 2,200 militants are housed in these camps. "After 26/11, many of these camps emptied out or relocated. Some are back to their original status now, while new ones have also come up", said on official.

With the Prime Minister declaring India wants Pakistan to take "strong, effective and sustained action" against the terror networks before it decides on resuming the composite dialogue process, the fate of these camps as well as that of the mastermind behind the 26/11 terror attacks in Mumbai is being tracked closely.

India of course, had rebuffed Pakistan's call for resumption of the dialogue process after 26/11. Even if India has signaled its interest in reviving the dialogue after Yekaterin burge meeting, New Delhi still remains cautious whether Pakistan will actually walk its talk.

While Pakistan is taking steps to crackdown on the Taliban-al-Qaeda nexus, faced as it with unrelenting heat from the U.S. the Jihadi factory against India continues to run with impunity. The MAC assessment says of the 2,200 militants in the 42 camps spread across Pakistan, some 300 belong to the LeT, 240 to JeM and 130 to HUJI, while the rest have "mixed" origins.

The "active' camps in PoK include the following :

| | |
|---|---|
| Kotli | Garhi Dupatta |
| Nikial | Forward Kahuta |
| Sensa | Peer Chinasi |
| Gulpur | Jhandi Chauntra |
| Bhimber | Abdullah Bin Masud |
| Barnala | Shavai Nallah |
| Skardu | Tatta Pani |
| Sawani | |

The NWFP province (now, Pashtunkhwa) is another hotbed of Jihadi activity, with the densely-forested hilly Manshera region, in particular, housing several *madrassas*, which also double up as training camps. These include the following :

| | |
|---|---|
| Jangal Mangal | Shinkiari |
| Andher Bela | Jalo Gali |

## Other NWFP camps include Boi, Oghi and Attar Shisha

The other camps in Pakistan and Northern Areas include Muridke, Sialkot, Beesian, Garhi Habibullah, and Jalo Gali. "Many of these camps are makeshift, which can be translocated very quickly to evade scrutiny. More over the real leaders of various *tanzeems* (organisations) are based in cities like Islamabad and Lahore."

## What a U.S. report foretells

An excerpt from Joint Operating Environment Report, 2008 of U.S. Joint Forces Command is reproduced below :

> "In terms of worst-case scenarios for the Joint Force and indeed the world, Pakistan bears consideration for a rapid and sudden collapse—Pakistan, in such an event, would be susceptible to a violent and bloody civil and sectarian war made more dangerous by concerns over the nation's nuclear arsenal. The perfect storm of uncertainty by itself might require U.S. engagement."

## Cult of suicide bomber : A weapon beyond Contest

A startling aspect of the patterns of violence witnessed across the country is the increasing frequency of suicide attacks. The magnitude of Pakistan's slide towards chaos is best illustrated by the fact that, between 22 March 2002 (the first suicide attack) and end-2006, there were 22 suicide attacks; in 2007 alone, there were 56 such attacks, rising to 59 in 2008.

Fidayeen (suicide squads) relentlessly targeted Army convoys and Check-posts, police stations and training units, Government officials, polling stations, schools, jirga meetings, hotels, restaurants, mosques, and various soft targets. Almost 11 per cent of total fatalities in Pakistan during 2008 were inflicted through suicide attacks.

More alarmingly, some Taliban clerics reportedly boasted of converting orderly persons into suicide-bombers "in six hours flat". "From the 26 suicide attacks where we recovered a head in 2007, we made a startling discovery...The vast majority (of suicide bombers) came from just one tribe, the Mehsuds of central Waziristan, all boys between 16 and 20", an analyst at the elite Special Investigation Group (SIG) told the Guardian. Qari Hussain, also known as the Ustad-e-Fidayeen (expert/teacher of suicide cadres), a Mehsud tribesman in his early 30s, is identified as the 'commander' who manages Baitullah Mehsud-led Taliban suicide bombing training centres and is directly responsible for indoctrinating youth for suicide missions. From "Pakistan Assessment 2009" (Courtesy : South Asia Terrorism Portal and Institute for Conflict Management).

## Suicide attack kill 8 Airmen; Troops kill 70 Ultras : November, 2007

A suicide attack on an Air Force bus killed eight people on 1 November, 2007 as security forces said they wiped out up to 70 militants in north-west Pakistan, fuelling talk that the beleaguered President, Gen. Pervez Musharraf, would invoke emergency powers to put off elections.

Nuclear-armed Pakistan is going through a period of intense uncertainty in the run up to a vote due in January (2008) that is supposed to transform the country into a civilian-led democracy, Javed Iqbal Cheema, head of the Interior Ministry's Crisis Management Cell, said : "With reference to extremists and terrorists, it is a bad situation.... It is a very serious threat to Pakistan's internal security."

The Pakistani Supreme Court added to tensions on 1 November by dragging out hearings on whether U.S. ally Gen. Musharraf was eligible to have stood for re-election while still the Army Chief in a vote in Parliament that he won easily early October 2007.

The Karachi Stock Exchange's benchmark index dropped nearly three per cent on 1 November, compounding declines earlier this week as investors turned tail in a market that is still 38 per cent up since the start of the year, 2007.

Before the market opened, a suicide bomber rammed a bus and killed eight personnel on their way to an air base in Sargodha in the central province of Punjab. Police said they had found the head of the bomber, and circled blood strains on the road with white chalk, while the handlebars of a motorbike used by the attacker lay on the tarmac.

"Separately, troops killed up to 70 militants as fighting flared in Swat Valley in the NWFP, where more than 180 people have died since last week as the military battles a pro-Taliban movement seeking to impose the strict Islamic law," says a Reuters report datelined Islamabad, 1 November, 2007.

The latest violence coincides with a visit by Adm William Fallton, commander of the US Central Command, for talks with the Pakistani military leadership.

Nearly 800 people have been killed in militant-linked violence and there have been more than 22 suicide attacks in the four months since Pakistani commandos stormed the Red Mosque in the capital, Islamabad, to crush a Taliban-style movement, which was aiming to impose Shariat laws on the country.

Al-Qaeda leaders Osama bin Laden and Ayman al-Zawahri, in audio and video tapes released in September 2007, exhorted their followers to wage war on Musharraf and Pakistan's security forces. "The last battle between Islam and the infidels is on. On the one side is Sheikh Osama, may Allah keep him safe," Maulvi Faqir Mohd, one of the most wanted militants in Pakistan told approving ranks of fighters in Bajaur tribal region, near Swat. "We assure him and Mullah Omar, and Mujahideen all over the world that we stand solidly behind you", he further announced.

Yet investors have been more concerned about the Supreme Court destabilizing Musharraf, who came to power in a coup eight years ago, than the burgeoning militant threat.

The court said it will adjourn after 2 November session until 12 November—just three days before Musharraf's present term expires, with the Parliament also coming to the end of its term.

## 60 Suicide attacks in Pakistan since 2002

Benazir Bhutto faced criticism for exposing her supporters to Jihadi bombers when she returned home in a convoy in Karachi on 18 October 2007. With the Tuesday, 30 October blast in Rawalpindi near the Musharraf Headquarters and Army House, Pakistan has suffered close to 60 suicide bombings since January 2002, of which the most deadly turned out to be the one aimed at Bhutto on the 18th.

In the context of the current jihadi maelstrom inside Pakistan, that 'distinction' is less important than the fact that these attacks have now become almost entirely directed at the armed forces. The present battle may have its immediate provocation in the fighting going on between the security forces and followers of Mullah Fazluallah of the Tehrik-e-Nifaz-e-Shariat-e-Mahammadi (TNSM) in Swat, but the 30th also marked the anniversary of an air strike in a Bajaur compound which had killed 80 militants.

Pakistan's jihad is coming home to its creators. Swat, Waziristan, Mingora, Mir Ali and Bajaur may be the breeding grounds of jihadis but their targets are increasingly Rawalpindi, military convoys, elite special services groups officers, and even as on 4 September in Rawalpindi, Pakistan's notorious intelligence agencies officials going to work.

Since the 12 July, 2007 Lal Masjid operation, the Pak Army has lost more than 250 officers and soldiers to Taliban, not to speak of 300 soldiers who "surrendered" to the Taliban militants without firing a shot, a horrible suicide bombing of Pakistan's elite SSG post in Tarbela, as well as continued attacks on Pakistani soldiers and Paramilitary forces in these areas.

In the latest incident of disgrace heaped on the Pakistani Army, pro-Taliban militants of Fazlullah on 2 November 2007 paraded captured para-military soldiers, who had surrendered their post near Charbagh town, 15 km north-east of Swat's capital Mingora, in front of the media at Charbagh in the restive Swat Valley. The militants later said they had freed all the captured soldiers.

The Pakistani Government is frantically trying to raise a frontier security force with locals, funding reportedly by the U.S. But recruitment been sparse, after the Taliban warned the locals against joining the Pakistan army. Demoralisation of the troops has been very high as they are being pushed more and more to fire at their own people.

Jihadi anger against Musharraf and, by extension, against Benazir is at an all time high. The provocation is not merely the U.S.—led war on terror or the serial bombings in Bajaur. The rise in violence can be attributed to the creation of a Pakistani Taliban, which is increasingly taking control of the lawless frontier tribal areas. Radical mullahs, using a combination of money and muscle power usurped the traditional authority of tribal chiefs and taken hold of vast tracts. In a nutshell, if traditionally Pakistani policies were aimed against giving space to the idea of Pashtunistan, the radicalisation of the frontier areas may have created something for worse—now called "Talibanisation" by writers like Jason Burke.

Former Indian intelligence chief Ajit Doval says : "The State and Islam are in direct confrontation in Pakistan and will be far a long time. The nature of the government in Islamabad is increasingly immaterial to this fight—democracy or military rule. Pakistan is now deeply entrenched in religious warfare." The focus has shifted from well-known jihadi groups to new entities like the TNSM, and its *amir* Mullah Fazlullah, who has been preaching Islamist hatred through an FM channel. The recent attacks by the Pakistani army have been against the followers of the Maulana and the latter are posing a stiff challenge to the state and its army in Swat.

It is no more an unlikely scenario that frontier tribal areas of Pakistan bordering Afghanistan—like North Waziristan, South Waziristan, Bajaur etc. in FATA and Swat Valley—will pass under the extremist Taliban supporting maulvis and mullahs like Fazlullah and the Qazi brothers of Lal Masjid. In one word, Pakistani frontier areas will pass under the control of Pakistani Tablean. The areas across the Afghan border, alongwith practically the entire east and southern Afghanistan, are already under the Afghan Taliban. Islamabad is in for a long, dreary winter.

## Lal Masjid Tests Musharra's Patience

The Lal Masjid (= Red Mosque) located in the centre of Pakistani capital of Islamabad had posed a serious challenge to the authority of the state for months on end. After a week-long stand-off between the security forces and the militants holed up inside the Mosque, Pak soldiers stormed it on 10 July, 2007.

The Lal Masjid was a symbol of the inconsistencies of the Pakistan Government. "For the past six months, the chief clerics of the mosque—Maulama Abdul Aziz and his brother Rashid Ghazi—and their followers had been openly flouting government's authority." One of Musharraf's excuses was the threat by Mosque's militants to resort to suicide bombings if government dared to use force.

The real reason might have been quite different : The Lal Masjid radicals served to divert attention from the embarrassing nationwide protests by the lawyers and civil society against Musharraf's dismissal of Pakistan's Chief Justice. Some critics have pointed to the link between the Pak military and clerics. Former President Zia-ul-Haq was known to be close to the then head of the Mosque, and a number of ISI officials are known to have been frequent visitors to the Mosque.

The sad story of the confrontation and the final storming of the Lal Masjid is briefly given in the following pages.

## Pak Women Commandos could Storm Madrassa

The Pakistan government was reported on 15 April, 2007 to be intent on deploying women's commandos to launch a crack down on a seminary housing militant girl students "who have stepped their campaign to impose Sharia law in the country backed by radical clerics. This was reported by the *Daily Times* Islamabad, quoting U.S. intelligence sources. Incidentally, Islamabad has been holding negotiation with the radical clerics of the Lal Masjid "that fixed a one-month dead line for the Government for imposition of Sharia law."

The madrassa, say these clerics, house about 3,000 girl students, majority of them hailing from poor families of the NWFP, or destitute children.

There were media reports about the Government having deployed several hundred male commandos at the nearby vacant buildings. But the government ruled out a crackdown in the immediate future fearing the political fall out of massive casualties to burqa clad girls, who themselves had threatened to resist with weapons and suicide attacks.

But the Government, negotiating with the clerics through the ruling PML (Q), "has failed to persuade the Islamists to give up their Taliban-style campaign in the capital.

## Lal Masjid Clerics' Demands Conceded

The government on 17 April, 2007 again went on the defensive in its stand-off with the clerics of Lal Masjid and Jamia Hafsa and allotted land for two of the seven mosques demolished by the Islamabad administration. The land for the two mosques has been allotted in two plots situated in Sector I-8 and Murree Road Orchard Scheme, respectively.

The local administration had demolished seven mosques in different areas of Islamabad recently. They were :

- Masjid Amir Hamza, Murree Road
- Masjid Syedna Ibn-i-Abbas, Orchard Road
- Masjid Amir Hamza, F-10/3
- Masjid Syedna Ali, G-10
- Masjid Umar bin Abdul Aziz, PM Staff Colony
- Masjid Safha (Hafsa), I-8
- Masjid Umar, G-8 Markez

The administrations of these mosques had opposed the demolition of the mosques and occupied a nearby children's library in protest. The Capital Development Authority (CDA) and the local administration had earlier refused either to rebuild the demolished mosques or to provide plots for new ones. But now the government has not only provided plots for the purpose but it has also promised to reconstruct these mosques. The CDA had declared as 'illegal' a total of 87 mosques in the city.

"Land for the other five demolished mosques would be provided in the next couple of days". Provision of land for the demolished mosques was one of the major demands of the clerics. The other demand pertains to enforcement of the Shariat in the country.

## Woman behind Radical Pak Cleric : April 2007

Behind Abdul Aziz, the cleric who wants to enforce *Shariah* (=

strict Islamic Code) in Pakistan's capital of Islamabad, stands a women, his wife Umm-e-Hassan, who is as fiery as he is...

In March 2007, Aziz threatened suicide attacks if the government used force to quell his campaign. Umm-e-Hassan says : "My female followers will not lag behind. If the government does not enforce' Islamic *Sahriah*, then we will resist. We do not ment to come to power, but we want to correct the system (of government) in Pakistan and that can't be done without *Shariah*." She told this to a journalist, who published the dails on 18 April, 2007. Zeeshan Haider, Reuters, cited, *Hindustan Times*, 19.4.2007.

Umm-e-Hassan heads Jamia Hafsa, a religious school (= madrassa for women), affiliated with the Lal Masjid (= Red Mosque), where her husband is the chief cleric.

A stand off with civil authorities erupted in January 2007 after she and her students seized a municipal library adjoining her madrassa to protest the demolition of (seven) illegally built mosques in the capital.

They made international news in March after they raided a brothel in the heart of Islamabad and held three women hostage in their madrassa for three days.

Prostitution is illegal in Muslim Pakistan, but many women and girls ply the trade across the country. The brothel raid was seen as a sign of growing influence of Islamists throughout the country, commonly dubbed as "Talibanisation" and posed a direct challenge to the government's authority.

Pakistan is constitutionally an Islamic Republic, operating parallel Islamic and civil legal system, but liberals and Islamists have long wrangled over the direction of society. While radicals like Umm-e-Hassan and Aziz want enforcement of a Taliban-style puritanical version of Islam, liberals want a progressive and modern caum.

And Umm-e-Hassan is not ruling out raiding other brothers if the government fails to act. "If people compel us to take action, then we will think we are asking the government to enforce Islamic *Shariah* so that we are not forced to take such action."

Pakistani madrassa, mainly for men, have long been seen as breeding grounds for religious militancy, especially those in the remote northern and western regions of the country, near the Afghan border, where the Taliban began.

But it is the female students of Jamia Hafsa who have taken the lead in launching the campaign for a Taliban-style system in Islamabad, causing huge embarrassment to the Musharraf Government.

The authorities have been heavily criticised for their lenient approach to the challenge thrown by the huge Lal Masjid Complex, which now resembles a rebel camp with gun-toting (female) students on the roof top.

Even after the Government has bowed, allotting the land for the mosques razed to the ground earlier and also promising construction of new mosques on these (new) plots, taking a u-turn on their earlier stance of refusing to do either, Aziz and Umm-e-Hassan have not relented on their main demand, next to restoration of these dismantled mosques; namely, imposing *Shariat* in Islamabad-Rawalpindi area.

Musharraf, a staunch front-line ally in the U.S.-led war on terrorism, has defended his policy in recent weeks, saying the government wanted to avoid confrontation with the Jamia Hafsa's "misguided" students. But Umm-e-Hassan is clearly determined : "The government must take the first step if there was to be a settlement."

Islamabad finds itself on a sticky wicket. The defiance displayed by the Lal Masjid is direct challenge to the government, which it cannot afford to ignore indefinitely. As of date (4 May 2007), the armed girl students, mostly in burqas/hijab, are still in occupation of the nearby library building. The gun-toting girl students, standing defiantly on the roof tops and guarding the Lal Masjid complex to face any government action to evict them by force, cannot be a soothing sight for any government's authority and self-respect! The fact is Islamabad is acutely concerned about the strong reaction in the Muslim world if it proceeds against the heavily armed and determined female students, who also have some suicide bombers among them. No one could be envious of Islamabad's helplessness! How it all ends up finally is not easy to predict.

## "Lal Masjid was Grooming Suicide Bombers"

Islamic students associated with the Lal Masjid have been indoctrinated and trained to mount suicide attacks, the MQM, the ruling coalition party claimed in a report released 23 April 2007. Its "unbiased research" disclosed that a large arsenal of unused weapons from Kalashnikov assault rifles to rocket-propelled grenades has been amassed at the Lal Masjid and two affiliated *madrassas*. The report also made the following points :

- "They (students) also think that in case of their martyrdom in suicide attacks, they will be welcomed by *hours* (virgins) with garlands in their hands and they will have entry into the heaven without accountability.
- "Independent witnesses have testified to the presence of automatic weapons on the premises, while members of terrorist group with a history of bombings have also joined the mosque's protectors."

The MQM (Muttehida Qaumi Movement) held April 2009 a rally of around 100,000 people against violent enforcement of self-defined Islamic laws.

## "Paradise Receipts" found in the Mosque : 8.7.2007

Pakistani security forces found a leaflet being distributed among the holed up militants in the besieged Lal Masjid, stating that their death while resisting the military operation would lead them to paradise.

A leaflet recovered 8 July 2007 from a 15-year-old boy, who managed to escape the Mosque complex through a damaged portion of a wall, stated that "it is a receipt to paradise". "Those who are killed while fighting would enter paradise directly," Online news agency quoted from the receipt.

The rescued boy said barricades had been erected in the Mosque to prevent students of the seminary from leaving.

## Violent Saga of Lal Masjid, Islamabad

A long-running confrontation between the Lal Masjid clerics and Pakistani government ended on 10 July 2007, with the troops mounting an attack to put an end to the 'rebellion' within the national capital of Islamabad. First a brief history of the mosque.

## The History

- The sprawling Lal Masjid is a rare mosque to have a name not connected with Islam. True to its name, it has remained a centre of defiance since it was constructed in 1965, though it was managed by the Pakistan government.
- Red is a colour militant Islamists shun because it is identified with Communists, or *Kafir* meaning infidel.
- The name was given by the Auqaf department that managed it, which many believe was due to its red walls and interiors. Over the years, it has played a major role in generating jihadis to fight the occupation of Afghanistan by the erstwhile Soviet Union. After that it became a centre of extremist Sunni ideology.
- Abdullah, father of the two top clerics—Abdul Aziz and his younger brother Abdul Rashid Qazi—was chosen as the first cleric of the mosque by Pakistan's frist military ruler General (later, Field Marshal) Ayub Khan.
- The clerics have been on the Pakistan government's pay roll ever since, receiving funds, salary, patronage.
- During Gen. Zia-ul-Haq's time, the mosque acquired a lot of state land in Islamabad to build its madrassas for boys and girls.
- Maulana Abdullah was gunned down outside Lal Majid in 1998, by suspected rival Shia militants.
- Masjid showed its street power for the first time in 2003 when radical Sunni leader Aziz Tariq was killed.
- It passed a controversial edict in 2004 against Pakistani soldiers fighting in Waziristan to flush out al-Qaeda and Taliban militants.
- According to the daily *Dawn*, this was the same year Lal Masjid's links with al-Qaeda were revealed with the arrest of Osama bin Laden's driver. The government at that time

accused Ghazi of masterminding attacks on government installations but he was mysteriously cleared of those charges.

- The mosque and its madrassas came under the scanner in 2005, when its girl students resisted a government operation. After the 7/7 attacks, UK had called on Pakistan to crack down on Islamic schools.

## Chronology of Clashes : July, 2007

- Tuesday-3 July, clashes erupt between students and security forces when some 150 students attack a security post at a government office near the mosque and snatch weapons.

  Death toll : 16

- Wednesday-4 July, Abdul Aziz, chief cleric of Red Mosque, is arrested while trying to escape clad in a woman's burqa upto 1200 students surrender.

- Thursday-5 July, Security forces fire the warning blasts near the mosque. Rebel cleric, Abdul Rashid Ghazi, offers surrender terms.

  Death toll : 19

- Friday-6 July, The Government rejects Ghazi's surrender terms and insists he release women and children held as human shields. Water, gas and power are cut.

- Saturday-7 July, President Pervez Musharraf tells Ghazi and his followers to surrender or die.

  Death toll : 20

- Sunday-8 July, Pakistani authorities issue a 'last warning'. Troops blast holes to provide escape routes to women and children in the mosque.

  Death toll : 21

- Monday – 9 July, Negotiations to end stand off fail.

- Tuesday – 10 July, Security forces launch operation to clear militants from the mosque.

Death toll : 54 (50 militants, 4 soldiers)

50 militants arrested

20 children escaped

(*Source :* Reuters)

## Army Mounts Operation to Clear the Mosque : 10 July, 2007

After a lot of dilly–dallying and heart–searching, because of religious emotions and sensitivities involved, Islamabad decided to proceed against the Lal Masjid defiance. Pakistani forces stormed the mosque compound in Islamabad on 10 July 2007, killing up to 50 militants as they fought their way through an Islamic school where women and children were feared to be detained/hiding. Abdul Aziz, the chief cleric of the mosque, had escaped earlier, before the 10 July storming of the mosque, but 43-year-old Abdul Rashid Ghazi, his younger brother, was killed during the operation on the 10th.

Once respected by the Pakistani establishment, the smooth-talking pro-Taliban cleric Ghazi killed in the mosque siege had pushed authorities too far with his sometimes bizarre drive to enforce strict Islamic law in the city, Islamabad.

As a student, Ghazi was regarded a moderate Muslim, but he was radicalised by the 1998 sectarian assassination of his cleric father. After 9/11, the emerged as an increasingly outspoken critic of President Musharraf's U.S.-backed government.

With his elder brother Abdul Aziz as chief cleric of the Lal Masjid, Ghazi cultivated links with Islamic militants and often lashed out at Pakistan's support of the U.S.—led war on terrorism tapping an antipathy shared by many in this conservative country.

But in 2004, he did something nothing short of an anathema to the Pakistani rulers—issuing a fatwa, or edict, declaring that funeral prayers should not be offered to Pakistani soldiers who died fighting al-Qaeda. Expectedly, it set him on collision course with the military government.

Greater provocation came in the name and form of a freelance vigilante campaign launched in early to impose Shariah (= Islamic Law) in the Pakistani capital, which mocked Musharraf's claim of combating religious extremists and directly challenged the government writ.

Stick-wielding student supporters of Ghazi kidnapped alleged prostitutes and police and warned vendors against selling music and movie CDs. That was a brash if somewhat symbolic attempt to impose Taliban-style rule in the city—the very capital of the nation. Such defiant action might have caused little physical harm, barring destruction and ransacking of some music stores, but it was a huge embarrassment for the national/federal government. But the threshold of forbearance was crossed when his followers on 4 November (2007) abducted seven Chinese at an acupuncture clinic which they claimed was a brothel.

It was a political and diplomatic challenge that triggered a military siege that culminated in a pre-dawn raid of the mosque. After all, China was not any other country. It was not only a key ally, but a time-tested all-weather friend.

15 hours after the assault began, officials reported that commandos had gunned down Ghazi in a fire-fight, after the cleric, alongside militants stuck in a basement inside the mosque complex, refused to surrender, repeated warnings not-withstanding.

Born in the village of Basti Abdullah in the southwestern province of Baluchistan, Ghazi later studies at two seminaries in Rawalpindi but was regarded less pious than his elder brother. He earned a masters degree in international relations from Islamabad prestigious Quid-e-Azam University, and later worked at the Education Ministry and according to some reports, for UNESCO.

Naeem Qureshi, a professor who taught Ghazi history in 1987-88, remembered him as a good student : religiously minded like many of his generation and motivated by the Mujahideen resistance to the Soviet occupation of Afghanistan. Ghazi's father, Mohd Abdullah, who became the prayer leader at the revered Red Mosque in 1960s, frowned on his son's secular appearance, according to a friend of Ghazi. The friend said : "Before his father's martyrdom, he (Ghazi) used to wear pants and shirt and a small beard. His life changed after his father's martyrdom. He became a religious man. He adopted his father's life."

## Lal Masjid, Islamabad Stormed Finally : 10 July, 2007

Radical cleric Abdul Rashid Ghazi, who led militants inside the pro-Taliban Lal Masjid in a tense week-long stand-off, was killed 18 July, 2007 with 88 of his associates when Pak troops stormed the premises to flush out heavily-armed hardliners holding women and children hostages.

Twelve commandos were also killed during 'Operation Silence', launched at 4 AM after talks with the radicals broke down.

43-year-old Ghazi, younger brother of the Captured Lal Masjid head Maulana Abdul Aziz, was killed by troops in the basement after he refused to surrender, even after receiving a bullet in his leg.

The death toll crossed 100 as the operation continued with well-armed militants engaging troops in pitched battle, said reports. "Troops are involved in room-to-room fighting to take control of layers and layers of the sprawling complex, stretching to several acres."

Umme Hassan, Ghazi's sister-in-law and Principal of the girls' madrassa attached to the mosque, and her daughter Asmma were taken into custody by troops who also rescued 134 people. Ghazi had not even allowed his aling mother to come out undergo treatment, said Pakistan Army spokesman Maj. Gen. Waheed Arshad, referring to Ghazi's claim that she was killed during the operation.

## Militant 'Wanted' by India Negotiated with Ghazi

Here is an interesting side story Fazal-ur-Rehman Khalil, who figures on India's list of 'most wanted' terrorists, was roped in by Pak authorities to persuade Ghazi to give up before troops stormed the mosque.

Journalist saw Khalil, head of the outlawed Harkat-ul-Mujahideen, driving into the mosque in the same car as the leader of the negotiating team, former Prime Minister Shujaat Hussain. Shunned until recently for his links with Qaeda and Taliban, Khalil smiled when the media noticed him sitting in Shujaat's vehicle.

## Pak Probes Lal Masjid-Militant Links

Pakistan authorities on Monday 16 July, 2007 were probing suspected links between radicals at the captured Red Mosque (= Lal Masjit) and militants in the north-west frontier, "where more than 70 people died in weekend suicide attacks and bombing."

Pak Interior Minister Aftab Khan Sherpa osaid the government was investigating whether the escalation of violence in the north-west was related to the raid on this Islamabad Mosque in which at least 100 people were killed. He did not elaborate on the possible links.

However, officials suggested that the Mosque's radical clerics had connections with the militants in the North Waziristan region, a Taliban and al-Qaeda strong hold on the Afghan border. Clerics and students at the mosque and its adjoining religious school had pressed for Taliban-style rule in Pakistan and launched a vigilante, anti-vice campaign in Islamabad.

Officials claimed that several foreign militants were among more than 100 killed during an 8-day army siege of the mosque but did not provide any evidence to support that.

The suicide attacks and bombings on the 14 and 15 July followed strident calls by extremists to avenge the government's bloody storming of the mosque and a declaration of jihad by at least one pro-Taliban cleric. Militants in North Waziristan also tore up a peace treaty with the Pakistan Government. Abdullah Farhad, a militant spokesman who announced the termination of the 10-month-old ceasefire, clarified that Taliban leaders made the decision after the government failed to withdraw troop from North-Waziristan.

The termination of the pact, the hopeful handiwork of Gen. Musharraf, put even greater pressure on him as he struggles with both Islamic extremists and a gathering pro-democracy movement.

The U.S. National Security Adviser, Stephen Hadley, expressed support for Musharraf but also voiced some criticism of his performance against the Islamic militants. Hadley told Fox news : "The action has at this point not been adequate, not effective. He is doing more, we are urging him to do more, and we are providing our full support of what he is contemplating."

## Taliban : Monsters of Terror

As the brutality goes, the Taliban beat the much-maligned (rightly of course) al-Qaeda, and they base their ideology on a narrow fundamentalist interpretation of Islam. The world still remember their most brutal rule over Afghanistan, 1994-2001.

## Origin, Rise and Spread of Pakistan's Taliban

Their origin lay in the FATA areas of Pakistan, where thousands of Afghans, mainly Pashtuns, had fled during the decade-long jihad against the Soviet army. A whole generation of boys grew up in refugee camps in these tribal areas, learning the ideology of hate and revenge. The camps and seminaries were organised by the Pakistani government, with funds received covertly from the U.S. (for fighting communism) and openly from Saudi Arabian armchair jihadists interested in spreading their strain of (wahhabi) Islam—a hard line one. As they are produce of *madrassa*, these fighters came to be known as the "Taliban", or students.

As the Soviets withdrew from Afghanistan with a bloody nose in 1989, and later the Najib government fell in Kabul in 1992, the Taliban continued operating from their bases in the camps of FATA areas—bidding their time as a vicious civil war raged in Afghanistan. As their popularity increased with successive victories in various areas, they finally moved in and captured Kabul in 1994.

Their ways and interpretation of Islam were shown to the world in their first public action in Qandahar in 1994. A local war lord had abducted two girls for serving his troops one night, a group of young, bearded Pashtuns, wearing black turbans, emerged from the darkness, stormed his base, hanged to warlord from the turret of a tank and rescued the girls. They were the Taliban.

Taking over Afghanistan in 1994, they declared their motherland the "Islamic Caliphate of Afghanistan". During their 7-year rule there, this fundamentalist brand of Islam spread not only in Afghanistan but also in areas bordering it. Drawing upon the public anger against the U.S. and Pak Government's inefficient and corrupt collusion, Taliban-like organisations spread in Pakistan.

Some of them are listed below :

- Jamaat-i-Islami and its associated outfits like Hizb-ul-Mujahideen.
- Deobandi Organisation like Harkat-ul-Mujahideen.
- Wahhabi groups like LeT and Jammat-ud-Dawa.

All these outfits subscribe to the global-jihad ideology. Today, Pakistani people are being held to ransom by extremist groups, ranging from global jihadist like remnants of al-Qaeda and the Taliban to the various Lashkars (armies) and mujahideen operating throughout the country. In 2008, 1,201 people died in 598 bombings. In 2009, only in first two months, 106 bombings took place. To briefly come to the present (August-2009), Pak Army had to attack the Lal Masjid, retake Swat from the Taliban, and are presently preparing to act in Waziristan.

After being thrown out of Afghanistan in 2001, they started regrouping themselves in 2003-4, and have been giving tough fight to the U.S. and NATO troops in Afghanistan particularly in Summers. Whenever under pressure, the Taliban went into hiding in villages on both sides of the Durand line. Mulla Umar who headed the Taliban government in Afghanistan, is most likely functioning from Quetta, ensconced in layers of safety provided by his acolytes as also the elements in state agencies which had created them in the first place.

In NWFP, the Taliban have been spreading their influence, especially in the FATA areas. Here, the local warlords and tribal chiefs either got assimilated into the fundamentalist fold or were systematically eliminated. In 2007, several fundamentalist groups made a joint front called the "Tehrik-e-Taliban Pakistan (TTP) led by Baitullah Mehsud, and supported by such local warlords as Maulana Fazullah of Swat and his father-in-law Sufi Mohd.

Under the garb of fighting terror, and to get another largesse from the U.S. Musharraf had targeted several fundamentalist groups pushing them further into the extremist arms. These include :

- Sunni groups such as the Lashkar-e-Jhangui, the Sipah-e-Sahaba Pakistan, Harkat-ul-Mujahideen al-Alami and Jundullah.
- Shia groups such as the Sipah-e-Muhammad.

Further down the line, these Sunni and Shia groups function on the sectarian or ethnic basis. Thus the TTP is largely a Pashtun or "Pathan" (as they are called in Pakistan) organisation. Pathans make up 15 per cent of the population and belong to the Sunni branch of Islam. Shias, the other major branch, comprise some 20 per cent of the population (Incidentally, the Sunnis are about 76 per cent of the Pakistani population).

While these groups have their differences on ideological or tactical issues, they share several commonalities. All are products of the Afghan jihad against the Soviet Union. They were nurtured by Gen. Zia-ul-Haq and received funding from Saudi and covert western sources in the early days. They were used for political gains by various governments in Pakistan as also for fighting in Kashmir.

More importantly/insidiously, all the outfits practice, preach and propagate a more hard line, rigid interpretation of Islam—in short, its Wahhabi version—opposing the more flexible and moderate South Asian way of Muslim life.

## Are Jihadis having Free Run in Pakistan?

A suicide bomber on Saturday, 27 January 2007, struck during a Muharram procession near a Shia mosque in Peshawar, killing at least 15 people, including Commissioner of Police, and wounding over 30. Since there is nothing new about the sectarian violence in Pakistan where Shias are regularly set upon by Sunni extremists, this blood bath should not come as a surprise.

But what should cause concern in both Islamabad and Washington is that it was the second suicide bombing over the weekend. On Friday, the 26th, another suicide bomber blew himself up at the Marriott Hotel in Islamabad, killing a guard and injuring some other. If it had not gone away, this suicide bombing would have extracted a terrible toll in life and limb. He arrived at the Marriott too early, lost his way and pressed the trigger in panic when confronted by a security guard.

Such repeated terrorist violence raises some urgent if dangerous questions. If the suicide bomber who struck during Saturday's Muharram procession was seeking martyrdom by laying to waste Shia lives, his compatriot was obviously aspiring for the same goal via a different route : Blowing himself up at the venue of the Republic Day Reception hosted by India's High Commissioner Satyabrata Pal. That he failed in his mission is no reflection on his commitment to jihad "although it demonstrated the contempt with which foot soldiers are treated by those who see themselves as commanders of this twisted holy war.

Pal did well by going ahead with the reception. Had he called it off, he would have signalled capitulation before those who flaunt there evil, hateful deeds as virtuous acts. Celebrating the republican ideas that nourish India's open and plural society is the most appropriate riposte to those who believe in intolerance and bigotry that understandably flourish on Pakistani soil.[1]

This continued terrorist violence should not only be a cause of concern to Pakistan's immediate neighbours, India and Afghanistan in particular, but also to the wider world beyond.

Not withstanding all his tall talk of "enlightened moderation" and loudly-claimed resolve to stamp out terrorism, Gen. Musharraf has dismally failed to even contain the extremist fringe which continues to grow in strength with each passing day. On the contrary, there is now ample evidence to prove that Pakistani establishment is working tandem with the resurgent Taliban to topple President Hamid Karzai's Government. There is equally strong evidence to suggest the protection extended to the Al Qaeda leadership. Not a single top Qaeda leader has been arrested or killed. But a Bugti, posing direct threat to Pakistan's integrity, was eliminated in no time. The contrast in dealing with two types of terrorist threat is self-obvious and instructive.

Gen. Musharraf's inability—or, more correctly, his reluctance—to deal with terrorists of various hues has been conceded by the U.S. National. Intelligence Director and has been widely commented upon in the Western media. NATO commanders and American operatives in Afghanistan have repeatedly highlighted Pakistani role in fostering cross border terrorism. It is therefore no surprise that the U.S. Congress is eager (January 2007) to bar military aid to Pakistan unless Islamabad demonstrates that it is genuinely waging a war on terror.

The U.S. seems to be stuck up in a cleft in Musharraf's Pakistan which has failed to deliver. It is aware of Musharraf's inability or reluctance to mount all-out offensive against the Taliban and Al Qaeda militants. At the same time, it is well aware that the General is its only bet. We are witnessing a strange spectacle' of Washington talking tough in private but heaping praises on him in public. The U.S. is convinced that Musharraf's replacement may be worse than him. So, it is a Hobson's choice as far as Gen. Musharraf is concerned. Even when the resurgent Taliban are having upper hand in southern and eastern Afghanistan, and are preparing to launch a spring (2007) offensive against the NATO and Afghan forces, all that the U.S. can do is to send Vice President Dick Cheney (26 February 2007) to issue a stern warning to Musharraf : Act against Taliban or face aid cuts!

## Taliban impose 'music fine' in Pakistan : February, 2007

Having banned music in Pakistan's tribal areas, the Taliban are now imposing a fine of Rs. 500 for any one playing it in public. The worst sufferers of the new "pay Rs. 500, if you play" regime are the taxi drivers who complain that even possession of a CD player in their vehicles is enough to invite punishment.

They have also intensified their attacks on shops and video stores selling music CDs and DVDs and cassettes of locally-made Urdu, English and Indian films.

The latest target was in Bannu, the home town of Akram Durrani, Chief Minister, NWFP. The attackers came in broad daylight, destroyed a video shop and damaged CDs, DVDs, and other material with impunity in front of the local police station.

More stringent punishment could be in the offing, local reports said.

The militants have distributed pamphlets in Pushto language warning drivers of public vehicles to avoid playing music or face "capital punishment."

"I was stopped by the Taliban at Sarband village near Bara, Khyber agency on 24 February. They searched my taxi and found some music cassettes," said Khanimullah, a Peshawar-based taxi-driver. He was fined Rs. 500. Another taxi driver faced the similar 'music' at Sangu, near the Khyber Agency border, mid-February 2007, when men claiming to be local Taliban fined him Rs. 500. They told him that music was a sin and prohibited in Islam.

The hardline Daawat-ul-Muhahideen had distributed pamphlets in Pushto saying music was banned in vehicles playing in Bajaur Agency.

## Pakistan gets serious about Taliban threat : 2009

Pakistan, somehow, seemed to have been reluctant to proceed against Taliban. In spite of failed peace deals with them in 2005 and 2006, Islamabad and NWFP government yet again made a peace deal with them through Sufi Mohd early 2009 in Swat. When they made inroads in Buner, a mere 60 miles from nation's capital region, taking advantage of the deal, the government bestirred itself and went after the recalcitrant terror outfit in Swat Valley in mid-April, 2009.

"1,224 Taliban have been killed in Pak military's operations against the militants in the country's restive north-west," Syed Kamal Shah, Interior Secretary, informed the parliament on 2 June, 2009.

## "300 Taliban Militants set to attack Pak Cities"

Pakistan's Interior Ministry had some alarming news for the press on 26 April 2009. The TTP chief Baitullah Mehsud "plans to carry out terror attacks in major cities, including Islamabad, Rawalpindi and Lahore. He is believed to have dispatched his top five commanders (Shikaari, Walid, Inayatullah, Mujahid and Abdali) from North Waziristan along with 300 terrorists and suicide bombers to execute the mission.

The five left North Waziristan for Islamabad on 11 April, 2009 along with an explosives-laden Toyota Corolla car with the registration number IDG-8720. Intelligence seems to be doing good job here. These commanders "would supervise the terrorist operations planned by Mehsud and Taliban Himayat Tehrik in these cities.

An official also said that law enforcement agencies were unaware whether the militants had reached their destination or postponed their operations.

But the Interior Secretary Kamal Saha confirmed the report and said foolproof security measures had been adopted to thwart the threats.

## U.S. Worried over Pak Nukes falling into Taliban Hands

The subject of the concern about the Pakistani nuclear arsenal falling into the hands of the extremist elements, especially al-Qaeda and Taliban, have been discussed among the academia and the commentariat for some time but it is the first time the U.S. Secretary of State, Hillary Clinton, has expressed her fears to the Fox News on 26 April, 2009.

Worried by the "worst" and "Unthinkable" possibility of this happening, the U.S. is pushing Islamabad hard to devise a strategy to regain control of the country, Clinton said. These fears mere evoked by the Taliban taking control of Buner district, a were 100 km from the capital region of Islamabad, in early April 2009. The development is believed to have stunned the Obama administration.

U.S. has raised its concern with Islamabad "that if the Taliban encouraged and supported by al-Qaeda and other extremists were to essentially topple the government for failure to beat them back—then they would have the keys to the nuclear arsenal of Pakistan",

Clinton told the news agency. Reacting to the Taliban march towards other Pakistan cities from their strong hold in Swat, she said the U.S. could not even contemplate that, and let go on any further.

However Clinton said U.S. had been assured by the Pakistani authorities and the military that their nuclear weapons were in "safe" hands.

## Pakistan : Surfeit of Terror Outfits

Pakistan arguably has the dubious distinction of a nation hosting largest number of terrorist groups. Epientre of the world terrorism lies within this country in tribal areas on its western border, contiguous to the eastern marches of Afghanistan and the area is better known by its acronym : FATA. It is no surprise that the U.S. administration feels that the next attack on its mainland will originate from the FATA region.

## Terrorist Groups

Several experts say it is difficult to determine how many terrorist groups are operating out of Pakistan. Most of these groups tend to fall into one of the five distinct categories laid out by Ashley Tellis, a senior associate at Carnegie Endowment for International Peace before the U.S. House Foreign Affairs Committee, early March 2009. The classification listed are :

- *Al Qaeda and its affiliates*

The outfit led by Osama and other non-South Asian terrorists believed to be ensconced in the FATA. Rohan Gunaratna of the International Centre for Political Violence and Terrorism Research in Singapore says other foreign militant groups such as the Islamic Movement of Uzbekistan, Islamic Jihad Group, the Libyan Islamic Fighters Group and the Eastern Turkistan Islamic Movement are also located in FATA.

- *The Pakistani Taliban*

Groups consisting of extremist outfits in the FATA, led by individuals such as Baitullah Mehsud, the chieftain of the Mehsud tribe in South Waziristan, Maulana Faqir Mohd and Maulana Qazi Fazlullah of the Tehrik-e-Nafaz-e-Shariat-Mohammadi (TSNM), and Mangal Bagh Afridi of the Lashkar-e-Islami in the Khyber Agency.

- *Anti-Indian*

Terrorist groups that operate with the alleged support of the Pakistani military and the intelligence agency ISI, such as the LET, JEM and the HUM.

- *Sectarian Groups*

Groups such as the Sunni Sipah-e-Sahaba, and the Shia Tehrik-e-Jafria which are engaged in violence within Pakistan.

- *Afghan Taliban*

The original Taliban movement and especially its Qandahari leadership centred around Mullah Mohd Omar, believed to be now living in Quetta.

## Pak-based Transnational Terrorist Organisations

1. Hizb-ul-Mujahideen
2. Harkat-ul-Ansar (now Harkat-ul-Mujahideen)
3. Lashkar-e-Tayyaba
4. Jaish-e-Muhammad
5. Al Badr
6. Lashkar-e-Jabbar
7. Jamait-ul-Mujahideen
8. Harkat-ul-Jehad-al-Islami
9. Muttahida Jehad Council
10. Tehrik-ul-Mujahideen
11. Ikhwan-ul-Mujahideen
12. Islamic Students League
13. Tehrik-e-Hurriat-e-Kashmir
14. Tehrik-e-Nifaz-e-Fiqr Jafaria
15. Al Mustafa Liberation Fighters
16. Tehrik-e-Jehad-e-Islami
17. Muslim Mujahideen
18. Al Mujahid Force
19. Tehrik-e-Jehad
20. Al Barq

(*Source :* South Asian Terrorism Portal)

## Major Terrorist Groups Operating against India

- HM
- LET
- JEM
- HUM

## Major Terrorist Groups Operating against Afghanistan

- Taliban
- LEJ
- HUM

## LET, JEM unite under one Banner in Pak Punjab

Banned terrorist groups in Pak Punjab province are gaining strength after joining hands under a new banner—Muslim United Army (MUA)—and have become a serious challenge for the government which lacks resources to effectively counter their activities. Reports in late April 2009 named three outfits—LET, JEM and LEJ—that came under the banner of MUA. A CID report says their activities are also in line with those of the Taliban.

Militancy has been rapidly taking roots in Punjab province, especially in the five districts of Muzaffargarh, Dera Ghazi Khan, Bahawalpur, Rahim Yar Khan and Bhakkar.

A senior CID official says : "As several members of these three banned groups have taken part in the Afghan war, they have developed a nexus with the Taliban. He further added : "In the suicide bombings of the Naval War College and Federal Investigation Agency office in Lahore and the terrorist attacks on the Sri Lankan cricket team and police training school in Manawan, the facilitators of the perpetrators were from these organisations operating in Punjab."

Officials also believe these three outfits had joined hands primarily to target the security forces.

## LET Chief Reappears to help Pak Government

Barely a few months after he went into hiding somewhere in North-West Pakistan to escape diplomatic Indian pressure for his arrest in the wake of the 26/11, JEM chief Maulana Masood Azhar is believed to have returned to his base in Bahawalpur in June 2009.

First the circumstances of his return. Federal Government wanted his help to settle a fierce dispute brewing over the ownership of Karachi's Binori mosque over the last some months. The trouble started in March-April 2009 with the powerful Pak Deobandis in Binori Mosque deciding to take over mosques belonging to the Bareilvis in the area. This provoked clashes with the MQM taking to streets, prompting government intervention. While one section of the Binori Mosque did relent largely due to the efforts of Maulana Fazl-ur-Rehman, but a smaller but more radical section was furious with the decision to return the mosques to the Barelwis.

While the mosques were vacated, the split inside Binori grew deeper and was becoming volatile because the radical groups had supporters among jihadi outfits willing to extend a helping hand. As the situation worsened in May 2009, Pak agencies felt the need to reach out to Azhar who has a strong influence over radical sections among the Pak Deobandis in the Binori Mosque.

Obliging the government, Azhar reached Karachi, addressed the hardliners, asking them not to fight among themselves. His appeal worked, with radicals backing off. Consequently, the issue stood somewhat settled for the moment.

It is believed Azhar was thence taken to Islamabad and has now returned to his headquarters in Bahawalpur. This was another addition to series of indications from Islamabad that it was not serious about India's concerns, given the way anti-India outfits are crawling back to existence. Prompted by all this and latest status of Azhar, India conveyed a strong message to the U.S. National Security Advisor Gen. James Jones 26 June, 2009 that Pakistan was being selective in its fight against terrorism.

There is a parallel move at the UN where India has moved a proposal to sanction Azhar under the Al Qaeda and Taliban Sanctions Resolution 1267. China came out to help its friend Pakistan—putting a hold on the resolution, demanding more evidence against Azhar. India is mustering more diplomatic support to undo the China-Pak nexus.

India can not trust Pakistan—not as yet.

## Rogues gallery of Terroristan (read, Pakistan)

Here follows the pens ketches of five men—terror leaders all—who hold the world hostages from somewhere in Pakistan; with or without the connivance of Islamabad is not known.

• **Hafiz Mohd Sayeed:** Founder of the Markaz Dawa-wal Irshad, and its terror arm, the LET, Sayeed is known for his vitriolic speeches against India, exhorting his audience/associates to "liberate" Kashmir from India's Control. Still active in Pakistan, his outfit maintains meticulous records of the jihadis it sent to Kashmir and other parts of India to launch terrorist strikes based in the Pakistani Punjab, the Lashkar is particular favourite of the Pak Army, especially the ISI.

India considers him among the masterminds behind the 26/11. Arrested under Indian pressure in December 2008, he has been granted bail by the Lahore High Court for lack of evidence. The Government went in appeal to the Supreme Court in July 2009, but the latter did not set aside the High Court's order and set a date for hearing the appeal. So he is walking a free man as a result.

It needs to be noted that Sayeed was put on the UN Al-Qaeda and Taliban sanctions list the Resolution 1267 post 9/11.

More importantly, a very senior and respected journalist of Pakistan, Najam Sethi, editor *Friday Times*, wrote June 2009 : "The arrest of Sayeed will have repercussions..." This not only shows helplessness of the Pak Government to proceed against a terror leader, but also advises New Delhi to understand ground realities in Pakistan on the issue.

• **Maulana Masood Azhar:** Released in exchange for the passengers of IC-814 in 1999, Azhar founded the JEM on return to Pakistan. A rabble rouser and fiery cleric, Azhar was whisked away from his residence in Bahawalpur to evade Indian pressure for his arrest post-26/11. He seems to have been rehabilitated after he helped the Pak authorities to settle Binori Mosque dispute, as explained earlier in the text. Even if Azhar was kept in wraps after 26/11, other Jaish factions were active in fomenting violence in Pakistan. One of its activists, Amjad Farooqui, was linked to the assassination attempts on Musharraf in 2003. Farooqui has now been eliminated by Pakistan's security forces.

• **Fazl-ur-Rehman Khaleel:** Leader of the Harkat-ul-Mujahideen, Khaleel was a close associate of Masood Azhar. Believed to be close to the Pak establishment, he was recently 2007 beaten up by some unknown persons near Peshawar. He was also employed as a mediator by the Pak government during Lal Masjid siege in Islamabad in June-July 2007. He remains at large and is seen as a key leader of jihadi outfits in Pakistan.

• **Ayman al-Zawahiri:** Number 2 in the al-Qaeda hierarchy, "Zawahiri has, of late, single out the Pakistani establishment and Musharraf as target for jihadi operations"—as of end-2007. He had announced it was duty of all Muslims to wage jihad against the infidel Musharraf regime. The dictator had obviously lost caste after he joined U.S. war on terror post 9/11. His whereabouts remain unknown, but he maintains a high profile in the Qaeda propaganda network. Zawahiri invited questions on a Qaeda website (mid-2007) to post replies. He gives interviews and posts his outpourings against the "enemies" of Islam or his network—replacing Osama in such cases.

• **Mullah Omar:** Founder of the Taliban, the one-eyed cleric is still at large somewhere in the border areas of Pak-Afghan. Some intelligence agencies believe he is ensconced in a safe house in Quetta. After all, Pakistan will need him once the U.S.—NATO troops pull out of Afghanistan, since the former has not given up its theory of creating a strategic depth in the latter.

A close associate of Osama, Omar was the Amir-ul-Momineen (leader of the faithful) in the period between 1996 and 2001 when the Taliban ruled over Afghanistan—over its large part, in any case—and hosted Osama as an honoured guest. Both fled Afghanistan, when the U.S. overthrew Taliban there in 2001, and are believed to be in hiding somewhere in the border areas of Pakistan.

Even if not much has been heard of Omar, the growing violence in Afghanistan since 2003 has often been attributed to the revived Taliban. They have been making larger gains during the summer fighting, especially since 2006 onwards. But the U.S. employment of drones seem to be getting better of the terrorist leaders hidden in tribal areas of Pak-Afghan border in the recent times—perhaps 2008 onwards.

## Macabre Statistics from (terror) War Zone

The world is paying a high price for the terrorist depredation for no obvious reasons. They seemed to be 'satans' personified engaged in mindless violence—murdering people often innocent, including children and women, destroying property and generally creating mayhem all over. They are the agents of death and destruction, working under some misperceived notions of wrongs and injustice done to them and their communities.

Pakistan possibly is the only country which, indeed, created terrorists and militants for reasons of "state policy". And today, the very same monsters are a serious threat to its sovereignty and integrity.

What follows are select data about the casualties suffered by Pakistan, collected from a variety of open sources.

## Deaths due to Terror Violence in Pakistan

| *Year* | *Fatalities* | *Year* | *Fatalities* |
|---|---|---|---|
| 2003 | 189 | 2006 | 1,471 |
| 2004 | 863 | 2007 | 3,599 |
| 2005 | 648 | 2008 | 6,715 |
| Total | 13,485 | | |

(*Source* : Institute for Conflict Management – SATP)

## Terror Tentacles Grip South-Asia

The region has become the epicenter of global terror. In 2008, Afghanistan, Pakistan and India accounted for a total of 5,395 killings—crossing that of Iraq (5,016). As the alarm bells were singing, the world was waiting to see if Obama's Af-Pak will be able to tackle this growing terror menace.

After Pakistan started facing Taliban challenge since April-May 2009, Af-Pak become Pak-Af. Tackling terror in Pakistan is the top priority for the world, if we are ever to seek an end to this scourge.

Terror deaths in Pakistan in 2008 were up by 70 per cent compared to 2007.

Three random data from 2008 for South Asia are given below :

**Suicide Attacks**

- There were 404 suicide attacks in 2008, only marginally down from 525 in 2007.
- 9 per cent of all suicide attacks in 2008 were by women. In Iraq, the equivalent figure was 15 per cent.

*2008 figure of terror casualties*

- 50,000 were injured and killed in terror attacks. Over 50 per cent of them were Muslims.

### Terror fatalities in South Asia

| *Year* | *Pakistan* | *Country* *Afghanistan* | *India* |
|---|---|---|---|
| 2005 | 338 | 682 | 1,357 |
| 2006 | 387 | 1,042 | 1,256 |
| 2007 | 1,335 | 1,966 | 1,093 |
| 2008 | 2,293 | 1,989 | 1,113 |

(*Source :* Hindustan Times, 2.5.09)

*Note :* It is to noticed that the Pakistani fatalities figures in this table are far less compared to those in the preceding table, where the data is from the SATP, maintained by the Institute for Conflict Management. It must be understood that the data from SATP is certainly more credible.

### Progressive figure for 2009 for Pakistan

| *Figures as of* | *Civilian* | *Security Forces* | *Total* |
|---|---|---|---|
| 1 March (SATP) | 469 | 100 | 569 |
| 29 March (SATP) | | | 815 |
| 25 May | | | 1,382 |
| 9 June (SATP) | | | 8,759 |

## Lal Masjid siege becomes a Landmark

Musharraf's military action against the Islamist fundamentalist holed up in Islamabad's Red Mosque was the first attack in the country against the religious extremists. It was dubbed Pakistan's Blue Star—Indian Army's military action in Amritsar's Golden Temple.

It was full one week after the Mosque was besieged by the troops that the General ordered attack on it on 10 July 2007 to avoid mass suicide by students holed inside as also to see that religious sentiment is not inflamed any further with the daily news about the casualties in and around the Mosque.

The siege of the Mosque became a sort of landmark as the following news blurb in the AFP story dated 20 February, 2009.

- "1600 people have been killed in suicide (and bomb) attacks across Pakistance *since* government forces besieged militants holed up in a radical (Red) Mosque in Islamabad in July, 2007".

The AFP news story is about a suicide bomber blowing himself up on 18 February 2009, killing 30 people and injuring many more, during the funeral procession of a Shia leader, Sher Zaman, at Dera Ismael Khan, a town at the edge of Pak's restive tribal areas, with a history of sectarian violence. Shia mob pumped bullets in the air, pelted stones at cars, ransacked shops, torched buses and set up road blocks with burning tyres in this dusty, low-rise town.

## Pakistan : Combating Terrorism a Tough Task

Combating terrorism is proving a very intractable task. Empirical experience has taught this bitter lesson to country's involved in countering the terrorism over the last few decades like India, Israel, Indonesia, Philipines etc, and countries like those in Europe and North America who fell victims to the scourge only in the recent years, to be more specific, since 9/11.

At every international gathering—like the UN, EU, ASEAN, Africa Union et al—resolutions are passed on the subject, pledging coordination in counter-terrorism war and resolving determination to win it.

This section deals with Pakistan's endeavours in this direction.

## Pakistan to set up Terror Watch-dog

The country has been under pressure to launch operations in a more vigorous manner to stem the tide of terrorism sweeping the land. Since Pakistan joined U.S. war on terror after 9/11, anti-American sentiment has been inflamed by the religious entities and the feeling in the nation's intellectual circles is that Pakistan is fighting others war under U.S. pressure. There is also no doubt that Pakistan has been facing worldwide demand to take action against the militant groups operating from its territory.

Over the last couple of years, particularly since Islamabad took military action to retake the Red Mosque on 10 July 2007, Pakistan itself has become a victim of terrorism. Consequently, it decided to establish a National Counter-terrorism Authority (NCA). Once it comes into existence, it will help the country to face the terror attacks more effectively.

Tariq Pervez, "who has just retired as the DG, FIA (Federal Investigation Agency) can head the new body", the *News* daily reported on 2 January, 2009.

"Pervez has been assigned the job of preparing the concept, structure and mandate of the NCA so that it could serve the purpose for which it is being established", an official told the daily. "The primary objective of the NCA will be maximum coordination among different tools and agencies of the government engaged in counter-terrorism."

The NCA is the brain-child of the Interior Ministry Advisor, Rehman Malik. So far counter—terrorism tasks were the preserve of intelligence agencies, primarily the ISI. The workload of these agencies increased manyfold after Pakistan joined global war on terrorism after 9/11. At the sometime lack of coordination among (various official) organs dealing with counter-terrorism chores also pointed towards some new instrument. Hence the decision on the NCA.

Most of the civilian governments in the past have been critical of the absence of any coordinating mechanism in this important field—and demanding it.

The decision on the NCA has not come a day too early.

## Pakistan—China to hold Anti-terror Exercises : December, 2006

Traditional allies, Pakistan and China will hold joint military exercises 'this week' aimed at helping the two countries fight terrorism, Pak military announced on 10 December 2006. A contingent of the PLA arrived in the garrison city of Rawalpindi on the 10th to take part in the exercise, named "Friendship-2006".

The focus of the joint exercise—the first by Chinese troops outside their country—will be to mutually benefit from each other's experience of planning and conduct of anti-terrorist operations. The two armies held such exercises in China in 2004.

## Pakistan Crackdown on Two Islamic Charities : 18 February, 2007

Pakistan on 18 February, 2007 ordered a renewed crackdown on two Islamic charities, al Rasheed and Al-Akhatar, already blacklisted for their suspected links with Al-Qaeda. The two charitable are on a UN list of entities linked to Al Qaeda and Taliban.

Headquartered in Karachi, the Al-Rasheed Trust is also linked to the JEM led by Masood Azhar, one of the three men freed by India during the 1999 Indian Airlines hijacking episode.

Orders have gone out to provincial governments to ensure that the offices, bank accounts, websites and publications of the two trusts do not operate. Pakistan had frozen accounts of Al-Rasheed and Al-Akhtar in 2002 and 2003 respectively. But from the government's fresh orders against them, it is obvious that they had continued to function.

The renewed action comes after a spate of suicide bomb attacks in Pakistan, "which claimed over 40 lives in the lost three weeks."

After the 17 February suicide bombing in Quetta in which 16 people were killed, the police had detained 25 people, mostly Afghans, for questioning.

Senior government official Ghulam Mohd Mahtaram told AFP : "offices of the two trusts have been sealed and their bank accounts frozen. They will not be allowed to give ads in the local papers for donations. The move followed reports that the two trusts were providing funds to other organisations involved in illegal activities. But there will be no restrictions on their welfare activity.

Al-Rasheed Trust was accused by the U.S. of links to the Al-Qaeda and Taliban. The Central Bank of Pakistan had frozen its accounts after the 11 September, 2001 attacks. However, a Pakistani court in August 2003 had overturned the bank's ban.

## Pak Shuts Two Newspapers for Links to Terrorists : 23 February, 2007

Pak authorities closed down publications of two Islamic charities—Al Rasheed Trust and Al-Akhatar Trust—on a list of organisation whose assets the UN says should be frozen because of their links to terrorism, officials said on 23 February, 2007.

Authorities had begun sealing offices of the two groups in different cities on the 18th, saying the action was required under UN Resolution 1267, which mandates all states to freeze the assets of people and organisation on the list established by the Resolution. Publication permits the two charities held were cancelled on the 22nd. This was disclosed by Pak Interior Secretary Gholam Mohtaram in the southern province of Sindh on the 23rd.

## "Attack on ISI Indicates Fight in Terror Front" : March, 2007

In a surprising development, and first of its kind, two senior Pakistan intelligence officers and three of their subordinates were killed on 27 March 2007 in an ambush sprung by jihadi terrorists in Bajaur Agency of FATA, NWFP, bordering Afghanistan.

So, Pakistan's dogs of war have started to bite the hand that fed them. In the incident, unprecedented till date, the Jihadi elements have attacked their long-time state patrons—the ISI. Chiddanand Rajghatta, *Times of India*, 29.3.07.

The U.S. intelligence is scrambling to make sense of the unprecedented clash, which it feels is "indicative of a change—especially given the historically close relationship" between jihadis and the ISI. It is not fully convinced that Islamabad has totally given up on terrorism as a state policy.

The intelligence group Stratfar commented in an assessment on 27 March, hours after the attack :

> "The travel itineraries of ISI officials are not easy to acquire. The only way the attackers could have gained access to such information is through a tip-off from some one within or close to the ISI office in which the officials worked. This lends credence to the suspicion that there are still ties between the agency and some Islamist militants, despite the purges and shake-ups the ISI has undergone since 11 September, 2000."
>
> "The clash has likely to do with Pakistani President Musharraf's move to rid the country's Pashtun areas of the Taliban, even as Islamabad continues to exploit the Afghan Taliban for its foreign policy objectives vis-à-vis Kabul."
>
> "Even now, certain elements within and close to the ISI are believed to maintain relations with militant Islamists."

The attack against the ISI officials took place a day after Pakistan's military regime signed a peace deal with the Salarzai and Utmankhel tribes under which the tribal leadership in Bajaur agreed to work with the government to rid the agency of foreign militants. The military junta has signed two other similar deals in South and North Waziristan which Washington initially accepted with skepticism but now says has aggravated cross-border terrorism.

In the case of Bajaur, the U.S. intelligence community feds the Pakistani military junta may have succeeded in creating a rift between the religious nationalists and Al-Qaeda elements and using the former to fight the latter. There appears to be a fault line running through the militant spectrum in the Pashtun areas, causing a rift between trans-national Al-Qaeda elements and religious nationalists, Stratfor noted.

## Jehadis in Pakistan are Defying Fatwas : Clerics : May, 2007

Pakistani clerics have accused the intelligence agencies in the country of supporting jihadi organizations whose actions now cannot be checked even by *fatwas* (= religious decrees), says a report in a daily, *Asian Age*, 8 May, 2007 datelined Peshawar, 7 May, 2007.

Legislator Qazi Fayyaz-ur-Rehman Alvi of Jamiat Uleme-e-Islam (JUI-F) said numerous jihadi organizations and people were terrorising the country and some of them had the support of the intelligence agencies. "The agencies are playing a dangerous game in the country", he said.

Another cleric, Maulana Mohd Hassan Jan, chief of Jamia Imdadul Uloom Al Islamia Darwaish Masjid, Peshawar, echoed the concerns of Qazi Alwi, saying : " we cannot force them (jihadi elements) to act upon our *fatwas*."

Clerics, who had issued a fatwa declaring suicide attacks *haraam* and illegal, are concerned that the existing volatile situation in the country has reached a point where even religious decrees cannot prevent such elements from carrying out their deadly actions.

A clerics convention organised by the JUI-F of the NWFP on 17 April (2007) had issued a *fatwa* that such suicide bombing was *haraam* in Islam and against the law of the land.

Over 2,000 clerics, including the leader of Opposition Maulana Fazl-ur-Rehman, had endorsed the *fatwa* against suicide bombing. However, the Charsadda suicide bomb attack recently in north-west Frontier Region in which at least 31 people were killed and Pakistan's Interior Minister Aftab Sherpao was critically injured seems to indicate that the clerics' decree had been ignored. Qazi Alvi said, "Fatwas do not work in troubled regions. The situation has progressed beyond them."

## How Pakistan Sold Bomb Secrets to North Korea

The question of North Korea successfully exploding a nuclear weapon is important and more dangerous for the international community than was the case when its 7 predecessors marched into the exclusive Nuclear Club. North Korea is a rogue nation not because President Bush pushed into axis of evil along with Iran and Iraq, but because it is in the grip of a paranoid Communist dictator who would rather starve his people and build an atom bomb. Its entire state structure can be dubbed dictatorial, and more accurately, terrorist. Not only because its rulers can use the bomb to terrorise its non-nuclear neighbours but also sell it to non-state actors for whim, fancy or profit. Besides from the fundamentalist terrorists, the world community also must reckon with the possibility of threat of nuclear terrorism from a state like North Korea. Hence the importance of a careful look at the nuclear explosion by this nation, and the path and means it employed to reach there. Aim here is to see not only the plight of its impoverished millions but also the human cost it paid to have nuclear weapons to its armoury.

"There was nothing to betray the feverish activity of North Korea's nuclear emerald green paddy fields to the heart of the hermit state. We saw women bent under firewood they were carrying along the unlit roads just outside the capital, Pyongyan, in scenes of unbelievable poverty".[7]

North Korea's 23 million people have been held hostage by a cruel dictorship since 1946. Unlike South Korea, which spent its energies on economic development of the country, the North, under its 'revered' founder Kim Il Sung, and his son and successor Kim Jong Il, subjected its people to repression and isolation. To ensure the safety of their regime—more accurately, their fiefdom—they had decided long ago to go nuclear. It was an insurance policy against the less-than-friendly states on their doorstep.

North was simply not equipped to achieve the desideratum on their own resource capital. They looked for help beyond their borders and had no difficulty in locating it.

They did it secretly, burying research facilities inside the impenetrable mountains and buying/bartering the hardware to build a bomb off the shelf in the international black market. They achieved this in the midst of a famine that killed unknown numbers, by accepting international aid and cynically diverting it to the military.

The young Pakistani scientist AQ Khan had returned home in 1975 after working in the uranium enrichment facility in the

Netherlands, and was looking for customers. He was about to launch himself on a road to subsequent infamy and disgrace. Khan, who developed the worlds first Islamic nuclear bomb—to borrow the evocative Bhutto phrase—for Pakistan in a top-secret programme, in the mid-1980s opened his own private 'walmart' of nuclear technology for sale to any one for right price.

One branch was based in his Pakistan laboratories, where 4-6 scientists were perhaps unwittingly involved. But the hub was in Dubai, which took care of procurement and distribution, with the help of European businessman.

One flight from Pakistan to North Korea carrying conventional weapons was intercepted by Pakistani government, acting on a tip-off that more sensitive material was on board. They found nothing, obviously because Khan's men had been informed in advance.

Similar flights had taken off for Iran, too. Tehran has confirmed receiving a centrifuge blueprint from Khan in the 1980s as part of a starter kit for its nuclear programme.

Through his network, Khan transferred to North Korea "nearly two dozen" P-1 centrifuges, and the more sophisticated P-11 centrifuges. This information comes from Gen. Musharraf, who debriefed Khan after his fall from grace, and has put it in so many words in his *Line of Fire*, published in September 2006. It is apparent that North Korea, along with Pakistan, constitutes a global web of nuclear proliferation, as one of its leading practitioners and beneficiaries.

But the world should not accept the proposition, as the U.S. has facilely done, that disgraced Khan could operate this entire complex network single handed. Certainly not in a country like Pakistan. It was not a simple cash and carry operation. It is known that Pakistan obtained missile technology know-how from North Korea, which, in turn, had procured from China. So it was nuclear bomb vs missiles. Khan's silence has been purchased through Presidential pardon. Even then, Pakistan can not trust him as a free man. He is under house arrest, though in a well-anointed palatial bungalow. That explains Pakistan's stubborn refusal to let America interrogate Khan on the question of his nuclear 'supermarket.'

## 15 October, 06

Disgraced father of Pakistan's nuclear bomb, Dr. Abdul Qadeer Khan shifted back to Islamabad from Karachi where he had undergone an operation on 9 September for prostate cancer. He had been diagnosed for disease on 22 August and moved to the Agha Khan Hospital in Karachi on 3 September.

## 4 Pak Atomic Energy Commission Officials Abducted : 14 January, 2007

At least four officials of the Atomic Energy Commission based in *Banda Daud* Shah tehsil of Karak district, NWFP, were kidnapped from their office by four armed men on the 14th. They also took away three vehicles.

The office was established a few years back, following discovery of high-grade uranium in the area.

## References

1. For more information, *see* Mohd Amir Rana, *A to Z of Jihadi organizations in Pakistan*, Marshall Books, Lahore, 2004.
2. Sumanta Bose, *The Change in Kashmir : Democracy, Self-Determination and* a Just Peace, 1997; and Hashim Quereshi, *Kashmir : The Unveiling* of *Truth*, Jedojuhd Publications, Lahore, 1999.
3. "Pakistan : 2005 overview," MIPT Terrorism Knowledge Base, at http://www.tkb.org/MorePatterns.jsp?CountryCd=Pk and year=2005.
4. "The State of Sectarianism in Pakistan", International Crisis Group (ICG), *Asia Report* 95, 18 April 2005.
5. Husain Haqqani, *Pakistan : Between Mosque and Military*, Carnegie Endowment for International Peace, Washington DC, 2005.
6. David Montero, "A Rebel's killing Rolls Pakistan", *Christian Science Monitor*, 28 August, 2006.
7. "Pakistan : The Worsening Conflict in Baluchistan", ICG Asia Report No. 119, 14 September 2006.
8. Vishal Chandra, "Politics in post-Taliban Afghanistan : "An Assessment", *Strategic Analysis*, 29 (2), April-June 2005, IDSA publication.
9. Peter Bergen, "Why the Taliban is back?", Afghanistan Watch, 19 September 2006, at http://the century of foundation.typed.com/aw/2006/09/peter-bergen-wh.html#more
10. Carlotta Gall, "Pakistan Allows Taliban to Train, a Detained Fighter says, *New York Times*, 4 August, 2004.

11. Harkat-ul-Mujahedeen. Some analysts have used the abbreviation HKUM for this outfit.
12. Mike collett-white, "Osama Probably Alive in Pakistan, Top Officials Say", *Reuters*, 27.9.2004.
13. "10 Questions for porter Goss", *Time*, 27.6.2005.
14. U.S. Counter-terrorism official Crumpton tells *CBS News*, Kabul, Afghanistan, 6.5.2006.
15. G Parthasarathy, "Afghanistan : The booming Dangers", *Business Lines*, 23 May, 2006.